Hugh Kelly

False Delicacy

A Comedy Adapted for Theatrical Representation

Hugh Kelly

False Delicacy
A Comedy Adapted for Theatrical Representation

ISBN/EAN: 9783744767026

Printed in Europe, USA, Canada, Australia, Japan

Cover: Foto ©Andreas Hilbeck / pixelio.de

More available books at **www.hansebooks.com**

Roberts del.   Audinet sc.

MISS DE CAMP as MISS RIVERS.

I wish he was come.

London, Printed for J. Bell, British Library, Strand, May 8, 1791.

PROLOGUE.

Written by DAVID GARRICK, Esq.*---Spoken by Mr. KING.

I'M vex'd—quite vex'd—and you'll be vex'd—that's
  worse;
To deal with stubborn scribblers! *there's the curse!*
Write moral *plays—the blockhead!—why, good people,*
You'll soon expect this house to wear a steeple!
For our fine piece, to let you into facts,
Is quite a sermon,---*only preach'd in* Acts.
You'll scarce believe me 'till the proof appears,
But even I, Tom Fool, *must shed some tears:*
Do, ladies, *look upon me---nay, no simp'ring---*
Think you this face was ever made for whimp'ring?
Can I, a cambrick handkerchief display,---
Thump my unfeeling breast, and roar away?
Why this *is* comical, *perhaps he'll say.---*
Resolving this strange aukward bard to pump,
I ask'd him what he meant?---He, somewhat plump,

---

* Mr. Kelly originally intended the prologue to be grave, and accordingly wrote
a serious one himself; but as Mr. King was to speak it, Mr. Garrick, with great
propriety, thought a piece of humour would be best suited to the talents of that
excellent actor, and therefore very kindly took the trouble of putting it into a form
so entirely different from the first, that it cannot with the least justice, be attri-
buted to any other author.

Now purs'd his belly, and his lips thus biting,
I must keep up the dignity of writing !
You may, but, if you do, sir, I must tell ye,
You'll not keep up that dignity of belly;
Still he preached on....' Bards of a former age
Held up abandon'd pictures on the stage,
Spread out their wit, with fascinating art,
And catch'd the fancy, to corrupt the heart :
But happy change!—in these more moral days,
You cannot sport with virtue, even in plays ;
On virtue's side, his pen the poet draws,
And boldly asks a hearing for his cause.'
Thus did he prance, and swell---The man may **prate,**
And feed these whimsies in his addle pate,
That you'll protect his muse, because she's good,
A virgin, and so chaste!—O, Lud ! O, Lud !
No muse the critic beadle's lash escapes,
Though virtuous, if a dowdy, and a trapes :
If his come forth, a decent likely lass,
You'll speak her fair, and grant the proper pass ;
Or should his brain be turn'd with wild pretences ;
In three hours time, you'll bring him to his senses ;
And well you may, when in your power you get him,
In that short space, you blister, bleed, and sweat him.
Among the Turks, *indeed, he'd run no danger,*
They sacred hold a madman, *and a* stranger.

FALSE DELICACY.

ACT I. SCENE I.

An Apartment at Lady *Betty Lambton's.* Enter
SIDNEY *and Lord* WINWORTH.

Sidney.

STILL I can't help thinking but Lady Betty Lambton's refusal was infinitely more the result of an extraordinary delicacy, than the want of affection for your Lordship.

L. *Win.* O, my dear cousin, you are very much mistaken; I am not one of those coxcombs who imagine a woman does n't know her own mind, or who, because they are treated with civility by a lady who has rejected their addresses, suppose she is secretly debating in their favour: Lady Betty is a woman of sense, and must consequently despise coquetry or affectation.

Sid. Why she always speaks of you with the greatest respect.

L. *Win.* Respect!—Why she always speaks of you with the greatest respect; does it therefore follow that she loves you? No, Charles—I have for some time, you know, ceas'd to trouble Lady Betty with my solicitations, and I see myself honour'd with her friendship, though I hav' n't been so happy as to merit her heart; for this reason, I have no doubt of her assistance on the present occasion, and, I am certain, I shall please her by making my addresses to Miss Marchmont.

Sid. Miss Marchmont is, indeed, a very deserving young woman.

L. *Win.* Next to Lady Betty, I never saw one so form'd to my wishes; besides, during the whole period of my fruitless attendance, she seemed so interested for my success, and express'd so hearty a concern for my disappointment, that I have consider'd her with an eye of more than common friendship ever since.—But what's the matter with you, Charles, you seem to have something upon your spirits?

Sid. Indeed, my lord, you are mistaken, I am only attentive.

L. *Win.* O, is that all!—This very day I purpose to request Lady Betty's interest with Miss Marchmont, for unhappily circumstanc'd as she is, with regard to fortune, she possesses an uncommon share of delicacy, and may possibly think herself insulted by the offer of a rejected heart:—Lady Betty, in that case, will save her the pain of a supposed disrespect, and me the mortification of a new repulse. But I beg your pardon, Charles, I am forgetting the cause of friendship, and shall now step up stairs to Colonel

Rivers about your affair.—Ah, Sidney, you have no
difficulties to obstruct the completion of your wishes,
and a few days must make you one of the happiest men
in England.   [*Exit.*

Sid. [*Looking after him.*] A few days make me one
of the happiest men in England—a likely matter truly!
little does he know how passionately I admire the very
woman to whom he is immediately going with an offer of his person and fortune. The marriage with Miss
Rivers I see is unavoidable, and I am almost pleased
that I never obtained any encouragement from Miss
Marchmont, as I should now be reduc'd to the painful alternative, either of giving up my own hopes, or
of opposing the happiness of such a friend.

Enter Mrs. HARLEY *and* Miss MARCHMONT.

Mrs. *Har.* O here, my dear girl, is the sweet swain
in *propria persona*: Only mind what a funeral sermon-
face the creature has, notwithstanding the agreeable
prospects before him. Well, of all things in the
world, defend me, I say, from a sober husband!

Sid. You are extremely welcome, Mrs. Harley, to
divert yourself——

Mrs. *Har.* He speaks too in as melancholy a tone
as a passing bell :—Lord, lord, what can Colonel Rivers see in the wretch to think of him for a son-in-
law. Only look, Miss Marchmont, at this love ex-
citing countenance :—Observe the cupids that ambush
in these eyes :—These lips, to be sure, are fraught
with the honey of Hybla :—Go, you lifeless devil you,

go, try to get a little animation into this unfortunate face of your's.

Sid. Upon my word my face is very much obliged to you.

Miss *March.* You are a mad creature, my dear, and yet I envy your spirits prodigiously.

Mrs. *Har.* And so you ought—But for all that, you and Lady Betty are unaccountably fond of those half-soul'd fellows, who are as mechanically regular as so many pieces of clock-work, and never strike above once an hour upon a new observation: who are so sentimental, and so dull, so wise, and so drowsy. Why I thought Lady Betty had already a sufficient quantity of led in her family, without taking in this lump to increase the weight of it.

Miss *March.* What can she possibly mean, Mr. Sidney.

Sid. 'T is impossible to guess, madam. The lively widow will still have her laugh, without sparing any body.

Mrs. *Har.* Why, surely, my dear, you can't forget the counter part of poor dismal here, that elaborate piece of dignified dulness, Lady Betty's cousin, Lord Hectic; who, through downright fondness, is continually plaguing his poor wife, and rendering her the most miserable woman in the world, from an extraordinary desire of promoting her happiness.

Miss *March.* And is n't there a great deal to say in extenuation of an error which proceeds from a principle of real affection?

Mrs. Har. Affection! ridiculous! but you shall have an instance of this wonderful affection :——T'o-ther day I din'd at his house, and though the weather was intolerably warm, the table was laid in a close room, with a fire large enough to roast an ox for a country corporation.

Sid. Well, and so————

Mrs. Har. In a great chair, near the fire-side, sat poor Lady Hectic, wrapp'd up in as many fur cloaks as would baffle the severity of a winter in Siberia :——On my entrance I express'd a proper concern for her illness, and ask'd the nature of her complaint. She told me she complain'd of nothing but the weight of her dress, and the intolerable heat of the apartment ; adding, that she had been caught in a little shower the preceding evening, which terrified Lord Hectic out of his wits ; and so, for fear she might run the risque of a slight cold, he exposed her to the hazard of absolute suffocation.

Sid. Upon my word, Miss Marchmont, she has a pretty manner of turning things.

Miss March. Really I think so.

Mrs. Har. Well ; unable to bear either the tyranny of this preposterous fondness any longer, or the intoler-able heat of his room, I made my escape the moment the cloth was removed ; and sha' n't be surprized, if, before the conclusion of the summer, he is brought before his peers, for having murdered his poor lady out of down-right affection.

Sid. A very uncommon death, Mrs. Harley, among people of quality.

Enter a Footman.

Foot. [*to* Sid.] Lord Winworth, sir, desires the favour of your company above: The person is come with the writings from the temple.

Sid. I 'll wait upon him immediately.

Mrs. Har. Ay, pray, do, you are the fittest company in the world for each other. If Colonel Rivers was of my mind, he 'd turn you instantly adrift, and listen to the overtures of Sir Harry Newburg.

Sid. I really believe you have a fancy to me yourself, you 're so constantly abusing me.   [*Exit.*

Mrs. Har. I, you odious creature!

Miss March. Now you mention Sir Harry, my dear, is n't it rather extraordinary for him to think of Miss Rivers, when he knows of the engagements between her and Mr. Sidney, especially as her father has such an objection to the wildness of his character.

Mrs. Har. What you are still at your sober reflections, I see, and are for scrutinizing into the morals of a lover. The women, truly, would have a fine time of it, if they were never to be married till they found men of unexceptionable characters.

Miss March. Nay, I do n't want to lessen Sir Harry's merit in the least, he has his good qualities as well as his faults, and is no way destitute of understanding; but still his understanding is a fashionable one, and pleads the knowledge of every thing right to justify the practice of many things not strictly warrantable.

Mrs. Har. Why I never heard any thing to his prejudice, but some fashionable liberties which he has taken with the ladies.

Miss March. And, in the name of wonder, what would you desire to hear?

Mrs. Har. Come, come, Hortensia, we women are unaccountable creatures, the greatest number of us by much love a fellow for having a little modish wildness about him; and if we are such fools as to be captivated with the vices of the men, we ought to be punished for the depravity of our sentiments.

Enter RIVERS *and* Lady BETTY.

Riv. I tell you, sister, they can read the parchments very well without our assistance; and I have been so fatigu'd with looking over papers all the morning, that I am heartily sick of your indentures witnessing, your forasmuch's, likewise's, also's, moreover's, and notwithstanding's, and I must take a turn in the garden to recover myself. [*Exit.*

Lady Betty. Nay, I only spoke, because I imagin'd our being present would be more agreeable to Lord Winworth. But I wonder Sir Harry does n't come, he promised to be here by ten, and I want to see his cousin Cecil mightily.

Miss March. What, Lady Betty, does Mr. Cecil come with him here this morning?

Lady Betty. He does, my dear——he arrived at Sir

B

Harry's last night, and I want to see if his late journey to France has any way improved the elegance of
his appearance.   [*Ironically*

Mrs. *Har.* Well, I shall be glad to see him too;
for notwithstanding his disregard of dress and freedom of manner, there is a something right in him that
pleases me prodigiously.

Miss *March.* A something right, Mrs. Harley!——
He is one of the worthiest creatures in the world.

Lady *Betty.* O, Hortensia, he ought to be a favourite of your's, for I don't know any body who possesses a higher place in his good opinion.

Miss *March.* 'T would be odd, indeed, if he was n't
a favourite of mine——he was my father's best friend;
gave him a considerable living you know, and, when
he died, would have provided very kindly for me, if
your generosity, Lady Betty, had n't render'd his
goodness wholly unnecessary.

Lady *Betty.* Poh! poh! no more of this.

Mrs. *Har.* I wish there was a possibility of making
him dress like a gentleman---But I am glad he comes
with Sir Harry; for though they have a great regard
for each other, they are continually wrangling, and
form a contrast which is often extremely diverting---

Enter a Footman.

Foot. Sir Harry Newburg and Mr. Cecil, madam.

Lady *Betty.* O, here they are! Shew them in.

                         [*Exit* Foot.

Mrs. *Har.* Now for it!

Miss March. Hush, they are here.

Sir Harry. Ladies, your most obedient.

Cecil. Ah, girls! give me a kiss each of you instantly. Lady Betty, I am heartily glad to see you: I have a budget full of compliments for you, from several of your friends at Paris————

Lady Betty. Did you meet any of them at Paris?

Cecil. I did, and, what was worse, I met them in every town I passed through; but the English are a great commercial nation, you know, and their fools, like their broad cloths, are exported in large quantities to all parts of Europe.

Sir Harry. What? and they found you a fool so much above the market price, that they have return'd you upon the hands of your country?—Here, ladies, is a head for you, piping hot from Paris.

Cecil. And here, ladies, is a head for you, like the Alps.

Sir Harry. Like the Alps, ladies! How do you make that out?

Cecil. Why it's always white, and always barren; 't is constantly covered with snow, but never produces any thing profitable.

Mrs. Har. O, say no more upon that head, I beseech you.

Lady Betty. Indeed, Sir Harry, I think they are too hard upon you.

Mrs. Har. Why, I think so too—especially my friend Cecil, who, with that unfortunate shock of hair, has no great right to be considered as a standard for dress in this country.

Cecil. Ah, widow, there are many heads in this country with much more extraordinary things upon them than my unfortunate shock of hair, as you call it:—what do you think of these wings, for instance, that cover the ears of my cousin Mercury?

Sir Harry. Death! do n't spoil my hair.

Cecil. You see this fellow is so tortur'd upon the wheel of fashion, that a single touch immediately throws him into agonies ;—now, my dress is as easy as it 's simple, and five minutes—

Sir Harry. With the help of your five fingers equips you at any time for the drawing room,—ha! ha! ha!

Cecil. And is n't it better than being four hours under the paws of your hair-dresser?

Lady Betty. But custom, Mr. Cecil!

Cecil. Men of sense have nothing to do with custom; and 't is more their business to set wise examples, than to follow foolish ones.

Mrs. Har. But do n't you think the world will be apt to laugh a little, Mr. Cecil ?

Cecil. I can 't help the want of understanding among mankind.

Sir Harry. The blockhead thinks there's nothing due to the general opinion of one's country.

Cecil. And none but blockheads, like you, would mind the foolish opinions of any country.

Lady Betty. Well! Mr. Cecil must take his own

way, I think---so come along, ladies,---let us go into the garden, and send my brother to Sir Harry to settle the business about Theodora.

Cecil. Theodora!---what a charming name for the romance of a circulating library!---I wonder, Lady Betty, your brother would n't call his girl Deborah, after her grandmother---?

Mrs. *Har.* Deborah!---O, I should hate such an old fashion'd name abominably--,-

Cecil. And I hate this new fashion of calling our children by pompous appellations.---By and by we shan't have a Ralph or a Roger, a Bridget or an Alice, remaining in the kingdom.---The dregs of the people have adopted this unaccountable custom; and a fellow who keeps a little alehouse at the bottom of my avenue in the country, has no less than an Augustus Frederic, a Scipio Africanus, and a Matilda-Wilhelmina-Leonora, in his family.

Mrs. *Har.* Upon my word, a very pretty string of christian names.

Lady *Betty.* Well, sir Harry, you and Mr. Cecil dine with us. Come, ladies let us go to the garden.

Mrs. *Har.* I positively won't go without Mr. Cecil, for I must have somebody to laugh at.

Cecil. And so must I, widow, therefore I won't lose this opportunity of being in your company.

[*Exeunt ladies, and followed by* Cecil, *who meets* Rivers *entering.*]

Cecil. Ah, colonel, I am heartily glad to see you.----

Riv. My dear Cecil, you are welcome home again.

Cecil. There's my wise kinsman wants a word with you.   [*Aside.*

Sir *Harry.* Colonel, your most obedient:---I am come upon the old business;---for unless I am allow'd to entertain hope of Miss Rivers, I shall be the most miserable of human beings.

Riv. Sir Harry, I have already told you by letter, and I now tell you personally, I cannot listen to your proposals.

Sir *Har.* No, Sir?

Riv. No, sir,---I have promised my daughter to Mr. Sidney----do you know that, sir?

Sir *Har.* I do; but what then? engagements of this kind, you know---

Riv. So then, you do know I have promised her to Mr. Sidney?

Sir *Harry.* I do; but I also know, that matters are not finally settled between Mr. Sidney and you; and I moreover know, that his fortune is by no means equal to mine, therefore------

Riv. Sir Harry, let me ask you one question before you make your consequence.

Sir *Harry.* A thousand, if you please, sir.

Riv. Why then, sir, let me ask you, what you have ever observed in **me,** or **my** conduct, that you desire **me** so familiarly to break my word: I thought, sir, you considered me as a man of honour.

Sir *Harry.* And **so** I do, sir, a man of the nicest honour.

Riv. And yet, sir, you ask me to violate the sanctity of my word—and tell me, indirectly, that it is my interest to be a rascal—

Sir *Harry*. I really do n't understand you, colonel: I thought, when I was talking to you, I was talking to a man who knew the world—and as you have not yet signed——

Riv. Why, this is mending matters with a witness! —And so you think, because I am not legally bound, I am under no necessity of keeping my word!—Sir Harry, laws were never made for men of honour;—they want no bond but the rectitude of their own sentiments, and laws are of no use but to bind the villains of society.

Sir **Harry**. Well! but my dear colonel, if you have no regard for me, shew some little regard for your daughter.

Riv. Sir Harry, I shew the greatest regard for my daughter, by giving her to a man of honour; and I must not be insulted by any farther repetition of your proposals.

Sir *Harry*. Insult you, colonel!---is the offer of my alliance an insult?---is my readiness to make what settlements you think proper——

Riv. Sir Harry, I should consider the offer of a kingdom an insult, if it was to be purchased by the violation of my word: besides, though my daughter shall never go a beggar to the arms of her husband, I would rather see her happy than rich: and if she has enough to provide handsomely for a young family, and something to spare for the exigencies of a worthy friend, I shall think her **as** affluent as if she was mistress of Mexico.

Sir Harry. Well, colonel, I have done; but I believe——

Riv. Well, Sir Harry, and as our conference is done, we will, if you please, retire **to** the ladies: I shall be always glad of your acquaintance, though I can't receive you as a son-in-law——for a **union** of interest I look upon as a union of dishonour; **and** consider a marriage for money, at best but a legal prostitution.

[*Exeunt.*

ACT II. SCENE I.

A Garden. *Enter* Lady BETTY, *and* Mrs. HARLEY.

Mrs. *Harley.*

LORD, Lord, my dear you're enough to drive one out of one's wits.——I tell you, again and again, he's as much yours as ever; and was I in your situation, he should be my husband to-morrow morning.

Lady Betty. Dear Emmy, you mistake the matter strangely——Lord Winworth is no common man, nor would he have continued his silence so long upon his favourite subject, if he had the least inclination to renew his addresses. **His** pride has justly taken the alarm at my insensibility, and he will not, I am satisfied, run **the** hazard of another refusal.

Mrs. Har. Why then, in the name of wonder, if he was so dear to you, could you prodigally trifle with your own happiness, and repeatedly refuse him?

Lady Betty. I have repeatedly told you, because I was a fool, Emmy. 'Till he withdrew his addresses, I knew not how much I esteemed him; my unhappiness in my first marriage, you know, made me resolve against another.—And you are also sensible I have frequently argu'd, that a woman of real delicacy should never admit a second impression on her heart.

Mrs. Har. Yes, and I always thought you argued very foolishly. I am sure I ought to know, for I have been twice married; and though I lov'd my first husband very sincerely, there was not a woman in England who could have made the second a better wife. Nay, for that matter, if another was to offer himself to-morrow, I am not altogether certain that I should refuse listening——

Lady Betty. You are a strange creature.

Mrs. Har. And are n't you a much stranger, in declining to follow your own inclinations, when you could have consulted them so highly, to the credit of your good sense, and the satisfaction of your whole family. But it is n't yet too late; and if you will be advis'd by me, every thing shall end as happily as you can wish.

Lady Betty. Well, let me hear your advice.

Mrs. Har. Why this, then: My lord, you know, has requested that you would indulge him with half an hour's private conversation some time this morning.

Lady Betty. Well!

Mrs. Har. This is a liberty he has n't taken these three months——and he must design something by it; now as he can design nothing but to renew his addresses, I would advise you to take him at the very first word, for fear your delicacy, if it has time to consider, should again shew you the strange impropriety of second marriages.

Lady Betty. But suppose this should not be his business with me?

Mrs. Har. Why then we 'll go another way to work: I, as a sanguine friend of my lord's, can give him a distant hint of matters, exacting, at the same time, a promise of the most inviolable secrecy; and assuring him you would never forgive me, if you had the least idea of my having acquainted him with so important a——

Lady Betty. And so you would have me——

Mrs. Har. Why not? This is the very step I should take myself, if I was in your situation.

Lady Betty. May be so: but it 's a step which I shall never take.——What! would you have me lost to all feeling? Would you have me meanly make use of chambermaid artifices for a husband?

Mrs. Har. I would only have you happy, my dear:——And where the man of one's heart is at stake, I do n't thing we ought to stand so rigidly upon trifles.——

Lady Betty. Trifles, Emmy! do you call the laws of delicacy trifles. She that violates these——

Mrs. *Har.* Poh! poh! **She** that violates :—what a work there is with you sentimental folks.——Why, do n't I tell you that my Lord shall never know any thing of your concern in the design ?

Lady *Betty.* But sha' n't I know it my self, Emmy! ——and how can I escape the justice of my own reflections!

Mrs. *Har.* Well, thank heaven my sentiments are not sufficiently refin'd to make me unhappy.

Lady *Betty.* I can 't change my sentiments, my dear Emmy, nor would I, if I could : of this, however, be certain, that unless I have Lord Winworth without courting him, I shall never have him at all.—— But be silent to all the world upon this matter, I conjure you ; particularly to Miss Marchmont, for she has been so strenuous an advocate for my lord, that the concealment of it from her might give her some doubts of my friendship : and I should be continually uneasy for fear my reserve should be consider'd as an indirect insult upon her circumstances.

Mrs. *Har.* Well, the devil take this delicacy; I do n't know any thing it does besides making people miserable:—And yet some how, foolish as it is, one can 't help liking it.——But yonder I see Sir Harry and Mr. Cecil.

Lady *Betty.* Let us withdraw then, my dear; they may detain us ; and, 'till this interview is over, I shall be in a continual agitation ; yet I am strangely apprehensive of a disappointment, Emmy—and if——

[*Going.*

Mrs. Har. Lady Betty.

Lady Betty. What do you say?

Mrs. Har. Do you still think there is any thing extremely preposterous in second marriages?

Lady Betty. You are intolerably provoking.————

[*Exeunt.*

Enter CECIL *and* Sir HARRY.

Cecil. Well, did n't I tell you the moment you open'd this affair to me, that the colonel was a man of too much sense to give his daughter to a coxcomb?

Sir Harry. But what if I should tell you, that his daughter shall be still mine, and in spite of his teeth?

Cecil. Pr'y thee explain, kinsman.

Sir Harry. Why suppose Miss Rivers should have no very strong objection to this unfortunate figure of mine?

Cecil. Why even your vanity can't think that a young lady of her good sense can possibly be in love with you?

Sir Harry. What, you think that no likely circumstance I see?

Cecil. I do really.----Formerly indeed the women were fools enough to be caught by the frippery of externals, and so a fellow neither pick'd a pocket, nor put up with an affront, he was a dear toad—a sweet creature—and a wicked devil; nay, the wicked devil was quite an angel of a man—and, like another Alexander, in proportion to the number of wretches which he made, he constantly encreas'd the lustre of his reputation, 'till at last, having conquer'd all his worlds, he sat down with that celebrated ruffian, and wept because he could commit no father outrages upon society.

Sir Harry. O, my good moralizing cousin, you 'll find yourself cursedly out in your politics ; and I shall convince you in a few hours, that a handsome suit on the back of a sprightly young fellow, will still do more among the women, than all your sentiment and slovenliness.

Cecil. What! would you persuade me that Miss Rivers will go off with you——?

Sir Harry. You have hit the mark for once in your life, my sweet temper'd mouther of morality. The dear Theodora——

Cecil. The dear Theodora! and so, Harry, you imagine, that by the common maxims of fashionable life, you may appear to be a friend to the colonel, at the very moment you are going to rob him of his daughter.——For shame, kinsman, for shame—have some pride if you have no virtue—and do n't smile in a man's face when you want to do him the greatest of all injuries.—do n't, Harry——

Sir Harry. Cecil, I scorn a base action as much as you, or as much as any man—but I love Miss Rivers honourably. I ask nothing from her father ; and as her person is her own, she has a right to bestow it where she pleases.

Cecil. I am answered—her person is her own—and she has a right to be miserable her own way. I ac-

C

knowledge it—and will not discover your secret to her father.

Sir *Harry.* Discover it to her father—why sure you would n't think of it. Take care, Cecil, take care— I do, indeed, love you better than any man in the world——and I know you have a friendship, a cordial friendship for me---but the happiness of my whole life is at stake, and must not be destroy'd by any of your unaccountable peculiarities.

Cecil. Harry---you know I would at any time rather promote your happiness than obstruct it. And you also know, that if I die without children——you shall have a principal part of my fortune; but damn it—— I wish you had not us'd the mask of friendship to steal this young lady away from her relations——'t is hard that their good nature must be turn'd against their peace; and hard, because her whole family treat you with regard, that you should offer them the greatest insult imaginable.

Sir *Harry.* Dear Cecil, I am more to be pity'd than condemn'd in this transaction. When I first endeavour'd to make myself agreeable to Miss Rivers, I imagined her family would readily countenance my addresses; and when I succeeded in that endeavour, I had not time to declare myself in form, before her father enter'd into this engagement with Sidney.—— the moment I heard it mention'd, I wrote to him, offering him a *carte blanche*; and this morning a repetition of my offer was treated with contempt.—I have, therefore, been forc'd into the measure you disapprove so much—But I hope my conduct, in the character of the son-in-law, will amply atone for any error in my behaviour as a friend.

Cecil. Well, well, we must make the best of a bad market; her father has no right to force her inclinations; 'tis equally cruel and unjust; therefore you may depend upon my utmost endeavours not only to assist you in carrying her off, but in appeasing all family resentments. For really you are so often in the wrong, that one must stand by you a little when you are in the right,—so I shall be ready for you, kinsman.

Sir *Harry.* Why, Cecil, this is honest——this is really friendly—and you shall abuse me a whole twelvemonth without my answering a syllable——but for the present I must leave you—yonder I see Miss Rivers, we have some little matters to talk of—you understand me—and now——   [*Exit.*

Cecil. For a torrent of rapture and nonsense.—What egregious puppies does this unaccountable love make of young fellows: Nay, for that matter, what egregious puppies does it not make of old ones?—*ecce signum.*—'Tis a comfort though, that nobody knows I am a puppy in this respect but myself.—Here was I fancying that all the partiality I felt for poor Hortensia Marchmont proceeded from my friendship for her father—when upon an honest examination into my own heart—I find it principally arises from my regard for herself.—I was in hopes a change of objects would have

driven the baggage out of my thoughts,—and I went
to France;—but I am come home with a settled resolution of asking her to marry a slovenly rascal of fifty,
who is to be sure a very likely swain for a young lad,
to fall in love with;—but who knows—the most sensible women have sometimes strange tastes ---and yet
it must be a very strange taste, that can possibly approve of my overtures. I'll go cautiously to work
however,---and solicit her as for a friend of my own
age and fortune;---so that if she refuses me, which is
probable enough---I shan't expose myself to her contempt.----What a ridiculous figure is an old fool sighing
at the feet of a young woman.----Zounds, I wonder
how the grey-headed dotards have the impudence to
ask a blooming girl of twenty to throw herself away
upon a moving mummy, or a walking skeleton.

[*Exit.*

SCENE II.

Changes to an Apartment in Lady Betty's *House.*

Enter Lady BETTY *and* Mrs. HARLEY.

Lady Betty. You can't think, Emmy, how my spirits are agitated?---I wonder what my lord can want
with me?

Mrs. Har. Well, well, try and collect yourself a
little---he's just coming up --- I must retire.----Courage,
my dear creature, this once---and the day's our own,
I warrant you. [*Exit.*

Enter Lord WINWORTH, *bowing very low.*

Lady *Betty*. Here he is !---Bless me, what a flutter I 'm in !

L. *Win*. Your ladyship's most obedient.

Lady *Betty*. Won't your lordship be seated ?---He seems excessively confus'd.   [*Aside*.

L. *Win*. I have taken the liberty, madam---How she awes me now I am alone with her !   [*Aside*.

Lady *Betty*. My lord !

L. *Win*. I say, madam, I have taken the liberty to---

Lady *Betty*. I beg, my lord, you won't consider an apology in the least---

L. *Win*. Your ladyship is extremely obliging---and yet I am fearful---

Lady *Betty*. I hope your lordship will consider me as a friend,---and therefore lay aside this unnecessary ceremony.

L. *Win*. I do consider you, madam, as a friend ;--- as an inestimable friend---and I am this moment come to solicit you upon a subject of the utmost importance to my happiness.

Lady *Betty*. [*aside*] Lord ! what is he going to say ?

L. *Win*. Madam !——

Lady *Betty*. I say, my lord, that you cannot speak to me on any subject of importance without engaging my greatest attention.

L. *Win*. You honour me too much, madam.

Lady *Betty*. Not in the least, my lord---for there is

C iij

not a person in the world who wishes your happiness with greater cordiality.

L. Win. You eternally oblige me, madam——and I can now take courage to tell you, that my happiness, in a most material degree, depends upon your lady-ship.

Lady *Betty.* On me, my lord?——Bless me!

L. Win. Yes, madam, on your ladyship.

Lady *Betty.* [*aside.*] Mrs. Harley was right, and I shall sink with confusion.

L. Win. 'T is on this business, madam, I have taken the liberty of requesting the present interview, and as I find your ladyship so generously ready——

Lady *Betty.* Why, my lord, I must confess—I say, I must acknowledge, my lord—that if your happiness depends upon me—I should not be very much pleas'd to see you miserable.

L. Win. Your ladyship is benignity itself; but as I want words to express my sense of this obligation —I shall proceed at once to my request, nor trespass upon you patience by an ineffectual compliment to your generosity.

Lady *Betty.* If you please, my lord.

L. Win. Then, madam, my request is, that I may have your consent——

Lady *Betty.* This is so sudden, my lord! so unex-pected!

L. Win. Why, madam, it is so; yet, if I could but engage your acquiescence——I might still think of a double union on the day which makes my cousin happy.——

Lady *Betty.* My lord—I really don't know how to answer: Doesn't your lordship think this is rather precipitating matters?

L. *Win.* No man, madam, can be too speedy in promoting his happiness: if, therefore, I might presume to hope for your concurrence—I wou'd n't altogether.——

Lady *Betty.* My concurrence, my lord! since it is so essentially necessary to your peace I cannot refuse any longer.——Your great merit will justify so immediate a compliance——and I shall stand excus'd of all.——

L. *Win.* Then madam, I don't despair of the lady's--

Lady *Betty.* My lord?

L. *Win.* I know your ladyship can easily prevail upon her to overlook an immaterial punctilio, and therefore——

Lady *Betty.* The lady, my lord?

L. *Win.* Yes, madam, Miss Marchmont; if she finds my addresses supported by your ladyship, will, in all probability, be easily induced to receive them, and then, your ladyship knows——

Lady *Betty.* Miss Marchmont, my lord!

L. *Win.* Yes, madam, Miss Marchmont.——Since your final disapprobation of those hopes which I was once presumptuous enough to entertain of calling your ladyship mine, the anguish of a rejected passion has render'd me inconceivably wretched, and I see no way

of mitigating the severity of my situation, but in the
esteem of this amiable woman, who knows how tenderly I have been attach'd to you, and whose goodness will induce her, I am well convinc'd, to alleviate
as much as possible the greatness of my disappointment.

Lady *Betty.* Your Lordship is undoubtedly right in
your opinion—and I am infinitely concern'd to have
been the involuntary cause of uneasiness to you ; but
Miss Marchmont, my lord—she will merit your utmost.

L. *Win.* I know she will, madam, and it rejoices
me to see you so highly pleas'd with my intention.

Lady *Betty.* O, I am quite delighted with it !

L. *Win.* I knew I should please you by it.

Lady *Betty.* You can't imagine how you have
pleas'd me !

L. *Win.* How noble is this goodness ! Then, madam, I may expect your ladyship will be my advocate.
The injustice which fortune has done Miss Marchmont's merit, obliges me to act with a double degree
of circumspection ; for when virtue is unhappily
plung'd into difficulties, 'tis entitled to an additional
share of veneration.

Lady *Betty.* [*Aside.*] How has my folly undone me !

L. *Win.* I will not trespass any longer upon your
ladyship's leisure, than just to observe, that though I
have solicited your friendship on this occasion, I
must, nevertheless beg you will not be too much my
friend. I know Miss Marchmont would make any

sacrifice to oblige you; and if her gratitude should appear in the least concern'd—this is a nice point, my dear Lady Betty, and I must not wound the peace of any person's bosom, to recover the tranquillity of my own. [*Exit.*

Enter Mrs. HARLEY.

Mrs. *Har.* Well, my dear, is it all over?

Lady *Betty.* It is all over indeed, Emmy.

Mrs. *Har.* But why that sorrowful tone, and melancholy countenance? Mustn't I wish you joy?

Lady *Betty.* O, I am the most miserable woman in the world! Would you believe it? The business of this interview was to request my interest in his favour with Miss Marchmont.

Mrs. *Har.* With Miss Marchmont!—Then there is not one atom of sincere affection in the universe.

Lady *Betty.* As to that, I have reason to think his sentiments for me are as tender as ever.

Mrs. *Har.* He gives you a pretty proof of his tenderness, truly, when he asks your assistance to marry another woman!

Lady *Betty.* Had you but seen his confusion——

Mrs. *Har.* He might well be confus'd, when, after courting you these three years, he could think of another; and that too at the very moment in which you were ready to oblige him.

Lady *Betty.* There has been a sort of fatality in the affair, and I am punish'd but too justly:—The woman that wants candour, where she is address'd by a man of merit, wants a very essential virtue; and she who can delight in the anxiety of a worthy mind, is little to be pitied when she feels the sharpest stings of anxiety in her own.

Mrs. Har. But what do you intend to do with regard to this extraordinary request of Lord Winworth; will you really suffer him to marry Miss Marchmont?

Lady Betty. Why, what can I do? If it was improper for me, before I knew any thing of his design in regard to Miss Marchmont, to insinuate the least desire of hearing him again on the subject of his heart, 't is doubly improper now, when I see he has turn'd his thoughts on another woman, and when this woman, besides, is one of my most valuable friends.

Mrs. Har. Well, courage, Lady Betty; we are n't yet in a desperate situation. Miss Marchmont loves you as herself, and would n't, I dare say, accept the first man in the world, if it gave you the least uneasiness.—I 'll go to her, therefore, this very moment—tell her at once how the case his; and, my life for it, her obligations to you——

Lady Betty. Stay, Emmy, I conjure you stay, and, as you value my peace of mind, be for ever silent on this subject. Miss Marchmont has no obligations to me; since our acquaintance I have been the only person oblig'd; she has given me a power of serving the worthiest young creature in the world, and so far has laid me under the greatest obligation.

Mrs. Har. Why, my dear——

Lady Betty. But suppose I could be mean enough

to think an apartment in my house, a place in my char-
riot, a seat at my table, and a little annuity in case of
my decease, were obligations, when I continually enjoy such a happiness as her friendship and her company ;—do you think they are obligations that would
make a woman of her fine sense reject the most amiable man existing, especially in her circumstances,
where he has the additional recommendation of an elevated rank and an affluent fortune :—This would be
exacting interest with a witness, for trifles ; and, instead of having any little merit to claim from my behaviour to her, I should be the most inexorable of all
usurers.

Mrs. Har. Well, but suppose Miss Marchmont
should not like my lord ?

Lady Betty. Not like him, why will you suppose an
impossibility ?

Mrs. Har. But let us suppose it, for argument sake.

Lady Betty. Why I cannot say but it would please
me above all things : for still, Emmy, I am a woman,
and feel this unexpected misfortune with the keenest
sensibility : it kills me to think of his being another's ;
but if he must, I would rather see him her's than any
woman's in the universe. But I 'll talk no more upon
this subject, 'till I acquaint her with his proposal,
and yet, Emmy, how severe a trial I must go through !

Mrs. Har. Ay, and you most richly deserve it.

[*Exeunt.*

ACT III. SCENE I.

Lady Betty's *Garden.* Sir HARRY, Miss RIVERS, *and*
SALLY, *cross at the head of the stage :* Colonel RIVERS
observing them.

Rivers.

In close conversation with Sir Harry this half hour,
at the remotest part of the garden!—Why, what am I
to think of all this? Does n't she know I have refused
him? Does n't she know herself engag'd to Sidney?
—There 's something mean and pitiful in suspicion :
But still there is something that alarms me in this affair, and who knows how far the happiness of my
child may be at stake? Women, after all, are strange
things; they have more sense than we generally allow
them, but they have also more vanity. 'T is not for
want of understanding they err, but through an insa-
tiable love of flattery. They know very well when
they are committing a fault, but destruction wears so
bewitching a form, that they rebel against the sense
of their own conviction, and never trouble themselves
about consequences till they are actually undone—But
here they come.—I do n't like this listening; yet the
meanness of the action must for once be justified by
the necessity.   [*Retires behind a clump of trees.*

Enter Miss RIVERS, Sir HARRY, *and* SALLY.

Miss *Riv.* Indeed, Sir Harry, you upbraid me very

unjustly. I feel the refusal which my father has given you severely ; nevertheless I must not consent to your proposal.—An elopement would, I am sure, break his heart ; and as he is wholly ignorant of my partiality for you, I cannot accuse him of unkindness.

Riv. [*behind.*] So! so! so! so!

Sir *Harry.* Why then, my dear Miss Rivers, would n't you give me leave to mention the prepossession with which you honour me, to the old gentleman?

Riv. The old gentleman!——

Miss *Riv.* Because I was in hopes my father would have listen'd to your application, without putting me to the painful necessity of acknowledging my sentiments in your favour ; and because I fear'd, that unless the application was approv'd, on account of it's intrinsic generosity, there was nothing which could possibly work upon the firmness of his temper.

Riv. Well said, daughter!

Sally. The firmness of your father's temper, madam! the obstinacy you should say.——Sir Harry, as I live and breathe, there is n't so obstinate, so perverse, and so peevish an old devil in all England.

Riv. Thank you, Mrs. Sally.

Miss *Riv.* Sally, I insist that when you speak of my father, you always speak of him with respect.—— 'T is n't your knowledge of secrets which shall justify these freedoms ; for I would rather every thing was discovered this minute, than hear him mention'd with so impudent a familiarity by his servants.

Sally. Well, madam, I beg pardon ; but you know

the Colonel, where he once determines, is never to be alter'd; so that call this steadiness of temper by what name you please---'tis likely to make you miserable, unless you embrace the present opportunity, and go off, like a woman of spirit, with the object of your affections.

Riv. What a damn'd jade it is!

Sir *Harry.* Indeed, my dear Miss Rivers, Sally advises you like a true friend; and I am satisfied your own good sense must secretly argue on her side the question. The only alternative you have, is to fly and be happy, or stay and be miserable.---You have yourself acknowledged, my ever adorable---

Riv. O, damn your adorables!

Sir *Harry.* I say, madam, you have yourself acknowledged, that there is no hope whatsoever of working upon the Colonel's tenderness, by acquainting him with our mutual affection :---On the contrary 'tis likely that had he the least suspicion of my being honoured with your regard, he would drag you instantly to his favourite Sidney, who is so utterly insensible of your merit, and who, if he has a passion for any body, is, I am confident, devoted to Miss Marchmont.

Riv. Why, what a lye the rascal has trumped up here against poor Sidney?

Miss *Riv.* Dear Sir Harry, what would you have me do?

Riv. There!---Her dear Sir Harry!

Sir *Harry.* My ever adorable Miss Rivers——

Riv. No, she can't stand these ever-adorables.

amiable, but it ought by no means to render you forgetful of what is due to yourself——Consider, madam, if you have been treated with tenderness, you have repaid that tenderness with duty, and have so far discharged this mighty obligation.

Riv. A pretty method of settling accounts truly!

Miss *Riv.* Don't, my dear Sir Harry, speak in this negligent manner of my father.

Riv. Kind creature!

Sir *Harry.* From what I have urg'd you must see, madam, that though you are so ready to sacrifice your peace for your father, he sets a greater value upon a trifling promise than upon your happiness :——Judge, therefore, whether his repose should be dearer to you than your own; and judge too, whether to prevent the breach of his word, you should vow eternal tenderness to a man you must eternally detest, and violate even your veracity to kill the object of your love?

Miss *Riv.* Good heaven, what shall I do?

Sally. Do——madam——go off, to be sure.

Riv. I'll wring that hussey's head off.

Sir *Harry.* On my knees, madam, let me beg you will consult your own happiness, and, in your own, the happiness of your father.

Riv. Ay, now he kneels, 'tis all over.

Sir *Harry.* The colonel, madam, has great sensibility, and the consciousness that he himself has been the cause of your unhappiness, will fill him with endless regret——Whereas, by escaping with me, the case will be utterly otherwise.—When he sees we are inseparably united, and hears with how unabating an assiduity I labour to merit the blessing of your hand, a little time will necessarily make us friends ; and I have great hopes that, before the end of three months, we shall be the favourites of the whole family.

Riv. You 'll be cursedly mistaken though.———

Sir *Harry.* But speak, my dear Miss Rivers—speak and pronounce my fate.

Miss *Riv.* Sir Harry you have convinc'd me ;———

Riv. Ay, I knew he would.

Miss *Riv.* And provided you here give me a solemn assurance, that the moment we are married you will employ every possible method of effecting a reconciliation———

Sir *Harry.* You consent to go off with me the first opportunity.———A thousand thanks, my angel, for this generous condescension !—and when———

Miss *Riv.* There is no occasion for professions, Sir Harry ; I rely implicitly on your tenderness and your honour.

Sally. Dear madam, you have transported your poor Sally by this noble resolution.

Riv. I dare say she has; but I may chance to cool your transport in a horse-pond.

Miss *Riv.* I am oblig'd to you, Sally, for the part you take in my affairs, and I purpose that you shall be the companion of my flight.

Sally. Shall I, madam ! you are too good ; and I am sure I should n't like to live in my old master's house, when you are out of the family.

Riv. Don't be uneasy on that account.

Sir *Harry.* Suffer me now, my dear Miss Rivers, since you have been thus generously kind, to inform you, that a coach and six will be ready punctually at twelve, at the side of the little paddock, at the back of Lady Betty's garden. There's a close walk, you know, from the garden to the place, and I'll meet you at the spot to conduct you to the coach.

Miss *Riv.* Well, I am strangely apprehensive, but I'll be there. However, 'tis high time for us now to separate, my father's eyes are generally every where, and I am impatient, since it is determined, 'till our design is executed.

Riv. O, I don't in the least doubt it.————

Sir *Harry.* 'Till twelve then, farewell, my charmer.

Miss *Riv.* You do what you will with me.

[*Exeunt separately.*

[Rivers *comes forward.*]

You do what you will with me! Why, what a fool, what an idiot was I, ever to suppose I had a daughter ————From the moment of her birth, to this cursed hour, I have labour'd, I have toil'd for her happiness, and now, when I fancy'd myself sure of her tend'rest affection, she casts me off for ever.————By and by, I shall have this fellow at my feet, entreating my forgiveness; and the world will think me an unfeeling monster if I don't give him my estate, as a reward for having blasted my dearest expectations. The world will think it strange that I should not promote his felicity, because he has utterly destroy'd mine;

and my dutiful daughter will be surpriz'd, if the tender ties of nature are not strictly regarded in my conduct, though she has violated the most sacred of them all in her own. Death and hell! who would be a father?————There is yet one way left, and, if that fails, why, I never had a daughter. [*Exit.*

SCENE II.

An Apartment. Enter Miss MARCHMONT *and* CECIL.

Miss *March.* Nay, now, sir, I must tax you with unkindness; know something that may possibly be of consequence to my welfare, and yet decline to tell me!————Is this consistent with the usual friendship which I have met with from Mr. Cecil?

Cecil. Look'ye, Hortensia, 't is because I set a very great value on your esteem, that I find this unwillingness to explain myself.

Miss *March.* Indeed, sir, you grow every moment more and more mysterious.

Cecil. Well then, Hortensia, if I thought you would n't be offended—I————

Miss *March.* I am sure, sir, you will never say any thing to give me a reasonable cause of offence.————I know your kindness for me too well, sir.

Cecil. Where is the need of sirring me at every word? I desire you will lay aside this ceremony, and treat me with the same freedom you do every body else; these sirs are so cold and so distant.

Miss March. Indeed, sir, I can't so easily lay aside my respect as you imagine, for I have long considered you as a father.

Cecil. As a father!—But that's a light in which I don't want to be consider'd——As a father, indeed! O she's likely to think me a proper husband for her, I can see that already. [*Aside.*

Miss March. Why not, sir?—your years, your friendship for my father, and your partiality for me, sufficiently justify the propriety of my epithet.

Cecil. [*Aside.*] My years!——Yes, I thought my years would be an invincible obstacle.

Miss March. But pray, sir, to the business upon which you wanted to speak with me: you don't consider I am all this time upon the rack of my sex's curiosity.

Cecil. Why then, Hortensia, I will proceed to the business, and ask you in one word, if you have any disinclination to be married?

Miss March. This is proceeding to business indeed, sir:—but, ha! ha! ha! pray, who have you design'd me as a husband?

Cecil. Why, what do you think of a man about my age?

Miss March. Of your age, sir!

Cecil. Yes, of my age.

Miss March. Why, sir, what would you advise me to think of him?

Cecil. That isn't the question, for all your arch significance of manner, madam.

Miss March. O, I am sure you would never recom-mend him to me as a husband, sir!

Cecil. —So!—and why not pray?

Miss March. Because I am sure you have too great a regard for me.

Cecil. She gives me rare encouragement. [*aside.*]— But do you imagine it impossible for such a hus-band to love you very tenderly?

Miss March. No—sir!—But do you imagine it pos-sible for me to love him very tenderly?——You see I have caught your own frankness, sir, and answer with as much ease as you question me.

Cecil. [*Aside.*] How lucky it was that I did not open myself directly to her!—O, I should have been most purely contemptible!

Miss March. But pray, sir, have you, in reality, any meaning by these questions? Is there actually any body who has spoken to you on my account?

Cecil. Hortensia, there is a fellow, a very foolish fel-low, for whom I have some value, that entertains the sincerest affection for you.

Miss March. Then, indeed, sir, I am very unhappy —for I cannot encourage the addresses of any body.

Cecil. No!

Miss March. O, sir! I had but two friends in the world—yourself and Lady Betty; and I am, with jus-tice, apprehensive, that neither will consider me long with any degree of regard. Lady Betty has a propo-sal from Lord Winworth of the same nature with yours, in which I fear she will strongly interest herself; and I must be under the painful necessity of disobliging you both, from an utter impossibility of listening to either of your recommendations.

Cecil. I tell you, Hortensia, not to alarm yourself.

Miss *March.* Dear sir, I have always consider'd you with reverence, and it would make me inconceivably wretched, if you imagin'd I was actuated upon this occasion by any ridiculous singularity of sentiment. I would do much to please you, and I scarcely know what I should refuse to Lady Betty's request; but, sir, though it distresses me exceedingly to discover it, I must tell you I have not a heart to dispose of.

Cecil. How's this?

Miss *March.* At the same time, I must, however, tell you, that my affections are so plac'd as to make it wholly impossible for me ever to change my situation. This acknowledgment of a prepossession, sir, may be inconsistent with the nice reserve which is proper for my sex; but it is necessary to justify me in a case where my gratitude might be reasonably suspected; and when I recollect to whom it is made, I hope it will be doubly entitled to an excuse.

Cecil. Your candour, Hortensia, needs no apology; but as you have trusted me thus far with your secret, may n't I know why you can have no prospect of being united to the object of your affections?

Miss *March.* Because, sir, he is engaged to a most deserving young lady, and will be married to her in a few days.—In short, Mr. Sidney is the man for whom I entertain this secret partiality; you see, therefore,

that my partiality is hopeless; but you see, at the
same time, how utterly improper it would be for me
to give a lifeless hand to another, while he is entirely
master of my affections.—It would be a meanness, of
which I think myself incapable; and I should be quite
unworthy the honour of any deserving hand, if, cir-
cumstanced in this manner, I could basely stoop to
accept it.

Cecil. You interest me strangely in your story, Hortensia!—But has Sidney any idea——

Miss March. None in the least.—Before the match
with Miss Rivers was in agitation; he made his addresses to me, though privately; and, I must own, his
tenderness, join'd to his good qualities, soon gave me
impressions in his favour.——But, sir, I was a poor
orphan, wholly dependant upon the generosity of
others, and he was a younger brother of family, great
in his birth, but contracted in his circumstances.—
What could I do?——It was not in my power to
make his fortune, and I had too much pride, or too
much affection to think of destroying it.

Cecil. You are a good girl, a very good girl;——
but surely if Lady Betty knows any thing of this matter, there can be no danger of her recommending
Lord Winworth so earnestly to your attention.——

Miss March. There, sir, is my principal misfortune.
—Lady Betty is, of all persons, the least proper to be
made acquainted with it.—Her heart is in the marriage between Miss Rivers and Mr. Sidney; and had
she the least idea of my sentiments for him, or of his

inclination for me, I am positive it would immediately frustrate the match. On this account, sir, I have carefully concealed the secret of my wishes, and on this account I must still continue to conceal it.—— My heart shall break before it shall be worthless ;— and I should detest myself for ever, if I was capable of establishing my own peace at the expence of my benefactress's first wish, and the desire of her whole family.

Cecil. Zounds, what can be the matter with my eyes !———

Miss *March.* My life was marked out early by calamity—and the first light I beheld, was purchas'd with the loss of a mother. The grave snatched away the best of fathers, just as I came to know the value of such a blessing : and had not it been for the exalted goodness of others, I, who once experienced the unspeakable pleasure of relieving the necessitous, had myself, perhaps, felt the immediate want of bread.——And shall I ungratefully sting the bosom which has thus benevolently cherished me ? Shall I basely wound the peace of those who have rescu'd me from despair ;— and stab at their tranquillity, in the very moment they honour me with protection ? O, Mr. Cecil! they deserve every sacrifice which I can make. May the benignant hand of Providence shower endless happiness upon their heads ; and may the sweets of a still encreasing felicity be their portion, whatever becomes of me !

Cecil. Hortensia, I can't stay with you.—My eyes

are exceedingly painful of late: what the devil can be
the matter with them ?—but let me tell you before I
go, that you shall be happy after all; that you shall, I
promise you.——But I see Lady Betty coming this
way—and I cannot enter into explanations: yet, do
you hear—do n't suppose I am angry with you for
refusing my friend; do n't suppose such a thing, I
charge you; for he has too much pride to force himself upon any woman, and too much humanity to
make any woman miserable. He is, besides, a very
foolish fellow, and it does n't signify.——   [*Exit.*

Enter Lady BETTY.

Lady *Betty.* Well, my dear Hortensia, I am come
again to ask you what you think of Lord Winworth?
——We were interrupted before——and I want, as soon
as possible, for the reason I hinted, to know your real
opinion of him.

Miss *March.* You have long known my real opinion
of him, Lady Betty. You know I always thought
him a very amiable man.

Lady *Betty.* [*with impatience.*] Do you think him
an amiable man?

Miss *March.* The whole world thinks as I do in
this respect—yet——

Lady *Betty.* Ay, she loves him, 't is plain; and
there is no hope after this declaration. [*aside.*] His
lordship merits your good opinion, I assure you, Miss
Marchmont.

Miss *March*. [*aside*.] Yes, I see by this ceremony that she is offended at my coolness to the proposal.

Lady *Betty*. I have hinted to you, Miss Marchmont, that my lord requested I would exert my little interest with you in his favour.

Miss *March*. The little interest your ladyship has with me——the little interest————

Lady *Betty*. Don't be displeased with me, my dear Hortensia—I know my interest with you is considerable.—I know you love me.

Miss *March*. I would sacrifice my life for you, Lady Betty : For what had that life been without your generosity?

Lady *Betty*. If you love me, Hortensia, never mention any thing of this nature.

Miss *March*. You are too good————

Lady *Betty*. But to my Lord Winworth.—He has earnestly requested I would become his advocate with you.—He has entirely got the better of his former attachments, and there can be no doubt of his making you an excellent husband.

Miss *March*. His Lordship does me infinite honour; nevertheless————

Lady *Betty*. [*eagerly*.] Nevertheless, what, my dear?——

Miss *March*. I say, notwithstanding I think myself highly honour'd by his sentiments in my favour, 'tis utterly impossible for me to return his affection.

Lady *Betty*. [*surprized*.] Impossible for you to return his affection!

Miss March. [*Aside.*] I knew what an interest she would take in this affair.

Lady Betty. And do you really say you can't give him a favourable answer?—How fortunate!   [*Aside.*

Miss March. I do, my dear Lady Betty; I can honour, I can reverence him; but I cannot feel that tenderness for his person, which I imagine to be necessary both for his happiness and my own.

Lady Betty. Upon my word, my dear, you are extremely difficult in your choice; and if Lord Winworth is not capable of inspiring you with tenderness, I don't know who is likely to succeed; for, in my opinion, there is not a man in England possessed of more personal accomplishments.

Miss March. And yet, great as these accomplishments are, my dear Lady Betty, they never excited your tenderness.——

Lady Betty. Why, all this is very true, my dear; —but, though I felt no tenderness,—yet I—to be sure, I—that is—I say, nevertheless.—This is beyond my hopes!   [*Aside.*

Miss March. [*Aside.*] She's distress'd that I decline the proposal.——Her friendship for us both is generously warm; and she imagines I am equally insensible to his merit, and my own interest.

Lady Betty. Well, my dear, I see your emotion, and I heartily beg your pardon for saying so much.— I should be inexpressibly concerned, if I thought you made any sacrifice on this occasion to me.——My lord, to be sure, possesses a very high place in my esteem—but——

Miss *March*. Dear Lady Betty, what can I do?—I see your are offended with me,—and yet——

Lady *Betty*. I offended with you, my dear!—far from it; I commend your resolution extremely, since my lord is not a man to your taste. Offended with you! why should I take the liberty to be offended with you?—A presumption of that nature——

Miss *March*. Indeed, Lady Betty, this affair makes me very unhappy.

Lady *Betty*. Indeed, my dear, you talk very strangely:—so far from being sorry that you have refus'd my lord—I am pleas'd, infinitely pleas'd——that is, since he was not agreeable to you.—Be satisfied your acceptance of him would have given me no pleasure in the world; I assure you it would n't: on the contrary, as matters are situated, I would n't for the world have you give him the smallest encouragement.

.[*Exit.*

Miss *March*. [*Alone.*] I see she's greatly disappointed at my refusal of an offer so highly to my advantage:——I see, moreover, she's griev'd that his lordship should meet with a second repulse, and from a quarter too, where the generosity of his proposal might be reasonably expected to promise it success.—How surpriz'd she seemed, when I told her he could not make an impression on my heart! and how eagerly she endeavour'd to convince me that she was pleas'd with my conduct; not considering that this very eagerness was a manifest proof of her dissatisfaction! She is more interested in this affair than I even thought she would be, and I should be completely miserable if she could suspect me of ingratitude.——As she was so zealous for the match, I was certainly to blame in declining it. 'T is not yet, however, too late. She has been a thousand parents to me, and I will not regard my own wishes, when they are any way opposite to her inclinations. Poor Mr. Cecil! —Make me happy after all!—How?—Impossible!— for I was born to nothing but misfortune.—   [*Exit.*

ACT IV. SCENE I.

An Apartment at Lady Betty's *House.* *Enter* Lady BETTY *and* Mrs. HARLEY.

Lady *Betty.*

THUS far, my dear Emmy, there is a gleam of hope. —She determined, positively determined, against my lord; and even suspected so little of my partiality for him, that she appeared under the greatest anxiety, lest I should be offended with her refusing him.——And yet, shall I own my folly to you?

Mrs. *Har.* Pray do, my dear; you'll scarcely believe it——but I have follies of my own sometimes.

Lady *Betty.* Why you quite surprize me!

Mrs. *Har.* 'T is very true for all that.——But to your business.

Lady *Betty*. Why then, greatly as I dreaded her approbation of the proposal,—I was secretly hurt at her insensibility to the personal attractions of his lordship.

Mrs. *Har.* I don't doubt it, my dear.—We think all the world should love what we are in love with ourselves.

Lady *Betty*. You are right—And though I was happy to find her resolution so agreeable to my wishes, my pride was not a little piqued to find it possible for her to refuse a man upon whom I had so ardently plac'd my own affection.—The surprize which I felt on this account, threw a warmth into my expressions, and made the generous girl apprehensive that I was offended with her.

Mrs. *Har.* Well, this is a strange world to live in. —That a woman without a shilling should refuse an earl with a fine person and a great estate, is the most surprizing affair I ever heard of.—Perhaps, Lady Betty, my lord may take it in his head to go round the family: If he should, my turn is next, and I assure you he shall meet with a very different reception.

Lady *Betty*. Then you wouldn't be cruel, Emmy?

Mrs. *Har.* Why no;---not very cruel.——I might give myself a few airs at first:---I might blush a little, and look down :---wonder what he could find in me to attract his attention ;---then pulling up my head, with a toss of disdain,---desire him, if ever he spoke to me on that subject again,——

Lady *Betty*. Well!

Mrs. Har. To have a licence in his pocket;---that's all.----I would make sure work of it at once, and leave it to your elevated minds to deal in delicate absurdities.---But I have a little anecdote for you, which proves, beyond a doubt, that you are as much as ever in possession of Lord Winworth's affection.

Lady Betty. What is it, my dear Emmy?

Mrs. Har. Why about an hour ago, my woman, it seems, and Arnold, my lord's man, had a little conversation on this unexpected proposal to Miss Marchmont; in which Arnold said,---' Never one of ' your Miss Marchmonts, Mrs. Nelson; between ' ourselves—but let it go no farther—Lady Betty is still ' the woman; and a sweet creature she is, that's the ' truth on 't, but a little fantastical, and does n't know ' her own mind—

Lady Betty. I'll assure you!---Why, Mr. Arnold is a wit.

Mrs. Har. Well, but hear him out :---' Mrs. Nelson, ' I know as much of my lord's mind as any body; let ' him marry whom he pleases, he'll never be rightly ' happy but with her ladyship; and I'd give a hundred ' guineas, with all my soul, that it could be a match.' ---These, Nelson tells me, were his very words.---Arnold is an intelligent fellow, and much in the confidence of his master.

Lady Betty. Indeed, I always thought my lord happy in so excellent a servant.—This intelligence is worth a world, my dear Emmy.——

Enter Miss MARCHMONT.

Miss *March.* I have been looking for your ladyship.

Lady *Betty.* Have you any thing particular, my dear Hortensia ?—But why that gloom upon your features ? —What gives you uneasiness, my sweet girl ? Speak, and make me happy by saying it is in my power to oblige you.

Miss *March.* 'Tis in your power, my dear lady Betty, to oblige me highly,—by forgiving the ungrateful disregard which I just now shew'd to your recommendation of lord Winworth ;——

Mr. *Har.* [*Aside.*] Now will I be hang'd if she does n't undo every thing by a fresh stroke of delicacy.

Lady *Betty.* My dear !

Miss *March.* And by informing his lordship that I am ready to pay a proper obedience to your commands.

Mrs. *Har.* [*Aside.*] O, the devil take this elevation of sentiment.

Lady *Betty.* A proper obedience to my commands, my dear ! I really don 't understand you.

Miss *March.* I see how generously you are concerned, for fear I should, upon this occasion, offer violence to my inclination :—But, lady Betty, I should be infinitely more distress 'd by the smallest act of ingratitude to you, than by any other misfortune.—I am therefore ready, in obedience to your wishes, to accept of his lordship ; and if I can 't make him a fond wife, I will, at least, make him a dutiful one.

Mrs. *Har*. [*Aside.*] Now her delicacy is willing to be miserable.

Lady *Betty*. How could you ever imagine, my dear Hortensia, that your rejection of Lord Winworth could possibly give me the smallest offence ?—I have a great regard for his lordship, 'tis true, but I have a great regard for you also; and would by no means wish to see his happiness promoted at your expence :—think of him, therefore, no more, and be assur'd you oblige me in an infinitely higher degree by refusing, than accepting him.

Miss *March*. The more I see your ladyship's tenderness and delicacy, the more I see it necessary to give an affirmative to lord Winworth's proposal.—Your generosity must not get the better of my gratitude.

Mrs. *Har*. Did ever two fools plague one another so heartily with their delicacy and sentiment ? [*Aside.*] Dear lady Betty, why don't you deal candidly with her ?————

Lady *Betty*. Her happiness makes it necessary now, and I will.

Mrs. *Har*. Ay, there's some sense in this.——

Lady *Betty*. Your uncommon generosity, my dear Hortensia, has led you into an error.————

Miss *March*. Not in the least, lady Betty.

Lady *Betty*. Still, Hortensia, you are running into very great mistakes.—My esteem for lord Winworth, let me now tell you,——

Enter Lord WINWORTH.

L. *Win.* Ladies, your most obedient.—As I enter'd, Lady Betty, I heard you pronounce my name:—May I presume to ask, if you were talking to Miss Marchmont on the business I took the liberty of communicating to you this morning?

Mrs. *Har.* [*Aside.*] Ay, now 'tis all over, I see.

Lady *Betty.* Why, to be candid, my lord, I have mentioned your proposal.——

L. *Win.* Well, my dear Miss Marchmont, and may I flatter myself that lady Betty's interposition will induce you to be propitious to my hopes?—The heart now offered to you, madam, is a grateful one, and will retain an eternal sense of your goodness.—Speak, therefore, my dear Miss Marchmont, and kindly say you condescend to accept it.

Mrs. *Har.* [*Aside.*] So—here will be a comfortable piece of work.—I'll e'en retire, and leave them to the consequences of their ridiculous delicacy.' [*Exit.*

Miss *March.* I know not what to say, my lord;—you have honour'd me, greatly honour'd me,—but lady Betty will acquaint you with my determination.—

Lady *Betty.* I acquaint him, my dear—surely you are yourself the most proper to---I shall run distracted! [*Aside.*

Miss *March.* Indeed, madam, I can't speak to his lordship on this subject.

Lady *Betty.* And I assure you, Hortensia, 'tis a subject upon which I do not chuse to enter.

L. Win. If you had a kind answer from Miss Marchmont, Lady Betty, I am sure you would enter upon it readily :—But I see her reply very clearly in your reluctance to acquaint me with it.——

Miss March. Why, madam, will you force me to—

Lady Betty. And why, Hortensia—What am I going to say ?——   [*Aside.*

L. Win. Don't my dear ladies, suffer me to distress you any longer :—To your friendship, madam, I am as much indebted [*addressing himself to Lady* Betty] as if I had been successful ;—and I sincerely wish Miss Marchmout that happiness with a more deserving man, which I find it impossible for her to confer on me.   [*Going.*

Lady Betty. [*Aside.*] Now I have some hope.——

Miss March. My lord, I entreat your stay.——

Lady Betty. Don't call his lordship back, my dear ; it will have an odd appearance.

Enter Lord WINWORTH.

Miss March. He is come back, and I must tell him what your unwillingness to influence my inclinations makes you decline.

L. Win. Your commands, madam.

Lady Betty. [*Aside.*] Now I am undone again !

Miss March. I am in such a situation, my lord, that I can scarcely proceed.—Lady Betty is cruelly kind to me, but as I know her wishes——

Lady Betty. My wishes, Miss Marchmont ! Indeed, my dear, there is such a mistake——

Miss March. There is no mistaking your ladyship's goodness ; you are fearful to direct my resolution, and I should be unkind to distress your friendship any longer.

Lady Betty. You do distress me indeed, Miss Marchmont. [*Half aside and sighing.*

L. Win. I am all expectation, madam !

Miss March. I am compell'd, by gratitude to both, and from affection to my dear Lady Betty, to break through the common forms impos'd on our sex, and to declare, that I have no will but her ladyship's.

Lady Betty. This is so provoking. [*Aside.*

L. Win. Ten thousand thanks for this condescending goodness, madam !—a goodness which is additionally dear to me, as the result of your determination is pronounced by your own lips.

Miss March. Well, Lady Betty, I hope I have answer'd your wishes now.

Lady Betty. You cannot conceive how sensibly I am touch'd with your behaviour, my dear. [*Sighs.*

Miss March. You feel too much for me, Lady Betty.———

Lady Betty. Why I do feel something, my dear: this unexpected event has filled my heart, and I am a little agitated. But come, my dear, let us now go to the company.

Miss March. How generously, madam, do you interest yourself for my welfare !

L. Win. And for the welfare of all her friends !

Lady Betty. Your lordship is too good.

L. *Win.* But the business of her life is to promote the happiness of others, and she is constantly rewarded in the exercise of her own benignity.

Lady *Betty.* You can't imagine how I am rewarded upon the present occasion, I assure your lordship.

[*Exeunt.*

SCENE II.

The Paddock behind Lady Betty's *Garden. Enter* Miss RIVERS *and* SALLY.

Sally. Dear madam, don't terrify yourself with such gloomy reflections.

Miss *Riv.* O, Sally, you can't conceive my distress in this critical situation!—An elopement even from a tyrannical father, has something in it which must shock a delicate mind——But when a woman flies from the protection of a parent, who merits the utmost return of her affection, she must be insensible indeed, if she does not feel the sincerest regret.—If he should n't forgive me!——

Sally. Dear madam, he must forgive you—are n't you his child?

Miss *Riv.* And therefore I should not disoblige him. I am half distracted, and I almost repent the promise I gave Sir Harry, when I consider how much my character may be lessen'd by this step, and recollect how it is likely to affect my unfortunate father.

Sally. But I wonder where Sir Harry can be all this time!

Miss *Riv.* I wish he was come.

Sally. Courage, madam, I hear him coming.

Miss *Riv.* It must be he; let's run and meet him.

Enter RIVERS. Sally *shrieks and runs off.*

Miss *Riv.* My father!

Riv. Yes, Theodora, your poor, abandon'd, miserable father.

Miss *Riv.* Oh, sir!——

Riv. Little, Theodora, did I imagine I should ever have cause to lament the hour of your birth; and less did I imagine, when you arrived at an age to be perfectly acquainted with your duty, you would throw every sentiment of duty off. In what, my dear, has your unhappy father been culpable, that you cannot bear his society any longer? What has he done to forfeit either your esteem or your affection? From the moment of your birth, to this unfortunate hour, he has labour'd to promote your happiness. But how has his solicitude on that account been rewarded?—— You now fly from these arms, which have cherish'd you with so much tenderness; when gratitude, generosity, and nature, should have twin'd me round your heart.

Miss *Riv.* Dear sir!

Riv. Look back, infatuated child, upon my whole conduct since your approach to maturity: Hav'n't I contracted my own enjoyments on purpose to enlarge

yours, and watched your very looks to anticipate your
inclinations? Have I ever, with the obstinacy of other
fathers, been partial in favour of any man to whom
you made the slightest objection? Or have I ever
shewn the least design of forcing your wishes to my
own humour or caprice? On the contrary, has n't the
engagement I have enter'd into been carried on seem-
ingly with your own approbation? And hav'n't you
always appear'd reconcil'd, at least, to a marriage
with Mr. Sidney?

Miss *Riv.* I am so asham'd of myself!

Riv. How then, Theodora, have I merited a treatment of this nature? You have understanding, my
dear, though you want filial affection; and my arguments must have weight with your reason, however
my tranquility may be the object of your contempt.—
I lov'd you, Theodora, with the warmest degree of
paternal tenderness, and flatter'd myself the proofs I
every day gave of that tenderness, had made my peace
of mind a matter of some importance to my child——
But, alas! a paltry compliment from a coxcomb un-
does the whole labour of my life; and the daughter
whom I looked upon as the support of my declining
years, betrays me in the unsuspecting hour of security, and rewards with her person the assassin who
stabs me to the heart.

Miss *Riv.* Hear me, dear sir, hear me!

Riv. I do not come here, Theodora, to stop your
flight, or put the smallest impediment in the way of
your wishes. Your person is your own, and I scorn

to detain even my daughter by force, where she is not bound to me by inclination. Since, therefore, neither duty nor discretion, a regard for my peace, nor a solicitude for your own welfare, are able to detain you, go to this man, who has taught you to obliterate the sentiments of nature, and gain'd a ready way to your heart, by expressing a contempt for your father. Go to him boldly, my child, and laugh at the pangs which tear this unhappy bosom.—Be uniformly culpable, nor add the baseness of a despicable flight to the unpardonable want of a filial affection. [*Going.*

Miss *Riv.* I am the most miserable creature in the world !

Riv. [*Returns.*] One thing more, Theodora, and then farewell for ever. Though you come here to throw off the affection of a child, I will not quit this place before I discharge the duty of a parent, even to a romantic extravagance ; and provide for your welfare, while you plunge me into the most poignant of all distress. In the doating hours of paternal blandishment, I have often promised you a fortune of twenty thousand pounds, whenever you chang'd your situation. This promise was indeed made when I thought you incapable either of ingratitude or dissimulation, and when I fancied your person would be given, where there was some reasonable prospect of your happiness : But still it was a promise, and shall be faithfully discharged. Here then, in this pocket-book, is a security for that sum. [*Miss* Rivers *shews an unwillingness to receive the pocket-book.*] Take it, but never see me more——Banish my name eternally from your remembrance; and when a little time shall remove me from a world which your conduct has rendered insupportable, boast an additional title, my dear, to your husband's regard, by having shortened the life of your miserable father. [*Exit.*

Enter SALLY.

Sally. What, madam, is he gone?

Miss *Riv.* How could I be such a monster, such an unnatural monster, as ever to think of leaving him!—But come, Sally, let us go into the house.

Sally. Go into the house, madam!—Why, aren't we to go off with Sir Harry?

Miss *Riv.* This insensible creature has been my confidante too!——O, I shall eternally detest myself.

Enter Sir HARRY *and* CECIL.

Sir *Harry.* I beg a thousand pardons, my dear Miss Rivers, for detaining you—an unforeseen accident prevented me from being punctual; but the carriage is now ready, and a few hours will whirl us to the summit of felicity. My Cousin Cecil is kindly here to assist us—and——

Miss *Riv.* Sir Harry, I can never forsake my father.

Sir *Harry.* Madam!

Miss *Riv.* By some accident he discover'd our design, and came to this spot while I was trembling with expectation of your appearance.

Sir *Harry.* Well, my dear creature!——

Miss Riv. Here, in a melancholy but resolute voice, he expatiated on the infamy of my intended flight, and mentioned my want of affection for him in terms that pierc'd my very soul. Having done this, he took an abrupt leave, and, scorning to detain me by force, forsook me to the course of my own inclinations.

Sir Harry. Well, my angel, and since he has left you to follow your own inclinations, you will not surely hesitate to————

Miss Riv. Sir Harry, unloose my hand; the universe wouldn't bribe me now to go off with you. O, Sir Harry! if you regarded your own peace, you would cease this importunity; for is it possible that a woman can make a valuable wife, who has prov'd an unnatural daughter?

Sir Harry. But consider your own happiness, my dear Miss Rivers!

Miss Riv. My own happiness, Sir Harry!—What a wretch must the woman be, who can dream of happiness, while she wounds the bosom of a father?

Cecil. What a noble girl!—I shall love her myself for her sense and her goodness.

Sally. [*Aside to Sir* Harry.] She won't consent, I know, Sir Harry; so, if the coach is at hand, it will be the best way to carry her off directly.

Sir Harry. Then, my dear Miss Rivers, there is no hope————

Miss Riv. Sir Harry, I must not hear you.—This parting is a kind of death.

Sir Harry. Part, madam!—By all that's gracious,

we must not part! My whole soul is unalterably fix'd upon you; and since neither tenderness for yourself, or affection for me, persuade you to the only measure which can promote our mutual felicity, you must forgive the despair that forces you from hence, and commit a momentary disrespect to avoid a lasting unhappiness.

Miss Riv. Hear me, Sir Harry; I conjure you to hear me!

Sir Harry. Let me but remove you from this place, madam, and I'll hear every thing.—Cecil, assist me.

Miss Riv. O, Mr. Cecil, I rely upon your honour to save and protect me!

Cecil. And it shall, madam.—For shame, kinsman, unhand the lady!

Sir Harry. Unhand her, what do you mean, Cecil?

Cecil. What do I mean! I mean to protect the lady. What should a man of honour mean?

Miss Riv. [*Breaking from Sir* Harry.] Dear Mr. Cecil, don't let him follow me.   [*She runs off.*

Sally. [*Following.*] I'll give her warning this moment, that's the short and the long of it.   [*Exit.*

Sir Harry. Mr. Cecil, this is no time for trifling— Didn't you come here to assist me in carrying the lady off?

Cecil. With her own inclinations, kinsman; but as they are now on the other side of the question, so am I too. You must not follow her, Sir Harry.

Sir Harry. Zounds! but I will.

Cecil. Zounds! but you sha'n't.—Look'ye, Harry, I came here to assist the purposes of a man of honour, not to abet the violence of a ruffian. Your friends of the world, your fashionable friends, may, if they please, support one another's vices; but I am a friend only to the virtues of a man; and where I sincerely esteem him, I always endeavour to make him honest in spite of his teeth.

Sir *Harry.* An injury like this——

Cecil. Harry! Harry!—don't advance: I am not to be terrified, you know, from the support of what is just; and though you may think it very brave to fight in the defence of a bad action, it will do but little credit either to your understanding or your humanity.

Sir *Harry.* Dear Cecil, there's no answering that. Your justice and your generosity overpower me. You have restor'd me to myself. It was mean, it was unmanly, it was infamous to think of using force. But I was distracted—nay, I am distracted now, and must entirely rely upon your assistance to recover her.

Cecil. As far as I can act with honesty, Harry, you may depend upon me; but let me have no more violence, I beg of you.

Sir *Harry.* Don't mention it, Cecil; I am heartily asham'd——

Cecil. And I am heartily glad of it.——

Sir *Harry.* Pray let us go to my house and consult a little. What a contemptible figure do I make!

Cecil. Why, pretty well, I think; but, to be less so, put up your sword, Harry.

Sir *Harry.* She never can forgive me.

Cecil. If she does, she will scarcely deserve to be forgiven herself.

Sir *Harry.* Do n't, Cecil; 't is ungenerous to be so hard upon me.—I own my fault, and you should encourage me, for every coxcomb has not so much modesty.

Cecil. Why, so I will, Harry; for modesty, I see, as yet sits upon you but very aukwardly.   [*Exeunt.*

ACT V. SCENE I.

An *Apartment at Lady* Betty's. *Enter* RIVERS *and* SIDNEY.

Sidney.

I AM deeply sensible of Miss Rivers's very great merit, sir;—but————

Riv. But what, sir ?————

Sid. Hear me with temper, I beseech you, colonel.

Riv. Hear you with temper!—I do n't know whether I shall be able to hear you with temper; but go on, sir.

Sid. Miss Rivers, independent of her very affluent fortune, colonel, has beauty and merit, which would make her alliance a very great honour to the first family in the kingdom.—But, notwithstanding my admiration of her beauty, and my reverence for her merit, I find it utterly impossible to profit either by her goodness or your generosity.

Riv. How is all this, sir! Do you decline a marriage with my daughter?

Sid. A marriage with Miss Rivers, sir, was once the object of my highest ambition; and, had I been ho-nour'd with her hand, I should have studied to shew my sensibility of a blessing so invaluable;---but at that time, I did not suppose my happiness to be incompatible with her's.----I am now convinc'd that it is so, and it becomes me much better to give up my own hopes, than to offer the smallest violence to her inclinations.

Riv. Death and hell, sir!—what do you mean by this behaviour?—Shall I prefer your alliance to any man's in England?—Shall my daughter even express a readiness to marry you?—And shall you, after this, insolently tell me you don't choose to accept her?—

Sid. Dear colonel, you totally misconceive my motive:—and I am sure, upon reflexion, you will rather approve than condemn it.----A man of common humanity, sir, in a treaty of marriage, should consult the lady's wishes as well as his own; and if he can't make her happy, he will scorn to make her miserable.

Riv. Scorn to make her miserable!—Why the fellow's mad, I believe.—Does n't the girl absolutely consent to have you?—Would you have her drag you to the altar by force?—Would you have her fall at your feet, and beg of you, with tears, to pity one of the finest women, with one of the best fortunes, in England?

Sid. Your vehemence, sir, prevents you from considering this matter in a proper light.----Miss Rivers is sufficiently unhappy in losing the man of her heart; but her distress must be greatly aggravated, if, in the moment she is most keenly sensible of this loss, she is compell'd to marry another.----Besides, colonel, I must have my feelings too.----There is something shocking in an union with a woman whose affections we know to be alienated ; and 'tis difficult to say which is most entitled to contempt, he that stoops to accept of a pre-engaged mind, or he that puts up with a prostituted person.

Riv. Mighty well, sir!---mighty well! But let me tell you, Mr. Sidney---that under this specious ap-pearance of generosity, I can easily see your motive for this refusal of my daughter ?---let me tell you I can easily see your motive, sir ?---and let me tell you, that the person who is in possession of your affections, shall no longer find an asylum in this house.

Sid. Colonel, if I had not been always accustom'd to respect you,---and if I did not even consider this in-sult as a kind of compliment, I don't know how I should put up with it. As to your insinuation, you must be more explicit before I can understand you.

Riv. Miss Marchmont---Sir.---Do you understand me now, sir ? If Miss Marchmont had not been in the case, my daughter had not receiv'd this insult.---Sir Harry was right ; and had not I been ridiculously besotted with your hypocritical plausibility, I might have seen it sooner ; but your cousin shall know of your behaviour, and then, sir, you shall answer me as a man.

Sid. Miss Marchmont, colonel, is greatly above this illiberal reflexion ; as for myself, I shall be always ready to justify an action which I know to be right, though I should be sorry ever to meet you but in the character of a friend. [*Exit.*

Riv. [*alone.*] Well!—Well!—Well!—but it does n't signify,—it does n't signify,—it does n't signify;—I won't put myself in a passion about it;---I won't put myself in a passion about it.----I'll tear the fellow piece-meal.----Zounds! I don't know what I'll do.

[*Exit.*

Enter Mrs. HARLEY, *and* CECIL.

Cecil. Why, this is better and better.

Mrs. *Har.* What a violent passion he's in.

Cecil. This is the very thing I could wish---'t will advance a principal part of our project rarely.----Well is n't Sidney a noble young fellow; and does n't he richly deserve the regard which my poor little girl entertains for him?

Mrs. *Har.* Why really I think he does.----But how secretly my lady Sentimental carried matters!---O, I always said that your grave, reflecting, moralizing damsels, were a thousand times more susceptible of tender impressions than those lively open-hearted girls who talk away at random, and seem ready to run off with every man that happens to fall into their company.

Cecil. I don't know, widow, but there may be some truth in this: you see, at least, I have such a good opinion of a madcap, that you are the first person I have made acquainted with the secret.

Mrs. Har. Well, and hav n't I return'd the compliment, by letting you into my design about Lady Betty and Lord Winworth?

Cecil. What a ridiculous bustle is there here about delicacy and stuff!—Your people of refin'd sentiments are the most troublesome creatures in the world to deal with, and their friends must even commit a violence upon their nicety, before they can condescend to study their own happiness.—But have you done as we concerted?

Mrs. Har. Yes; I have pretended to Lady Betty that my lord desires to speak with her privately on business of the utmost importance; and I have told his lordship that she wants to see him, to disclose a secret that must entirely break off the intended marriage with Miss Marchmont.

Cecil. What an aukward figure they must make! each imagining that the other had desir'd the interview,—and expecting every moment to be told something of consequence.—But you have not given either the least hint of Hortensia's secret inclination for Sidney?

Mrs. Har. How could you possibly suppose such a thing?

Cecil. Well, well, to your part of the business then, while I find out the colonel, and try what I can do with him for my rattle-pated Sir Harry.

Mrs. Har. O, never doubt my assiduity in an affair of this nature!   [*Exeunt.*

Enter Lady BETTY *in another Apartment.*

Lady Betty. What can he want with me I wonder?

—Speak with me again in private, and upon business
of the utmost importance! He has spoken sufficiently
to me already. upon this business of importance to
make me miserable for ever.----But the fault is my own,
and I have nobody to blame but myself.----Bless me!
here he is.

Enter Lord WINWORTH.

L. *Win.* Madam! your most devoted: I come in
obedience to your commands to——

Lady *Betty.* My commands, my lord!

L. *Win.* Yes, madam, your message has alarmed me
prodigiously;—and you cannot wonder if I am a little impatient for an explanation.

Lady *Betty.* Impatient for an explanation, my lord!

L. *Win.* Yes, madam, the affair is of the nearest
concer to my happiness, and the sooner you honour
me with——

Lady *Betty.* Honour you with what, my lord?

L. *Win.* My dear lady Betty, this reserve is unkind,
especially as you know how uneasy I must be 'till I
hear from yourself——

Lady *Betty.* Really, my lord, I am quite astonish'd
—Uneasy 'till you hear from myself!—Impatient for
an explanation!---I beg your lordship will tell me what
is the meaning of all this?

L. *Win.* Surely, madam, you cannot so suddenly
change your kind intentions.—

Lady *Betty.* My kind intentions, my lord!

G

L. Win. I would not, madam, be too presuming, but, as I know your ladyship's goodness, I flatter myself that——

Lady Betty. Your lordship is all a mystery!—I beg you will speak out;—for upon my word I don't understand these half sentences.——

L. Win. Why, madam, Mrs. Harley has told me.——

Lady Betty. [*with eagerness.*] What has she told you, my lord?

L. Win. She has told me of the secret, madam, which you have to disclose, that must entirely break off my marriage with Miss Marchmont.

Lady Betty. Has she then betray'd my weakness?——

L. Win. Madam, I hope you won't think your generous intentions in my favour a weakness: for be assur'd that the study of my whole life——

Lady Betty. I did not think that Mrs. Harley could be capable of such an action;—but since she has told you of the only circumstance which I ever wish'd to be conceal'd, I cannot deny my partiality for your lordship.

L. Win. Madam!——

Lady Betty. This secret was trusted with her, and her alone; but though she has ungenerously discovered it, her end will still be disappointed. I acknowledge that I prize your lordship above all the world;——but even to obtain you I will not be guilty of a baseness, nor promote my own happiness by any act of injustice to Miss Marchmont.

L. Win. I am the most unfortunate man in the

world!—And does your ladyship really honour me with any degree of a tender partiality?

Lady *Betty.* This question is needless, my lord, after what Mrs. Harley has acquainted you with.

L. *Win.* Mr. Harley, madam, has not acquainted me with particulars of any nature———

Lady *Betty.* No!

L. *Win.* No.—And happy as this discovery would have made me at any other time, it now distresses me beyond expression, since the engagements I have just entered into with Miss Marchmont, put it wholly out of my power to receive any benefit from the knowledge of your sentiments. O, Lady Betty! had you been generously candid when I solicited the blessing of your hand, how much had I been indebted to your goodness! But now, think what my situation is, when, in the moment I am sensible of your regard, I must give you up for ever.

Enter CECIL *and* Mrs. HARLEY *from opposite places.*

" Mrs. *Har.* [*repeating ludicrously.*] Who can be-
" hold such beauty, and be silent!

" *Cecil.* [*in the same accent.*] Desire first taught us
" words.———

" Mrs. *Har.* Man, when created, wandered up and
" down,

" *Cecil.* Forlorn and silent as his vassal beasts;

" Mrs. *Har.* But when a heaven-born maid like
" you appear'd,

G ij

" *Cecil.* Strange pleasure fill'd his eyes, and seiz'd
" his heart.

" Mrs. *Har.* Unloos'd his tongue,

" *Cecil.* And his first talk was love." [*both*, ha! ha!
ha!]

L. *Win.* Pray, Mr. Cecil, what is the meaning of
this whimsical behaviour?

Lady *Betty.* The nature of this conduct, Mrs. Harley, bears too strong a resemblance to a late disingenuity, for me to wonder at.

Mrs. *Har.* What disingenuity, my dear?

Lady *Betty.* Why, pray, madam, what secret had I
to disclose to his lordship?

Mrs. *Har.* The secret which you have disclos'd, my
dear,——   [*courtseying.*

Cecil. I beg, my lord, that we may n't interrupt
your heroics, " when in the moment you are sensible
" of her regard, you must give her up for ever."——
A very moving speech, Mrs. Harley!—I am sure it
almost makes me cry to repeat it.

L. *Win.* Mr. Cecil, listening is——

Mrs. *Har.* What are we going to have a quarrel?——

Cecil. O, yes; your lover is a mere nobody without
a little bloodshed: two or three duels give a wonderful addition to his character.

Lady *Betty.* Why, what is the meaning of all this?

Cecil. You shall know in a moment, madam;——
so walk in, good people——walk in, and see the
most surprising pair of true lovers, who have too

much sense to be wise, and too much delicacy to be happy.

Mrs. Har. Walk in——walk in.

Enter RIVERS, Miss RIVERS, Miss MARCHMONT, SIR HARRY, *and* SIDNEY.

Lady Betty. O, Emmy! is this behaving like a friend?

Mr. Har. Yes, and like a true friend, as you shall see presently.———

Riv. My lord, I give you joy, joy heartily.—We have been posted, for some time, under the direction of Marshal Cecil and General Harley, in the next room, who have acquainted us with every thing; and I feel the sincerest satisfaction to think the perplexities of to day have so fortunate a conclusion.

L. Win. The perplexities of to-day are not yet concluded, Colonel.

Miss March. O, Lady Betty, why would n't you trust me with your secret? I have been the innocent cause of great uneasiness to you, and yet my conduct entirely proceeded from the greatness of my affection.

Lady Betty. I know it, my dear,—I know it well; but were you to give up Lord Winworth this moment, be assured that I would n't accept of any sacrifice made at the expence of your happiness.

Cecil. At the expence of her happiness! O, is that all? Come here, master Sobersides [*to* Sidney] and come here, Madam Gravity, [*to* Miss Marchmont] come here, I say;—I suppose, my Lord, I suppose,

Lady Betty, that you already know from what very manly motives—Sidney, here, has declined the marriage with Miss Rivers?

L. Win. I do; and though I lament the impossibility of a relation to the colonel's family, I cannot but admire his behaviour on that occasion.

Lady *Betty.* And I think it extremely generous.

Mrs. *Har.* Come, Cecil, stand by a little; you sha'n't have the whole management of this discovery.

Cecil. Did you ever see such a woman!

Mrs. *Har.* Well, my lord and Lady Betty, since we have agreed thus far, you must know that Mr. Sidney's behaviour has produc'd more good consequences than you can imagine. In the first place, it has enabled Colonel Rivers, without a breach of his word——

Cecil. To give his daughter to my foolish kinsman.

Mrs. *Har.* You won't hold your tongue.

Cecil. And in the next place, it has enabled Mr. Sidney——

Mrs. *Har.* To marry Miss Marchmont.

Cecil. Ay, she will have the last word.——For it seems that between these two turtles there has long subsisted——

Mrs. *Har.* A very tender affection——

Cecil. The devil's in her tongue!—she has the speed of me.

L. Win. What an unexpected felicity?

Lady *Betty.* I am all amazement!

Riv. Well, well, my dear sister, no wondering about it——at a more convenient time you shall know particulars; for the present let me tell you, that now I am cool, and that matters have been properly explained to me, I am not only satisfied, but charm'd with Mr. Sidney's behaviour, though it has prevented the first wish of my heart; and I hope that his Lordship and you, by consenting to his marriage with Miss Marchmont, will immediately remove every impediment in the way of your own happiness.

L. Win. If my own happiness was not to be promoted by such a step, I should instantly give my consent;—and therefore, my dear Miss Marchmont, if I have Lady Betty's approbation and your own concurrence, I here bestow this hand upon as deserving a young man as any in the universe.——This is the only atonement I can make for the uneasiness I have given you; and if your happiness is any way proportioned to your merit, I need not wish you a greater share of felicity.

Sid. What shall I say, my lord?

L. Win. Say nothing, Charles; for if you only knew how exquisite a satisfaction I receive on this occasion, you would rather envy my feelings than think yourself under an obligation.—And now, my dear Lady Betty, if I might presume.

Lady *Betty.* That I may not be censur'd any longer, I here declare my hand your lordship's, whenever you think proper to demand it; for I am now convinced the greatest proof which a woman can give of her own worth, is to entertain an affection for a man of honour and understanding.

L. Win. This goodness, madam, is too great for acknowledgment.

Lady Betty. And now, my dear Theodora, let me congratulate with you: I rejoice that your inclinations are consulted in the most important circumstance of your life; and I am sure Sir Harry will not be wanting in gratitude for the partiality which you have shewn in his favour.

Miss Riv. Dear madam, you oblige me infinitely.

Sir Harry. And as for me, Lady Betty, it is so much my inclination to deserve the partiality with which Miss Rivers has honoured me, as well as to repay the goodness of her family, that I shall have little merit in my gratitude to either. I have been wild, I have been inconsiderate, but I hope I never was despicable; and I flatter myself I sha'n't be wanting in acknowledgment only to those, who have laid me under the greatest of all obligations.

Riv. Sir Harry, say no more.——My girl's repentance has been so noble; your cousin Cecil's behaviour has been so generous; and I believe you, after all to be a man of such principle—that next to Sidney I do n't know who I should prefer to you for a son-in-law. But you must think a little for the future, and remember, that it is a poor excuse for playing the fool, to be possessed of a good understanding.

L. Win. Well, there seems but one thing remaining undone:—I just now took the liberty of exercising a father's right over Miss Marchmont, by disposing of her hand; 't is now necessary for me——

Cecil. Hold, my lord ;—I guess what you are about, but you sha' n't monopolize generosity, I assure you. —I have a right to shew my friendship as well as your lordship ; so, after your kinsman's marriage, whatever you have a mind to do for him shall be equalled, on my part, for Miss Marchmont ; guinea for guinea, as far as you will, and let's see who tires first in going through with it.

L. *Win.* A noble challenge, and I accept it.

Lady *Betty.* No, there's no bearing this.

Miss *March.* Speak to them, Mr. Sidney, for I cannot.————

Sid. I wish I had words to declare my sense of this goodness.

Riv. I did n't look upon myself as a very pitiful fellow, but I am strangely sunk in my own opinion, since I have been a witness of this transaction.

Cecil. Why, what the devil is there in all this to wonder at? People of fortune often throw away thou-sands at the hazard table to make themselves miser-able, and nobody, ever accuses them of generosity.

L. *Win.* Mr. Cecil is perfectly right ; and he is the best manager of a fortune, who is most attentive to the wants of the deserving.

Mrs. *Har.* Why, now all is as it should be—all is as it should be!—This is the triumph of good sense over delicacy.—I could cry for downright joy.——I wonder what ails me !—this is all my doing !

Cecil. No—part of it is mine; and I think it extremely happy for your people of refined sentiments to have friends with a little common understanding.

Riv. Sister, I always thought you a woman of sense.———

Mrs. *Har.* Yes, she has been a long time intimate with me, you know.

Cecil. Well said, sauce-box!

Sir *Harry.* If this story was to be represented on the stage, the poet would think it his duty to punish me for life, because I was once culpable.

L. *Win.* That would be very wrong. The stage should be a school of morality; and the noblest of all lessons is the forgiveness of injuries.

Riv. True, my Lord.—But the principal moral to be drawn from the transactions of to-day is, that those who generously labour for the happiness of others, will, sooner or later, arrive at happiness themselves.

[*Exeunt Omnes.*

EPILOGUE.

Written by DAVID GARRICK, Esq. Spoken by Mrs.
DANCER.

*W*HEN *with the comic muse a bard hath dealing,*
The traffic thrives, when there's a mutual feeling;
Our author boasts, that well he chose his plan,
False Modesty !—*Himself an* Irishman.
As I'm a woman, somewhat prone to satire,
I'll prove it all a bull, what he calls nature;
And you, I'm sure, will join before you go,
To maul False Modesty—*from* Dublin *ho!*
Where are these Lady Lambton's *to be found?*
Not in these riper times, on English ground.
Among the various flowers which sweetly blow,
To charm the eyes, at Almack's *and* Soho,
Pray does that weed, False Delicacy, *grow?*
     O, No.——
Among the fair of fashion; common breeding,
Is there one bosom, where Love *lies a bleeding?*
In olden times your grannams unrefin'd,
Ty'd up the tongue, put padlocks on the mind;
O, ladies, thank your stars, ther's nothing now confin'd.
In love you English *men,—there's no concealing,*
Ere most, **like** Winworth, *simple in your dealing;*
But Britons, **in** *their natures as their names,*
Are different **at** *the* Shannon, Tweed, *and* Thames,
As the Tweed *flows, the bonny* Scot *proceeds,*

Wunds slaw, and sure, and nae obstruction heeds ;
Though oft repuls'd, his purpose still hauds fast,
Stecks like a burr, and wuns the lass at last.
The Shannon, *rough and vigorous, pours along,*
Like the bold accents of brave paddy's tongue :
Arrah, dear creature—can you scorn me so ?
Cast your sweet eyes upon me, top and toe !
Not fancy me ? Pooh !—that's all game and laughter,
First marry me, my jew'l—ho !—you 'll love me after.
Like his own Thames, *honest* John Trot, *their brother,*
More quick than one, *and much less bold than t'other,*
Gentle not dull, *his loving arms will spread ;*
But stopt—in willows hides his bashful head ;
John *leaves his home, resolv'd to tell his pain ;*
*Hesitates—I—love—*Fye, sir—'t is in vain——
John *blushes, turns him round, and whistles home again.*
Well ! is my painting like ?—Or do you doubt it ?
What say you to a trial ?—let 's about it.
Let Cupid *lead* three Britons *to the field,*
And try which first can make a damsel yield ;
What say you to a widow ? *Smile consent,*
And she 'll be ready for experiment.

THE END.

A

WORD TO THE WISE.

A

COMEDY,

By Mr. HUGH KELLY.

ADAPTED FOR

THEATRICAL REPRESENTATION,

AS PERFORMED AT THE

THEATRE-ROYAL, COVENT-GARDEN.

REGULATED FROM THE PROMPT-BOOK,

By Permission of the Manager.

The Lines distinguished by inverted Commas, are omitted in the Representation.

LONDON:

Printed for the Proprietor, under the Direction of
JOHN BELL, British Library, STRAND,
Bookseller to His Royal Highness the PRINCE of WALES.

THIS

COMEDY

IS INSCRIBED TO

ROBERT LADBROKE, ESQ.

AS A PUBLIC TESTIMONY

OF THE

VERY HIGH ESTEEM

IN WHICH

THE AUTHOR HOLDS HIS FRIENDSHIP,

AND A SINCERE MARK

OF THE

VERY JUST RESPECT HE ENTERTAINS

FOR

HIS PRIVATE CHARACTER.

PROLOGUE.

Written by Mr. KELLY. Spoken by Mr. KING.

WELL, here you are, and comfortably squeez'd——
But do you come quite willing to be pleas'd?—
Say, do you wish for bravo—fine—encore——
Or—hiss—off, off—no more—no more—no more——
Though for true taste I know the warmth you feel,
A roasted poet is a glorious meal——
And oft I've known a miserable wit,
Through downright laughter fasten'd on the spit,
Basted, with cat-call sauce, for very fun,
Not till quite ready——but till quite undone——

And yet you serv'd the puppy as you ought——
How dare he think to tell you of a fault——
What fair one here from prudence ever strays,
What lover here e'er flatters or betrays?
What husband here is ever found to roam,
What wife is here that does not doat on home?
In yon gay circle, not a blooming face
From Club's rude king could point you out the ace;
No sober trader, in that crowded pit,
'Till clear broad-day, will o'er his bottle sit;
Nor, while our commerce fatally decays,
Erect his villa, or set up his chaise——

Nay, you above, in cake-consuming bow'rs,
Who through whole Sundays munge away your hours;
You are so mild, so gentle, that ev'n here,
Your sweet ton'd voices never wound the ear;
Ne'er make the house for tune or prologue ring,
Roast beef—roaf beef—the prologue, prologue—King——

    Why then, thus weigh'd in truth's severest scale,
Shall each pert scribbler impudently rail,
With dull morality disgrace the stage,
And talk of vices in so pure an age;
Your wise forefathers, in politer days,
Had ev'n their faults commended in their plays,
To cheat a friend, or violate a wife,
Was then true humour, comedy, and life——
But now the bard becomes your highest boast,
Whose ill-bred pen traduces you the most;
Whose saucy muse can hardily aver
That still a lady possibly can err;
That still a lord can trick you at a bet,
And fools and madmen are existing yet——

    Be rous'd at last—nor, in an age so nice,
Let these grave dunces teize you with advice——
What, though some taylor's oft protracted bill
May hang all-trembling on the author's quill,
Regard it not, remove the growing evil—
A well drest poet is the very devil——

Do taverns dun him—That, can scribblers treat ?
Fine times, indeed, when scribblers think to eat——
*Do justice then—to-night, **ten minutes here***
*May blast the **bard's** whole labour of a year——*
*What **do I see !**—resentment in your eyes?*
*'Tis **true,** the fellow at your mercy lies;*
***And of** all wreathes, the Briton's noblest crown,*
***Is** ne'er to strike an enemy when down——*

Dramatis Personae.

COVENT-GARDEN.

Men.

Sir GEORGE HASTINGS,	Mr. Lee Lewis.
Sir JOHN DORMER,	Mr. Hull.
WILLOUGHBY,	Mr. Aickin.
Captain DORMER,	Mr. Whitfield.
VILLARS,	Mr. Lewis.
Footman,	Mr. Ledger.

Women.

Mrs. WILLOUGHBY,	Mrs. Jackson.
Miss WILLOUGHBY,	Mrs. Hartley.
Miss DORMER,	Mrs. Whitfield.
Miss MONTAGUE,	Mrs. Bulkley.
JENNY,	Miss Stuart.
LUCY,	Mrs. Poussin.

A

WORD TO THE WISE.

ACT I. SCENE I.

An Apartment in Sir John Dormer's *House.* *Enter* Sir
JOHN DORMER, MISS DORMER *and* MISS MONTAGU.

Sir John.

WELL but, my dear Caroline, though I grant you
that Sir George Hastings has his peculiarities, still you
must grant me that he has many very amiable qualities.

Miss *Dor*. I never denied Sir George's merit, sir,
but all his good qualities cannot conceal his unaccountable coxcombry; his attention is constantly centered
in himself, and there is no enduring a man who
fancies that every woman must, at first sight, fall
violently in love with him.

Sir *John*. Do you hear her, Miss Montagu?

Miss *Mon*. Why, Sir John, there is no accounting
for inclination, you know; however, I cannot look
upon Sir George in the very ridiculous light he appears to Miss Dormer.

Miss Dor. No—why he is a Narcissus that continually makes love to his own shadow, and I can't bear the idea of a husband, in whose affection I am likely to be every moment rival'd by the looking-glass.

Miss Mon. Nay now, my dear, you are rather hard upon him.—Sir George may possibly be a little **too** fond of himself.

Sir John. But that does n't prevent him from entertaining very tender sentiments for Caroline Dormer.

Miss Mon. He may be unnecessarily attentive to the niceties of dress————

Sir John. But then he is attentive to every law of justice and generosity.

Miss Mon. And if his foibles provoke us to an occasional smile, his worth must always excite our warmest admiration.

Miss Dor. Upon my word, Harriot, a very florid winding up of a period, and very proper for an elevated thought in a sentimental comedy; but I tell you I should relish these encomiums on Sir George well enough, if he was not so particularly recommended to my attention. I really can't support the imagination of vowing honour and obedience to the object of my own ridicule, and it would mortify my pride beyond conception, to see my husband the constant jest of his acquaintance.

Sir John. My dear Caroline, do n't be too difficult in your choice, nor entertain any romantic idea of finding a husband, all perfection.—The expectation of too much before marriage, frequently imbitters the

ınion after ;—and as the best men will have their lit-
le blemishes, we may surely number those among the
ɔest, in whose characters we can discover nothing
nore than a few trifling peculiarities.

Miss *Dor.* **I see, sir,** you make a point of this affair.

Sir *John.* I would not make a point of any thing,
my dear, which I thought would be in the least repugnant to your happiness:—but, really, when I
consider this proposal in **every respect,** when I consider the rank, the fortune, and **what is** above all, the
merit of the man, I cannot but wish that you would
give him a favourable reception; and this the more
especially, **as I am** convinced, if the match should
take place, that your fine sense and sweetness of temper, will easily mould your husband to your wish,
and quickly remove every trace of those foibles, which
are at present the only reason of your objection.

Miss *Dor.* You are very good, sir.

Sir *John.* This morning, my dear, Sir George purposes to declare himself in form.—If you can receive
his addresses, you will make him happy, and oblige
me exceedingly; but if you cannot, deal ingenuously,
and reject him; the justice which I owe to him, **as**
well as the tenderness which I have for you, makes
this **advice** doubly requisite.

Enter a Servant.

Ser. Mr. Willoughby, **sir.**

Sir *John.* I'll wait upon him instantly. [*Exit* Ser.]
Think, therefore, seriously, Caroline, before you de-

termine, for I neither wish to cheat my friend into the possession of a reluctant heart, nor to sacrifice my daughter to the object of her aversion.   [*Exit.*

Miss *Dor.* Well, Harriot, what shall I do?—You hear he has actually mention'd him to me in the most serious terms, and that this very morning he is to make a formal declaration.

Miss *Mon.* And what then, does n't **Sir** John desire you to reject him, if he is really disagreeable?—Can **you** possibly wish for a greater degree of indulgence?

Miss *Dor.* And yet that very indulgence, my dear Miss Montagu, is likely to render me extremely miserable.

Miss *Mon.* **Why** indeed, Miss Dormer—remember, child, you complimented me first with the cold respectful epithet of miss—the men in general say, that the surest way of making a woman wretched, is to indulge her inclinations——But pray, my dear, why is this liberty which Sir John allows you, of promoting your own happiness, so very likely to make you miserable.

Miss *Dor.* Ah, Harriot! do n't you see that while he is so generously anxious to consult my wishes, I am bound by gratitude, as well as justice, to pay the greatest regard to his **expectations.**

Miss *Mon.* You are really an excellent girl, my dear. But pray **answer** me one question seriously.

Miss **Dor.** What is it?

Miss *Mon.* Is this dislike, which you entertain to your father's choice, entirely the result of your aversion to Sir George? or is it, be honest now, the consequence of a secret partiality for somebody else!

Miss *Dor.* A secret partiality for somebody else?—Pray, my dear, for whom is it likely I should entertain a partiality?

Miss *Mon.* Caroline, Caroline, this reserve is ill-suited both to the nature of our friendship and the customary frankness of your temper—yet, notwithstanding the secrecy you have hitherto so unkindly observed, I can easily see that Mr. Villars——What, conscious, Caroline?

Miss *Dor.* O, Harriot, spare me—nor be offended that I have endeavoured to keep a secret from you, which I absolutely shudder to whisper to myself—to deal candidly, my dear, I must acknowledge that your charge is but too just—and notwithstanding every effort of my pride, and every argument of my prudence, I find this humble yet deserving Villars possesses a much higher place in my esteem than can be consistent with my happiness.

Miss *Mon.* Why, to do the young fellow justice, he is really very agreeable, and has something in his manner that would do credit to a more eligible situation——but——

Miss *Dor.* Ay, Harriot, there's the misfortune—agreeable as he is in every respect, he is still a total dependent on m. father, and thinks himself extremely happy that his talents have obtained him even a temporary establishment in an opulent family.

Miss Mon. Well, **my** dear, Sir John is generous, and Mr. Villars is very useful to him in his literary researches; besides, I am not a little **pleased** at the distinction with which he, as well as the Captain, constantly treats Mr. Villars.

Miss Dor. I do n't **know how** it is—Mr. Villars has a manner of commanding respect **from** every body; he is humble without servility, and spirited————

Miss Mon. Oh! he is every thing **that 's** amiable, **no** doubt————and the stars have been exceedingly relentless in not giving him a large fortune————however, **if I** have any skill **in** the business of the heart, Villars **is** to the full as uneasy upon your account as you can possibly be on his—he is always contriving excuses for conversing with you, yet when he does, **he** is in visible confusion; and it was only yesterday evening, when I beg'd he would put a letter for me into the Post-Office, that he stammer'd out, in the utmost perplexity, ' I shall take particular care, madam, to deliver it to Miss Dormer.'

Miss Dor. **If** this **be** the case, Harriot, I must indeed behave with particular circumspection to him; and yet, though I see the impossibility of ever being his, he has given me an insuperable aversion to the **rest of** his sex.

Miss Mon. What then do you intend to do with Sir George?

Miss Dor. To reject him; but still to do it without giving any offence to my father.

Miss Mon. And how do you propose to manage it?

Miss *Dor*. By throwing myself honestly upon Sir George's humanity, by telling him my affection is engaged, and by begging of him to withdraw his addresses in such a manner as shall appear to be the result of his own choice, and not the consequence of my disinclination——Sir George, notwithstanding his egregious vanity, is uncommonly good-natured—but let us retire to my room, my dear, I am unfit for company at present, and here we are likely to be broken in upon——O, Harriot.

Miss *Mon*. And O, Caroline, what a **very** foolish figure does a woman make, when she is lamentably in love.   [*Exeunt.*

Enter Sir George Hastings *and* Captain Dormer.

Dor. Well, my brother-in-law elect, you are very splendidly dress'd **this morning.**

Sir *George*. Why, **Jack, I think, I** do make a pretty tolerable appearance.

Dor. And **do you** think this appearance calculated to make an impression upon a woman of spirit.—— Zounds, man, give up your pretensions, **for** nothing but a fellow of life is likely to succeed with my sister, I can promise you.

Sir *George*. A fellow of **life,** Jack; that is, I suppose, **a fellow of** profligacy:—truly, **you** pay your sister a very pretty compliment.

Dor. And why, pray, do you necessarily connect the idea of life with the idea of profligacy?

Sir George. Because, in the vocabulary of libertines, like you, Jack, the word life always means, a round of every thing that is foolish or unwarrantable.

Dor. Why, what the devil are you turned fanatic, George, that you begin to deal so much in second-hand morality?

Sir George. In short, your fellows of spirit never allow a man a scruple of common **sense, till** he has entirely prostituted his understanding; **nor** suppose him **to** be fit for a commerce with the world, till he abso-.lutely merits **to** be hunted out of society.

Dor. Well but, George, there is one excess of which you yourself have **been** guilty; and I have known the time, when you took **a** bottle **so** freely, that you were generally made toast-master **of** the company.

Sir George. Yes, but I soon found out that drinking was detestable, and toasting the greatest of all absurdities.

Dor. Why how would you wish to pass an evening? —Can any thing exceed the pleasure of society, with a few select friends of good-nature and vivacity?

Sir George. O, nothing to be sure is **so** delightful as guzzling down half a dozen bottles, and enjoying the rational discourse—of where does the toast stand—— **with** you, Sir William—no, with you, **Sir** George— fill him a bumper, Captain Dormer—fill him to the top.——O, an evening spent in this manner must be delectable, especially **if** a couple of fools should happily quarrel **in** their cups, and cut one another's throats to prove the superiority of their understanding.

Dor. Ha! ha! ha!—But was this all your objection to the bottle?

Sir *George.* No, for it made my head ach, and disordered my dress beyond bearing.

Dor. Disorder'd your dress, ha! ha! ha! what unaccountable coxcombry.

Sir *George.* Why to be sure it's a very ridiculous thing for a man to shew a little regard to decency.

Dor. Well, notwithstanding you are a coxcomb systematically, I am sure the character will not be a strong recommendation to my sister.

Sir *George.* Your sister, Jack, is a woman of sense, and must see that she has a much stronger chance of being happy with me, than poor Miss Montagu has of being happy with her brother.——My heart is unadulterated, and is, therefore, worth any woman's acceptance.

Dor. O, no doubt it is a very valuable acquisition.

Sir *George.* Whereas, you fellows of life, hawk about your hearts from commoner to commoner, till they become quite contemptible; and then with the additional merit of broken constitutions—tottering limbs —pale cheeks, and hollow eyes, you politely offer the refuse of the stews to ladies of fortune, family, and character.

Dor. And so your affection is unadulterated;—— ha! ha! ha!

Sir *George.* Ay, laugh on and welcome;—but who have we here?

Dor. Mr. Willoughby, who will keep you in countenance with maxims of musty morality.

Sir George. What, my good-natur'd optimist, who thinks every thing happens for the best?

Dor. Ay, Candide to perfection, who is continually blessing his stars the more they load him with misfortunes;—and pray Heaven his business here this morning has not been to talk with **Sir John** about my intimacy in his family. [*Aside.*]

Enter WILLOUGHBY.

Will. Sir George, your most obedient.—Captain, I am your humble servant.

Sir George. Mr. Willoughby, yours. How do the ladies, sir?—the **good** Mrs. Willoughby, and your amiable daughter.

Will. Why my daughter, Sir George, is very well; and my wife is as usual, continually embittering every comfort of life, and lamenting the miseries attendant on mortality.

Sir George. I wonder she does not choose to follow the sensible example you set her, and endeavour rather **to** lessen, than to aggravate the measure of unavoidable misfortunes.—She's a young woman, and misanthropy at her age is rather out of character.

Will. Why yes, Sir George, she's twenty good years younger than I am, and yet she is twenty times more impatient under the smallest disappointment.

Sir George. But, **my** good friend, you don't think her youth a very unfortunate circumstance?

Will. O, Sir George, my principle is to think every thing for the best.

Dor. Well said, Mr. Willoughby.

Will. It wasn't her youth, however, that struck me, but the sobriety of her conduct, and her affection for my daughter;---she was besides a distant relation of my first wife's—liv'd with us in the same house; and some how I lik'd her, because having no fortune, it gave her but little expectation of a better husband.

Sir *George.* But why don't you teach her, to adopt some part of your own fortitude under disappointment?

Dor. Perhaps it is not in her power to exercise so desirable a philosophy.

Will. My dear captain, life has misfortunes énough without our being industrious to encrease the number of them—when an accident therefore happens, we should consider that, bad as it may be, it might have been still worse; and instead of arrogantly murmuring at the dispensations of Providence, we should thankfully acknowledge the goodness that did not plunge us into a deeper degree of affliction.

Sir *George.* Upon my word I think there is much reason in this argument.

Will. Ay, and much policy too, Sir George——we should always imagine-that every thing happens for the best—about ten years ago I broke my leg by a fall from a horse.

Dor. And pray did this prove a fortunate accident?

Will. Yes; for your father, who generously pitied my situation, got my place continued to my family;

so that if I drop off to-morrow, there's a comfortable provision for them——Indeed, when the accident happened I could n't foresee this consequence, however I made the best of matters, was thankful that I had n't broke both my legs, and drew a kind of negative good fortune from a stroke of real calamity.

Sir *George*. Why what the **devil is this** fellow Dormer laughing at ?

Dor. Why how the devil can I help laughing, when **the** very evils of life are made so many indirect **in**struments of happiness.

Will. Oh ! let him laugh, Sir George; he can by no means joke me **out of** my sentiments.—Why, when my son **was** stolen from me in his infancy, I found a consolation **in** reflecting that I had not lost my daughter **too ;** and though **I** have never since been able to hear any account **of** my poor boy, I am satisfied he was taken from me **for the** best, and I bear my lot with resignation.

Dor. How ! do you set down the loss of your son **in** the chapter of fortunate accidents ?

Sir *George*. Negatively he may, Dormer; for he might have turned out a libertine like yourself, and in that case his being lost is indeed **a very** fortunate circumstance.

Dor. Very smart, truly—but I suppose you bear your lot **with** resignation too, Sir George, for you have lately got a good two thousand a year by the death of this young fellow's godfather, old Webly the humourist; and it is your interest to pray that he never may be found, as there is a certain clause in the will you know, which——

Sir *George.* Which obliges me to invest him with this estate if ever he is discovered, a mighty hardship really; and you must be a very pretty fellow to suppose it any way difficult for an honest man, to do a common act of justice.

Will. All for the best still, captain. Sir George we are certain will do good with his fortune, whereas had it been possessed by my boy, how am I sure that it would not be applied to very different purposes:——yet who knows that it might either; who knows but—— however [*Stifling his emotion.*] I am positive every thing happened for the best——and so——and so a good morning to you.   [*Exit.*

Sir *George.* Poor man, how sensibly he feels the loss of his son, notwithstanding his endeavours to be cheerful. But what am I throwing away my time upon you for, when I have business of so much importance with your sister? Good bye, Jack, and now let us see if profligates only are to meet encouragement from the ladies.   [*Exit.*

Dor. Ha! ha! ha! was there ever such a compound of sentiment and vanity. Caroline must keep the fellow in a glass-case, or he'll kill himself before the honey-moon is over, with the fatigue of seeing company.   [*Going,*

Enter Sir JOHN DORMER.

Sir *John.* Jack, Jack, come back a little---I want a word or two with you.

Dor. I fear'd as much [*Aside.*] What are your commands, sir?

Sir *John.* Why, Jack, I need not tell you how anxious I am to have you settled in the world, nor is it necessary for me to put you in mind of the engagement I entered into with my late worthy friend, Sir Ralph Montagu.

Dor. I know your obliging solicitude for me **extremely** well, sir, and I feel it with the most grateful sensibility, but sure there is yet time enough before I undertake the important charge of a family.

Sir *John.* Come, come, you have seen enough of the world to become, if you please, a useful member of society; besides, Miss Montagu is now without a father, and should be treated with an additional degree of attention.—Nothing, therefore, can be more improper than to keep a young lady of her merit and fortune waiting for the result of your determination, when you ought to think it a very great honour that she can be prevailed upon to receive you as a husband.

Dor. Miss Montagu, sir, will, I dare say, be no way offended at the delay, if I can judge from the indifference with which she constantly behaves to me.

Sir *John.* And how can she behave otherwise, when you constantly treat her with indifference? To be plain with you however, Jack, I fear you are too wild, too dissipated, to think seriously?——you moreover possess a spirit of gallantry, which gives me many an uneasy moment, and I am not a little troubled at your continual visits **to Mr.** Willoughby's.

Dor. To Mr. Willoughby, sir, to your own particular friend!

Sir *John.* **Yes,** and the more I esteem him, the more uneasy I must naturally be at your visiting there so frequently. **Miss** Willoughby has a fine person, and a feeling **heart;** she thinks, besides, I have obliged her father, and may, in the fullness of her gratitude, imbibe sentiments for the son of his benefactor. Take care, therefore, take care; gallantry, though **a** fashionable crime, is **a** very detestable one; and the wretch who pilfers from **us** in the hour of his necessity, is an innocent character, compared to the plunderer who wantonly robs us of happiness and reputation.

Dor. I hope, sir, I shall never do any thing to bring a reflection upon the honour of my family.

Sir *John.* I hope not, Jack, and therefore I could wish you were not a man of gallantry: to engage the confidence of the innocence on purpose to betray it, is as mean as it is inhuman.

Enter a Servant.

Ser. Every thing is ready in the library, sir.

Sir *John.* Very well. [*Exit* Servant.] Come, Jack, think a little on what I have said; in my son let me for once find a friend; the honour of my family is now materially trusted in your hands, and though my tenderness for you may feel at any prostitution of that honour, be assured that my justice will never allow me to pardon it. [*Exit Sir* John.

Enter VILLARS.

Dor. Well, Villars, I fancy Willoughby has at last made a complaint to my father, for I am commanded, in the most positive terms, to think of an immediate marriage with Miss Montagu.

Vil. And is n't it by much the most sensible course you can follow ?—Miss Montagu is a very fine young lady.

Dor. True—but you have never seen Miss Willoughby.

Vil. Besides the great fortune——

Dor. Miss Willoughby.

Vil. That courts your acceptance, if I may so express myself.——

Dor. Miss Willoughby.

Vil. Oh---I see how it is ; and are you then determined to marry Miss Willoughby ?

Dor. Not so fast—not quite so fast, my dear Villars, I beg of you : Miss Willoughby certainly possesses a greater share of my affection than any other woman in the world ; and I do n't know, if my father could be brought to approve of such a match, that I should find the least disinclination to marry her : but as matters stand at present there 's no likelihood of such a circumstance, and therefore I would n't choose to disoblige Sir John in so material a point, especially as my wishes with regard to Miss Willoughby may possibly be indulged without so considerable a sacrifice.

Vil. I do n't understand you.

Dor. Why, Miss Willoughby knew all along of my engagement with Miss Montagu, and consequently had no reason to suppose that my intentions could be very matrimonial; besides, she let nobody into the secret of my addresses but her ridiculous step-mother, who is a miserable compound of avarice and affectation: Indeed, to do the young lady justice, it was a considerable time before she would hear a syllable of a tender nature from me, on account of my connection with Miss Montagu.

Vil. And how did you manage it at last?

Dor. Why, in the customary manner: I talk'd a damn'd deal of nonsense with a very tragical tone and a very melancholy countenance—exclaim'd against the tyranny of fathers who wanted to force the inclinations of their children from despicable motives of interest---and curs'd the poor stars for giving her so much beauty, and making me so sensible of it: then pressing her tenderly by the hand, I usually ran out of the room, as if in violent emotion, affecting to gulp down a torrent of tears, and left her own pity to be my advocate the moment she recovered the use of her recollection.

Val. What, and did this answer your purpose, sir?

Dor. Oh, perfectly; the women are inconceivably fond of the pathetic, and listen to you with rapture if you talk about death or distraction——spring but the mine of their pity, you soon blow their hearts into a flame—and reap more service from an hour of com-

C.

pleat substantial misery than from a whole year of the most passionate adoration.

Vil. Well, captain, and may I presume to ask what use you intend to make of Miss Willoughby's partiality for you?

Dor. Why faith, Villars, that's a very puzzling question upon the whole; notwithstanding all my levity, you know I have the deepest reverence for my father, and he must not be disobliged upon any account, though, to deal honestly with you, I have no mighty inclination to Miss Montagu.

Vil. And what must become of poor Miss Willoughby?

Dor. Why I should n't like to be a rascal there neither, yet what can one do; where a woman's weak enough to encourage the addresses of a man whom she knows to be pre-engaged, she gives him a kind of title to deceive her: besides, Villars, Miss Willoughby has herself shewn a genius for duplicity in this affair which should make a man of any sense a little considerate.

Vil. How so, pray?

Dor. Don't you recollect she has deceived her father through the whole transaction? and it is a maxim with me that the woman who can forget the sentiments of nature, has half an inclination to forget the sentiments of virtue.

Vil. Poor Miss Willoughby!

Dor. You are mightily concern'd for a woman you never saw in your life; however, be easy, I am as sentimental for a libertine, you know, as any fellow in the kingdom, and it shall be Miss Willoughby's own fault if matters are carried to extremities.—But, Villars, step with me to my agent's, and we'll talk farther on this subject: few people despise money more than myself, and yet there are few to whom a snug sum would, at this moment, be more acceptable.

Vil. You promise me then that in this affair of Miss Willoughby's——

Dor. Zounds, Villars, I won't brag too much neither, I am still flesh and blood, and these make a very dangerous composition in the hour of love and, opportunity.

Vil. My dear captain, this is no jesting matter—the happiness of a deserving young lady is at stake, and a laugh will but poorly repay a violation of your honour, or a breach of your humanity.   [*Exeunt.*

ACT II. SCENE I.

Willoughby's *House.   Enter* Mr. *and* Mrs. WIL-LOUGHBY.

Mrs. *Willoughby.*

AND so my prudent, sage, considerate dear, you have actually advised Sir John Dormer to restrain his son's visits to our house?

Will. Yes, that was my business at Sir John's this morning.

Mrs. *Will.* And you imagine this wise measure will turn out for the best I suppose?

Will. I do really————

Mrs. *Will.* What? You think it for the best to let your poor family continue always in obscurity;—and look upon it as a great unhappiness, whenever they have the least chance of rising in the world?

Will. And you think I have done a mighty foolish thing in preserving the peace as well as the honour of my poor family, from the greatest of all misfortunes?

Mrs. *Will.* From the greatest of all misfortunes! did any body ever hear the like?——Why I tell you Captain Dormer is in love, passionately in love with your daughter.

Will. So much the worse.————

Mrs. *Will.* So much the worse! this is the only thing in which you ever forgot your all for the best principle.—So much the worse! so much the better I tell you; and in all likelihood he might have married her, if your ridiculous fear of being happy, had not put Sir John upon his guard, to prevent so desirable **a circumstance.**

Will. What, madam, would you have me trepan the only son of my benefactor, into a marriage with my daughter, and at a time too **when I** know him to be engaged to a lady **of** Miss Montagu's family and fortune.—O, Mrs. Willoughby, **I am** ashamed of these arguments; and if there is no way to be rich without being despicable, let us look upon poverty as the most eligible of all situations.

Mrs. *Will.* Don't tell me of Miss Montagu's family, Mr. Willoughby, your daughter is not her inferior in

that respect ;---besides, a woman of beauty, educated
as I have educated Cornelia, even if she has not altogether so much money, has merit enough to deserve
the first man in the kingdom. I am sure if I was a
single woman again.———

Will. You have been a single woman, madam, and
are now married to a fellow old enough for your father.

Mrs. *Will.* I don't deserve to be reproach'd by
you, Mr. Willoughby ; you are at least a gainer, by
my pity.

Will. I think so, my dear—I think all for the best.

Mrs. *Will.* What all for the best ; my marrying a
man as old as my father ?—Have a little gratitude, Mr.
Willoughby.

Will. Well, well, my dear, 't is foolish for a man
and wife to quarrel, because they must make it up
again.—However, we were here talking of Captain
Dormer, and what is our girl's beauty and education
to the purpose ?

Mrs. *Will.* Very much to the purpose.—They shew
there would have been no impropriety in suffering
Captian Dormer to marry Cornelia, and they shew
that you behav'd very absurdly in striving to prevent
the advancement of your own daughter.

Will. Madam, madam, young women are apt enough
to err of themselves, but a father has indeed a great
deal to answer for, who exposes his daughter to unnecessary temptations—Captain Dormer has been already too successful in some families of our acquaintance ; and if, while we are contriving to trap him into

a marriage with Cornelia, he should find it possible to rob her of her honour, we shall be very properly punished for the baseness of our designs.

Mrs. Will. And do you think that possible, after the share I have had in her education?——though I am but her mother-in-law————

Will. My good wife, it is by supposing our own children wiser than the children of **other** people, that so many are constantly ruined. If we **are** desirous, therefore, of preserving them unsullied, we should always keep them out of danger; but our ridiculous partiality, constantly paints them in the most flattering colours of perfection, and we never suppose them capable of committing the smallest mistake, till they are totally undone.

Mrs. Will. Well, it is in vain to talk with you;—but remember I say, you will always be the enemy of your own family.

Will. I shall always endeavour, madam, to act as becomes a father, but I shall also strive to act as becomes an honest man, and therefore Captain Dormer shall have no more interviews with my daughter.

Mrs. Will. No?————

Will. No.——My avarice shall neither lead me to injure the happiness of my friend's family, nor shall my weakness betray the honour of my own.—Every thing will, I dare say, turn out for the best; though if the worst should happen, I shall still find a consolation in having taken every justifiable method to prevent it.

[*Exit.*

Enter Miss WILLOUGHBY.

Miss *Will.* O, madam, I have heard **all:**---what will become of me?

Mrs. *Will.* **Ah,** my poor dear child, was there ever so preposterous a fool as your father!

Miss *Will.* Dear madam, say something to comfort me.---You have kindly made yourself the confidant of my sentiments for Captain Dormer, and I must be the most miserable creature in the world, if my father is inflexibly determined to drive him from the house.

Mrs. *Will.* I can say nothing to you, Cornelia, but what must add to your regret:---there is no hope of any favourable turn in the affairs of our family :----- day after day produces fresh disappointments; and instead of having any agreeable prospect to cheer us as we go on, the view becomes more and more cloud- ed with misfortunes.-----No, there's no enduring life upon these terms; no, there's no possibility of en- during it.

Miss *Will.* O, that I had never seen Captain Dormer, or that he had been less amiable !-----

Mrs. *Will.* Ah, my dear child, I know but too well **how** to pity your distress :-----I have been in love my- self; strangely as he now neglects my advice, I was once very desperately in love with your father: He was the first man that ever said a tender thing to me; and Mexico, if he was dead to-morrow, would not purchase a single glance of regard for another, nor the mines of Peru obtain **a smile of** approbation.

Miss *Will.* Well, madam, it is happy for me that you have yourself been susceptible of the softer impressions, since **that** susceptibility has induced you to assist **me** during **my** acquaintance with Captain Dormer.

Mrs. *Will.* It is happy for you, Cornelia, and it shall be happy for you. My tenderness is more than the tenderness of a step-mother, and there is nothing I admire so much as constancy in love. My thoughts, therefore, have not been idle on this affair, and I believe you will allow my understanding to be tolerable.

Miss *Will.* The whole world concurs in an opinion of your good sense, madam, but few entertain a higher idea of it than Captain Dormer.

Mrs. *Will.* The Captain, my dear, is a man of taste and discernment.

Miss *Will.* And yet I must give him up for ever.

Mrs. *Will.* 'Tis your own fault; why won't you take my advice, and make him yours securely? there is but one way——

Miss *Will.* O, madam, you know my abhorrence of an elopement——I have often told you——

Mrs. *Will.* Yes, and I have often told you, that you father's forgiveness may be easily obtained; but that Dormer once married to that Harriot Montagu, is lost for ever. Do you imagine, child, I would advise you to **an** impropriety?

Miss *Will.* But how can I betray the dignity **of** my sex, in proposing so bold a measure to the Captain?

Mrs. *Will.* To be sure **it's** very bold in a woman who has given away her heart, to make an honourable offer of her hand to a lover.——However, stay, child— let poor Dormer be forc'd into this marriage with Miss Montagu, let him be torn irrecoverably from you--- and let **your obstinacy**, like your father's, continua'ly counteract the happiness of your family ; were you once Mrs. Dormer, very handsome things might be done for Mr. Willoughby.

Miss *Will.* O, madam, **don't** attack me in so tender a point!

Mrs. *Will.* Come up stairs, child ; suspecting your father's **business to** Sir John Dormer's this morn..g, and dreading **the** consequence, I have packed up all your things ready for an expedition to Scotland:—— you must determine, therefore, instantly:—and if you determine to have Dormer, you must act instantly too.

Miss *Will.* What will become of me!

Mrs. *Will.* I don't know what will become of you, if you don't take **my** advice ; and I am sure, on the present occasion, I give you advice that would be very agreeable to half the young ladies within the bills of mortality. [*Exeunt.*

SCENE II.

Changes to a Room at Sir John Dormer's. Miss Dor-
MER *and* Sir GEORGE *discovered.*

Sir *George.* Nay, **my** dear Miss Dormer, there is no
bearing so unjust an insensibility to the power of your
own attractions.

Miss *Dor.* Indeed, Sir George, you over-rate my
little merits exceedingly ; and probably **the** greatest I
can boast, is my consciousness of their being contracted within a very limited circle.

Sir *George.* Well, madam, the very modesty which
induces you to decline every pretension to the admiration of the world, is but a fresh proof how greatly you
deserve it.

Miss *Dor.* You have much politeness, Sir George,
but politeness is your peculiar characteristic————

Sir *George.* At least, madam, I have much sincerity;
and if Sir John's mediation in my favour, together
with as fervent an attachment as ever warmed the bosom, can obtain a look of approbation **from Miss** Dormer, she may rest satisfied that the business **of my**
life will be an unremitting solicitude for the advance-
ment of her happiness.

Miss *Dor.* I am infinitely honoured by this declaration, and I believe there are not many ladies————

Sir *George.* Why, madam, if the vanity may **be** ex-
cused, I flatter myself there **are** not many ladies who

would highly disapprove my addresses.—I have more than once resisted some flattering overtures, and from very fine women too ; but my heart was reserved for Miss Dormer, and she will make me the happiest man existing, by kindly condescending to accept it.

Miss *Dor.* I am very sensible how just a value should be placed upon such an affection as yours, Sir George, and it gives me no little————

Sir *George.* [*Aside.*] So the Captain imagined I should not succeed with her.

Miss *Dor.* You will pardon my confusion, Sir George, but the declaration I am going to make————

Sir *George.* **Will** demand my everlasting gratitude, madam.

Miss *Dor.* I shall be very happy to find you really of this opinion.

Sir *George.* I must be eternally of this opinion;—condescension and benignity, madam, are animating every feature of that beautiful face, and I am satisfied you will **be** prevail'd **upon**, not utterly to disregard the heart that so passionately solicits your acceptance.

Miss *Dor.* Indeed, Sir George, I must own you are possess'd of extraordinary merit.

Sir **George.** This goodness is too much, madam.

Miss *Dor.* Your understanding is enlarg'd.

Sir *George.* Dear Miss Dormer !

Miss *Dor.* Your person is unexceptionable.

Sir *George.* You distress me, madam, by this excessive generosity.

Miss *Dor.* Your manners are amiable.

Sir *George.* I want words to thank you, madam.

Miss *Dor.* And your humanity is unbounded.

Sir *George.* What I am, madam, take me: I am yours, and only yours; nor should the united graces, if prostrate at my feet and soliciting for pity, rival you a moment in my affection.—No, Miss Dormer, your happiness will ever be the ultimate object of my attention, and I shall no longer wish to exist, than while I am studious to promote it.

Miss *Dor.* Sir George, I fear you misunderstand me, and yet it is in your power to make me very happy.

Sir *George.* How can I misunderstand you, my dearest creature, if it is in my power to make you happy.

Miss *Dor.* 'Tis in your power indeed, Sir George.

Sir *George.* Bewitching loveliness, how you transport me ;———so the Captain thought I should not succeed with her. [*Aside.*]

Miss *Dor.* But if you would wish to see me happy ————you must withdraw your addresses.

Sir *George.* Miss Dormer!

Miss *Dor.* It is impossible for me ever to return your affection.

Sir *Geo.* Miss Dormer!

Miss *Dor.* And I shall be miserable beyond belief by a continuance of your solicitation.

Sir *Geo.* Miss Dormer!

Miss *Dor.* O, Sir George, to the greatness of your

humanity let me appeal against the prepossession of your heart. You see before you a distressed young creature, whose affection is already engaged; and who, though she thinks herself highly honoured by your sentiments, is wholly unable to return them.

Sir George. I am extremely sorry, madam, to have been—I say, madam—that—really I am so exceedingly disconcerted, that I don't know what to say.

Miss Dor. O, Sir George, you have no occasion for apologies, though I have unhappily too much; but I know the nicety of your honour, and I depend upon it with security. Let me then entreat an additional act of goodness at your hands, which is absolutely necessary, as well for my peace as for my father's:— this is to contrive such a method of withdrawing your addresses, as will not expose me to his displeasure.— Let the discontinuance of them appear, not to be the result of my request, but the consequence of your own determination; he is a zealous advocate for you, and I should incur his severest resentment, if he was to be acquainted with the real impediment to the match. You are distressed, Sir George, and I am sinking with confusion—I shall, therefore, only add, that I trust you with more than life, and that I conjure you to compassionate my situation. By this conduct you will engage my eternal esteem, and merit that happiness with a much more deserving woman, which it is impossible for you ever to enjoy with me.

[*Exit.*

Sir George. What is all this!—a dream!——No,

't is no dream, and I feel myself awake but too sensibly. What then, am I rejected, despis'd, where I suppos'd myself certain of success and approbation.— This is too much ; neither my pride nor my tenderness can support the indignity, and I shall—what shall I do? Shall I meanly betray the poor girl who has generously thrown herself upon my humanity, and convince the world by such a conduct that she was right in refusing me :—no, damn it—I scorn a littleness of that nature, and I must shew myself worthy of her affection, though her unfortunate pre-engagement would not suffer me to obtain it. But how, in the name of perplexity, shall I manage the matter ?— A refusal on my side necessarily incurs the general resentment of the family, and the censure of the world into the bargain ; so that in all probability I shall not only have the honour of risquing my life but my reputation, and this for the happiness of giving the woman I admire to the arms of my rival.——Really the prospect is a very comfortable one. [*Exit.*

Enter Miss MONTAGU *and* Miss DORMER.

Miss *Mon.* Upon my word, Caroline, you have acted a very heroic part ; but this unaccountable love is able to carry the most timid of the romantic ladies through the greatest difficulties.—Now had I been in your situation, I could no more have ask'd the man to take my fault upon himself, than I could have made downright love to him.

Miss *Dor.* Ah, Harriot, you little know to what

extremities a strong prepossession is capable of driving a woman, even where there is the most evident impossibility of ever obtaining the object of her inclinations.

Miss *Mon.* O, my dear, I see very plainly that it is capable of driving a woman to very great extremities.

Miss *Dor.* Well I am convinc'd that if any thing was to prevent your marriage with my brother, you would, notwithstanding this seeming insensibility, look upon the rest of his sex with the utmost aversion.

Miss *Mon.* I wonder, Caroline, after my repeated declarations of indifference with regard to your brother, that you can imagine I consider him with the smallest partiality—There was indeed a time when I might have been prevailed upon to endure the creature, but his negligence quickly alarmed my pride, and prevented me from squandering a single sentiment of tenderness upon a man, who seem'd so little inclin'd to deserve it.

Miss *Dor.* Well, my dear, I am in hopes that you will have but little reason to blame his negligence for the future, because I know he intends this very day to solicit your approbation.

Miss *Mon.* O, he does me infinite honour, and I suppose you imagine he is entitled to one of my best curtsies for so extraordinary an instance of his condescension; but, Caroline, I am not altogether so critically situated as to be glad of a husband at any rate, nor have I such a meanness of disposition as to favour any addresses which are made to me with a visible reluctance.

Miss *Dor.* A visible reluctance, my dear?——

Miss *Mon.* Yes, Caroline, a visible reluctance——
'T is true indeed there are a good many kind-hearted
creatures who can stoop to flatter a fellow's vanity,
even while he treats them with contempt; but I
am made of different materials, my dear——I love
to mortify the presumption of those confident puppies,
who ask my hand with as much familiarity as if they
ask'd for a pinch of snuff, and seem to say, ' so
child, I want to make you the upper servant of my
family.'

Miss *Dor.* You are a whimsical creature, Harriot,
but how can you contrive to invalidate the contract
between my brother and you, if you are even serious
in your determination?

Miss *Mon.* If I can guess right, your brother will
himself find a very expeditious method of breaking it.
However, **if** he should not, I am in no great hurry
for a tyrant, and my Strephon's impudent brow shall
be pretty well loaded with wrinkles, before he finds
me in the humour of saying, ' whenever you please,
good sir, and I am very much oblig'd to you.'

Miss *Dor.* Well, well, Jack must solicit for himself, and I am sure, notwithstanding this pretended
want of feeling, you are no way destitute of good-
nature and sensibility.

Miss *Mon.* Good-nature and sensibility, Caroline
——ay, 't is this good-nature and sensibility that
makes the men so intolerably vain, and renders us
so frequently contemptible. If a fellow treats us with

ever so much insolence, he has only to burst into a passionate rant, and tell a gross lie with a prodigious agitation; in proportion as he whines we become softened; till at last bursting into tears, we bid the sweet creature rise, tell him that our fortune is entirely at his service, and beg that he will immediately assume the power of making us completely miserable.

Miss *Dor.* What a picture!

Miss *Mon.* While he, scarcely able to stifle his laughter, retires to divert his dissolute companions with our weakness, and breaking into a yawn of insolent affectation, cries, ' poor fool she 's doatingly fond of me.'—However, Caroline, to convince you at once with regard to my sentiments for your brother—

Miss *Dor.* Well!

Miss *Mon.* Let me tell you now you have determin'd against Sir George, that this very coxcomb as you call him, this Narcissus, who can love nothing but himself, according to your account——

Miss *Dor.* Astonishment!

Miss *Mon.* Is the only man I shall ever think of seriously—There, wonder, be amaz'd that I do n't see with your eyes, and despise my want of taste; I am a mad girl, you know, and possibly I like Sir George for his peculiarities—but still foibles are less culpable than faults, Caroline, and the vanities even of a coxcomb are more easily cured than the vices of a libertine.

Enter a Footman.

Foot. Mr. Villars, ladies, sends his compliments,

and is ready, if you are disengaged, to play over the new air which you commended last night at the Opera.

Miss *Dor.* O, we 'll wait upon him instantly.

[*Exit* Footman.

Miss *Mon.* [*Ludicrously.*] O yes, we 'll wait upon him instantly!

Miss *Dor.* How can you be so provoking, Harriot?

Miss *Mon.* What, provoking to wait upon your Corydon instantly. Come, my sweet shepherdess, let me shew it to the parlour.   [*Exeunt.*

SCENE II.

Changes to Willoughby's   *Enter* Mrs. WILLOUGHBY.

Mrs. *Will.* Mr. Willoughby is return'd, I find, and has got the letter Cornelia left for him.—Well, by this time she's with her husband that is to be, and will, I suppose, be speedily on her journey.—The Captain can't recede now, and let his father be pleased or displeased, he is still heir to his title and fortune.—What a difficulty I had to shew her the necessity, nay the propriety of this measure;——fond as she is of Dormer, it was hardly possible to engage her in it, and she seem'd at one time more determin'd to give him up for ever, than betray the dignity of the female character. Dignity indeed—I think I know what belongs to female dignity, as well as most people;—— these very young girls, however, are strange creatures; their nicety is not in the least wounded when they tell a man they love him. But O, 'tis a deviation from dignity to own they wish him for a husband. Here comes Mr. Willoughby; he must n't know my share in this transaction till he finds himself happy in the good consequences, and owns that there is at least one sensible head in the family.

Enter WILLOUGHBY, *speaking to a* Servant *behind*.

Will. Let a coach be call'd directly——she must certainly be gone off to this libertine Dormer.

Mrs. Will. Well, have your elevated notions done you any service, or has all turned out for the best now?

Will. Madam, madam, don't distract me, don't distract me—I am sufficiently miserable without these unnecessary reproaches.

Mrs. Will. O you are! I am heartily glad of it——

Will. Yet something whispers at my heart that all will still turn out for the best——

Mrs. Will. Indeed!

Will. Yes, the dispensations of Providence are always founded on justice; and none are ever sufferers in the end, but those who have merited the utmost severity from its hands.

Mrs. Will. Fine philosophy, truly; and I suppose you would have thought it for the best if you had lost me as well as your daughter?

Will. [*Ironically.*] I would have tried at least, madam, to be as easy as possible under so great a misfortune.

Mrs. Will. You would, you barbarous man—but you are miserable enough without such a circumstance, and that's some comfort to me. Your obstinacy has made your only child desperate, and you have thought it better to run the hazard of her ruin, than to establish her happiness on a certain **foundation.**

Will. I tell you, madam, any distress is preferable to the perpetration of a crime ; and there **was** no way of acting upon your principles, without the blackest ingratitude to the common benefactor of my family.— I feel for the indiscretion of this unhappy girl with the severest poignancy, but I rejoice that my partiality for her led the father into no action that could impeach the probity of the man.

Mrs. Will. Mighty fine.

Will. This, madam, is a consolation, a great consolation in this hour of affliction ; and let me tell you, that in the severest trials, the truly honest feel a satisfaction, which is never experienced in the most flattering moments of a guilty prosperity.

Mrs. Will. Well, well, follow your own course, and answer for the consequences.——Had my advice been taken, but who indeed takes sensible advice now-a-days; **you never** took my advice in your life, and you see what the effect has proved to your unfortunate family.

Will. A truce with your wisdom, madam, I beseech you ; for if it only teaches you to be worthless, it would be happy for you to be the greatest idiot in the kingdom :—but I have no time to waste in words, every possible measure must be taken for the recovery of this infatuated girl——

Mrs. *Will.* And suppose you should not be able to recover this infatuated girl as you call her, what medicine will your philosophy in that case administer for so great a misfortune.

Will. The best of all medicines, the consciousness of having never deserv'd it.   [*Exit.*

Mrs. *Will.* Why, you ill-bred brute, won't you take me along with you—I must go with him to see that every thing is conducted with propriety.   [*Exit.*

ACT III.   SCENE I.

The Park. VILLARS *alone.*

Villars.

INTO how very hopeless a situation has my fortune at last plunged me, and how unluckily has the very accident which I consider'd as the most happy circumstance of my life, turn'd out a source of disappointment and distress.—Here, while I was rejoicing on being entertained by Sir John Dormer, was it possible for me to suppose that his amiable daughter would have made so absolute a conquest of my heart. But on the other hand was it possible to see so much sweetness, affability, and merit, without the warmest admiration ? Yet to what purpose do I continually indulge myself in

thinking of Miss Dormer? My lot in life is as precarious as it is poor, whereas she is entitled to cherish the
noblest expectations.———'T is true, indeed, Captain
Dormer has favour'd me with his friendship, and I
am **in** hourly hope of an ensigncy by his means. And
will an ensigncy———No———I 'll lock the secret eternally in my bosom, and since **I cannot** raise myself
up to the importance of her prospects, she shall never
be reduced to the penury of mine:

Enter Captain DORMER.

Dor. All alive and merry, my dear Villars, I am
now in cash enough ; but here, my boy, is the commission I have been soliciting for you. 'T is just
sign'd, **and you** must do me the additional favour of
accepting **this** note to buy regimentals.

Vil. You overwhelm me with this generosity———

Dor. Nay, no hesitating———you shall give me **a**
draft upon the agent for the money, or do any thing
your ridiculous nicety requires, so you only condescend to oblige me.

Vil. I am at a loss for words to———

Dor. I am very glad of it, as I don't want to be
thank'd for an act of common justice; the necessities
of the worthy have a constant claim upon the super-
fluities of the rich, and we in reality only pay a debt,
where the world imagines we confer an obligation.

Vil. This way of thinking is so noble, that———

Dor. Poh, poh, poh man, let 's have none of these
elaborate acknowledgements, especially at this time,

when I have news for you; such news, would you believe it, Miss Willoughby has actually left her father,
and is now at my private lodgings in Pall-mall.

Vil. You astonish me!

Dor. Read this lettter, and it will inform you of
every thing.

Vil. [*Reads.*] ‘ My dearest Dormer, my unrelenting
father has this morning commanded me, never to receive a visit from you more——

Dor. There’s a touch of the **pathetic**, Villars.——
My unrelenting father has this morning commanded
me, never to receive a visit from you more.

[*Ludicrously.*]

Vil. ‘ But there’s no possibility of existing without
my Dormer——

Dor. But there’s no possibility of existing without
my Dormer.

Vil. ‘ I have, therefore, sent some clothes, and a
few ornaments, to the house in Pall-mall, where I
have occasionally met him, and shall follow them immediately myself——

Dor. And shall follow them immediately myself—
Ay, there she drops the heroic; and sensibly proceeds
to business.

Vil. ‘ If my Dormer’s passion is as sincere and as
honourable as I think it, he will take instant measures
for carrying me to Scotland——

Dor. No—Scotland is too far to the north, Villars—too far to the north—but mind what follows.

Vil. ‘ And put it out of the power of the most ma-

Dor. There she's in heroics again, Villars.

Vil. ' To rob him of his Cornelia Willoughby.'

Dor. To rob him of his Cornelia Willoughby.   O, you must speak that with all the emphasis of tragedy tenderness, man :——your voice must be broken, your bosom must be thump'd, your eyes must be fix'd. zounds, it will never do without a deal of the passionate.

Vil. How can you turn a woman into ridicule, whose partiality for yourself, is the only cause of her indiscretion ?

Dor. And how can you suppose that her partiality for me, should render me blind to the impropriety of her conduct ?—I can see when a woman plays the fool with myself, as soon as when she plays it with other people.

Vil. Well, but what do you intend to do, you see her elopement is upon an absolute supposition of your intending to marry her ?

Dor. I don't know that, nor do I see how I am bound to take more care of a lady's honour, than she chooses to take herself.   But even admitting the force of your supposition, what can I do ? It is not in my power to marry her, she knows herself it is not in my power, and I should cut a very ridiculous figure in the eye of the world, if after a fine girl threw herself voluntarily into my arms, with a perfect knowledge of my situation, I was to read her a lecture of morality with a prim, puritanical phyz, and to cry, ' you sha'n't stay with me, Miss, you must go home and be dutiful to your papa.'

Vil. My dear captain, a fond woman always judges of her lover by herself; and Miss Willoughby imagines, because she is ready to run any risk for your sake, that you will as readily run any hazard for her's ——she therefore trusts you————

Dor. Zounds, Villars, how preposterously you argue; does n't every woman who trusts entirely to the discretion of a lover, trust a robber with her purse, and an enemy with her reputation? A woman of real principle will never put it into a man's power to be perfidious, and I should not care to trust any of these eloping damsels with my honour, who are such miserable guardians of their own.

Vil. You are a very extraordinary man indeed, to think meanly of a woman, for giving you the greatest proof which she can possibly shew of her affection.

Dor. I must think meanly of any woman who gives me an improper proof of her affection, though I may be inclined to take an advantage of it.

Vil. Indeed!

Dor. O, Villars, if the women did but know how we doat upon them for keeping us at a sensible distance, and how we despise them where they are forwardly fond, their very pride would serve them in the room of reason, and they would learn to be prudent even from the greatness of their vanity.

Vil. So then you think Miss Willoughby fair game, now she has————

Dor. Undoubtedly; formerly, indeed, I had some scruples on her father's account, but now she has gone

this length, there is no resisting the temptation. As
I told you before, Villars, she knows I can't marry
her, she knows I am already engag'd, and what the
devil do you think she wants with me—hey?

Vil. Why but——

Dor. Why but——why but what? Only consider,
man, what a mind a woman must have, who can plunge
her whole family in wretchedness **for** any fellow's
sake; honour believe me, Villars, never took root in
a bosom which is dead to the feelings of nature; nor
are those in the least to be pitied who are willingly
destroyed.

Vil. Well, well, I stay still——

Dor. But well, well——I hav'n't time to hear what
you would say, for I want you to go to Pall-Mall directly to see that Miss Willoughby is properly accom-
modated.——I know the moment she is missed I shall
be suspected, so I 'll go to my father's and be in the
way there, to save appearances as much as possible.

Vil. Why ha'n't you been in Pall-Mall to receive her?

Dor. Yes, but I had only time to take a few trifling
liberties, and I am now going to make love very much
against my inclination to Miss Montagu——My father read me a damn'd severe lecture this morning,
and the best way of preventing any suspicion from
fastening on me about Miss Willoughby, is to shew
every mark of readiness to comply with his inclinations; but go, my dear boy, about the business, and
I 'll do as much for you whene'er a pretty woman
brings you into difficulties.

Vil. O, I am much oblig'd to you.

Dor. The people of the house will admit you directly; and remember that a trifling lie or two must choak neither of us, if any body should question us about the little run-away.   [*Exeunt severally.*

SCENE II.

Changes to Sir John Dormer's. *Enter* Sir GEORGE.

Sir *George.* Why how the plague shall I act in this affair, or with what face can I possibly tell Sir John that I am desirous of declining an alliance with his family, after I have so repeatedly solicited his influence with Miss Dormer.——I promised to wait till he return'd from the Cocoa-tree——I wish he was come back with all my heart—for my present situation is none of the most agreeable.——Upon my word it was a mighty modest request of the young lady, at the very moment she refus'd me, to desire I would take the whole blame upon myself.——Your women of sentiment, however, have a very extraordinary manner of doing things——O, but here comes Sir John, what the devil shall I say to him.

Enter Sir JOHN DORMER.

Sir *John.* Sir George I give you joy a thousand times.—I met Caroline as I was coming up stairs, and by her silence as well as blushing, I read her readiness to comply with my wishes, and find her the excellent girl I always imagin'd her.

Sir *George.* She is a very excellent young lady, indeed, and I am very much obliged to her.

Sir *John.* You can't now, conceive the transport of my heart at her cheerful concurrence, but I hope you will one day experience, that a dutiful child is the first of all human felicities.

Sir *George.* It must be a very great happiness, indeed, Sir John.

Sir *John.* Well, Sir George, our lawyers shall meet this very evening, and every thing shall be settled to our mutual satisfaction.

Sir *George.* Yes, Sir John, I wish to settle every thing to your satisfaction.

Sir *John.* There will be no great occasion for expensive preparations.

Sir *George.* O, none in the world, none in the world.

Sir *John.* I don't see any necessity you have to move out of our present house in Berkeley-square.

Sir *George.* Nor I either.

Sir *John.* You have room enough there.

Sir *George.* Plenty.

Sir *John.* Why, what's the matter, Sir George, you speak with an air of coolness and embarrassment that surprizes me?

Sir *George.* Sir John, I am incapable of a duplicity.

Sir *John.* Well.

Sir *George.* And notwithstanding my wishes for Miss Dormer are as ardent as she is deserving——a circumstance has happen'd, which must for ever deny me the blessing of her hand.

Sir John. You astonish me!——but what circumstance——she **is ready**——

Sir George. Yes, yes, she is very ready, Sir John.

Sir John. Then pray acquaint me with the impediment.

Sir George. My dear Sir John, a point, a very nice point of honour prevents the possibility of my indulging you in this request: you may, however, safely assure yourself that I am now no less worthy of your good opinion, than when you favoured me with the warmest recommendation to Miss Dormer.

Sir John. Mighty well, **Sir** George, mighty well, **and so** you come into my house to solicit my influence **in** your favour, over the affections of my daughter, obtain her approbation, and then, without producing one cause for a change in your sentiments, affront us both in the grossest manner, **by** instantly receding from your engagements.

Sir George. You are warm, Sir John.

Sir John. Have I not abundant cause for warmth, when you deny a reason for the affront which on this occasion you have offered to my family. If you know **any** thing in my daughter's conduct that renders her unworthy of your alliance, pronounce it freely—and I shall myself be the first to approve your rejection of her. But, Sir George, if you capriciously decline a treaty which you yourself took so much pains to commence, without assigning a sufficient cause for your

behaviour; be assured I will have ample satisfaction.
——Nor shall the altar itself protect you from the
united vengeance of an injured friend and an insulted
father.

Sir *George*. Sir John, I easily conceive the purport
of this menace: but whatever measures you intend to
take, let me tell you, I shall one day have your thanks
for the conduct which now excites your indignation;
and, let me also tell you, that the very moment in
which your hand is raised against my, life, will be the
moment in which I shall prove myself the truest
friend to your family.

Sir *John*. Away, away, you are all profession and
falsehood.—My daughter told me that you were incapable of loving any thing but yourself.

Sir *George*. I thank her very heartily, sir.

Sir *John*. And that the wishes of your heart were
entirely centred in the admiration of your own adorable person.

Sir *George*. O, I am infinitely obliged to her.

Sir *John*. But insignificant, as she justly represented you——

Sir *George*. Insignificant!

Sir *John*. That insignificance shall **not** be your protection.

Sir *George*. My protection!——So, I want to be
protected.

Sir *John*. Therefore, unless you would prove yourself as destitute of courage as of honour, meet me at
the Cocoa-tree in an hour; we can easily have a pri-

vate room, and, if you fail, I shall set such a stigma on the coward, as will render him a scorn even to the greatest profligate in the kingdom.   .   *[Exit.*

Sir *George.* So——now I am engaged in a pretty piece of business—and must hazard my life for a woman, who has not only rejected my addresses, but mentioned me with coutempt; and danger joined to insult is my reward, where, in reality, I ought to meet with thanks and approbation, la la la la lalla, [*Hums a French air.*] Well, be it as it will, Miss Dormer's secret shall be inviolably preserved.—A thrust through the guts is, to be sure, disagreeable enough, but if fellows every day hazard it in defence of the basest actions, there can be no mighty heroism in running a little risque, to support the cause of honour and generosity.   *[Exit.*

SCENE III.

Dormer's *Lodgings in Pall Mall.* *Enter* Miss WILLOUGHBY.

Miss *Will.* Where shall I hide my miserable head, or how shall I avoid the stroke of impending destruction. The man who should have been the guardian, is himself the person that attacks my honour, and the unlimited confidence which I rashly repos'd in his affection, is now made use of to cover me with disgrace.——O that my unhappy sex would learn a little prudence, and be well convinced, when they fly from the imaginary oppression of a father, that they are not seeking protection from the most cruel of all enemies, those who mean to sacrifice their peace, and blast their reputation.

Enter **LUCY.**

Lucy. Madam, there is a gentleman from Captain Dormer come to wait upon you.

Miss *Will.* What can he want with me?

Lucy. I really can't say, madam.——But, **if you** please, I'll send him up, and then you can know his business from himself.

Miss *Will.* [*Walking about disorderly.*] How am I insulted and expos'd! But the woman deserves no respect from others, who does not shew a proper regard for her own character.

Lucy. [*Aside.*] Lord! what a mighty fuss we make, though I don't see we are a bit handsomer than other people. Well, madam, what shall I say to the gentleman?

Miss *Will.* Shew the gentleman up.

Lucy. [*Pertly.*] Yes, madam.   [*Exit.*

Miss *Will.* Whoever he is he cannot increase my fears, and may possibly bring me **some** intelligence to mitigate their severity.

Enter **VILLARS.**

Vil. Madam, your most obedient.——I wait upon you with Captain Dormer's respects, to apologize for his unavoidable absence a few hours and to hope that every thing here is quite to your satisfaction.

Miss *Will.* As the captain, sir, has engaged your good offices on this occasion, I suppose you are acquainted with the history of **my** indiscretion.

Vil. The captain, madam, gave me no particular account **of** matters, but only sent me as a friend, on whose **secrecy** he could rely, to apologize for his absence, and to enquire how you approved of this situation.

Miss *Will.* [*With emotion.*] Sir, I don't approve of this situation at all.

Vil. I should be sorry, madam, that my presence distressed **you.**

Miss *Will.* 'T is not your presence, sir, which distresses me, 't is the consciousness of my own folly ; 't is the danger to which I have exposed myself.——— But, sir, your appearance is the appearance of humanity ; and I think you look with compassion on an unhappy young creature, whom the perfidy of a man too tenderly esteem'd, has devoted to destruction ; if you do, sir, save me———I conjure you, by all you hold most dear, to save me from dishonour. I have been indiscreet, but not criminal, and the purity of my intention has some claim to pity, though the rashness of my flight may be wholly without excuse.

Vil. Be compos'd, madam———Pray be composed— You affect me exceedingly.———And you shall find a protector in me, if you have any just cause to apprehend the least violence from Captain Dormer.

Miss *Will.* If I have any cause, sir.—Why, instead of proceeding with me to a place where we might be securely united, am I detained in this unaccountable house ?---Why did he here attempt liberties, that must be shocking to the mind of sensibility ?---And why at his departure did he give the people here **or-**ders to confine me to these apartments.

Vil. You feel too strongly, madam.

Miss *Will.* Can I feel too strongly, **sir**, where my everlasting peace of mind **is destroyed ; and** where the man who declared he only existed for my sake, is cruelly industrious to plunge me into infamy ?———Unknowing in the ways of the world, I could not distinguish between the language of sincerity, and the voice of dissimulation.---By my own integrity I judged of his truth, and could not think that any man would be monster enough to return a tender partiality for himself with disgrace and destruction.

Vil. Madam, there is something in your manner---there **is** something in this generous indignation that disposes me very warmly to serve you, and if you really desire to leave this house, you shall leave it instantly ; the people have directions to obey me in every thing, and I do not think myself obliged to answer Mr. Dormer's expectations, where his demands are evidently contrary to the principles of virtue.

Miss *Will.* Sir, you charm me with these sentiments.

Vil. Madam, they are sentiments which should regulate the conduct of every man; for he who suffers a bad action to be committed when he has the power of preventing it, is, in my opinion, as guilty as the actual perpetrator of the crime.

Miss *Will.* I am eternally indebted to this generosity, sir.

Vil. Not in the least, madam. For, abstracted from my general abhorrence of what is indefensible, I find, I know not how, an irresistable inclination to serve you. But we lose time. I'll order a coach directly to the door, and leave you at perfect liberty to follow your own inclinations.

Miss *Will.* I have a fix'd reliance on your honour, sir, and only lament that I have nothing but thanks to shew my gratitude for this goodness.

Vil. My dear madam, your thanks are more than I deserve. What I have done humanity made my duty; and the most contemptible of mankind, is he who declines the performance of a good action because he has not an expectation of being rewarded.

ACT IV. SCENE I.

Sir John Dormer's.   *Enter* DORMER, *followed by* WILLOUGHBY.

Willoughby.

CAPTAIN Dormer, don't keep me on the rack, but give me my daughter.

Dor. Sir, I have repeatedly told you——

Will. Yes, sir, you **have** repeatedly told me, that you are wholly unconcerned in her flight—But this is the only thing in which I could find it any way difficult to believe you.

Dor. Mr. Willoughby, this doubt of my veracity is neither kind nor delicate.

Will. Don't insult me, Captain Dormer, while you are loading me with calamity, or possibly I may forget that you are the son of my benefactor.——However, sir, I do not come here to menace, but to supplicate. ——I do not come here to provoke the warmth of your temper, but to interest the sensibility of your heart. ——You see me a distress'd, unfortunate, miserable old man. The whole happiness of my life is wrapp'd up in the inconsiderate girl you have stolen from my arms ——and if she is not instantly return'd, my portion will be distraction.——Restore her therefore, I beseech you, and restore her while she is innocent.——The blow is a barbarous one, which is aim'd at the bosom of a friend; and the triumph is despicable indeed, which is purchased at the expence of humanity.

Dor. [*Aside.*] Why, how contemptible a rascal is a libertine!

Will. For pity's sake give **me** back my child; nor destroy, in your giddy pursuit of pleasure, the eternal peace of a man who would **readily** risque his life for the advancement of your happiness.——You have generosity, Captain Dormer, and you have understanding---yet **you combat** the natural benevolence of your heart, and oppose **the** evident sense of your own conviction: You are cruel, because it is gallant; and you are licentious, because it is fashionable. But, sir, let my distress, my anguish, restore you to yourself, and teach you, in some measure, to anticipate the feelings of a father. Early in life an only son was taken from me; and the evening of my days is now to be marked with the pollution of an only daughter. O! Mr. Dormer, you men of pleasure know not how wide a ruin you spread in the progress of your unwarrantable inclinations. You do not recollect, that, besides the unhappy victim sacrific'd, there is a family to participate in her injuries; a mother, perhaps to die at her destruction, and a wretch like me to madden at her disgrace.

Dor. I cannot be the rascal I intended. [*Aside.*] Sir, ———Mr. Willoughby, be satisfied. Miss Willoughby is safe and well———nor shall I ever entertain a wish to disturb your happiness, or to injure her reputation.

Will. Eternal blessings on you for this generous declaration. But, if you speak your real sentiments, conduct me instantly to my child.

Dor. With pleasure, sir———and I have great reason to imagine, that the anxiety she has suffer'd in consequence of this little indiscretion, will make her additionally worthy of your affection.

Will. Why, I always said that every thing happens for the best; and that many accidents are really blessings in disguise, which we lament as absolute misfortunes.

Dor. Your philosophy will be justified in the present case, I assure you.

Will. Give me your hand, captain.———I esteem you more than ever. But come; I am impatient to see my poor girl. Her fault was the result of her inexperience; and if we were all to be punished for the errors of indiscretion, what would become of the best of us?

Dor. Justly considered, sir.

Will. Come along, come along, man: I want to be gone---and my miserable wife, whom I did n't care to bring in, for fear she should be clamorous, waits for me in a coach at the end of the street.

Dor. I attend you, sir---yet, if half the gay fellows about town were informed of the business I am going upon.---I fancy they'd laugh at me pretty heartily.

Will. Ah! Captain! a man of sense should despise the ridicule of the profligate, and recollect, that the laughter of a thousand fools is by no means so cutting as the severity of his own detestation.   [*Exeunt.*

SCENE II.

Changes to another Apartment in Sir John Dormer's.
Enter Miss Montagu *and* Miss Willoughby.

Miss *Will.* Thus, my dear madam, have I given you the whole history of my infatuation; and I have now only to repeat my sincere concern for thinking it pos- sible that Captain Dormer could be insensible of your very great merit, and to intreat the favour of your interposition with my father.

Miss *Mon.* My dear girl, there is no occasion what- soever for this generous apology.

Miss Will. Indeed, madam, there is---I was unpardonably vain in attempting to dispute a heart with you, and I was extremely culpable, in forgetting how much the completion of my own wishes might disturb the peace of a family, to which my father had so many obligations.

Miss Mon. My dear Miss Willoughby, we women are all fools when we are in love, and it is but natural that our own happiness should be more immediately the object of our attention, than the happiness of other people. But I want to ask you a question about this recreant of ours, to which I beg you will give me an ingenuous answer.

Miss Will. Pray propose your question, madam.

Miss Mon. Then, my dear, suppose matters could be so brought about, that Sir John would approve the captain's attachment to you, could you, tell me candidly, forgive the insolent use which he has just made of your generosity?

Miss Will. Dear Miss Montagu, why do you ask me such a question?

Miss Mon. Because I am pretty sure you may still have him, if you think him worth your acceptance.

Miss Will. I really do n't understand you.

Miss Mon. You shall understand me then—I never will marry Captain Dormer.

Miss Will. Madam!

Miss Mon. He 's not a man to my taste.

Miss Will. No!

Miss Mon. No—he is worse to me, to make use of

an affected simile, than prepar'd chicken gloves, or almond paste.

Miss *Will.* Indeed!

Miss *Mon.* Yes—he is more offensive than Naples dew, or Venitian cream, the essence of daffodil, or the Imperial milk of roses.

Miss *Will.* You can't be serious surely—not like him!

Miss *Mon.* No, positively I do not like him.

Miss *Will.* Why, where can there be so————

Miss *Mon.* O, bravo.

　　' Is he not more than painting can express,
　　' Or youthful poets fancy when they love.'

Miss *Will.* You reprove me very justly, madam, and I blush to speak of a man with softness, whom I should always consider with indignation.

Miss *Mon.* Come, come, my dear, the captain is a very agreeable young fellow after all. But I know he is as indifferent about me, as I can possibly be about him, and I should never have a syllable of the tender kind from him, if he was not extremely unwilling to disoblige his father.

Miss *Will.* Has he yet declar'd himself, madam?

Miss *Mon.* Why, not expressly, but I expect him every moment to open with the usual formality, and if you please, we cannot only render the scene a whimsical one, but make him smart very sensibly for the liberties of this morning.

Miss *Will.* In what manner, pray?

Miss *Mon.* Why, the moment he comes, you shall retire into this closet, and in the midst of all his professions to me, I shall take an opportunity of mentioning your name with an air of jealous resentment.

Miss *Will.* Well!

Miss **Mon.** This I am sure will induce him to make violent protestations, that this heavenly face of mine alone is the object of his adoration; and, as the men think it no way dishonourable to tell a trifling little fib to a woman, I shall soon have him vowing everlasting fidelity and swearing,

‘ *The envious moon grows pale and sick with grief,*
‘ *That I, her maid, am far more fair than she.*’

Miss *Will.* I conceive the whole design, madam.

Miss *Mon.* Well then, when he is in the meridian of all his nonsense---do you steal softly out of the closet and sit in that chair---I'll take care that he does n't see you---If he forswears his passion for you, give him a gentle pull by the sleeve---and, looking him stedfastly in the face, leave all the rest to accident.

Miss *Will.* I am afraid I sha'n't have spirits to go through with it.

Miss *Mon.* Courage, child; ha'n't I given you spirits enough in declaring that I'll never marry him? ——I think you said my woman let you in, and that you saw nobody else.

Miss *Will.* Yes.

Miss *Mon.* Why then she shall keep your being here a secret from every body, and I warrant we'll pay the captain off pretty handsomely——but why so melancholy?.

Miss *Will.* Why, my dear Miss Montagu, I don't know, if in justice to you, I should think any more of Dormer—he has so many accomplishments——

Miss *Mon.* Well, my dear, to make you entirely easy, there is a man in the world who is, in my opinion, much more accomplished ; but not a word to any body on this matter for your life---I only mention it to you in confidence, and to shew the probability of your yet being happy with Dormer.

Enter JENNY.

Jenny. Madam, the pens and paper are laid in the next room.

Miss *Mon.* Very well---go---and, Jenny——

Jenny. Madam.

Miss *Mon.* Don't give the least hint to any of the family that Miss Willoughby is here.

Jenny. By no means, madam.   [*Exit.*

Miss *Mon.* And now we'll prepare a letter to your father----But come, my dear girl, you must not be so dejected—Your little error is amply atoned for by the generosity of this conduct ; and there are some faults which, like happy shades in a fine picture, actually give a forcible effect to the amiable light of our characters.   [*Exeunt.*

SCENE III.

Changes to the Pall-Mall Apartments. Enter WIL-
LOUGHBY, Mrs. WILLOUGHBY, DORMER, *and*
LUCY.

Dor. Come in, my dear sir---come in --do n't be
alarmed Miss Willoughby --your father is prepared
to overlook every———Why, she is n't here!

Lucy. **Pray**, sir, did n't I tell you so?

Mrs. *Will.* What, is n't she here?

Lucy. No, madam.

Will. No!

Lucy. Lord bless you, sir, did n't I tell you so as
you came up?

Dor. And where is she gone to?

Lucy. Do you desire I should tell the truth?

Will. Ay, speak the truth, child, and fear nothing---
But let 's take a peep into this room.

                                    [*Goes into another room.*

Lucy. Then the truth is———

Mrs. *Will.* That 's a good girl, speak up.

Lucy. The truth is, I do n't know where she 's gone.

Dor. Death and confusion, where can she be gone
to?

Lucy. That I do n't know, as I said before---But
she went with your friend---the gentleman you sent
here on a message to her.   [*Exit.*

Mrs. *Will.* O, she 's gone away with a friend of

your's, is she---for shame, Captain Dormer---you a
tender lover---you animated with that exquisite softness which souls of sensibility feel.

Dor. Death, madam, why will you teaze me in this
manner---I tell you I have been betray'd———

Re-enter WILLOUGHBY.

Will. No, sir, it is I who am betrayed. And so a
friend of his has carried her off. [*To Mrs.* Willoughby.

Mrs. *Will.* Yes, and every thing happens for the
best now---does not it?

Dor. Mr. Willoughby, hear me.

Will. Captain Dormer, after this re-iterated insult,
this aggravated cruelty—'t is infamous to talk with
you.---However, sir, old as you think me, and little
as you dread my resentment, you shall feel it heavily.
———No! injured as I am, you shall never receive a
stroke from me.---I am too miserable myself by the
loss of a child, to stab my best benefactor even in the
person of a worthless son.---You are, therefore, safe
---Safe as the fears of cowardice can wish. But, if
you have feelings, to those feelings I consign you.---
They will wake a scorpion in that bosom to avenge
my wrongs.--For know, though bad men may find
it possible to elude the justice of a whole universe,
they are yet utterly without means of flying from
their own recollection.

Dor. Mr. Willoughby, let me only explain the
matter———

Will. Sir, I'll talk to no monsters.

Dor. Dear, Mrs. Willoughby, your husband is so impetuous——

Mrs. *Will.* Don't speak to me, sir,---don't speak to me.----A perfidious lover shall never gain an audience from Mr. Willoughby.---But, my dear, what do you intend doing!

Will. Pray, madam, don't teaze me.

Mrs. *Will.* Why, your ill-natured---but I won't forget the bounds of propriety, especially as you are not mad man enough to fight---It would be little for the better if you were killed.

Will. Death, madam, any thing would be for the better, that set me free from your intollerable impertinence.　　　　　　　　　　　　　　[*Exit.*

Mrs. *Will.* Did the world ever hear such a vulgar fellow---But these husbands have no more breeding! ---And here he is gone without giving me his hand. In a little time I suppose the fair sex will be entirely neglected. [*Going, returns.*] But, sir, a word in your ear. You are a base man.---I would not violate propriety for the world---but you are a base man. Sir John shall know every thing instantly,---'T was I that urg'd my poor girl to repose that implicit confidence in your honour---and since my advice has lost —my assiduity will do any thing to recover her. [*Exit.*

Dor. Why, how just is it that profligacy should be constantly attended with punishment, and how reasonable is it, that those who make no scruple of wounding the happiness of others, should be conspicuously miserable themselves.---How shall I look my

father in the face, when this matter comes to be
known; or how shall I see this unhappy old man,
whom I have so infamously wronged. What **a poor**,
what a paltry, what a merciless passion is this passion
of gallantry; yet it reflects no scandal whatever **upon**
its followers, though it begins **in** the most despicable
falsehood, **and** terminates in the most irreparable destruction. A man of gallantry, **is** the only wretch
who can despise the sense of shame, and stifle the
feelings of gratitude without reproach; take him into
your house, he attempts the sanctity of your bed;---
load him with obligations and he betrays the purity **of**
your daughter. The sensible world however allows
him to be a man of honour all the time, and he stabs
you with impunity to the heart for presuming to
complain of your wrongs. Why did not I see the
blackness of this character a little earlier. But---no
---my cursed pride would resist the arguments of my
conviction. And for a pitiful triumph over an unsuspecting innocent, I must basely divest myself both of
reason and humanity. Where can this girl be fled
to ?---Villars I am sure is incapable of betraying me,
and as she came here with her own consent she was
prepared for the consequences of course.

Enter VILLARS.

My dear Villars you are come most luckily here,
Miss Willoughby is gone off, and the people of the
house have the impudence to say, by your means.

Vil. Well, and they say very justly.

Dor. How's this?

Vil. I suffer'd her to escape---I assisted in her escape ---and am now ready to answer for the consequences.

Dor. Indeed!

Vil. But first, sir, let me return you the commission, and the note with which you were this morning so kind as to present me. I do not mean to keep your favours while I counteract your views, and I scorn to profit by the generosity of any man, unless upon terms that merit my approbation.

Dor. Death and the devil, sir, how dare you use me in this manner: how dare you betray my confidence so scandalously, draw, and give me instant satisfaction.

Vil. I came here on purpose to give you satisfaction ---but before I draw suffer me to ask a question or two in my turn. And now, sir, how dare you suppose that I was to be made the instrument of your licentiousness; how dare you suppose that I would be the pander to your vices, and join with you in a barbarous contrivance of destroying a young creature, whose inexperience was her only crime?

Dor. Here's a fellow!

Vil. But I suppose you insulted me on account of my situation, and imagined because I was poor that I was consequently worthless; however, sir, be now undeceived, and, in the midst of your affluence, and my poverty, know that I am your superior, for the best of all reasons, because I disdain to commit a despicable action.

Dor. I am astonish'd at the very impudence of his rectitude, and can't say a syllable to him.

Vil. When I came here, instead of a willing victim to your wishes, I found Miss Willoughby in the utmost affliction, conscious of her indiscretion in flying from her father, and shuddering with apprehension of violence from you. She soon inform'd me of her fears, and lamented, in the most pathetic terms, how greatly she had been deceiv'd in the object of her affection.--- She imagin'd an honourable union with you, would have been the consequence of her flight; and little supposed that the man she lov'd would make use of her partiality for himself to cover her with disgrace.--- Thus disappointed, thus betray'd, she ask'd for my protection, she receiv'd it; and now, sir, [*Drawing.*] take your revenge.

Dor. Yes, sir, I will take my revenge, but it shall be thus——[*Throwing down his sword, and shaking* Villars *by the hand.*] Thus, my dear Villars, let me thank you for the superiority of your principles; I am myself just awakened to a sense of true honour, and cannot, now I know the real motive of your conduct, resent, as an injury, what I must look upon with the highest admiration.

Vill. How agreeably you surprize me, sir.

Dor. Dear Villars, take these trifles again, or I shall not think you forgive me. [Villars *accepts the commission, &c.*] But, my poor girl—and so she has principle after all—what a rascal have I been! Do tell me where she 's gone.

Vil. Indeed I cannot—I only saw her into a coach; but I suppose she is returned to her father's.

Dor. No, she is not—her father is but just gone—he came to me, as I suspected, on the very first knowledge of her flight; and shew'd so deep a dis.ress, that I could n't persevere in my design of seeming wholly ignorant of her elopement.

Vil. Well!

Dor. I therefore brought him here to give her back; and the poor man was actually in extacies; but when he found she was gone, he lost all patience; and, naturally enough, imagining that she was carried off by my contrivance, treated me with a freedom, which nothing but the conviction of my guilt could enable me to endure, even from the father of Miss Willoughby.

Vil. Upon my word, this affair has drawn you into a very disagreeable situation.

Dor. Into a disagreeable situation! into a damn'd one, and I shall hate the word gallantry as long as I live.—My friend's daughter too!—shame—shame—shame—zounds! Villars, a man ought to be good even from policy, if he is not so from inclination.—Damn it, you don't know half the perplexities of my situation.

Vil. No!

Dor. No. Distracted as I am, I must assume a calm unruffled face immediately, before Miss Montagu.

G

Vil. What, are you going to Miss Montagu directly?

Dor. Yes, instantly—I have myself requested a tete a tete, to make a formal declaration, and truly I am in a pretty frame of mind to make love to a woman of her vivacity.

Vil. Why, indeed, your hands are pretty full of business.

Dor. Yes, yes, I have business enough: and my father will know every thing presently. But I must be a man of gallantry, and be damn'd to me!—Villars, you now see, that the greatest of all idiots is he who makes himself despicable to destroy his own happiness.　　　　　　　　　　　　[*Exeunt.*

SCENE II.

Changes to a Room at the Cocoa-tree. Sir GEORGE *alone.*

Sir *George.* Well, here I am; and a pleasant affair I have to go through!—I wish it was well over:—— For, though there may be a great deal of bravery in venturing one's life, I can't say that there is a great deal of satisfaction.

Enter a Waiter.

Wait. Sir John Dormer, sir.

Sir *George.* Shew Sir John up. Now for it.

The Waiter *returns, introducing* Sir JOHN, *and exit.*

Sir *George.* Sir John, your most obedient.

Sir *John.* Well, Sir George; I see you are a man of courage, at least; and so far I find you worth my resentment.

Sir *George.* No reproaches now, my dear Sir John: for the greatest enemies make a point of being perfectly well bred, when they are going to cut one another's throats.

Sir *John.* Then, Sir George, that I may answer your ideas of politeness, let me beg of you to draw instantly.

Sir *George.* There is no refusing a request which is made with so much civility; and now, sir, I am all obedience to your commands.

Sir *John.* And now to punish the infamous insult which has been offered to my family:

Miss DORMER *rushes from a door at the head of the stage, and, falling upon her knees, exclaims,*

Then punish it here, sir, for I alone am culpable.

Sir *John.* How's this!

Miss *Dor.* O sir, hear me with pity; for the dread of your resentment is insupportable.

Sir *George.* A lady upon her knees! Pray, madam, suffer me to raise you up.

Miss *Dor.* No, Sir George: this attitude best becomes a creature like me, who has not only exposed her benefactor to danger, but even rais'd a sword against the life of her father.

Sir John. Rise, Caroline. But tell me, in the name of wonder, what I am to understand by this ?

Miss Dor. My indiscretion, sir—my disobedience. For, though you have ever treated me with the most unbounded indulgence, I have nevertheless ungratefully disappointed your views, and plac'd my affections upon an object that can never be entitled to your approbation.

Sir George. So my throat seems to be pretty safe this time.

Sir John. Go on.

Miss Dor. Actuated by my regard for this object, though utterly despairing to obtain him, I trusted Sir George with the secret, in the fulness of my heart, and begg'd he would not only withdraw his addresses, but withdraw them in such a manner, as might save me even from the suspicion of any unwillingness to pay an implicit obedience to your commands.

Sir John. This is very extraordinary.

Sir George. Yes, but it's very true for all that.

Miss Dor. Sir George saw my distress, and kindly complied with my request; and had n't I accidentally overheard the altercation which produc'd this meeting, the best of fathers or the noblest of men [*Pointing to Sir George.*] had perhaps fallen a sacrifice to the unhappy prepossession of an inconsiderate daughter.

Sir George. I never knew so sensible a woman in my life.

Miss Dor. Distracted at the extremity to which matters were carried, I knew not how to act—the moment I was capable of resolving, I resolv'd to fly here and wait for your arrival, not coming to any determination till you, sir, and Sir George had quitted the house; here I hinted to the people my apprehension of a misunderstanding between you, and desir'd to be plac'd in the next room to that which he told me was reserv'd for your use; the rest is already known, and I am now to entreat Sir George's forgiveness, for the danger to which his unexampled greatness of mind has nearly expos'd him, and to implore your pardon, sir, for daring to entertain even a hopeless prepossession, when I knew it must combat with the favourite object of your inclinations.

Sir George. Come, Sir John, what the devil are you dreaming of; you and I are friends now, and therefore we need not stand altogether upon ceremonies.

Sir John. I am considering, Sir George, whether I ought most to be pleas'd, or offended with my daughter.

Sir George. Zounds, man, be pleas'd with her, for it will be most to your own satisfaction.

Sir John. Then, Caroline, let me tell you that I am charm'd with your frankness upon this occasion—though I am sorry it was not shewn a little earlier—had you ingenuously told me the situation of your heart when I talk'd to you this morning, you would have sav'd yourself much anxiety, and prevented me from behaving in a manner to Sir George that I must

Miss Dor. Indeed, sir, if you knew **my** motive——

Sir George. Come, come, my dear Miss Dormer, do n't let us pain ourselves with the recollection of past anxieties, when we may indulge ourselves with the prospect of future happiness—I have no notion of the wisdom that makes us miserable, and, therefore, Sir John must, and shall, if he expects **me** to overlook his cavalier conduct of to-day, do me the favour to consult your inclinations.

Miss Dor. You are too good, Sir George—but——

Sir John. Speak up, my dear, and tell us candidly who you **have** distinguished with your approbation— I am not one of the fathers who wish **to maintain a** despotic authority, nor will I make my daughter wretched, to convince **the** world that I am master in my family.

Sir George. O fye, Sir John, there are a great many good fathers who never refuse any thing but happiness to their children.

Miss Dor. I am so overwhelm'd with this goodness, it is at present too much for me. As **we go home in** the coach, I shall endeavour to let **you know** every thing, especially as the object of **my** choice is——

Sir John. Is he a man of merit, my dear—is he a good man—he that is worthy in himself, is above the despicable necessity of stealing a reputation from the virtue of his progenitors ; the riches of the heart are the noblest of all possessions.

[*Exeunt Sir* John *and Miss* Dormer.

the riches of the heart are the noblest of all possessions, and I do n't think that, on the present occasion,
I have proved myself the poorest fellow in the kingdom, notwithstanding my recent insignificance.

[*Exit.*

ACT V. SCENE I.

Sir John Dormer's *House. Enter* Miss MONTAGU,
and Miss WILLOUGHBY.

Miss Montagu.

WHY, what can keep this hopeful Corydon of our's.

Miss Will. Possibly some other attachment.

Miss Mon. Jealousy, Miss Willoughby, rank jealousy, my dear girl. O that we should be such fools
as to bestow a single thought upon these wretched fellows, who are not sensible of the obligation.

Enter JENNY.

Jenny. Madam, madam, Captain Dormer is coming
up.   [*Exit.*

Miss Mon. To your ambush, my dear, and be sure
you watch a proper opportunity of annoying the
enemy.

Miss Will. [*Retiring into a closet.*] O you sha'n't have
any occasion to question my generalship.

Enter DORMER.

Dor. Miss Montagu, your most obedient.

Miss Mon. Captain Dormer, your most devoted humble servant.

Dor. I am come my dear Miss Montagu——

Miss Mon. I see you are, my dear Captain Dormer.

Dor. The amiable vivacity of your temper, madam, has always **been** an object **of my admiration**—but I **come now** to solicit you in regard to a subject———

Miss Mon. Upon which it is criminal, I **suppose**, to exercise my amiable vivacity.

Dor. I need not inform you, madam, of the engage-ment which, so happily for me, subsists between our families; nor need I remind you———

Miss Mon. Why then do you give yourself this trouble, sir, if the information is so very unnecessary ?

Dor. That I may tell you, madam, I am inexpres-sibly fortunate in the honour of this interview, and that I may assure the most charming of her sex, the whole felicity of my life materially depends upon her approbation.

Miss Mon. Upon **my** word, **a very** pretty speech, Captain, and very **tolerably** express'd ; **but** do you know now, that I look upon the **w**hole business of making love to be mighty foolish, and have no notion of a woman's sense, who is to be flatter'd out of her li-berty, by a flimsy compliment to her person.

Dor. This liveliness is charming, but you must not however rally me out of my purpose—suffer me, there-fore, my dear Miss Montagu, **to** implore———

Miss Mon. No, possitively I must stop you, for there is no bearing the insolence of this humility.

Dor. What insolence, my dear Miss Montagu.——
Is it insolence thus to fall at your feet?—Is it insolence————

Miss Mon. For heaven's sake, Dormer, do n't make a fool of yourself, for I tell you the humblest suppli-
cations with which you men can possibly teaze the women, are an unaccountable mixture of pride and absurdity.

Dor. There is something so very new in this opi-
nion, madam, that I should be glad you'd let me know how it is to be supported.

Miss Mon. O, 'tis very easily supported, if you only suffer me to put the general purport of all love addresses, from the time of the first pair, down to the present hour, into something like plain English.

Dor. Pray do.

Miss Mon. Why then, suppose that a tender lover, like you, should offer up his adoration at the altar of some terrestial divinity like myself, let me ask you if this would not be the meaning of his pretty harrangue, however he might study to disguise his design with the plausible language of adulation.

Dor. Now for it.

Miss Mon. Do n't interrupt me. Madam, your beauty is so exquisite, and your merit is so transcen-
dent, that emperors themselves might justly tremble to approach you, and languish in the deepest despair of being allied to so much perfection.

Dor. Well said.

Miss *Mon.* Yet, though all hearts are your's, and though you were born to triumph over an admiring world, I desire you will instantly appoint me the master of your fate ; my happiness depends upon your being a slave, and I must be eternally wretched, without the power of making you miserable ; you must, therefore, promise to know no **will** but my humour, and no pleasure but my inclination——Your present state of freedom you must exchange for the most mortifying dependence, and throw your whole fortune at my feet, for the honour of managing the domestic con-, cerns of my family. If you——

Dor. What the devil is there more of it ?

Miss *Mon.* If you behave well, that is, if you put up with every caprice of my temper, and every irregularity of my conduct ; if you meanly kiss the hand that strikes at your repose, and treat me with reverence when I offer you the grossest indignities, you shall have an occasional new gown, and sometimes the use of your own chariot——Nay, if you are very good indeed, I may carry my kindness still farther, and use you with nearly as much civility as any of my servants.

Dor. What hav'n't you done yet ?

Miss *Mon.* O, I could go on for an hour. But what do you think of this specimen ; isn't it a true translation of all the love speeches that have been made since the commencement of the world, and aren't you men a set of very modest creatures, to suppose that an address of this elegant nature is calculated to make an instant conquest of our affections?

Dor. This spirit is bewitching, and increases my admiration though it treats me with severity.

Miss Mon. Well, notwithstanding the frightful idea which I entertain of matrimony, I am, nevertheless, half afraid I shall be at last cheated out of my freedom as well as the rest of my sex—but then I must be perfectly convinc'd of my admirer's sincerity.

Dor. A decent hint that, though I wish **it had been** spar'd. [*Aside.*] And can you, my dear **Miss Montagu**, possibly doubt the sincerity of my professions, and cruelly turn away those irresistible eyes when I vow an everlasting fidelity? What, still silent, my angel, not a word, not one word to rescue me from distraction—but be it so—if Miss Montagu decrees my fate, I submit without murmuring, for death itself is infinitely preferable to the idea of offending her. [*Going.*] I think I am pretty safe now. [*Aside.*]

Miss Mon. Now, who would believe that this fellow could lye with so very grave a countenance.— [*Aside.*] Why you are in a violent hurry, Captain Dormer.

Dor. O, zounds, she calls me back does she?—— [*Aside.*] What, **my** dear Miss Montagu, do you relent, do you feel the least compassion for the distresses of a heart that adores you?

Miss Mon. Sit down, captain.—Sit down here—I am a strange, foolish creature, and cannot disguise my sentiments. But if I thought myself the only ob-

Dor. **By** all my hopes——

Miss *Mon.* Well, do n't swear—I must believe you. And yet I am strangely apprehensive, that in the extensive circle of your acquaintance you must have form'd some attachments. The world has been talking, and 'tis no secret that Miss Willoughby has accomplishments.

Miss WILLOUGHBY *enters unobserv'd* **by** Dormer, *and sits down.*

Dor. Yes, madam, Miss Willoughby has accomplishments, but they are very trifling.

Miss *Mon.* Then you never entertained any tenderness for her, I suppose.

Dor. For Miss Willoughby, madam. O, my dear Miss Montagu, you do n't think me altogether destitute of understanding ?

Miss *Mon.* Why, you just now own'd that she had accomplishments.

Dor. Yes, I said that she had trifling ones.

Miss *Mon.* And no more ?

Dor. The baby's face is regular enough, **and might serve** very well for the window **of a toy**-shop.

Miss *Mon.* Then I find there is nothing to be apprehended **on** her account.

Dor. On her account, my angel, you shan't lessen the merit of you own attractions so much, as to admit the possibility of supposing it.

Miss *Will.* [*Giving him a pull by the sleeve.*] I am very much obliged to you, sir.

Miss *Mon.* [*Ludicrously.*] 'Not a word, not one word to rescue me from distraction———'

Miss *Will.* 'The baby's face is regular enough, and might serve very well for the window of a toy-shop.'

Miss *Mon.* 'But be it so—if Miss Montagu decrees my fate, I submit without murmuring.'

Miss *Will.* I don't think the gentleman altogether destitute of understanding.

Miss *Mon.* 'For death itself is infinitely more preferable to the idea of offending her'———There, Miss Willoughby, is a man of honour for you.

Miss *Will.* And are these the men who value themselves so much upon their veracity?

Miss *Mon.* O, my dear, they have veracity to a very prudent degree, for they never tell a falshood to any body who is capable of calling them to an account. But come, Miss Willoughby, let us leave the gentleman to himself; he has a very pretty subject for a reverie, and it would be cruel to disturb him in his agreeable reflections. Sir, your most obedient.——— Give it him home, my dear girl; have no mercy on him.　　　　　　　　　　[*Aside to Miss* Willoughby.

Miss *Will.* Sir, your most respectful.

Miss *Mon.* That's right. Sir, your most oblig'd,

Miss *Will.* Your most faithful.

Miss *Mon.* Bravo! And most devoted humble servant.　　　　　　　　　　　　　[*Exeunt laughing.*

Dor. [*After a long pause of confusion.*] So, I have had a hopeful time on't; my evil genius has been a long arrear in my debt, and now pays me off with a

witness. What a sneaking, what a pitiful puppy do
I appear—thus detected, and thus laughed at—But I
deserve it all—I would n't see the infamy of practising
deceit upon a woman—I must even think myself called upon to betray, because the object was a woman;
and laugh at the anguish I gave a worthy heart, because it was lodged in a female breast——Notwithstanding all my mortification, however, I am overjoy-
ed at finding Miss Willoughby safe——I may now
perhaps prevent the matter from reaching my father's
ears—not that I fear he will discard...but what is infinitely worse, if he knows it, will eternally despise
me. How merry the girls were with me---Sir, your
most respectful—Sir, your most obliged---Sir, your
most faithful————

Enter Sir JOHN DORMER.

Sir *John.* Sir, your most devoted humble servant—
Dor. [*Aside.*] O! now I am completely done for—

Sir *John.* Well, sir, what can be urged for you
now ?—Is this the reformation I was to expect---and
is this the regard which you entertain for the credit of
your family ?

Dor. If you 'll give me leave to clear this matter up,
sir————

Sir *John.* 'T is already cleared up—Mr. Willoughby——Miss Montagu have cleared it up——And now
suppose Mr. Willoughby, listening only to the dictates
of his rage, and not to the pleadings of his friendship
for me, had demanded reparation for his wrongs, how,

after robbing him of his daughter, could you come prepared against his life——And how, after destroying a young lady's reputation, could you attempt to embrue your hands in the blood of her father?—— But, sir, you are a man of spirit, you are a man of honour, and that spirit, and that honour are to be sufficient pleas for every violence offered to justice, and every outrage committed upon humanity. You have a title to be guilty, because you have the character of being brave, and you may perpetrate the blackest crime with impunity, because you have the diabolical resolution to defend it.

Dor. There is so much propriety in this reproach, Sir—that I feel myself unable to answer it——

Sir *John.* That sword I gave you, sir, to be exerted in the cause of honour, not to be drawn in the support of infamy---I gave it to be used in the defence of your country, not to be exercised in the violation of her laws---but why do I talk of honour to him who looks with admiration upon shame, and thinks himself accomplished in proportion as he becomes profligate---why do I reason with a man who glories in the prostitution of his understanding, and imagines he exalts his character as he destroys the peace of society?—Perhaps, in his ideas of bravery he may be obliged even to raise his arm against my bosom, and perhaps he may punish a reproachful mention of his vices, though it comes from the lips of his father.

Dor. Sir I have been culpable---extremely culpable

---but my present intention is to remove Mr. Willoughby's distress---not to defend the injury I offered
him---and I can with truth affirm, that the principal
part of my misconduct in this affair, originally proceeded from the great veneration which I entertained
for that very father, who now thinks me so profligate
and unnatural.

Sir *John*. Mighty well!

Dor. I loved Miss Willoughby, sir, tenderly loved
her, before you entered into an engagement about
Miss Montagu. But fearful of disobliging you, I
kept the circumstance of my passion a secret, as I did
not suppose you would countenance a union, where
there was so material a disparity of situations.

Sir *John*. And, pray, sir, **how** dare you suppose
that I should be more offended at the performance of a good action, than at the commission of a
dishonourable one?---How dare you imagine I should
be displeased at your marriage with Miss Willoughby,
and that I should not be infinitely more displeased at
this scandalous seduction?---But it was your regard
for me which led you to betray the confidence of your
friend, as well as to attempt the innocence of his
daughter---Yes, sir, your regard for me is extremely
evident---You knew how much my happiness depend-
ed upon your reputable rise in the world, and how
warmly I expected you would be a credit to your
country, as well as an ornament to your family------
Your natural advantages were great, and your education has been liberal.--Yet, instead of the flattering

prospects with which my imagination was once delighted, I have now nothing before me but a gloomy scene of disappointment and regret.---Instead of hearing my son's name with joy, and exulting in the growing dignity of his character, I am hourly mortified with some fresh accounts of his licentiousness, and hourly trembling lest the hand of well-grounded resentment, or the sword of public justice, should cut him off in the perpetration of his crimes---Instead of finding him the support of my age, he incessantly saps the foundation of my life, and instead of kindly nourishing the lamp of my existence with his virtues, he sinks me down into the grave, an equal victim of sorrow and disgrace.

Dor. [*Falling at his father's feet.*] No more, sir, I beseech you no more---nor suppose me such a monster ---My life hitherto has been a scene of folly and dissipation, and I reflect, with the deepest concern, upon the anxiety which the best of fathers has suffered on my account---but if he can be prevail'd upon to forgive the past, the future, I will boldly say, shall merit his approbation---for I am now satisfied that nothing can be consistent with the principles of honour, which is any way repugnant to the laws of morality.

Sir *John.* Rise, and be my son again---there is a candour, there is a generosity in this acknowledgment which engages my confidence, and I still flatter myself with a belief, that you will answer my warmest expectations.

Dor. Your are too good, sir---But the freedom with

which I shall communicate the most unfavourable circumstances of this affair, as well as my readiness to
fulfill all your commands, shall in some measure prove
the certainty of my reformation.

Sir John. Why, Jack, this is speaking like my son.
And to let you see that your inclination is the only
object of my wishes, Miss Willoughby's hand now
waits to crown your return to virtue.

Dor. Miss Willoughby's, sir!

Sir John. Yes, Miss Montagu, just as I entered, acquainted me with the whimsical distress of your
courtship scene, in terms equally consistent with her
usual good-nature and vivacity, and on account of
your attachment to Miss Willoughby, as well as her
own fixed disinclination to be your's, requested I
would not think any longer of the treaty between our
families---Finding her determined in the solicitation, I would by no means force her wishes---and am
now rejoiced at so lucky an opportunity of reward-
ing, as you yourself could desire, the merit of your
present character.

Dor. There is no doing justice to the generosity of
your sentiments, sir———

Sir John. Poh, poh, man, the parent that makes
his children happiest always gives them the best fortunes—We'll now join the company cheerfully---
But remember for the future, my dear boy, what
every son should constantly have in view, that more
than your own happiness and your own honour are
trusted to your care, and that you cannot experience

a misfortune, nor suffer a disgrace, without sensibly
wounding the bosom of your father.   [*Exeunt.*

SCENE III.

Another Room at Sir John Dormer's. *Enter* Sir GEORGE.

Sir *George.* So then, it seems, I am not quite detesti-
ble after all.----It seems there are some women, though
I have been rejected, who can still think me amiable
---and declare, if ever they change their situation, I
must positively be the man. Villars had **the** secret
from Miss Dormer, and Miss Dormer had the acknowledgment of Miss Montagu's regard for me,
from Miss Montagu herself; her refusal of Dormer
moreover corroborates the intelligence, even **if** there
was any thing very improbable in my having engaged
a lady's affection. Upon my soul I don't see but
Harriot is to the full as handsome as Caroline; and
then her understanding---Yes, I think 'tis pretty **evi-**
dent that she has the advantage in understanding------
Ay, but can I so readily forget Caroline---Can I so
quickly remove my addresses, and offer up that heart
at the shrine of the one which has been so recently
rejected at the altar of the other. Why, to be sure,
there will be nothing extremely gallant in such an
affair. But, at the same time, there will be nothing
extremely preposterous. It doesn't follow, because
I have been repuls'd **by one** woman, that I should
forswear the whole sex; and, in a fit of amorous

lunacy, like the knight errants of old, nobly dedicate my life to despair, because I unfortunately lost the original object of my affections.---Besides, at the present period, changing hands is all the fashion; and while **it is** so meritorious in men of quality to part with their wives, it cannot surely be very criminal to part with our mistresses——Here, by all that's opportune, she comes; what a bewitching girl——O! 't would be barbarous to let her pine. I'll give her encouragement at once, and put an end to her anxiety.

Enter Miss MONTAGU.

Miss *Mon.* O! there's no bearing their loves, and their joys——their tears, and their congratulations—— Sir John has joined the hands of another couple—and Caroline has now Miss Willoughby to keep her in countenance. But pray, Sir George, wasn't poor Villars overjoy'd when you told him of Sir John's design of receiving him as a son-in-law.

Sir *George.* He was, both with gratitude and astonishment---however, I carried him immediately to Sir John; here Miss Dormer was sent for, and, without the least hint of her private sentiments, Sir John, who had properly sounded the young fellow's inclinations, introduced him as a man whom he found worthy to be his son-in-law, and her husband.

Miss *Mon.* I pitied her situation most heartily.

Sir *George.* I pity the situation of every lady in love, madam.

Miss *Mon.* I am sure. Miss Dormer thinks herself much indebted to your generosity.

Sir *George.* Perhaps, madam, I may yet have obligations to the prepossession of Miss Dormer.

Miss *Mon.* Prepossessions **are** strong things, Sir George.

Sir *George.* And, in a lady's bosom, madam, very troublesome.

Miss *Mon.* Not where the object is attainable——

Sir *George.* True, madam—and he must be a barbarian who, conscious of a lady's tenderness, **possesses** the ability without the inclination to return it——I think that hint will give her some consolation. [*Aside.*

Miss *Mon.* The men, I believe, Sir George, have but few opportunities of exercising such a barbarity— Indications of tenderness seldom first proceed from the ladies.

Sir *George.* I don't know that, madam—but was I happy enough to be the object of a lady's esteem—I would sacrifice much to remove her anxiety.——This will make her speak, or the devil's in't.   [*Aside.*

Miss *Mon.* Kind creature! and so you'd condescend to take pity on her.

Sir *George.* I would do every thing to make her happy, madam——why, what the plague **must** she be in love, and is the courtship to come entirely from my side?   [*Aside.*

Miss *Mon.* Well! you are a whimsical creature, and so I leave you——

Sir *George.* Stay, Miss Montagu——

Miss *Mon.* For what?

Sir *George.* I will be generous and spare her blushes [*Aside.*] I have something very serious to say to you.

Miss *Mon.* Serious indeed, if one may judge by your gravity.

Sir *George.* Miss Montagu, I am inexpressibly concerned——I say inexpressibly concerned to see you of late so melancholy.

Miss *Mon.* To see me of late so melancholy! Why, Sir George, I never had better spirits.

Sir *George.* No!

Miss *Mon.* No——really——

Sir *George.* I could not imagine it.

Miss *Mon.* And why so, pray?

Sir *George.* Why so, madam? Nay, I have no particular reason—but Miss Montagu, I should be sorry to see you labour under the smallest uneasiness——I have the highest opinion of your merit, madam—— and——

Miss *Mon.* Surely Caroline has not—[*Aside.*] I shall be always proud of possessing a place in the good opinion of Sir George Hastings.

Sir *George.* You do possess the principal place in my good opinion, madam—and——

The back Scene thrown open, discovers Sir JOHN, *Captain and* Miss DORMER, VILLARS, *Mr. Mrs. and* Miss WILLOUGHBY.

Sir *George.* Zounds, this interruption is abominable.

Dor. Ay this is right; now the rooms are thrown

together, we shall have space enough for a country dance in the evening—Villars, we now are brothers.

Vil. To my unspeakable transport.

Sir *John.* [*To* Willoughby, *who seems in private con-versation with* **him**.] Nay, no acknowledgement, my dear Mr. Willoughby, I am acting no more than an interested part, and consulting my own wishes in the wishes of my children.

Will. [*To his* Wife.] Does n't every thing happen for the best now ? **And** is n't this excellent young man, to **whom** I probably **owe** my child, another proof, that if **we** are desirous of happiness, we must labour to deserve it.

Mrs. *Will.* [*Aside.*] My Scotch scheme has help'd the business greatly for all that.

Sir *John.* We 'll have a public wedding, the friends of all **our** families shall be invited, and, Mr. Villars, let not any humility in the situation of your's, pre-vent you from calling the worthy to be witnesses of the justice which fortune **renders** to your merit.

Vil. **Sir, your** goodness is unbounded, **but** justice obliges me to tell you, that the man thus honour'd with your esteem, is even more humble than you think him ; that he has no family, no relations, and, out **of** this company, no friends.

Will. How 's this ?

Sir *John.* Pray, was n't Mr. Villars, the clergyman in my neighbourhood, your uncle ?

Vil. He was the best of men ; and more than a fa-ther to me in every thing but the actual relation.

Will. [*Impatiently.*] Stand out of the way.

Mrs. *Will.* My dear, I desire you won't forget the rules of propriety.

Will. You said, sir, you were ignorant of your family.

Vil. I did, sir.

Will. Some unhappy father, like me, now bleeds for the loss of a son. Pray go on.

Mrs. *Will.* My dear———

Vil. At an early stage of infancy, some wandering miscreants stole me from my friends, and carried me into a distant part of the country, where a woman, who call'd herself my mother, being committed to prison for a theft, fell ill of a fever, that put a period to her life—with her dying breath she related this circumstance, and would have told more, but the last agonies taking away her utterance, prevented the possibility of any farther declaration.

Sir *John.* How unfortunate!

Miss *Dor.* How extremely unfortunate!

Vil. It would have been still more unfortunate, had n't the good Mr. Villars, who kept a little academy in the place, attended the poor wretch with medicines, and look'd with an eye of compassion on my helpless situation. Mr. Villars was the universal friend of mankind, the rich never mention'd him without reverence, and the poor never beheld him without joy—but his income was too narrow for the extent of his benevolence, and he was involv'd in continual distresses from the uncommon excellence of his heart.

Sir *George.* Zounds, no person doubts his being a

Vil. Mr. Villars, without hesitating, ordered me to be taken care of, and, as soon as I was capable of instruction, receiv'd me into his house, where I was educated in common with the rest of his pupils, and at last grew sufficiently qualified to be his assistant; but his necessities encreasing with the exercise of his virtues, notwithstanding my utmost assiduity, he was oblig'd to sell his academy, and I had at last the mortification of closing his eyes in the very prison, from which I was originally rescu'd by the greatness of his humanity.

Miss *Dor.* And was it just at this time that Sir John bought the seat in your neighbourhood?

Vil. It was, madam; and it was at this time also, that hearing Sir John had an occasion for an assistant in some literary employments, I procur'd the recommendation to him which has given me the honour of being known in this family. The only trace of what I ever was, is this picture; which was by some means in my possession when I was stolen, as the woman who stole me declar'd in the course of her imperfect narration; fearing to dispose of it, she kept it to the hour of her death, and then delivered it up as a possible means of finding out my family.

Sir *John.* Let me see this picture.

Will. No, let me see it for the love of heaven—O Sir John, Sir John, this was Lady Dormer's picture, she made a present of it to my first wife, and here on

Sir John. I remember it perfectly, I myself ordered the letters to be engrav'd.

Vil. I can scarce speak.

Will. While I have power to ask, tell me, sir, what is your age.

Vil. Twenty-two.

Will. Receive my thanks, receive my thanks, kind heaven!—O, my boy, my boy! Providence still orders all things for the best, and I am in reality your father.

Vil. O, sir! bless your son, and assure him he has a father.

Miss *Will.* [*Embracing him.*] My brother my deli verer too!—this is happiness, indeed.

Mrs. *Will.* Let me embrace you too. Your sister will tell you what a mother-in-law I am, and how much she is indebted to my lessons of propriety.—— Well! I begin myself to think every thing happens for the best, after the unexpected good fortune of this morning.

Dor. Not to Sir George, I am sure—for he loses a good estate by this unexpected discovery.

[*Here Miss* Montagu, *Miss* Dormer, *Sir* John, *and* Dormer *seem congratulating* Villars—*so does Sir* George.]

Sir George. What, you begin to crow again, do you?—But, let me tell you, I think every accident happens for the best, which enables me to do an act of justice, and advance the welfare of the deserving.

George—few people, I believe, would give up a fortune so easily.

Sir *George*. Why, my friend Jack there, if he lost
both an estate and a mistress in a couple of hours,
would hardly set so good a face upon matters, notwithstanding he is much my superior in serenity of
countenance.

Sir *John*. And perhaps, Sir George, even you, may
be a considerable gainer in the end, if we can but contrive to make an actual comedy of to-day's adventures,
by your marriage with a certain lady in this company.

[*Looking at Miss* Montagu.

Sir *George*. And possibly that might be yet effected,
through your interposition, Sir John, with Miss Montagu.

Miss *Mon*. What! is your denouement to be produc'd at my expence; upon my word, I should be
much oblig'd to Sir John's interposition for such a
purpose!

Sir *George*. I should at least, madam, and though
I come rather with an ill grace after so recent a rejection.

Dor. Your affection is not unadulterated now, Sir
George.

Sir *George*. Why, no---but I hav'n't yet told Miss
Montagu, that death itself is infinitely preferable to
the idea of offending her—[*Ludicrously.*]—though I
would readily risk my life to purchase her favourable
opinion.   [*Turning to her.*

Miss *Mon*. Well, do n't talk to me on this subject
now, Sir George. You have, to be sure, merited

much, and you are in every respect so greatly the opposite of my confident swain there, who thought I
must fly into his arms the moment he condescended to
receive me; that, however, I won't hear a syllable
from you now—if you can make a tolerable bow to
me, do, but do n't let me hear a syllable of nonsense,
I beg of you.

Sir *George.* This goodness———

Dor. Did n't the lady say she wou'd n't hear a syllable of nonsense.

Sir *George.* And so you begin to talk to her do you?

Mrs. *Will.* Mighty fine! is it nonsense to make a
grateful acknowledgement for the kindness of a lady.
What will the men come to at last?

Sir *George.* So he thinks, madam. Though, Vil-
lars, [*Aside to* Villars.] 't is a little hard, because Miss
Montagu chooses to consult her own happiness, that
I am to acknowledge the receipt of an obligation.

Sir *John.* My dear Sir George, Miss Montagu has
too much discernment not to see the value of so deserving a lover—address her, therefore, certain of
success, and look securely for happiness according to
Mr. Willoughby's principle, because you richly merit it.

Will. Right, Sir John—Providence looks down delighted on the actions of the worthy, and, however
it may command adversity to frown on the beginning
of their days, they will acknowledge with me, that
all it's dispensations are full of benignity in the end.

EPILOGUE.

Spoken by Mrs. BARRY.

MODISH *divines, at court and in the city,*
Are in their pulpit humourous, gay, and witty———
They've now chang'd hands, the stage and pulpit teaching,
Sermons are plays, **and** *plays are merely preaching*———
A **Word** *to* the **Wise,** *a pretty pert adviser !*———
As if 't were possible to make you wiser :
Yet as each *here may think the poet labours*
Not to *teach him, but to instruct his neighbours ;*
As the *bright* **tenants** *of that splendid* **row**
Sneer on the pit, **for** *beings much below ;*
And these in turn, as things **in** *order move,*
Toss up the sneer to those who mount above :
The gods **look** *down and let their pity fall*
On *front, side, green, stage-boxes,* **pit,** *and all.*
Let me, before your carriages appear,
Breathe one short word, ye wise ones, in your ear.
You, stop your *chairs,* [to the side boxes] *you backs,* [to
the pit] *won't* **run** *away ;*
And ladies, [to the gallery] **put** *not on your pattins pray :*
And first, ye soft, **ye sweet** *romantic maids,*
Who die for purling **streams,** *and sylvan shades,*
And think for better **and for** *worse, to take*
The best of husbands in a darling rake :

Who brings a shatter'd fortune to the fair,
With mind and body wanting vast repair;
Shall I for once your tender thoughts reveal?
'Tis fine to hear him swear, to see him kneel;
His tongue with worn out extacies will run,
'Till he has triumph'd, 'till the wife's undone;
And then that tender strain, so love-creating,
Turn to, ' Death, madam, hold your cursed prating——
' You quite distract me—pr'ythee farther stand————
' I won't be teaz'd—Zounds, take away your hand—'
This is a sad change, ladies, but 'tis common,
Man will be man, and woman will be woman;
For Villars is a phœnix, where's his brother?
'Twill take a hundred years to find another.
Yet you, ye sires, whom time should render wise,
You act as if each moment it could rise;
Forgetting all what you yourselves have been,
You trust your girls with Dormers at fifteen;
Throw your poor lambkins in the tyger's way,
Then stare to find a rake—a beast of prey.
Learn prudence here—and, O! you precious blades,
Whether cockaded, or without cockades;
Whether haranguing for the public good,
You shake St. Stephen's—or the Robinhood——
Who ring our charms for ever in our ears,
Yet inly triumph in a virgin's tears;
Be now convinc'd—the libertine disclaim,
And live to honour, if not dead to shame.
What is the plaudit of a fool when mellow,

Will that repay you for the bosom stings ?
Damn'd honest fellows, *oft are worthless things——*
But I'll *stop here,* I *will not sermonize——*
A *foolish woman can't instruct the wise.*

Roberts pinx.   Lerey sc.

Mrs DAVENPORT as **MISS WINIFRED EVANS.**

Miss Win.—— *I'll no longer be accountable for measures*

THE

SCHOOL FOR RAKES.

A

COMEDY,

By Mrs. ELIZABETH GRIFFITHS.

ADAPTED FOR

THEATRICAL REPRESENTATION,

AS PERFORMED AT THE

THEATRE-ROYAL, DRURY-LANE.

REGULATED FROM THE PROMPT-BOOK,

By *Permission of the Manager.*

The Lines distinguished by inverted Commas, are omitted in the Representation.

LONDON:

Printed for, **and** *under the Direction of*

GEORGE CAWTHORN, British Library, STRAND,

MDCCXCV.

TO

DAVID GARRICK, ESQ.

SIR,

DEDICATIONS are generally meant to do honour
to the Patron, by revealing their private virtues, or
recording their public merits. But neither of these
subjects occasioned the present address; for while the
undivided applause of a nation, proclaims the latter,
my small plaudit must be lost, in the general voice;
and while the friendship and esteem, of so many of
he first personages of the age, are, at once, the
strongest testimony, and most pleasing reward of the
former, my simple concurrence must be deemed su-
perfluous.

To neither of these motives, then, is to be attri-
buted my publicly placing this play, under your patronage; but to a desire of acknowledging my gratitude, for the great trouble you have taken with it,
and of indulging a much higher vanity, than that of
being its author; by declaring to the world, that you
are my friend, and that I am, sir,

Your much obliged,

And most humble servant,

THE AUTHOR.

January, 1769.

ADVERTISEMENT.

THE hint of this Comedy was taken from a much admired performance of Monsieur Beaumarchais, stiled Eugenie, which Mr. Garrick was so kind to put into my hands some time ago. I was immediately struck with the elegant simplicity of language, and sentiment, which characterizes that work, and which, indeed, should do the same, in all dramatic writings, where neither the persons, or situations of the **drama** are elevated above the common degrees of life.

I immediately adopted the plan, and set about adapting it to the English Stage. But, as I proceeded in this work, I found I had great difficulties to encounter; for, though Mons. Beaumarchais had laid the scene of his play in England, he had, unluckily, adopted Spanish manners. This circumstance appeared an unsurmountable obstacle to me, and I should have immediately relinquished all hopes from my project, if Mr. Garrick had not, in the most friendly manner, lent me his assistance, to overcome this otherwise insuperable difficulty.

How far I have succeeded, in rendering this piece worthy of the English Stage, must be left to the candor of the public. I shall only add, that the characters of Frampton, Willis, Loyd, I may add Mrs. Winifred, also, are of English growth. The character of Lord Eustace, too, has received some additions; and, I hope that his compunction, for the crime he had committed, will render him more worthy the favour of a British audience, whose generous natures cannot

brook the representation of any vice upon the stage, except
in order to have it punished, or reclaimed. As the situation
of Harriot would not admit of any change, I have not at-
tempted to deviate from the gentle, and interesting Eugenie,
of Monsieur Beaumarchais.

I had written thus far, before I could have been informed
of the very kind and favourable reception with which the
public have honoured this piece; and I think myself extremely happy at having this opportunity of assuring them,
that I shall ever retain the most grateful sense of their indulgence to me.

I am particularly bound to Mrs. Clive, on this occasion,
who undertook the study of a new part, at a time when she
had determined to quit the stage, and whose kindness to the
Author, and attention to the public, made her hazard her
health, by performing it-- I need not say how well---when
her physicians would have confined her to her chamber.

I acknowledge myself also much obliged to the rest of the
performers in my play, for having acquitted themselves so
much to the advantage of the piece, and the approbation of
the public; to whom I have the honour to be,

A much obliged, and

Most obedient Servant,

THE AUTHOR.

PROLOGUE.

Written by a FRIEND, Spoken by Mr. KING.

THE scribbling gentry, ever frank and free,
To sweep the stage with prologues, fix on Me.
A Female representative I come,
And with a Prologue, which I call a broom,
To brush the critic cobwebs from the room.
Critics, like spiders, into corners creep,
And at new plays their bloody revels keep;
With some small venom, close in ambush lie,
Ready to seize the poor dramatic Fly:
The weak and heedless soon become their prey;
But the strong Blue Bottle will force its way,
Clean well its wings, and hum another day.
Unknown to Nature's laws, we 've here one evil,
For Flies, turn'd Spiders, play the very devil!
But why choose me to fill a woman's place?
Have I about me any female grace,
Sweetness of smile, or lily-dimpled face?
Whate'er I have, I 'll try my winning ways,
Low'ring my voice, and rising from my stays;
Warm with anxiety, this hat my fan,
I'm now an Auth'ress, and no longer man.

The ladies, I am sure, my brat will spare,
For I'm not young, nor am I over fair;
Assemblies, balls, deck'd out, I ne'er appear at,
My husband is the only man I leer at.
Ye Beaux, *whose minds are flimsy as your shapes,*
Who scorn all writings as the fox the grapes;
Let not a woman's faults ill humours breed,
I own my failings——I both write and read.   [Cries.
Sit still two hours, for one not fair nor young !—
You would not wait for Venus, *half so long.*
Could I please *You, *and* †You, *more patient folks,*
With some small nature, and some harmless jokes;
These ‡ *splendid rows would not their mite deny,*
They will, as well as you, both laugh and sigh,
Sigh when you laugh, and laugh whene'er you cry.
Ye Soldiers, Sailors, *valiant as you're free,*
O lend your aid, protect my babe and me!
Cowards spare none; but you, the truly brave,
Women, and children, will for ever save!
Here ends my task—and for our last expedient——
The auth'ress makes you this [Curtseys.] *and this*
        [Bows.] *Your most obedient.*

* Pit. † Gallery. ‡ Boxes.

Dramatis Personae.

DRURY-LANE.

Men.

Lord EUSTACE, - -	Mr. Cautherley.
Sir WILLIAM EVANS, -	Mr. Holland.
Colonel EVANS, - -	Mr. Palmer.
Mr. FRAMPTON, -	Mr. Reddish.
Captain LOYD, - -.	Mr. King.
WILLIS, Valet to Lord Eustace,	Mr. Dodd.
ROBERT, - -	Mr. Baddeley.

Women.

Mrs. WINIFRED, - -	Mrs. Clive.
HARRIOT, - -	Mrs. Baddeley.
BETTY, Servant to Harriot,	Mrs. Smith.

THE

SCHOOL FOR RAKES.

ACT I. SCENE I.

An Apartment in Lord Eustace's *House. Enter* Mr.
FRAMPTON *and* WILLIS.

Mr. *Frampton.*

WELL, Willis, they are come!

Wil. Yes, sir, but I am quite of opinion, they will
soon begone again, at least out of this house; for as I
assisted in carrying in their trunks, and band-boxes,
merely to contemplate their countenances, I could
perceive the strongest marks of dissatisfaction in Sir
William's face; and when the servants retired from
the parlour, I overheard him, and his sister Winifred,
in high disputation—Both their Welch bloods were
up, and a fine splutter there was between them; but,
though you might have heard them into Hyde-Park,
they spoke so quick, that I could only pick up an odd
word here and there, as if Sir William did not like
this part of the town.

Fram. I wish they had staid in the country, with all my heart.

Wil. I believe there are more people of that mind, than you, sir. I fancy my lord would give a good round sum, **that they had** remained fixed to the free-hold **at** Langwillan.——**Though,** to be sure, Miss Harriot is, by many degrees, the handsomest girl that ever his lordship was fond of.

Fram. You must not, Willis, talk of her, in that stile—She **is a** young woman both of charaƈter, and family.

Wil. So much **the better** for her, sir, if she has a good family of her own, for I am pretty sure she never will belong to ours.

Fram. I must again desire you, Mr. Willis, not to speak so lightly of this affair——the real friends of your lord will not be much inclined to mirth or ridicule, upon this occasion, I can tell you.

Wil. As we were both placed here, by my lord, to manage this matter for him, I thought there could be no great harm to argue a little upon it, Mr. Frampton.

Fram. I am not, at present, in a humour for conversation.

Wil. O, sir, another time will do as well.

Fram. I would have you go immediately, and acquaint Lord Eustace with their arrival—Let him also know, that I shall wait upon the ladies, and make his apology, for not being here to receive them.

Wil. You have been very obliging to his lordship, upon many such occasions, **Mr.** Frampton; but I

fancy he never stood more in need of your assistance
and mine too, than he does at present.

Fram. Though in the same cause, I believe our
services will tend to different purposes——I shall not
flatter his vices.

Wil. Lord, Mr. Frampton, you are grown so pru-
dish of late!

Fram. You are grown too familiar, Mr. Willis——
You'll oblige me, and obey your lord's commands,
at the same time, by going directly with the message
I desired you.

Wil. I did not mean to offend you, sir, by observing how useful your friendship has been to my lord.——
Has your honour any farther commands?

Fram. None, but those I gave you.

Wil. Here's more to do with these shabby, ruined,
hangers-on of my lord's, than all the family beside.
I think myself as good a man as he, and if he had not
a little too much spirit for me, I would tell him as
much. [*Aside.*]   [*Exit grumbling.*

Fram. To what a state have I reduced myself, when
even such a wretch as that dares to upbraid me! What
now remains of all the scenes of mirth and revelry,
which I have been partaker of beneath this roof! A
ruined fortune, a disturbed mind, and a broken constitution, are the only mementos that are now left me
——Yet I think I have fortitude sufficient to bear all
these—but to be obliged to minister to another man's
vices, for a wretched subsistence, is to degrade human nature below the brutes.——Thank heaven,

however, I have escaped being concerned in this iniquitous affair; and though my friendship for Lord Eustace, will not suffer me to desert him, in his present difficulties, I am determined to proceed no farther, than is consistent with my honour, and my peace.——I have consented to see the lady, and excuse his absence.——I must wait for Sir William's going out, and then hasten to fulfil my promise. [*Exit.*

SCENE II.

Changes to another Apartment. Discovers Sir WILLIAM, *Mrs.* WINIFRED, *and* HARRIOT, *in travelling dresses—trunks, cloak-bags, &c.* BETTY *attending.*

Sir W. I tell you, again and again, sister Winifred, I am not satisfied.

Mrs. Win. As to that matter, brother, you know you never are satisfied, with what any person does, but yourself. I shall, therefore, make myself perfectly easy, on that head.

Sir W. That's more than I shall be, while I am in this house, I can tell you——I have very solid objections to staying here—A young, idle, rakish lord—

Mrs. Win. What a vulgar objection! I declare, Sir William, if I were not acquainted with your ancestry, I should suspect you to be descended **from** mechanics. But I hope the family of Ap Evans, is known to be

Sir *W*. Adam at least, sister——But let me now inform you, that Lord Eustace is placed in a much higher rank, than any of your boasted ancestors have ever been; and that I hate obligations to persons above me; for the only satisfaction I ever felt in receiving favours, arose from the prospect of repaying them.

Mrs. *Win*. Pride, absolute pride, brother!

Sir *W*. It is an honest one, at least, you must allow, that inclines persons to discharge their debts of honour, as well as of law.

Mrs. *Win*. Pray, Sir William, give me leave to ask you—where is the mighty matter of interchanging civilities, between persons of a certain rank? Lord Eustace spent some months at your house in the country——

Sir *W*. Not by my invitation, sister, but yours——You know I was at my estate in Devonshire, the greatest part of the time he spent at Langwillan——I have, therefore, neither right nor inclination, to accept of his house——Besides it is extremely inconvenient to me, as I have so much business to transact in Lincoln's Inn.

Mrs. *Win*. You should have written to your broker, then, to provide you apartments in some of the stoves on t'other side of Temple Bar, Sir William; but as to my niece and me, we don't choose to be suffocated, I must inform you.

Sir *W*. Why, this place, as you say, is airy enough. When I was last in London, about twelve years ago, there **was** not a house within a mile of it---but all the fools of the nation have now crouded up to the capital, and made the head too large for the body; and this very place, where I used to send my horses to graze, begins now to look something like a street.

Mrs. Win. Like a street, Sir William!

Sir W. Let us have done with wrangling, sister; I **give it** up—This air may be better **for** my girl——I shall stay here, therefore, for the short **time** I remain in town, though I don't like it——You **are** content, I hope—But what says **my** Harriot? Why so grave? I expected to have seen you as blithe, as one of the kids upon our mountains, at your arrival in London.

Har. I find myself a little fatigued, sir.

Sir W. You were all life and spirit, during our journey---the bad air of this **town** can't have affected you already, child. But tell me how you like this house?

Har. I think **it** very retired, sir.

Mrs. Win. Why, really, Miss Harriot, I don't believe my lord intended following business, or opening shop, when he took it; but surely, **for** persons of distinction, it is the very spot **one would** desire. I am astonished at your want of taste, child---Sir William, I know, loves noise.----I think there is nothing else to wish for here.

Har. Except the owner of the mansion.   [*Aside.*

Betty. Pray, madam, which is to be my young lady's apartment?

Mrs. Win. That upon the right hand, child.——

you had better go with her, Harriot, and adjust your dress.----O, Betty, bid them look into the coach for my snuff-box; they 'll find it on the seat or in the pockets. [*Exit* Harriot *and* Betty. Do n't you think you shall be full late for your lawyers, Sir William?

Sir *W*. Yes, as I have so far to go to them---Who is there?

Enter BETTY, *with the snuff-box.*

Betty. Here 's the box, madam.

[*Gives it to her, and exit.*

Enter ROBERT.

Sir *W*. Send David for a hackney-coach---Take this key, and bring me a parcel of papers, which you will find tied up in my strong box, Robert.

Rob. Yes, sir. [*Exit* Robert.

Mrs. *Win.* I hope, Sir William, you have your **ad**-dress written upon your cards, and that you have ordered your letters to be directed to Lord Eustace's house. As his lordship honours me with his friend-ship, I think it necessary that our acquaintance should be informed of his great politeness.

Sir *W*. His lordship honours me with his friendship! how well the traffic is kept up, in that phrase, between vanity and vanity! [*Aside.*]---I had ordered my letters to Serle's Coffee-house; but since it is determined that I must stay here, I shall direct them to be sent to me.

Mrs. Win. I must beg, Sir William, that you will ord:r all the newspapers and magazines to be sent here also. My mental faculties are quite at a stand--- I have not had the least political information, these four days.

Enter ROBERT.

Rob. Here are the papers, sir.

Mrs. Win. Are they of this day, Robert ?

Sir W. They are of much older date, sister, and will not, I fancy afford you much entertainment.—— Get my hat and cane : do you know, Robert, where Captain Lloyd lodges?

Rob. In Craven-street, sir ; they told me at Tre-vallin.

Sir W. Direct the coachman there. [*Exit* Robert.

Mrs. Win. For Heaven's sake, Sir William, what do you loiter for ? It will be monstrous late before you can return—you won't be back by dinner.

Sir W. You seem so very impatient for my setting out, sister, that I cannot imagine you should be very anxious for my coming back again. I shall go first to Captain Lloyd's.

Mrs. Win. You are, doubtless, at liberty to go where you please, Sir William, but I hope you will not think of incumbering us with his visits here.

Sir W. You amaze me! Not receive the uncle of the man who is to marry my daughter ?

Mrs. Win. That may be sooner said than done, I fancy, Sir William.

Sir *W*. You are mistaken, I never yet have falsified my promise.

Mrs. *Win*. A pretty alliance, truly, for my niece and your daughter. But let me tell you, sir, if Harriot had not a shilling, her family and her beauty would intitle her to a much better match, than your colonel ; who has nothing but an old tottering castle, a scarlet coat, and a sword, to settle by way of jointure.

Sir *W*. Your absurdity distracts me. What has your family and beauty done for you ? And I dare say you once rated them as high as you do Harriot's.

Mrs. *Win*. You 'll pardon me, brother, I understand genealogy better than so.---Though there is not a very great difference between my niece's years and mine, she has one generation more in her table than I ; which, let me tell you, is of no small consequence to those who know how to set a proper value upon family.

Sir *W*. Family! Nonsense ! Let those who have no other merit to support them, build on that; but, know, that I despise it ; and to make an end of this ridiculous altercation for ever, I shall inform you, that eight years ago, when Harriot was but a child, and the colonel was sent young abroad, to serve his country, I liked him so well, that I promised his father, if the young fellow returned with his life and honour, my daughter should be his.

Mrs. *Win*. I have ever disapproved of that method of affiancing young persons.----Have you no idea that it is possible the colonel may dislike your daughter?

Sir *W.* I am not very apprehensive on that account.

Mrs. *Win.* Have **you** no fears of her refusing him?

Sir *W.* None.----Bred up in retirement, and inno-cence, she can have formed no attachment; and her obedience to a fond father, will certainly incline her to dispose of both her hand and heart where his prudence shall direct.

Enter ROBERT.

Rob. Sir, the coach is ready.

Sir *Win.* [*Looking at his watch.*] 'T is later than I thought it was – Why, I sha'n't be back to dinner——I shall go no where but to the captain's; if I don't meet with him, I shall return, directly. Put up these papers, Robert   [*Exit Sir* William.

Mrs. *Win.* Desire Miss Evans to come to me, and pray, good Robert, send out for the last Gazette, directly. There may be a thousand treaties on foot, that **I am** ignorant of. [*Exit* Robert.] What an ab-surd man, is my brother! His ideas are dreadfully confined. His daughter's hand and heart will follow her obedience! thank heaven they are not now to be disposed of.

Enter HARRIOT.

What, not begun to dress, niece?

Har. My spirits are too much agitated, madam, to think **of** dress.

Mrs. *Win.* For Heaven's sake, child, don't talk in this doleful strain to me—I can easily conceive that your father's presence may distress you, as he is so totally ignorant of your good fortune, but with me it appears ridiculous.

Har. I am, indeed, madam, infinitely distressed, by my father's ignorance of my situation.

Mrs. Win. What a fuss is here about your father? You know he would never have given his consent to your marrying Lord Eustace, if he had been asked, he hates men of quality; and as my lord is not yet in possession of his fortune, I doubt if he would even have thought it a good match.

Har. I wish he were acquainted with it, be it good or bad.

Mrs. Win. I tell you, child, I lost two excellent matches myself, by waiting for advice; and by that means giving time to the parties to consider of it, so it came to nothing; but I now tell you, that by my prudence, your good fortune does not admit of a doubt.

Har. Would to heaven it did not!

Mrs. Win. You are the very counterpart, of your father; never content with any thing—Are you not intitled to *supporters* and *coronets* upon your coach? And when the Evans's arms are quartered with my lord's, and well emblazoned, there won't be so handsome an equipage in London.

Har. Yet the possessor may be wretched, madam!

Mrs. Win. Wretched, and a countess!—I think that scarce possible. But what is it you would have, child? Have I not, with the greatest address imaginable, managed matters, with my headstrong brother, and triumphed over his obstinacy? Are you not at this instant lodged in your husband's house?

Har. What is his house, while he is absent from it? I hoped to have met him here—My letters must have informed him——

Mrs. Win. Perhaps his and your father, my Lord Delville, Harriot, may have claimed **his** lordship's attendance. It is only people of no consequence, who are masters of themselves; and therefore pretend to dignify their insignificance, with the title of independence. But persons of quality, my dear, never presume to rebel against the laws of subordination.—But this is a political secret which you are yet ignorant of, child.

Har. He appeared to be perfect master of his own time, when we were first acquainted; nor did his engagements seem to interfere with his inclinations, till after you had commanded me to receive his hand.

Mrs. Win. 'Till after I commanded you!—Really, Miss Evans, any person who was to hear you talk in this manner, might suppose that I had compelled you, to marry Lord Eustace; but, perhaps miss, you had rather have been sacrificed to your father's ridiculous attachment to Colonel Llody, and been buried alive in the old castle of Trevallin.

Har. Notwithstanding all your attention to my happiness, madam, if my lord no longer loves me, I must be miserable.

Mrs. Win. Can he hinder your being a countess,

simpleton? But, pr'ythee, what can have put all these melancholy thoughts into your head? Did ever any man appear to be more in love than he?

Har. O, no! he was all tenderness; he wept our parting: I wept too, yet found a pleasing softness in that grief he seemed to share.——What a change!

Mrs. Win. Revolutions are common in all states, child; and if you understood politics, you would not be so much surprized at them.

Enter ROBERT.

Rob. Mr. Frampton, madam, desires to see my young lady.

Har. Mr. Frampton! I don't know such a person: do you know him, Robert?

Rob. I know nothing more of him, madam, than that he lives in this house, and has a fine man to attend him. There are a power of people coming and going, but I can't tell who they be.

Mrs. Win. He must certainly be a friend or relation of your lord's. I think we had better step into the parlour to receive him, lest your father's return should interrupt us. [*Aside to* Harriot.]—We will see the gentleman below, Robert, and wait on him directly.   [*Exeunt.*

SCENE III.

Changes to a Garden Parlour. Enter Mr. FRAMPTON.

Fram. I feel myself extremely shocked at this affair, both for Lord Eustace and the unhappy girl, it is an infamous business, and I am certain it must turn out ill.

Enter ROBERT.

Rob. The ladies will wait on you immediately, sir.

[*Exit* Robert.

Fram. Would the interview were over!——If she is but half so amiable, as Lord Eustace has described her, I fear I shall acquit myself but indifferently of his commission.——Beauty, that makes most men knaves, makes me honest; for I hold it the lowest baseness to be capable of admiring and betraying an innocent creature in the same moment.

Enter Mrs. WINIFRED *and* HARRIOT.

Fram. I come, madam, from Lord Eustace to your ladyship——

Mrs. *Win.* By accosting my niece in that manner, sir, I suppose you are one of his lordship's particular friends; but pray be more guarded, sir, and do not call my niece ladyship—That time is not yet come.

Fram. I stand corrected, madam.

Har. How does Lord Eustace, sir? I hope he is well.

Fram. Perfectly so, madam, though extremely concerned at having it not in his power, to receive your ladyship——

Mrs. *Win.* Again, sir !

Fram. ——The moment of your arrival ; but his attendance on his father, who is at present ill in Berkshire, prevented him that happiness.

Mrs. *Win.* Aye, I knew it——Did not I tell you so, Miss Harriot ?

Har. Pray, sir, when may we expect to see Lord Eustace ? I hope his father's illness is not dangerous ?

Fram. No, madam, I hope not ; though old **men's** lives are certainly precarious. I am sure your lord will leave him the first moment it is possible, as I well know he burns with impatience to throw himself at your feet.

Mrs. *Win.* I hope your mind is easy now, child ?—— She may be a countess sooner than I thought for ; and if my lord can get into the ministry, I may be of some consequence to my friends.   [*Aside.*

Har. I am much obliged **to you**, sir, for the trouble you have taken.——I by no means wish that Lord Eustace should neglect his duty to Lord Delville, or distress himself in any other way on my account ; though I sincerely desire the happiness of seeing him.

Fram. His inclinations, madam, I am satisfied, more than keep pace with yours ; and you may, with great probability, expect to see his lordship either to-day or to-morrow morning.

Mrs *Win.* You alarm me vastly, sir ; I would not have **his** lordship catch us in this dishabille for any

consideration. I beg, child, you will go to your toilet
——Bless me, what figures we are!

Har. I shall attend you, madam. You have made
me very happy, sir—but do you think that he will come
to night?

Fram. I fear it is not in his power, madam.

Har. Come when he will, I shall rejoice to see him.

Mrs. *Win.* Pray, niece, come away, now. Sir, your
humble servant——You do n't know but his lordship
may be here in a few minutes. [*To* Harriot.

[*Exit Mrs.* Win. *and* Har.

Fram. I never lied with a worse grace—By heaven
that girl is an angel, and Lord Eustace, of course, a
devil! What a delicate sensibility in her countenance!
what softness in her voice! The man who could first
injure and then forsake such a woman, deserves to be
marked as the most infamous, because he must be the
most cruel of his sex——I have some consolation in
thinking that Lord Eustace, though ten years younger,
is ten times a greater——

Enter Lord EUSTACE *behind.*

Lord *Eust.* —What, what, Frampton!——I will lay
ten thousand pounds that is impossible, though you
did not finish the sentence——Do you think I should
lose, Frampton?

Fram. I certainly do, my lord, though you were to
determine the bet yourself. But this is no time for
fooling. I am astonished at your imprudence——I
thought you had determined not to come this night;
what can have changed your purpose?

Lord *Eust.* Have you seen Harriot, Frampton, and can you ask that question? My mind, restless, distracted, and impatient, has impelled me hither—— But tell me have you seen her?

Fram. I have seen Lady Eustace.

Lord *Eust.* You startle me! Do n't talk so loud--- Are you sure that no one can overhear us?

Fram. Not a creature---Sir William is gone abroad; and the ladies are retired to dress.

Lord *Eust.* What said Harriot to my absence?

Fram. The tears which seemed to have dimmed her lovely eyes, reproached you silently; but not an angry word escaped her lips.

Lord *Eust.* Do not add to my distress, Frampton! By Heaven, my heart bleeds for the unhappy Harriot! Had I, like you, been born a private man, and not at once bound down, by the vile trammels of family and dependence, the world should not have bribed me, to forsake her.

Fram. The sense, you now seem to have of your own situation should have operated sooner, my lord, and prevented your involving an innocent young woman, in certain ruin.

Lord *Eust.* No, Frampton, no! that was beyond my power; I loved her to distraction——nay, I do love her still——But let us talk no more upon this subject; it softens me to weakness; and as I am dependent on my father, I must obey him——I hope she has not heard of my intended marriage.

C

Fram. No, no! the devil is too great a gainer by your schemes to blast them.

Lord *Eust.* Don't you think it too late in the day for you to turn methodist, Ned?

Fram. It is never too late, my lord, for a man **to** condemn and forsake his follies; and young as you are, I heartily wish this was **the** time appointed for your doing so likewise.

Lord *Eust.* These sentiments have at least the grace of novelty to recommend them from you, Mr. Frampton.

Fram. My sentiments, my lord, are of little consequence to you: but the time draws near, when you must justly suffer in the opinion of one who ought to be dear to you. Miss Evans cannot be much longer deceived—and when I reflect upon the vile artifices that were used to draw her into a feigned marriage, by Heaven I cannot help detesting you, and every one of the infernal agents **who** were any way concerned in it.

Lord *Eust.* O, Frampton! my heart tells me that I deserve your detestation—Why, why were you not with me, to save me from the sad effects of my wild youthful passions! The wretches who were near me but inflamed them.

Fram. The attachments of mean persons, are always founded in self-interest, my lord, nor was there ever yet a solid friendship form'd in vice.

Lord *Eust.* Don't upbraid me with my miseries, Frampton, but think what a situation is **mine**. Though

I feel the errors of my conduct, and would repair them, I am so much involved in my own toils, that I find it impossible to break them. —What would I not give even to postpone this fatal marriage!

Fram. Postpone it! aye, for ever!

Lord *Eust.* Could I do that, I might yet be happy, Frampton; but matters are gone too far——every thing was settled, between my father, and Lady Anne's guardians, before I came to town, and I am certain he never will be brought to relinquish the great advantage of her immense fortune.

Fram. And can you, my lord, be brought to consider those advantages, as an equivalent, for your peace, and honour?

Lord *Eust.* What would you have me do?

Fram. Avow your situation to Lord Delville.

Lord *Eust.* Were it a common folly I had committed, Frampton, I might hope for his forgiveness; but the infamy which must deservedly attend my conduct, in this affair, would probably make him cast me from his heart, and fortune, for ever.

Fram. You are certainly in very difficult circumstances, my lord, nor can I discover **any** means of extricating you from them.

Lord *Eust.* The only miserable hope I have now left, is founded on the gentleness of Harriot's nature, which may enable me to prevail on her to return into the country, before she hears of my intended marriage.

Fram. It is rather shameful, my lord, to erect a sanctuary for our vices, upon the virtues of others.

Lord *Eust.* I acknowledge it, Frampton; but were Harriot removed from the probability of hearing of this hateful marriage, my mind would be more at ease, and I might then possibly think of some expedient to break it off.

Framp. There is some merit in that thought, my lord; and now let me know how I can serve you.

Lord *Eust.* You shall hear——That villain Langwood, my father's steward, who persuaded me into this sham marriage, and personated the clergyman, on that occasion, is now dying, and writes me word, that he is distracted with the horrors of his conscience, and is determined to ask the young lady's forgiveness ——a letter from him to the family would discover all.

Fram. That would, indeed, be fatal; but how can I prevent it?

Lord *Eust.* You must remain in this house, and take care that my servants prevent their receiving any letters, without bringing them first to you. I will order Willis to intercept them.

Fram. He is fit for the office; but this is a very odious affair, my lord. However, I have promised to assist you, and if I can prevail upon myself, I will go so far as to prevent Langwood's hastening the catastrophe, which I much fear will be a sad one.

Lord *Eust.* You know not how you torture me! But let me now indulge my fond impatience, and see my lovely Harriot.

Fram. You must not think of it; I would advise you to retire directly.

Lord *Eust.* It is impossible I should obey you! I long, yet dread, to see her, Frampton.

Fram. It will require a good deal of courage, my lord, to support the interview; for I really think, that an injured, innocent woman, is a very formidable object. But though you may be brave enough for the encounter, I must prevent it for the present, as I have but just now apologized for your absence, by telling her you were in Berkshire, with your father; and the inconsistency of your immediate appearance might justly alarm her. I would, therefore, have you withdraw, immediately, lest any of the family should see you.

Lord *Eust.* You have a right to direct me; and, at your desire, I'll defer my visit for a little time; but I can have no rest till I behold her.

Fram. I don't fancy your meeting will contribute much to the quiet of your mind.

Lord *Eust.* I do not hope it should——But never yet was that mind so distressed, since it had first the power of thinking.

Fram. Peace and guilt seldom cohabit, my lord.

Lord *Eust.* True, Frampton, true——and if young men, like myself, would but calculate the pains and difficulties, which are the natural consequences of vice, and how much they over-balance its transitory joys, they would be shocked at a traffic, where certain loss must be the reward of their industry.

Fram. The being sensible of our errors, is the first step to amendment; for no man ever sets seriously

about getting out of debt, till he is thoroughly ap-
prized of the vast sum he owes.——But come, my
lord, let us retire immediately ; I hear some of the family in motion—this way quickly.   [*Exeunt.*

ACT II. SCENE I.

A Drawing-Room in Lord Eustace's *House.* Enter *Lord*
EUSTACE.

Lord Eustace.

I feel the force of Frampton's sentiments, and tremble
at the thoughts of seeing Harriot ; and yet, I cannot
deny myself this last indulgence. If my father were
acquainted with my distress, perhaps——O no ! I must
not think of that.—Cursed ambition ! detested pride
of family ! that makes us sink the man to aggrandize
the peer.

Enter ROBERT,

Rob. The ladies will wait on your lordship, immediately.   [*Exit.*

Lord *Eust.* I am glad the aunt comes with her——
Her folly and impertinence will help to interrupt what
I most dread, my Harriot's tenderness, and sensibility.
She comes—I feel her superiority, and shrink to nothing.

Enter HARRIOT ; *she runs a few steps towards Lord*
Eustace, *then stops suddenly, in confusion.*

Lord *Eust.* My Harriot's first motion was, surely

natural, why then does she restrain the feelings of her heart? Have I been so unfortunate, as to deserve this coldness?

· *Enter* Mrs. WINIFRED.

Lord *Eust.* I hope, madam, [*To Mrs.* Winifred] you will be so good as to excuse my absence, at the time of your arrival, and that you have found every thing in this house agreeable and convenient to you.

Mrs. *Win.* Ceremony, my lord, is quite unnecessary, among persons of rank and breeding; especially where they have the honour of being so close allied to your lordship. And I have great reason to believe, that every thing in your house, is, like your lordship, perfectly complete.

Lord *Eust.* You are very polite, madam; and if my Harriot knew what I had suffered————

Har. I might then have been more concerned than I am at present, and that, my lord, is needless.

Mrs. *Win.* I hop'd we should have had an end of your sighs, and your tears, when you saw Lord Eustace——I declare, child, you are a perfect Niobe!—— One would imagine that you were the most unhappy creature in the world.

Lord *Eust.* You alarm me extremely, madam—— Speak, my love, and tell me what affects you?

Har. Your lordship may remember with what great reluctance I consented to a private marriage.

Lord *Eust.* My Harriot's scruples cost me too many sighs ever to forget them.

Har. Yet your too powerful persuasions conquer'd them; and while you remained in Wales, your presence silenc'd my reflections, nor suffered even a painful thought to intrude into that heart which was ingrossed by you. What a delirium!

Lord *Eust.* May it last for ever!

Har. It fled with you, my lord——Left to myself, the offence I had committed against an absent father —the clandestine air which accompanied the awful ceremony——

Mrs. Win. Pray, niece, could that be avoided?

Har. The painful necessity of your absence——

Lord *Eust.* Let me, I entreat you, flatter myself, that my presence now may be sufficient to remove the anxiety my absence caused——What would I not do to make my Harriot happy! Command me; task my power.

Har. I would intreat, but not command, my lord.

Lord *Eust.* Then name the soft request, and think it granted.

Har. Since you permit, I wish you to employ that dear persuasive art, which you possess so amply, to reconcile my father to our marriage.

Lord *Eust.* You, madam, sure will join us, and assist in bringing about an event, which cannot longer be deferred, without injury to your honour and my peace.

Mrs. Win. I am his lordship's guarantee, that this treaty shall be kept secret, Harriot; and I shall preserve my promise as inviolably as if the peace of Eu-

rope were concerned. And to avoid the least in-
fringement of the articles, I will prevent Sir William's
surprizing you, in this state of altercation, and give
you notice of the enemy's approach.   [*Exit.*

Har. If ever I was dear to you, my lord, this is
the time to prove it: remove the veil of mystery,
which I blush to wear, and give that love, which is
my highest boast, a sanction to the world.

Lord *Eust.* Never was man so embarrassed. [*Aside.*]
I will obey my Harriot, though in opposition to my
own judgement, which had determined me not to reveal the important secret to Sir William till our return
into the country; lest the warmth of his resentment,
for what he will stile an act of disobedience, might
tempt him to discover our marriage to my father.

Har. Must it be ever kept a secret then? And must
we always live thus separated?

Lord *Eust.* By no means—I can make a pretence to
my father, of joining my regiment, and then can I
retrace those paths that brought me first to Langwillan; and the moment I arrive there, Sir William
shall be made acquainted with my happiness.

Har. Do you mean to come there soon, my lord?

Lord *Eust.* I should have been there in a few days
if you had not come to town.

Har. Why did you not tell me so? the least hint
of your design would have prevented my coming to
London.

Lord *Eust.* Does my Harriot think I would delay

my own happiness, by deferring an interview I so ardently desired, even for an hour?

Har. You can persuade me to any thing. I acquiesce in your determination.——There is but one thing more disturbs my mind, but that's a trifle.

Lord *Eust.* It cannot **be so,** in my estimation, if it affects you.—Let me know it.

Har. Where there is much sensibility, the heart is easily alarmed——It has appeared extraordinary to me, that your lordship, in any of **your letters to me,** has never honoured me with the title of your wife.

Lord *Eust.* And can my Harriot blame me for such caution, meant to secure her happiness? If my fortunes only were at stake, I should now boast what I so much endeavour to conceal, nor fear the consequence of Lord Delville's resentment. The miscarriage, **or interception** of a letter, signed your husband, would precipitate the discovery of our marriage, and ruin me with my father.

Har. I would not have you suffer for my sake.

Lord *Eust.* It is only through you that I can suffer. Had my fortune been independent, I should, at once, have asked you of Sir William. Nay, situated as I am, I can forego all the advantages of wealth without regret, and, blest with you, only lament its loss for your dear sake. You weep, my Harriot! Let me kiss off those tears.

Har. No, let them flow, my lord—joy has its tears as well as grief, and these are tears of joy.

[Embracing him.

Lord *Eust.* My lovely softness!—How severely she distresses me!   [*Aside.*

Har. I will not trust this simple heart again, and blush to think it was so easily alarmed.

Enter Mrs. WINIFRED, *in a hurry.*

Mrs. *Win.* Softly, softly! here comes my brother— have done with your love-prate——What, always a pouting, Harriot?

Enter Sir WILLIAM, *speaking to* ROBERT.

Sir *W.* Give the coachman half-a-crown, and, do you hear, Robert, let there be springs put to our coach, every one has them now—Luxury! luxury!— Every alderman and apothecary skims over this new-fangled pavement, without so much as a jolt. One of these city sparks would be shook to death, if he were to ride my Bay Bolton a fox chase.

Mrs. *Win.* My brother is always his own herald, and proclaims himself by the noise he makes—How detestably vulgar! how unlike a man of fashion!—— Here is Lord Eustace come to wait upon you, Sir William.

Sir *W.* I am glad to see your lordship, you have been a good while absent from quarters—but you young men of quality can have leave of absence when you please, I suppose; and all you have to do, is to appear handsomely on a field day, or at a review. It was not so in my time——But discipline of every kind is relaxed now-a-days.

Lord *Eust*. I have been a truant, Sir William; but I mean to make up for lost time, and return immediately to your regiment, and then look to your partridges.

Sir *W*. You shall be welcome to my manor, my lord. How does my Harriot? I think you look pale. Don't you think her altered, my lord?

Lord *Eust*. Rather improv'd, sir.

Sir *W*. She used to be remarkably lively: but as girls grow up, they affect gravity, in **order to** appear women before their time. Her brother and she are all I have left, and when Harriot is married——

Mrs. *Win*. Lord, Sir William, are you entering into family matters!

Sir *W*. Well, well, we won't talk of that now; but since we are upon the subject, I think I ought to congratulate your lordship.

Lord *Eust*. It must be then, Sir William, upon the happiness I at present enjoy in the company of these ladies.

Har. What does my father mean?   [*Aside*.

Sir *W*. No, no, my lord, I meant to give you joy of your approaching marriage.

Har. Surely my ears deceive me!   [*Aside*.

Lord *Eust*. You jest, Sir William!

Sir *W*. By no means, I assure you; I have it from undoubted authority.

Mrs. *Win*. Ridiculous!

Sir *W*. I tell you, sister, that it is in one of to-day's papers—I know what I read, sure.

Mrs. *Win.* Did it mention how things go in the Mediterranean? that is an article which concerns us more—we shall not have a port left us there soon.

Sir *W.* I speak only of domestic news, and mind no other. The paragraph I saw, ran thus—' We hear ' there is certainly a treaty of marriage on foot between ' Lord Eustace, and Lady Anne Mountfort, which will ' be concluded in a few days'——and then a great deal more, my lord, about both your accomplishments, which I have forgot.

Mrs. *Win.* I never knew any thing come of a *We hear*, yet. But I wish you had brought home the paper.

Lord *Eust.* Ha, ha, ha!——And is that your undoubted authority, Sir William? Why, at this season of the year, when occurrences are rare, the news writers couple half the nobility in England to fill up their papers——But, as there are no other papers filled up by the parties themselves, your marriages in print are not allowed good in law.

Mrs. *Win.* How can you be so easily disconcerted, child?   [*Aside to* Harriot.

Sir *W.* I think it highly insolent in them, my lord, to take these liberties without authority, as such reports may sometimes happen to be prejudicial to one party or the other.

Lord *Eust.* The freedom of the press, Sir William, though sometimes injurious to individuals, must never be restrained in this land of liberty. 'Tis the very *Magna Charta* of freedom.

Mrs. *Win.* So it is, my lord.

Lord Eust. However, there have been some slight grounds for the report you mention.

Sir W. So I should imagine.

Lord Eust. Lady Anne's large fortune was rather a desirable object to my father—he did, therefore, propose my paying my addresses to her; but, upon my declaring that love should be my first motive in an engagement of that nature, and that my heart had never given me the least hint of her ladyship, he had the goodness to sacrifice his project to my happiness.—— The affair had been whispered in our family, and even whispers have echoes, Sir William.

Sir W. Your lordship has taken more pains than was necessary, to explain this matter to us. For though you should not marry Lady Anne, it is to be supposed that you 'll soon marry a Lady Betty, or a Lady Mary, Somebody. Such an accomplished young nobleman will not be suffered to remain long single.

Mrs. Win. Lord, Sir William, how can you talk so oddly? There are many instances of persons who have lived single in spite of temptation and solicitation too, and that to your certain knowledge, I believe.

Sir W. You 'll pardon me, sister; I am really not acquainted with any of these coy, these sensitive plants.

Mrs. Win. You seem inclined to be witty, brother, and therefore I shall retire.

Lord Eust. I should oppose the severity of that resolution, madam, but that an engagement of business calls me away at this moment. May I hope for your permission to wait upon you frequently, while you stay

Mrs. *Win.* Your lordship's visits must always be considered by us, both as an honour and an obligation.

Lord *Eust.* My sweet Harriot!—Ladies, your servant.——I hope we shall often meet, Sir William.—[*Bows to* Harriot.] Nay, no ceremony.

Sir *W.* Your lordship must excuse me.

[*Exit Lord* Eust. *and Sir* W.

Mrs. *Win.* With what nice delicacy and honour has my nephew explained away this idle report! But I am amazed, how you could be affected with it, child.

Har. Chide me as you please, I own I deserve it, for doubting the most amiable of men. Yet when my father hinted the subject, I should have fainted, if the tenderness of my lord's looks, even more than his words, had not convinced me of his love and truth.— Our fears are proportioned to our treasure; you cannot, therefore, condemn my apprehensions without lessening his worth.

Mrs. *Win.* That I shall never do. Persons of a certain rank in life are always worthy. But come, child, I am in a monstrous dilemma at present.

Har. What's the matter?

Mrs. *Win.* I want your assistance, to calculate the distance from Persia to America; for I have great apprehensions that the Sophy may join the Czarina, sail down the Baltic together, and strip us of all our settlements.

Har. Dear madam, how can you trouble yourself with things so foreign, either to your knowledge or interests?

Mrs. Win. I beg your pardon. Why, niece, now that you are married to my satisfaction, I know nothing in the domestic way worth being concerned for; and one's affections you know, child, cannot lie **idle,** therefore, I beg you will go immediately, and search for 'Salmon's Geography,' which I believe you will find in my trunk, along with 'Colins's Peerage,' which are books I never travel without; and which no person can pretend to keep company, without being thoroughly conversant in.   [*Exeunt.*

Enter Sir WILLIAM *and* ROBERT.

Sir W. Pr'ythee, Robert, was that man in the hall my lord's valet de chambre? Of what use can he be to his master, here!

Rob. Of a great deal I fancy, sir. There are numbers of people come here after his lordship. A fine lady just now wanted to gain admittance; but Mr. Willis had dacity enough to make her disbelieve her own senses, and persuaded her that his master was down at Bristol, though she said her eyes saw him come into the house. O, these Londoners are cunning folks!

Sir W. You told me of another person that lives here, a gentleman, I think———

Rob. Yes, poor fellow, I believe he may be an honest man, because Willis don't seem much to like him. But it **is** hard to say which is good or bad amongst them.

Sir W. There is something very mysterious in all this [*Aside.*]———I desire, Robert, that you will have as little communication as possible with his lordship's servants, and that you will prevent the rest of my family from having any also.

Rob. Your honour need not fear.—They are not kindly to any of us.

Sir W. I am glad of it.—Civility, is the most dangerous mask of art.——My sister's folly in forcing us into this house, can only be equalled by my own, in submitting to come to it. But I will get out of it as fast as I can. [*Aside.*] I hope, Robert, to finish my business in a few days, and I shall not remain in London an hour after.

Rob. Your honour makes my heart glad.

Sir W. Do you know where Harriot is, Robert? I left her here just now.

Rob. I saw her go up stairs with Madam Winifred, as we came hither, sir. I think, with submission, our young lady likes London as little as either your worship or myself; she mopes mightily to be in the country again.

Sir W. She sha'n't mope long for that, Robert, nor when she is there neither, for I intend to settle her soon, both to her happiness and my own, by marrying her to Colonel Lloyd immediately. And when the wedding is over, and I am once more sat down safe at Langwillan, I shall think all my troubles are at an end. I'll go to Harriot, directly, and talk the matter over with her.

Rob. And I'll go and write the good news to my friends in Wales. [*Exeunt.*

SCENE II.

Mr. Frampton's *Apartment.* Enter Mr. FRAMPTON *and* WILLIS.

Fram. To barricade the doors, and deny admittance to their friends!

Wil. These were his lordship's orders, sir.—' Willis ' (says he, with an arch look, which I understand pretty ' tolerably) you must be my Cerberus, and not suffer ' the devil himself to get through the key-hole, for a ' few days. But as soon as I am married, and gone off ' to the country your care will be needless.' ' Yes,' says **I to his** lordship, ' I will then make my escape out of the ' gulph, leave the doors open for all the devils to enter, ' and pursue your lordship to the Elysian fields.'

Fram. You are very poetical, Mr. Willis. But I fancy his lordship is rather over cautious, and that you will have no great employment **for** your extraordinary talents ; for I don't think the family have any acquaintance in London.

Wil. More is the pity, for the girl is devilish handsome——It would be a good deed to bring her a little into life. I should like to have the introducing her.

Fram. Stop your licentious tongue! I have already told you, that this is no common affair. She is a young lady of unblemished character.

Wil. This is the old story, Mr. Frampton; I never knew a woman in my **life** who had not an unblemished character, till she **lost** it. This fellow is turned puri-

tan; he 'll preach presently—But I hope his canting
will not be able to corrupt my lord.—This would be
no place for me then. I fancy he likes the girl himself.

[Aside.

Fram. Believe me, Willis, Lord Eustace will find
it a very difficult matter to get clear of this unhappy
adventure. Sir William is a man of sense and spirit,
and the young lady has, besides, a brother in the army,
who is esteemed a brave young man.

Wil. As to Don Pedro, the father, I think my lord
had better get Commodore Lloyd, to take a short walk
with him upon the quarter-deck; and as to the young
Spaniard, his Lordship can't well refuse to take a bout
of tilting with him, if he should insist upon it. But I
have been pretty well used to things of this sort, as
you know, Mr. Frampton; and I never yet knew a
wounded reputation cured by a sword or a pistol——
Perhaps they may think as I do, and so let the matter
rest in peace.

Fram. I should imagine their sentiments to be very
different from yours upon this occasion. But, pray, who
is this Captain Lloyd, that you talk of, for Sir William's antagonist?

Wil. There I was out a little——I forgot his being
a Welchman, and a particular friend of the Ap Evans's.

Fram. But how came he connected with Lord
Eustace?

Wil. They were acquainted before the captain went
to sea, and a jolly buck he was. But he has now lost
his ship; and, to solicit another, he is as constant at

Lord Delville's levee as an old maid at her parish church. The simile holds farther too; for his head is cast in so peculiar a mould, that he believes every thing he hears, and repeats it as a matter of fact.

Fram. What an infinite deal of falsehood must this honest man utter in the course of a summer's day !

Wil. I will save his poor conscience, for this one day at least, by keeping him out of our fortress.

Fram. It will be more necessary for your purpose to prevent his telling truth at present, I imagine.

Will. Your honour knows it is not to be spoken at all times. He has told a thousand for my master himself. [*Aside.*] [*Knocking at the door.*] I must fly to my post, sir.   [*Exit.*

Fram. A fit one for such an office ! It is such wretches as these that corrupt us all; that clear the thorny paths of vice, and strew them o'er with roses. These agents for perdition can remove mountains that obstruct our passage, till we are sunk in the abyss of guilt, and then their weight falls on us ! I would willingly persuade myself that Lord Eustace is not so far gone in baseness as to conclude his marriage with Lady Anne, and desert this amiable unfortunate. Yet can I not, at present, foresee how it may be possible for him to avoid it. There is some time, however, to think about it. I'll seek him out directly, and try how his heart beats after his interview with Harriot.

[*Exit.*

SCENE III.

Sir William's *Apartment.* Sir WILLIAM *and* HARRIOT *discovered.*

Sir *W*. I am sorry to find you so cold upon this sub-ject, Harriot. But I flatter myself when you come to know the colonel, you will have no objections to him. Believe me, my child, he is the only man, I know, deserving of an heart like yours, untainted with the follies or vices of the world, and unsullied with the image of any other man.

Har. This is too much; I cannot bear it. [*Aside.*] ——Sir.——

Enter ROBERT.

Rob. Captain Lloyd is come to wait upon your honour.

Sir *W*. Desire him to walk in. And do ye hear, Robert? [*They walk aside.*

Har. To be obliged to compound with my duty!—— Ashamed to look my father in the face! To blush at his confidence, and be humbled by his kindness! To feel the irksomeness of receiving praise which I am conscious I do not merit! What a state for an ingenuous mind! [*Exit* Robert.

Enter at opposite doors, Mrs. WINIFRED *and* Captain LLOYD.

Mrs. *Win.* O heavens, that monster here!—But 'tis impossible now to escape. [*Aside.*

Capt. Good morrow, my good friend. Fair ladies your servant.

Sir *W*. I am extremely glad to see you, captain.

Capt. Why so I thought you would be, baronet, or I should not have been here ; and yet it has not been without some difficulty that we are met. I fancied just now that I should have been obliged to tack about without seeing you.

Sir *W*. I don't understand you, captain.

Capt. Why, to say the truth, Sir William, I don't rightly comprehend it myself; but one **of** your lazy hall furniture—the most obstinate puppy ! I have seen him before, though I can't now recollect where, took **it** into his head to deny **me** admittance, and if old **Robert had** not come to the door, and cleared the deck **of this** fellow, I should have sheer'd off directly.

Sir *W*. What can this mean ! Was it your orders, sister, that we should be denied ?

Mrs. *Win.* As our arrival in town has not yet been announced to any one, I did not expect visitors so soon ; and, therefore, gave no orders about the matter——Though I wish to keep him and all his family out of the house. [*Aside.*

Sir *W*. There is something very extraordinary in this proceeding. [*Aside.*

Capt. Since the wind sits so, I am glad I came aboard you ; I should not choose to run foul of a lady's orders, especially any that belong to you.

Sir *W*. You seem to have forgot these ladies, captain ; this is my sister, and this will soon be your niece, I hope.

Capt. They are both much altered since last I saw them—for one is grown a young woman and the other an old one.

Mrs. *Win.* You are not grown a brute, for you always were one.

Sir *W.* Have **a** care, captain, you are very near splitting on a rock.

Capt. Not at all—time brings every vessel into port, at last, that does not founder—But, faith, my nephew has had an excellent look **out;** I could almost envy him such a station. A fine full sail, truly!—Well, prosperous gales attend their voyage! But' where is **Harry?** I expected to have seen him here.

Sir *W.* Whom do you speak of, captain?

Capt. Why, of your son, the young colonel. I met him yesterday in the Park, not in **his** regimentals though ; for he told me he was a little *incog* at present, and had even changed his name, for fear of being known. I think it **was** Weston he called himself—as he had quitted quarters without leave of absence, and at the hazard of losing **his** commission.

Sir *W.* And he deserves it—What can have brought him here?

Har. I rejoice at the thoughts of seeing him ; does he look well, good captain?

Mrs. *Win.* **Do** you know where my nephew lodges, sir?

Capt. I should have as many tongues as there are swivels on the quarter-deck, to answer such a broadside of questions ; but one at a time, I beseech you.—

As to you, madam, I answer no; and to you, fair lady, yes; and as to you, Sir William, I think one need not have doubled the Cape to be able to find out his errand hither. A fair woman and a fair wind certainly brought him from Ireland.

Sir W. Rash, inconsiderate boy!

Capt. That may not be quite the case, neither, Sir William. But I should not have mentioned this matter to you, if I had not thought it had been all above-board between him and you, for Harry was never kept under hatches, I know.——But never fear, man, keep a stout heart, and I warrant you he shall weather it; he shall not lose his commission.

Mrs. Win. I fancy, sir, it may require the interest of a person of rather more consequence than you to preserve it. But there are those who are ready to interest themselves for any one who belongs to my family; the Ap Evans's are neither unknown, nor unallied to the nobility.

Capt. As to that, madam, I should think the Lloyds——

Sir W. For shame! for shame!——Can you, who are a man, be infected with this folly?

Capt. Why, 'tis not right, or becoming a man of war to attack a frigate, to be sure. But the Lloyds, Sir William——

Sir W. Psha!

Mrs. Win. Pray, brother, let the gentleman value himself upon what he pleases; but 'tis rather unlucky that a person of his weight and importance should not

be able to inform us where my nephew lodges, as that
is the only thing in which the captain could be any way
serviceable to us.

Capt. Not so fast, Miss Winifred, if you please;
there are many people in this town who are apt to
make offer of their services, without either will or
power to be of the least use to us. Now, if you will
tell me, madam, who those people are that you reckon
upon, I shall be better able to judge of your interest
with the great.

Mrs. Win. What **do you** think of Lord Eustace?—
Did you ever hear **of** him, captain?

Capt. I suppose I may; why, he is one of my most
intimate friends, madam, and I'll speak to him about
the business directly.

Mrs. Win. Pray now, good captain, spare yourself that trouble, for he is one of *my most intimate
friends* also. It is he who has been so obliging to lend
us this house, while we stay in London.

Capt. I do remember this place now as well as my
own cabin—but the impertinence of that footman,
whom I now recollect **to be** his, put it out of my head.
Yes, my lord and I have had some jovial parties here.

Sir W. What, in this identical house?

Capt. Why aye—this used to be the place of ren-
dezvous——But those days must be all over with him,
now that he is going to be married.

Mrs. Win. and Har. How! married!

Capt. Yes—the ceremony is to be performed immediately; he'll soon be in the bilboes.——But you seem

E

surprized——'T is odd enough, truly, that he has
not mentioned it to you, Miss Winifred, in particular,
who **are** one of his *most intimate friends*. When did
you see him, **pray?**

Mrs. *Win.* What! again alarmed at the same story?
                                          [*Aside to* Harriot.

Sir *W.* He was here this morning, and I knew it
was so then, though my sister chose not to believe it.

Mrs. *Win.* Nor do I now.—But pray, Mr. *Intel-*
ligencer Extraordinary, to whom is Lord Eustace to
be married?

Capt. Why really, madam, it is no extraordinary
intelligence that he is to marry Lady Anne Mountfort,
for it is just as public as the arrival of a king's ship in
the Downs, or an Indiaman at Blackwall. The newspapers tell these things, and every one in London
knows them.

Har. Gracious heaven! Where shall I hide my head?
                                           [*Aside.*

Mrs. *Win.* We have heard this choice account before, sir; but though I have as implicit a faith in the
veracity of the public prints as any person can have,
I would, however, stake my life on't that this is a
falsehood.

Capt. You are not serious, madam? But if you
choose **to** deny the fact, I have nothing further to say
about it.

Sir *W.* It is very odd that Lord Eustace should dis-
own it to me, and yet 't is certain that he did so.

Capt. That may be possible; but I, who am every

day at his father's, and have seen the liveries, equipage, and jewels brought home for the wedding, cannot easily be persuaded, that all this rigging should be prepared before there is a bottom on the stocks for it.

Har. 'Tis too true! Undone, unhappy Harriot!
   [*Aside to Mrs.* Winifred.

Sir *W.* What think you now, sister?

Mrs. *Win.* That the captain has dreamed all he has said, or may be, perhaps, infected with a calenture; for I think I have very good reason to know, that Lord Eustace is otherways engaged.

Capt. Aye, aye, engaged to be sure; say rather that he has taken another frigate in tow to add to his squadron; I know the man pretty well. I now recollect my having heard, some time ago, that he had an attachment to a pretty country girl. He was a long time absent from London.

Mrs. *Win.* A country girl, truly!

Sir *W.* Some poor simple creature, I suppose, who had youth and beauty enough to attract his inclinations, but neither sense or virtue sufficient to preserve herself or them.

Capt. This is probably the real truth of the matter.

Sir *W.* Though I lament the unhappy victims of their own folly, I cannot say that I am sorry such adventures happen sometimes, as these examples may possibly have their effect, in abating the presumption of young women, who are often too apt to fancy themselves much wiser than their fathers and mothers.

E ij

Har. I can no longer sustain the agonies I suffer!

[*Aside.* Faints.

Sir *W.* My Harriot! my dear child! what's the matter?

Har. I am suddenly taken ill; I hope you'll excuse me, sir.

Mrs. *Win.* Was there ever any thing so absurd?— Let us retire, my dear, and leave these wonder-making gentlemen to compose some other marvelous anecdotes. 　　　　　　　　[*Exit Mrs.* Win. *and* Har.

Sir *W.* I am extremely alarmed. [*Aside.*] You'll be so good as to excuse my staying longer with you, captain, at present. Harriot's illness distresses me extremely.

Capt. Doubtless, Sir William.——I will now go and give chace to the colonel, and if I can hail him, shall pilot him hither.

Sir *W.* I shall be much obliged to you.

Capt. But you must not play old square-toes upon us, baronet. Remember you were once as young, and I'll warrant as frolicsome too as any of us. Your servant, your servant, Sir William. 　　　　[*Exit.*

Sir *W.* There is something very singular in this affair of Lord Eustace. My sister's absurdity in denying the fact I can account for, from the peculiar obstinacy of her character. But why should Harriot be affected with it? Her aunt's folly may have operated there also; perhaps persuaded her, that his lordship's common address of gallantry and politeness, was a professed declaration of passion for her. But this marriage will soon put an end to such illusion, and restore my child to her sense and duty again. I will, therefore, go now and sooth, not wound her mind with my surmises.——The foibles of youth should be rather counteracted than opposed, lest, in endeavouring to weed them out, we may destroy a kindred virtue. [*Exit.*

ACT III. SCENE 1.

Frampton's *Apartment.* *Enter* FRAMPTON.

Frampton.

It was unlucky I could not meet with Lord Eustace. I perceive I am more anxious about this affair than he appears to be. Youth and dissipation buoy him up against those consequences, which I cannot help **fore**seeing.

Enter WILLIS, *with a parcel of* **letters.**

Wil. Here they are, sir; and if **you** knew what pains and address it cost me to get them into my hands, you would say, ' Willis, you deserve **to** be rewarded.'

Fram. With a halter. [*Aside.*

Wil. I was forced to swear to the fellow who brought them, that I was Sir William's own servant; and as the devil would have it, he was a Monmouth-

shire lad, waiter at Serle's Coffee-house, and had
come on purpose to ask a thousand impertinent questions about Gillian and John, James and Mary Le-
wellins, Ap-Griffiths, Ap Owens, and the Lord knows
who. Then my terrors about Robert surprizing us---
but luckily he was out of the way; so I carried the
lad to a beer-house, killed one half of his kindred,
and married the other, without knowing one of the
parties.

Fram. What an ingenious rascal! [*Aside.*] You
have acquitted yourself of your commission very **well.**
Leave the letters.

Wil. I hope, sir, you honour will be so kind to let
my lord know the pains I have taken for his service,
since you don't choose to take any notice of it yourself.—Industry should be rewarded, Mr. Frampton.
You used to be generous, sir; but——

Fram. How the fellow wounds me! [*Aside.*] Your
services will be repaid; you have no cause to doubt of
your lord's generosity.

Wil. No, really, sir——If you don't prevent it.
[*Aside.*] I fancy, **now, I** could guess **pretty** nearly to
the contents of these epistles. I wish I could keep
them in my possession, 'till I gave them to my lord,
and then I should be sure of being paid the postage.
[*Aside.*] **Let** 's see—To Sir William Evans, baronet; the
post-mark, Monmouth; this probably comes from his
steward, and may possibly contain an account of a
strayed sheep, or a cur hanged.——This, to the same,
from Ireland; from his son, I presume, the young

hero you talked of, about fighting my master—but I
think we are pretty safe, while he's at that distance.

Fram. I hope he may remain there, 'till this unhappy business is over.

Wil. To Mrs. Winifred Evans; post-mark, Here-
ford; 'tis Langwood's hand—This must be the letter
of letters.—Am I right, sir?

Fram. Pr'ythee leave them and your impertinence.
You have no right to pry into their secrets.

Wil. I ask pardon, **sir**; I have been trusted with
a great many secrets, before now, and I believe your
honour knows I never betrayed them.——And,
though **I am** not a gentleman, sir, I believe my lord
will give me the character of being faithful to him;
he never had any cause to repent his confidence in me
——Whatever he may—— [*Aside.*

Fram. Leave the room this moment, lest I should
be tempted to forget myself, and chastize your insolence as it deserves.

Wil. I wish I had the letters again, and the devil
should have them, before that sneaking puppy. [*Aside.*
. [*Exit.*

Fram. What a mean light do I appear in, at this
moment, to myself! Involved in an infamous confidence, with an insolent footman! Let me keep clear
of the looking-glass, that I may not be shocked at
my own features.—And can I persist in an action that
the least remains of honour or conscience must revolt
against? No, let beggary, rather than infamy, be my
portion. My indiscretions have deserved the first,

but let not the baseness of my conduct ever set a seal to the last. I will go and deliver them instantly to Sir William.

As he is going out, Enter Lord EUSTACE.

Lord *Eust.* Well, my dear Frampton, have you secured the letters?

Fram. Yes, my lord, for their rightful owners.

Lord *Eust.* As to the matter of property, Frampton, we wo'n't dispute much about that. Necessity, you know, may sometimes render a trespass excusable.

Fram. I am not casuist sufficient to answer you upon that subject; but this I know, that you have already trespassed against the laws of hospitality and honour, in your conduct towards Sir William Evans and his daughter. And as your friend and counsellor both, I would advise you to think seriously of repairing the injuries you have committed, and not increase your offence by a farther violation.

Lord *Eust.* 'T is actually a pity you were not bred to the bar, Ned: but I have only a moment to stay, and am all impatience to know, if there be a letter from Langwood, and what he says.

Fram. I shall never be able to afford you the least information upon that subject, my lord.

Lord *Eust.* Surely, I do n't understand you.---You said you had secured the letters---Have you not read them?

Fram. You have a right, and none but you, to ask me such a question.---My weak compliance with your first proposal, relative to these letters, warrants your thinking so meanly of me.—But know, my lord, that though my personal affection for you, joined to my unhappy circumstances, may have betrayed me to actions unworthy of myself, I never can forget that there is a barrier, fixed before the extreme of baseness, which honour will not let me pass.

Lord *East*. You'll give me leave to tell you, Mr. Frampton, that where I lead, I think you need not halt.

Fram. You'll pardon me, my lord; the consciousness of another man's errors can never be a justification for our own—and poor, indeed, must that wretch be, who can be satisfied, with the negative merit, of **not** being the worst man he knows.

Lord *East*. If this discourse were uttered in a conventicle, it might have its effect, by setting the congregation to sleep.

Fram. It is rather meant to rouze, than lull your lordship.

Lord *East*. No matter what it is meant for; give me the letters, Mr. Frampton.

Fram. Yet, excuse me———By Heaven, I could as soon think of arming a madman's hand, against my own life, as suffer you to be guilty of a crime that will for ever wound your honour.

Lord *East*. I shall not come to you to heal the wound; your medicines are too rough and coarse for me.

Fram. The soft poison of flattery might, perhaps, please you better.

Lord *Eust.* Your conscience may, probably, have as much need of palliatives as mine, Mr. Frampton ; as I am pretty well convinced, that your course of life, has not been more regular than my own.

Fram. With true contrition, my lord, I confess part of your sarcasm to be just. Pleasure was the object of my pursuit, and pleasure I obtained, at the expence both of health and fortune---but yet, my lord, I broke not in upon the peace of others ; the laws of hospitality, I never violated; nor did I ever seek to injure or seduce the wife or daughter of my friend.

Lord *Eust.* I care not what you did; give me the letters.

Fram. I have no right to keep, and therefore shall surrender them, though with the utmost reluctance ; but by your former friendship I intreat you not to open them.

Lord *Eust.* That you have forfeited.

Fram. Since it is not in my power to prevent your committing an error, which you ought for ever to repent of, I will not be a witness of it—There are the letters.   [*Lays them on the table.*

Lord *Eust.* You may, perhaps, have cause to repent your present conduct, Mr. Frampton, as much as I do our past attachment.

Fram. Rather than hold your friendship upon such terms, I resign it for ever.———Farewell, my lord.
            [*Exit.*

Lord Eustace *takes up the letters;* WILLIS *appears at the side of the Scene.*

Wil. I am glad they have quarrelled, I shall have my lord all to myself now.   [*Aside.*

Lord *Eust.* I have been to blame—but yet 't was cruel in him to distress me, when he knows the difficulties of my situation—he has shocked me so extremely, I find it impossible to touch the letters.

Wil. Then we are all ruined, and I shall never be paid for the carriage.   [*Aside.*

Lord *Eust.* Yet if Langwood's letter should fall into their hands I must be undone.

Wil. In order to strengthen his lordship's conscience, I 'll make my appearance. [*Aside.*] [Willis *comes forward.*] I hope Mr. Frampton has given your lordship the letters I took so much pains to get for you------there is one from Langwood to Mrs. Winifred————

Re-enter Mr. FRAMPTON.

—The devil! he here again! there is no doing any business with these half gentlemen.   [*Aside.*

Fram. My lord!

Lord *Eust.* Mr. Frampton!---Leave us, Willis.

Wil. So, I have lost my labour.   [*Aside.*] [*Exit.*

Fram. Ill treated as I have been, my lord, I find it impossible to leave you surrounded by difficulties.

Lord *Eust.* That sentiment should have operated sooner, Mr. Frampton—recollection is seldom of use

to our friends, though it may sometimes be serviceable to ourselves.

Fram. Take advantage of your own expression, my
lord, and recollect yourself.--Born and educated as I
have been, a gentleman, how have you injured both
yourself and me, by admitting and uniting, in the same
confidence, your rascal servant?

Lord *Eust.* The exigency of my situation is a sufficient excuse to myself, and ought to have been so to
the man who *called* himself my friend.

Fram. Have a care, my lord, of uttering the least
doubt upon that subject; for could I think you once
mean enough to suspect the sincerity of my attachment to you, it must vanish at that instant.

Lord *Eust.* The proofs of your regard have been
rather painful of late, Mr. Frampton.

Fram. When I see my friend upon the verge of a
precipice, is that a time for compliment? Shall I not
rudely rush forward, and drag him from it? Just in
that state you are at present, and I will strive to save
you.--Virtue may languish in a noble heart, and suffer her rival, vice, to usurp her power; but baseness
must not enter, or she flies for ever---The man who
has forfeited his own esteem, thinks all the world has
the same consciousness, and therefore is, what he deserves to be, a wretch.

Lord *Eust.* Oh, Frampton! you have lodged a
dagger in my heart.

Fram. No, my dear Eustace, I have saved you from
one, from your own reproaches, by preventing your

being guilty of a meanness, which you could never have forgiven yourself.

Lord *Eust.* Can you forgive me, and be still my friend?

Fram. As firmly as I have ever been, my lord.

Lord *Eust.* You are, indeed, my best, my truest friend. [*Embracing him.*] But yet, I fear you will despise me, Frampton---You never loved to that excess that I do, and therefore cannot pardon the madness of that passion which would destroy its dearest object.

Fram. We must not **judge** of the strength of our passions, **by the miseries** they bring on others, **but** rather by the means we use to save them from distress ---But let us at present hasten to get **rid of** the mean business we are engaged in, and forward the letters we have no right to detain.

Lord *Eust.* Here, take them; do what you will with them: I will be guided by you—Yet this affair of Langwood's letter———

Fram. Will make dreadful confusion. my lord—— Let me think a little—I have it---Suppose we delay the delivery of it for a few days; something may happen in that time that may save the unhappy Harriot **the** pain of such a discovery.

Lord *Eust.* Though I have little hopes on that account, yet would I not precipitate her wretchedness: it was to save her from it, Frampton, that first induced me———

Fram. Talk no more of it, my lord—Mr. Willis—

Enter WILLIS.

Wil. So they are friends again, I see. [*Aside.*]——
Did your honour call, Mr. Frampton?

Frám. Take these letters and give them to Sir William's servant, to be delivered immediately.

Wil. What, all of them, my lord?

Fram. No, this one must be kept back. Lock it
up carefully, 'till I call for it.

Lord *Eust.* Come, my dear Frampton, I have a
thousand obligations to you, and a thousand things to
speak to you about.   [*Exeunt Ld.* Eust. *&* Fram.

Wil. My dear Frampton!——There's a fellow for
you, that, without half a crown in his pocket, talks
as much stuff about honour, and such nonsense, as if
he were a duke---They have not broke the seal, I
find; that's Frampton's fault: if he had not returned the instant he did, I would have satisfied my lord's
curiosity, and my own---Well, cannot I do so now?
A good servant should prevent his master's wishes---
My lord, I am sure, would be glad to know the contents; egad, and so should I too---but how shall I
come at 'em?---This cursed seal [*flirts it with his
finger.*] Zounds, what have I done?---what an accident! why, the letter's open!---Why, if it is, one may
read it without offence---So, by your leave, good Mrs.
Winifred---[*Reads.*] 'Madam, as I am sensible the
' dreadful moment now approaches, when I must ren-
' der an account of all my actions.' A steward's ac-
' count will be tolerably long, I suppose. [*Continues*

reading.] ‘ I wish, even by this late confession, to
‘ atone for the crime I have been guilty of, in aiding
‘ Lord Eustace to impose upon your niece by a feigned
‘ marriage.’---The devil! This is a confession, indeed!
for which, like all other mean-spirited, whimpering
rascals, he deserves to be hanged. My lord was in
the right to look sharp after this business---We must
have been blown up, if it had come to light. But as
I hope to be well paid for the contents of this, I may
let the others go free.   [*Exit.*

SCENE II.

Changes to Sir William Evans's *Apartment*, HARRIOT,
seated on a Couch, leaning on her Arm.

Har. I cannot pierce through the mystery in which
I am involved: I strive in vain to recover confidence
in Lord Eustace. These fatal reports unhinge my
very soul.——Yet nothing can abate my love. One
false step has involved me in a thousand difficulties.
I can endure my situation no longer ; and let the consequence be what it may, I will reveal the secret to
my father. But then my lord's intreaties, and my
aunt's commands---why, even they must be sacrificed
to filial duty——Wretch that I am, how did I dare to
break that first of moral ties!—Heavens! he is here!

Enter Sir WILLIAM EVANS, *with a letter in his hand.*

Sir W. I have just received a letter from your bro-
F ij

ther, Harriot, which I should have had, ten days ago, had I been at home.

Har. Does he assign a cause for coming to London, sir?

Sir *W.* Yes, yes, 'tis as Lloyd guessed, an affair of gallantry, **but** an honourable business though——I long 'till ye are both married, that I may hear no more of romances. I hope when Harry has led the way, you will have no objection to follow him.

Har. What shall I say to him?   [*Aside.*

Sir *W.* I wish I knew who my future daughter-in-law is to be. Harry tells me she has a great fortune; but that, I suppose, is a sweetener——But if she has worth and virtue sufficient to make him happy, I shall be content.----But what's the matter, Harriot? I thought your illness was quite gone off---you look as if you had been weeping---My sister, I suppose.——

Har. No, sir; indeed her goodness to me, as well as yours, is graved upon my heart.

Sir *W.* She is a very odd woman------She would fain persuade me that I distressed you, by jesting with Captain Lloyd about Lord Eustace's mistress——I begin to think that she is in love with **him** herself--- Of what consequence are his gallantries to her? I dare say he has had a hundred of the same sort; and that the lady, to whom he is now going to offer his hand, can have but a very small remnant of his heart.

Har. I have heard him say, sir, they should never be divided.

Sir *W.* Fine talking for a libertine, truly!---How-

ever, I agree with you that it is not right to make a
a jest of those unfortunate women he may have ruined
---And I commend your delicacy upon this occasion,
as I well know it is the result of the most amiable female virtues, modesty and compassion.

Her. O, sir!   [*Rises.*

Sir *W.* What ails my child?

Har. [*Falls at his feet.*] My father!

Sir *W.* What is the matter? You amaze me, Harriot!

Har. I am——

Sir *W.* What?

Har. You see before you, sir——

Sir *W.* **Do** n't distract me! Whom do I see?

Har. I am---Lord Eustace---my father!——

Sir *W.* Speak; go on---Lord Eustace!---What of
him?

Har. I am his wife!——

Sir *W.* What—Lord Eustace's wife!—Then you
are a wretch, indeed!

Har. Yet pardon me, sir!

Sir *W.* I cannot pardon you, Harriot—you have undone yourself.

Har. O, do not say so, sir, when it is in your power
to make me happy.

Sir *W.* I would it were—but there is very little prospect of happiness for a virtuous woman, who is connected with a libertine.

Har. I hope, sir, you have mistaken his character;
and when you know him better, I am sure you will be
sorry——

Sir W. It is you, child, that I fear will have cause to be sorry, for having mistaken his character—young women are but bad judges of their lovers morals.

Har. My aunt, sir——

Sir W. Aye, aye, she, I suppose, was privy to the match; he is a lord, and that's enough for her. I might have expected such a stroke from her intolerable vanity—But how have I been deceived, in my opinion, both of your duty and affection to me!

Har. My future conduct, sir, shall prove them both.

Sir W. O, Harriot! What a disappointment is mine? I hoped to have seen you united to a man of sense and worth, who would have respected as well as loved you —Instead of that, you are now joined to one, who, from his too intimate knowledge of the vicious part of your sex, is likely to despise them all.

Har. I flatter myself, sir, that the goodness, both of his heart, and understanding, will make him readily renounce any light errors he may have fallen into.

Sir W. I wish it most sincerely——but——

Har. Do not, sir, injure him, by doubting it.

Sir W. I fear, my child, you flatter yourself in vain, with any change in your husband's conduct— that last amour, which Captain Lloyd spoke of——

Har. How blest am I, to be able to acquit my lord! —Though blushing I avow it, it was his mysterious attachment to his wife, that caused that vile report. ——O, sir! let me again, upon my knees, entreat you to pardon what is past, and give Lord Eustace leave to prove the sincerity of his affection to me, by his respectful tenderness and gratitude towards you.

Sir W. Rise, rise, my Harriet. Since it is so——I forgive, and bless you. *[Embraces her.*

Har. You have made your daughter happy—how will Lord Eustace be transported!

Sir W. Would I could see occasion for this joy! *[Aside.]*—Retire, my child; compose your spirits, and let me compose mine.—I wish to be alone.

Har. It is almost impossible, sir!——I am too, too happy! *[Exit.*

Sir W. Why was this marriage huddled in the dark? It shall not be kept secret——Mystery is the fit mask for vice; my daughter needs it not—I am impatient till I see Lord Eustace.

Enter ROBERT.

Rob. It is not long, sir, since he went from hence.

Sir W. No matter; leave me, Robert.

Rob. If your honour would hear a few words that I have to say.——

Sir W. I cannot hear you now; my thoughts are all engaged.——I must write to Colonel Lloyd directly. ——I shall have a sad piece of work with the old gentlemen at Trevallin——he doats upon my girl as if she were his own child.——

Rob. Aye, sir, and so does every one who knows her, except some of the folks in this house.—I wish, indeed I do, that we were fairly out of it.

Sir W. Well, we shall leave it soon---but for the present, Robert——

Rob. Your honour little knows what's going forward in it---such quarrelling, such high words! aye, and such fine words too, as I never heard before; though, if I understand them right, they have but a black meaning.

Sir *W.* Robert, we'll talk of this, some other time. ---I say again, I am not at leisure now.————

Rob. I can't be easy, 'till I tell you, sir; as I am sadly afraid there is something a plotting against your honour, or my young mistress.————I have heard that wicked Willis talking of her to his fellow servant.---- O, sir, that fellow knows all his lord's secrets; he is at the beginning, and ending of all mischief; and he says as how Miss Harriot has been only imposed upon. [*Sir Wil. starts.*]---Yes, sir, imposed upon--- and that his master will be married to a fine lady in less than a month's time.————   •   ,

Sir *W.* How! imposed upon! What can this mean? Lord Eustace dare not think of any thing so base.———— I injure both myself and him by the suspicion.

Rob. All I know of the matter is, sir, that the gentleman that lives here (whom I believe to be a very honest man, though Willis calls him a poor rogue) and my Lord Eustace had a sad quarrel, and they talked so loud, that I could not help overhearing Mr. Frampton—for I scorn to listen---reproaching my lord with having behaved very ill both to you and your daughter---but they were friends afterwards, and went out together.------But Willis said a great deal more to James, my lord's footman, to the same sense

---and whatever mischief there is a brewing, I am sure
he knows all about it.

Sir *W*. I cannot comprehend the meaning of all this.
------Imposed upon!------I will be satisfied---His scoundrel servant talk of my daughter, and of his marriage
with another lady!---I have not patience to wait the
meeting with Lord Eustace---Is that fellow in the
house? That Willis, Robert?

Rob. Yes, sir, James and he have been taking a
hearty glass, I believe; he looks pure and merry.

Sir *W*. Bid him come to me directly.

Rob. I am afraid he will be too cunning, for your
worship.

Sir *W*. Do as I bid you.

Rob. I will, sir.   [*Exit* Robert.

Sir *W*. The happiness or misery of my child, seem
now suspended in an equal balance.------Let my impatience to turn the scale in her favour, excuse me to
myself, for condescending to enquire into another's
secrets, though they so nearly concern me.

Enter WILLIS.

Wil. Your valet de chambre told me, sir, that you
desired to speak with me.

Sir *W*. Our conversation will be but short, Mr. Willis.   [*He shuts the door.*

Wil. I am in a rare humour to bam this Welsh
Baronet.   [*Aside.*

Sir *W*. I say our conversation will be but short, Mr.
Willis; but I should wish it to be sincere.

Wil. There he has hit the mark. [*Aside.*]—O, to be sure, sir! I have been remarkable for truth and sincerity all my life, sir. My mother taught me, from a child, never to tell a lie.

Sir *W.* Truth is certainly the foundation of every other virtue, and I hope I may depend upon yours, to answer a few questions that I shall ask you.

Wil. O yes, you may depend upon me.—What the devil is he about! He is certainly going to hear me my catechism.   {*Aside.*

Sir *W.* I shall think myself obliged to you, if you will acquaint me with what you know, in relation to Lord Eustace's marriage.

Wil. Me, sir! How is it possible I can tell?—All's out, I suppose—O, that cursed Langwood!   [*Aside.*

Sir *W.* No trifling with me, friend; I will be answered.

Wil. Yes, to be sure, sir, all servants ought to give civil answers to gentlemen; but really, sir, I cannot possibly tell you any thing about it.

Sir *W.* Since fair means will not prevail upon you, this shall extort the truth.   [*Draws his sword.*

Wil. For Heaven's sake, sir, don't terrify an evidence, in this land of liberty——You will either frighten what I do know out of my head, or make me confess something without knowing any thing at all of the matter.

Sir *W.* No prevarication, sir——Men like you, who are bred up in vice and idleness, are to be influenced by nothing but their fears---Therefore tell me,

Wil. Yes, yes, they have had another letter from. Langwood; so I may as well make a merit of giving up ours, since there can be none in keeping it from him. *[Aside.*

Sir W. What are you muttering, villain? Don`t urge me farther; I have lost my reason, and will not answer for the consequences.

Wil. I will do any thing, sir, if you will be pleased to drop the point of that ugly piece of cold iron.——— What you have heard from Langwood is most certainly true. But a good servant, you know, sir, ought to keep his master's secrets, till his life is in danger.

Sir W. **Langwood**!—Master's secrets!——Explain yourself this moment.

Wil. Dear sir, be patient---What need you have the trouble of hearing it over again, when you know it all already?

Sir W. Dare you again insult me with your trifling!.

Wil. Why really, sir, I can't say it was a right thing of my lord, but none of his servants were in fault, except Langwood; we must do what our masters bid us; and he, poor devil, is sorry enough, as you know, sir, and may see, sir. *[Takes the letter out of his pocket, Sir William snatches it.]*

Sir W. Langwood, again!——Who is Langwood? And what has he to do with your lord's marriage? And what is this letter?

Wil. It is for Mrs. Winifred, sir; and as to Langwood, he was the mock-doctor, the counterfeit parson, that married my lord; I was only the clerk, indeed,

sir; and I hope your honour will be so good to forgive me, and not leave all the sin and the shame too,
upon my poor conscience.

Sir *W.* Why, villain! rascal! what is all this stuff?
If your lord be married to my daughter, how dare he
think of any other wife?

Wil. So, I have made **a** fine piece of work on 't! I
find he did not know it was a sham marriage, till now.
—[*Aside.*] Why, really, sir, you terrify me so, that I
do n't rightly understand you; I thought you knew
all about it, before I opened my lips to you.

Sir *W.* I asked you, wretch, about your lord's intended marriage.

Wil. O lord, sir, it was very unlucky I did not understand you. I shall be obliged to fly my country;
my lord will never let me live in England after this.
I shall **lose an** excellent place, **sir.**

Sir **W.** Begone, thou profligate! Fly from my sight
this moment.

Wil. I am an undone scoundrel, that 's the truth of
it!—But this comes of muddling in a morning——
Had I been sober, I should have been an over-match
for his worship, or any justice of peace in England.
I 'll e'en retire, till my master and this Welch family,
have so reconciled matters between themselves, that a
gentleman may **be able** to live with some satisfaction
amongst them. [*Aside.*]   [*Exit.*

[*Sir* William *reading the letter.*

Sir *W.* What am I now to think! My child is dishonoured! Let me contain my rage a moment longer,

and be yet more fully satisfied, from their own lips.—
Robert!

Enter ROBERT.

Go, call my sister, and---I cannot name her.

Rob. Miss Harriot, sir?

Sir *W.* Aye, bid them come hither.

Rob. I never saw my master so disturbed before.
[*Aside.*]   [*Exit* Robert.

Sir *W.* Of what can they inform me? Do I not
know my daughter is undone?

Enter Mrs. WINIFRED *and* HARRIOT.

Mrs. *Win.* Pray, my lady, go first.

Sir *W.* Where are these wretched, these unhappy
women, that have brought shame and sorrow on themselves, and infamy on me?

Mrs. *Win.* Hey day! What's **the** matter now?
Harriot told me she had just left you in a heavenly
temper; what can have happened to discompose you
since; but *Much Ado about Nothing* is your play, from
morning 'till night.

Sir *W.* Read that.   [*Gives her a letter.*

Mrs. *Win.* A broken seal!——What can be the
contents?

Har. **Dear** sir, what is the matter?

Sir *W.* **Do** not talk to me, unhappy girl! Lord
Eustace has deceived you—you are not his wife.

Har. All gracious Heaven!   [*Sinks upon a couch.*

G

Sir W. Rage and madness! O women, women, what have ye done!

Mrs. Win. Vastly well, I think.

Sir W. Do not provoke me.

Mrs. Win. You are enough to provoke a saint, your-self.---What **is all this** stuff, this letter, this forgery, this nonsense! He personate a parson! I think I should know a clergyman in any dress. I am not quite so easily imposed **upon as you, Sir** William.

Sir W. I will not answer you---But thou, undutiful, unhappy girl! what can'st thou say?

Mrs. Win. I wish you would hear reason, and spare your reproaches, Sir William.

Har. No---give them vent---I only fear to live, not die---Let loose your rage upon me: I implore it; I will endure it all.

Sir W. You have deserved it. Your own deceit has fallen upon your head: you are betrayed, dishonoured, and abandoned, both by your villain husband, and your wretched father.

Har. O, sir! have pity on my anguish and despair!

Sir W. I cannot bear your sight——My being, life itself, is hateful to me. [*To Mrs.* Win.] This is your pride, your rage for quality!---You have undone my child, and I renounce you both! [*Exit.*

Har. Will you forsake me, also?

Mrs. Win. Forsake you! no, child: this is a per-fect chimera of your father's.

Har. O, let us go this moment, implore his goodness to forgive our fault, and fly for ever from this hateful dwelling.

Mrs. Win. By no means; I don't approve of your quitting your husband's house. I would have you write to him immediately, and desire him to come to us this evening.

Har. I write to him! You make me shudder at the thought.

Mrs. Win. It must be done, child—I insist upon it. This is some trick, meant to impose upon us.

Har. I feel the imposition here————Lord Eustace has betrayed us.

Mrs. Win. I tell you, Harriot, it is impossible——he is at least the ninth peer of his family, in a direct line.

Har. Though honours may be————honour is not hereditary, madam.

Mrs. Win. No matter; write to him, I say: you are and must be Lady Eustace, at any rate, I tell you.

Har. And can you think me vile enough, after such perfidy, to receive his hand? Can I vow to honour the man whom I no longer esteem? Shall I go to the altar with him, and swear to be faithful to a perjured wretch? again repeat my vows of everlasting love for him who has abandoned, and undone me? No; I would sooner die a thousand, thousand deaths!

Mrs. Win. You are just as obstinate as your father—Now you have taken this into your head, nothing can get it out again.

Har. Do you think my father could be so inhuman,

G ij

without just grounds, to stab me to the heart? It is, it is too true!

Mrs. *Win.* I will not believe a word of it.------I never was mistaken in my life; my brother is ever in the wrong.------I desire, Harriot, you will write to Lord Eustace directly.

Har. Indeed I will not.   [*Exit.*

Mrs. *Win.* Then, positively, I will---I am determined to know the truth from him. I own I begin to be a little doubtful about this matter myself. This letter may be forged---but those eternal reports confound me---'T is impossible he should dare to deceive me---but if he has, he shall find that the Ap Evans's are not to be injured with impunity.

ACT IV. SCENE I.

The Park. Enter Captain LLOYD, *and* Col. EVANS.

Colonel Evans.

My father in London! you surprise me, captain----What can have brought him here?

Capt. Nay, as to the matter of surprise, my young hero, your father was quite as much astonished at hearing of your being in the same port, as you can be; and as to your aunt Winifred, she stared with as much amazement, as the sailors that spied the first Patagonian. You sister, indeed, seemed more pleased

than any of them, at the news, and inquired whether
I had met you in healthy condition, and if I knew your
moorings.

Col. My gentle Harriot!—I am impatient to see her.

Capt. Hoist sail, and away, then; I'll be your con-
voy, though I should like better to drop anchor, and
take in refreshment, for an hour or so, at the Admi-
ralty Coffee-house, where I have appointed Captain
Blast of the Boreas, and some other jolly lads to
meet me.

Col. I am much obliged to you, captain, but will
by no means suffer you to break your engagement.—
I have a little business to dispatch, before I can see
my father, and shall easily find out the house, without
troubling you.

Capt. Why, that you may readily do, as it is in-
closed by a very high wall, and has a large handsome
gate-way, with a bell at the door.——Aye, aye, that
bell was not placed there to call the crew to prayers,
but to prevent the neighbours from knowing who
comes in and out, as they might do, if there was a
rapper only.

Col. I can't see why that caution should be necessary.

Capt. It is of no great use at present—But time has
been——Harke me, Harry; there is a devilish storm
brewing over your head; you may look for dirty
weather, I can tell you.---Your father is in a con-
founded passion at your having quitted the regiment,
and is strongly persuaded that you'll spring a leak,
my boy.

Col. I wrote to my father, some time ago, to acquaint him with my motives; I have also written to
my colonel, to account for my conduct.

Capt. Never fear, I'll take care of you, as I am
sure you did not desert from cowardice——But it was
a silly trick, Harry.—Some girl, I suppose, is in the
wind; they make fools of the wisest of us.—I remember, when I was stationed at Gibraltar, a Donna
Isabella——

Col. Would you were there now: I know not how
to get rid of this tiresome man.   [*Aside.*

Capt. A Spaniard, you may guess by the name,
had a devilish mind to come off with me, as she said,
to see foreign parts.---But I weighed anchor slily, one
moon-light night, and left the poor signiora on shore
——But all men have not the gift of discretion:
though I **was** a younker then, Harry, not much turned
of thirty, I'll assure you——

Col. I think it was rather cruel in you to forsake the
lady, captain.

Capt. Why, I did hear afterwards, that there was a
ballad made about it, intitled *The Cruel Captain's Garland*, and set to a very woeful tune——I laugh at these
things, Harry; but I find you are a truer lover, and
have come here in spite of wind and tide, in pursuit
of your mistress---You can't expect, however, that
Sir William will be highly delighted, if you should
happen to make a losing voyage of it.

Col. I hope, sir, it will be the most prosperous one
of my life, and I shall **be** able to give my father a sa-

Capt. Why, if your mistress be well freighted, a sixty thousand pounder or so, he will have no objection, I suppose. But come, my boy, tell me a little about it: is she maid or widow, Harry? I like to hear love stories mightily.

Col. She is a maiden, young and beautiful, and **of a** rank and fortune beyond my expectation, captain.--- We have loved one another long; **her** guardians are upon the point of disposing of her to another; she has desired me to free her from their tyranny, and accept of her hand as **my** reward—Glorious recompence!

Capt. Why, Harry, this is running before the **wind,** with **a vengeance**—Not so fast, not so fast, my boy, you **go** at the rate of twelve knots an hour——This story sounds a little romantic though, and puts me in mind of the lady that the flying man comes to save from the monster——But 'tis odd enough that I should not know this lady; pr'ythee, Harry, what's her name?

Col. You must excuse my not answering that question, captain, as you might possibly become my rival.

Capt. Why, to **be** sure, if she had applied to me, she should have been far enough from her guardians by **this;** we'd have run gunnel to **all** the way, my boy, and left them and you on the dry land, Harry.

Col. I shall **tell** her **of your** intended gallantry, captain; and I **hope** you and she will be better acquainted---for the present, I must wish you a good evening.

Capt. Nay, if you have **a** mind to sheer **off,** colonel,

I wish you a fair gale.----I never grapple with any
but a pretty lass, or an enemy; and so your servant,
your servant, colonel.   [*Exit* Capt.

Col. My meeting with this blundering sailor, was
unlucky, as my father may, perhaps, be displeased at
my not waiting on him, the moment I knew of his
being in London.----But I cannot break my engagement with Lady Anne----every thing must give way
to that charming woman----I will fly to her directly,
and if possible, find time to pay my duty to my father
before I sleep.   [*Exit.*

SCENE II.

Sir William's *Apartment.* Enter Mrs. WINIFRED *and*
ROBERT.

Mrs. *Win.* **He** will come, then?---You have staid a
great while, Robert.

Rob. My lord **was** not at home, madam; and as
you desired I should bring an answer, **I was** obliged to
wait his coming---Every thing seems **in** confusion, in
the family; his lordship, it seems, **is to be** married in
a few days; they are all packing **up,** and the servants
scarce knew where to find pen, ink, and paper.

Mrs. *Win.* This alarms me---'T is but too plain I
have been deceived. [*Aside.*]————Hearken to me,
Robert, and do exactly what I command you---go
and place yourself by the private door, in the garden,

and the moment you hear a key turn in the lock, come and tell me.

Rob. I shall obey you, madam.—I am sure all is not right.   [*Aside. Exit.*

Mrs. Win. I must, if possible, prevent Sir William's knowing of this interview——But here he comes.

Enter Sir WILLIAM.

I hope you have vented all your rage, brother, and that one may talk a little calmly to you now?

Sir W. O yes: I have great reason to be calm.

Mrs. Win. I can tell you that a little more of your outrageous **fury** would have killed your daughter; nor do I know what fatal effect it might have had upon **my own** constitution.

Sir W. That is not very easily shocked, I believe.

Mrs. Win. That is more than you know, at least, brother; but a person so entirely given up to their passions, never once reflect upon consequences.

Sir W. I wish you had reflected upon consequences; but those who have err'd themselves are ever ready to reflect on others.

Mrs. Win. A truce with reflections on all sides; and in case that there should be any truth in this infamous story, let us set about forming some scheme for redressing the affront that he has dared to offer to our family.

Sir W. I shall not stand in need of your assistance. I am determined how to act.

Mrs. Win. Pray, Sir William, do not be headstrong, but for once be advised by me.—I have thought of a scheme, and I am sure it will answer.

Sir *W.* What is it?

Mrs. *Win.* It is happy for my family that I have a little sense, brother, though I do not boast of it.

Sir *W.* Your wisdom in this matter has been conspicuous; but what new proofs of it are we to expect at present?

Mrs. *Win.* Suppose we were to send for Lord Eustace, and try what effect Harriot's tears and my reproaches would have upon him. He has always had the greatest deference for my opinion.

Sir *W.* Your opinion!—Is this your boasted scheme? He will not come; base as he is, it is impossible he could endure her sight.

Mrs. *Win.* Your affected sagacity is enough to set one mad. You are mistaken, as you always are.

Sir *W.* I know it cannot be; the consciousness of his vile treachery will keep him far from hence. He dare not see her.

Mrs. *Win.* I cannot bear this contradiction. [*Aside.*] For once let conviction conquer your obstinacy: I wrote to him myself in Harriot's name; I have had his answer; he will be here this night.

Sir *W.* And shall my daughter sue to him for justice? Implore him to receive the hand he has rejected, and the heart he has betray'd? Shall she be sacrificed to make his peace? I tell you no—I will have other vengeance.

Mrs. *Win.* I see these horrid punctilios will ruin

all——If we can make up this matter quietly, what does it signify whether he be a man of honour or no?

Sir *W.* I never must forget that I am one.

Mrs. *Win.* I wish you would have a little patience, and hear me out. If this should fail, I have another project in my head which I am certain must succeed. My imagination has not been idle, and I think it full as active as your own.

Sir *W.* I believe it may be rather more so. But I have no leisure for imaginary matters now. [*Going.*

Mrs. *Win.* Pray, Sir William, don't be so positive —you know Lord Eustace has a place at Court.

Sir *W.* What then?

Mrs. *Win.* I would, at least, let the king know what a servant he has about him; and as I may reasonably suppose that his majesty may have heard of our ancestors, though he knows nothing of you, Sir William, I would advise you to throw yourself at his feet. He is himself a father.

Sir *W.* Blest may he long be in that honoured title! though I am rendered wretched by the name. But what can he do for me?

Mrs. *Win.* Disgrace and displace the man who has wronged you, although he be a lord.

Sir *W.* What is his title? has he not debas'd it—— But know, there is no difference of rank before the throne—degrees of elevation are only seen by those who look above them: kings must look down, and therefore see all equal; and in our monarch's sight, the rights even of the meanest subject are precious as

Mrs. *Win.* Though I can never believe that a knight baronet is upon a par with a lord, Sir William.

Sir *W.* Absurd distinctions! I will hear no more—The man who has the means of justice in his own hands, and seeks for it elsewhere, deserves to be the sport of chance, and dupe of his own weakness. Then let him come this night—I 'll meet him as I ought.

Mrs. *Win.* You are exactly in the same case of the Diffidents at Warsaw ; nothing but force of arms will content you ; and like them too you may be undone by it. Suppose you were to meet Lord Eustace, and he should kill you ?

Sir *W.* I shall not then out-live my honour. [*Exit.*

Mrs *W.* This self-will'd man distresses me extremely, he is for ever disconcerting my schemes—There never was such a race of idiots as the family of the Ap Evans's, myself excepted—there is not a head in this house but my own.—To be sure I have been a little over-reach'd in this affair of the wedding ; but the greatest politicians are liable to mistakes—I hope to repair all yet, and make my niece a woman of quality one way or another.

Enter ROBERT.

Rob. Madam, I have just now heard the private door of the garden unlock, and ran to tell you.

Mrs. *Win.* Vanish! [*Exit* Rob.] I must not let my brother and Lord Eustace meet till every thing is settled. [*Exit.*

SCENE III.

Garden Parlour. Enter Lord EUSTACE *and* Colonel EVANS, *with their Swords in their hands.* Lord Eustace *lays his on a Chair.*

Lord *Eust.* You are here in safety, sir, and may put up your sword; this house is mine, notwithstanding the mysterious manner of my entrance. I hope you are not wounded?

Col. Thanks to your courage and generosity, sir, I have escaped unhurt. I thought our police was better conducted than to suffer our lives to be endangered by footpads.

Lord *Eust.* These accidents are less frequent in this country than they used to be; but no code of laws was ever yet framed that could make all men honest. I am extremely happy at having come so opportunely to your assistance.

Col. I shall ever be grateful for the obligation, sir; but may I not know to whom I am obliged?

Lord *Eust.* Do not mention the matter as a favour, I intreat you——You would, doubtless, have done the same for me; and had I happened to have come first, I should have stood in need of your assistance.—— I am called Lord Eustace.

Col. I shall remain indebted to your lordship, and wish you a good night. What a rencontre! [*Aside,*

H

Lord *Eust.* I could wish you not to leave me, sir; 't is late, and therefore unsafe for either of us to return alone—The fellows who attacked you may lye in wait for you—I shall not stay here a quarter of an hour; and as I wish to be better acquainted with you, I should be glad to know your address.

Col. I am extremely obliged to your lordship. I am called Colonel Weston; you 'll hear of me at the hotel in Pall Mall.   [*Going.*

Lord *Eust.* Let me entreat you not to leave me—I am at present in a very difficult and disagreeable situation.

Col. Your lordship has a right to command me; but I hope you will not stay longer than the time you have mentioned, as I have some business to transact this night.

Lord *Eust.* If that be the case, I will not trespass upon you; perhaps there may be something similar in our circumstances; for your business, at this hour, must, in all probability, be with a lady, and you may reasonably suppose, by my being alone and on foot, that I am come to meet one here.

Col. Let me entreat your lordship not to lose such precious minutes, but fly to the expecting fair one.— This is an odd discovery.   [*Aside.*

Lord *Eust.* The matter is not as you imagine, sir.

Col. There is perhaps a jealous husband, or an old cross father, my lord.

Lord *Eust.* Neither, colonel. But matches made for interest only, too often break the most delightful ties, the union of fond hearts—The lady who lives here is the most amiable of her sex, and I adore her; yet am on the point of marrying one whom I can never love.

Col. This is a sad affair indeed, my lord.—I could save you a great deal of trouble if I were at liberty to tell you Lady Anne's intentions.   [*Aside.*

Lord *Eust.* I fear the unhappy girl has heard of my intended marriage, as she has written to me to come here this night—I never was so embarrassed or distressed.

Col. Some girl you keep, I presume, my lord.

Lord *Eust.* By no means; she is a woman of family and character—I am almost distracted about her. I will now step and see if the coast be clear, as there are some of the family that I should not choose to encounter at this late hour, and return to you, sir, instantly—You see what confidence you have already inspired me with.   [*Exit.*

Col. A confidence indeed! but of what use can it be to me, who am bound in honour not to betray it? [*Looks at his watch.*] Bless me, it is now past eleven— the time I spent with Lady Anne stole unperceived away. It will certainly be too late to go to my father's to-night; I must defer my visit till to-morrow; and as Lord Eustace do n't seem in a great hurry to be married, I shall have time enough to get Lady Anne out of her guardian's power, and prepare my father for her reception. But here comes my new friend.

Re-enter Lord EUSTACE.

Lord *Eust.* All is quiet; I must therefore take the opportunity of conveying you safe out again; and I hope to have the pleasure of being better known to you.

Col. Your lordship's inclination does me honour.

[*Exeunt.*

SCENE IV.

Another Apartment.   *Enter* Mrs. WINIFRED, *leading* HARRIOT.

Mrs. *Win.* You obstinacy is enough to distract me; I say you shall see him.

Enter Lord EUSTACE,

Har. Support me, gracious Heaven!

Lord *Eust.* My dearest Harriot, your billet has alarmed me more than I can express—I have made the utmost dispatch that was possible to fly to you; and the moments that have passed since I received your commands, have been the most painful of my life.

Mrs. *Win.* Your lordship need not enter into a defence of your punctuality.

Lord *Eust.* Why is my Harriot's brow overcast— and her eyes quenched in tears? Why is she silent?

Mrs. *Win.* Ask your own heart!

Lord Eust. Is it possible that the idle report of my marriage can have distress'd her thus?

Har. Horrid dissembler!   [*Aside.*

Mrs. Win. **Do** not exhaust your spirits, my dear Harriot; give me leave to talk to him [*Aside to Harriot.*] So then, my lord, what we have heard upon the subject is but an idle report, without the least foundation?

Lord Eust. If you will but recollect what has pass'd between your niece **and** me, madam, you must be fully convinced it can **be** nothing more.

Mrs. Win. And yet, my lord, you seem confused.

Lord Eust. Why really, madam, the doubts you seem to entertain of my veracity are a little distressing —But **let** me hope my Harriot will believe me, while I swear——

Har. Away, my lord! I can believe no more—— Could I have thought that either my wrongs or my resentment were capable of increase!

Lord Eust. Really, madam, I do not clearly understand the meaning of this conversation, and I must say, I think it rather severe to be condemned unheard.

Mrs. Win. I can contain my rage no longer; read that.   [*Gives him* Langwood's *letter.*

Lord Eust. Langwood's letter! All is discovered then!   [*Aside.*

Mrs. Win. I perceive that even a man of quality may be disconcerted—Your lordship did not use to be at a loss for an answer.

H iij

Lord *Eust.* Have patience, madam; I confess that appearances are against me.

Mrs. *Win.* Aye, and realities too, my lord.

Lord *Eust.* I do not mean to justify myself—No, I plead guilty. The fear of losing you, my Harriot, whom I loved more than life, and the apprehension of disobliging my father, tempted me to make you mine in an illegal manner—But here I swear I will repair the injury.

Mrs. *Win.* I think it will do; matters are in a right train **now,** if I can but prevent Sir William from interrupting them.   [*Aside. Exit.*

Lord *Eust.* You are offended, Harriot, and have cause—but let not your resentment turn against yourself.

Har. Could I forgive myself, my lord, I then might pardon you; but while I think my punishment severe, I own I have deserved it.

Lord *Eust.* You judge yourself too hardly——Has either your virtue or your delicacy suffered by my crime? Nay, even your reputation is still free from stain; and if you will now condescend to accept my hand, my future life shall be devoted to your happiness.

Har. And can you think I'll be again deceived?

Lord *Eust.* By heaven you shall not!

Har. Nay, I will not—your poor evasions have no weight with me—leave me, for ever leave me. I will not be united to you by any ties.   [*Going.*

Lord *Eust.* Yet hear me, Harriot.

Har. Would I had never **heard** you. But though

I were to listen to you now, you cannot shake my purpose.—No—I can die!——   [*Exit.*

Lord *Eust.* No, live my Harriot! Live to make me
happy.——

Sir *W.* [*Within.*] Where is he? I must and will see
him!

Lord *Eust.* Ah! Sir William! This is unlucky!—
I am not prepared for this encounter.   [*Aside.*

Enter Sir WILLIAM.

Sir *W.* What! is it possible that you should dare to
enter underneath this roof?

Lord **Eust.** What should I fear, Sir William?

Sir *W.* Your own base heart, and my much injured
honour; which calls upon you now for justice.

Lord *Eust.* So then, I find the pride of injured virtue was assumed. Your daughter would secure me
by compulsion—but I despise assassins!

Sir *W.* Do not, my lord, insult my patience farther;
I did not know you were without a sword: on
that account I put up mine; but know, young man,
I shall not rest till it has done me justice.

Lord *Eust.* Sir William, though I cannot pretend
to justify the injuries I have done your daughter, I
neither must, nor will be compelled to make the reparation; I should indeed be unworthy to become her
husband, if fear could make me so.

Sir *W.* At the first hour you saw her, sir, I should
have deemed you so—'t is not your birth, young man,
can varnish over vices such as yours—your rank renders them the more **obnoxious.**

Lord *Eust.* I readily allow myself to blame, Sir William.

Sir *W.* You cannot then be base enough to refuse the sole atonement which is now within your power.

Lord *Eust.* I will confess I felt my heart subdued by Harriot's grief and tenderness—they had more power than armies. She might have triumphed over me, but————

Sir *W.* You surely do **not think I mean to** give my daughter to you! What! to reward **your vices** with a heart like hers—to have my child become a second time a sacrifice to that vain idol, Title!—No, sir, it is another kind of reparation I demand, and I will have it.

Lord *Eust.* A brave man, Sir William, never **thinks** meanly of another's courage; and as I know you to be so, I hope you will not think me otherwise if I decline your offer.

Sir *W.* On what pretence, **my lord?** Have you not wronged me?

Lord *Eust.* For that reason only I cannot, dare not, draw my sword against you.

Sir *W.* These are new rules of honour, formed on the principles of fear, my lord.

Lord *Eust.* Fear, Sir William!

Sir *W.* Yes, my lord, I say it; none but a coward ever will decline to meet the man he has injured; and should you still persist in your refusal, I will proclaim you one.

Lord *Eust.* This is too much—But consider, sir, you are—my Harriot's father.

. Sir *W*. That consideration would brace a nerveless
arm. But look upon me, sir; I am not bent beneath
the weight of years—my mind and body both are firm
as yours; and the first shock that ever reached my
heart, except her mother's loss, is the disgrace you
have brought upon my child. The stain must be ef-
faced, my lord.

Lord *Eust*. I know not how to act; should I declare my intention to marry Harriot, he would despise me; and if I fight him, that renders it impossible.

                                             [*Aside.*

Sir *W*. Come, come, my lord, this is no time for
pausing—you must determine instantly to give me the
satisfaction I require, or see your title posted up, with
the honourable addition of coward to it.

Lord *Eust*. Nay then, Sir William, though with
reluctance, I must accept your offer. Name your
time, sir.

Sir *W*. At eight to-morrow morning.

Lord *Eust*. I 'll call upon you, sir, and bring a
friend—But let me once more add, that you are the
only man on earth that I should fear to meet upon
such terms.   [*Exit.*

Sir *W*, I am glad my son is ignorant of this affair.
Had he been here, he must have fought Lord Eustace.
He has, I hope, a long and happy life before him ;—
mine, though not quite worn out, is of less value ;
and if I lose it in defence of my child's honour, 't is
well disposed of,

Enter Mrs. WINIFRED

Mrs. *Win.* So she was, or might have been, very well disposed of, but for your intemperance. You have managed your matters very cleverly to be sure. You have driven Lord Eustace away, and the family of the Ap Evans's are disgraced for ever.

Sir *W.* Thou weak, vain woman! whose folly has undone me and my child.

Mrs. *W.* Not I truly, Sir William—It is her own high-flown principles that have ruined her. My lord offered to marry her over and over again, it seems, but she, with her nonsensical, romantical notions, affected to despise him, and refused to be his wife on any terms.

Sir *W.* Has she? I rejoice to hear it.—

Mrs. *Win.* Rejoice, at what! at her being a mad woman? I think, in her situation, she need not have been so nice. It would have been much better for her to have been Lady Eustace, even against his will, than Miss Harriot Evans against her own.

Sir *W.* How nearly pride and meanness are allied! You would obtrude your niece upon a man who has abandoned and dishonoured her; then vainly think she might receive distinction from a title, which force, not choice, bestowed.

Mrs. *Win.* Brother, I neither understand logic nor sophistry, but I am very sorry matters are as they are., As to Harriot, I believe it will be of no great consequence to her; she will soon break her heart, I imagine. But the scandal of this affair will rest upon the survivors. I do n't think I shall ever be able to shew my face at Monmouth again.

Sir W. Away! The moments now are too precious to be wasted. Where is Harriot?

Mrs. Win. In her chamber, like a distracted wretch, tearing herself to pieces. I endeavoured to comfort her as much as I could, by telling her how wrong she had acted, and that she might have lived to be a countess, if she had followed my advice.

Sir W. Was this the consolation you offered to her grief? How could you be so barbarous? The proper spirit she has shewn in refusing that worthless lord, has replaced her in my heart—I will go try to comfort her. [*Exit.*

Mrs. Win. Aye, so you may; you are the fittest to go together. For my part, I disclaim the mismanagement of the whole affair, and remember, *I 'll no longer be accountable for measures that I am not suffered to guide.* [*Exit.*

ACT V. SCENE I.

Mr. Frampton's *Apartment.* Lord EUSTACE *and* Mr. FRAMPTON *discovered.* Lord *Eustace rises from a Table, as if writing.*

Frampton.

YOUR meeting with Sir William was extremely unfortunate.

Lord *Eust.* I most sincerely wish we had not met ; but that is past————

From. Then I suppose you think the worst is over.

Lord *Eust.* No, Frampton, 'tis to come.——Sir William has insisted upon **my** meeting him this morning.

Fram. Impossible, my lord! you must not fight him. Think on the consequences ; **if you** should be so unhappy as to kill the father of **the woman** you have highly injured, the world would certainly unite against you, and drive you from society.

Lord *Eust.* In that case I should be but ill qualified for solitude I confess.——Now, my dear Frampton, as I know you are my friend, and as I would not wish any other person should be **acquainted** with this story, I must desire you will be my second.

Fram. It is much beneath a man **of** honour to make professions either of his friendship **or** his courage ; but, on this occasion I must tell you, that I would hazard my life for your service in any other cause ; but I will not be concerned in this infamous affair ; and I say again, you must not raise your arm against Sir William.

Lord *Eust.* You do not know how **I am** circum-stanced. He has compelled me to this duel ; said he would brand me for a coward if I declined it. What would you have me do ?

Fram. Marry his daughter.

Lord *Eust.* No——Though I love her with the truest fondness, I will not wed her upon such terms;

nor suffer her to think so meanly of me, as to suppose I poorly bartered a coward's hand to save this worthless life.

Fram. **Yet,** consider, my lord, that let the consequences **of this** duel be what they may, nothing can **acquit you of that** justice **you** owe both to her and yourself.

Lord *Eust.* I own that I have greatly wronged her.

Fram. It is now within your power to make reparation, by becoming her husband; **but** should you deprive her of a father, she never can be united to the man who **killed him.**

Lord *Eust.* I will not kill him, Frampton——Urge me no farther——My mind is torn to pieces.

Fram. **Believe me,** my lord, you are not **in a** right **course to heal it.**

Lord *Eust.* **No matter; you have** refused **to** be **a** witness **of** my conduct, Mr. Frampton.

Fram. And do so still: I never had the least reason to doubt your bravery; and as this is an affair, in which only principals can be concerned, I hope it will be no imputation upon mine if I decline seeing your lordship engaged in a strife where **I cannot** wish you success.

Lord *Eust.* I shall **not press you;** but have yet a request **to make.**

Fram. Name it, my **lord.**

Lord *Eust.* **If I** should fall, deliver this letter to my father; **and if** there be any circumstance of my misconduct left untold, which may do Harriot justice,

I

inform him of it fully.——I must now go seek for a
less cautious friend than Mr. Frampton.

Fram. **Your** lordship will **scarcely** ever find **a sin-**
cerer. [*Exit Lord* Eustace.] Of what opposite qualities is this young man compounded ? What a mixture
of good and evil ! But are we not **all** made of the same
materials ? The devil himself cannot always mislead a
man that has principles ; they **will** recur **in** spite of **him,**
and make their owner act rightly **upon** trying occasions. This letter **to** his father **shews him to** be a man
of honour.——Something must be done **to** preserve
him.——I cannot give him up. An experiment,
though a hazardous one, must be made directly. [*Exit.*

SCENE II.

Sir William's *Apartment. Enter* HARRIOT *and* Mrs.
WINIFRED.

Har. When shall my tortured mind find rest !——
Gracious Heaven, preserve me from distraction ! Perhaps in a few moments my father's sword may pierce
my husband's heart. Why has that tender name escaped my lips ? Resentment should have stopt its passage to my tongue, and sighs opposed it utterance.

Mrs. *Win.* I do n't see any harm, child, in your
calling him your husband, though to be sure he is not
so in law.—But I would have you hope for the best,
Harriot.

Har. No, I will hope no more——What should I hope?—My pride, my reason might have scorn'd him living, but I will love him, and lament him dead! —Would I had died the hour before I listen'd to your counsel, and set at nought the authority of my father!—Your cruel kindness has undone me!

Mrs. Win. I should not have thought of meeting such a return, for that kindness, from you, Miss Evans.

Har. Forgive and pity my distraction, madam! 'Tis I that have brought ruin on you all——But if you ever loved me, think of some means, to find my brother out: he may prevent this duel, and save me from the lowest depth of misery.

Mrs. Win. Really, child, you are extremely ignorant; you talk as if you were at Monmouth, where our family are known, and properly respected—— but in such a place as London, it may possibly be as difficult to find out an Ap Evans, as any of those mushroom gentry, whose *table* does not contain above three generations.

Har. My dearest aunt, do not place bars before my only hope; let all our servants be sent out to seek him.

Mrs. Win. Well, child, if it will make you easy, they shall go directly; though I am of opinion it will be but a fruitless inquiry. But the being too easily prevailed upon, is my greatest foible——I wish I had a little of Sir William's obstinacy about me.

Har. Consider, madam, I am on the rack; do not lose time, I beg of you.

Mrs. Win. Well, be composed, I will send them;

I ij

they shall search all the genteel coffee-houses, at the
West End of the town—it is impossible he **should** be
in the **City.**——But do n't let your father know that I
told **you** of the duel: **he** thinks women are never to be
trusted with any thing; and has no more respect for
the Empress-queen, or the Czarina, than I have for a
country justice.   [*Exit Mrs.* Winifred.

Har. How can she be insensible to griefs like mine!

Enter Sir WILLIAM EVANS.

Sir *W.* What, up so early, Harriot! **who has** disturbed your rest?

Har. O, sir! where is that **powerful opiate to** be
found, that can restore it?

Sir *W.* The consciousness of your own heart, and
my forgiveness of your only fault, should set your mind
at peace.

Har. What! while that fault endangers your dear
life, and robs my brother of the best of fathers?—unworthy as I am to call you by that name.

Sir *W.* Her grief almost unmans me. [*Aside.*]——
Why are you agitated thus?

Har. O, do not make my brother hate me too!——
Will he not call me parricide?—or if——

Sir *W.* Who has acquainted you with this affair? I
did not think there was a heart so brutal. But do
not, Harriot, thus alarm yourself—all may yet be
repaired.

Har. Never, sir, never! for here I vow, that should
Lord Eustace arm his hand against your life, no power

Sir *W.* Harriot, the laws of *honour* must be satisfied; and when I was first blest with the fond name of father, *yours* then became my most peculiar care; nor life, nor aught on earth, is half so dear to me.—Nay, Harriot, do not weep, I blame you not; your youth and innocence, have been deceived.

Har. You are too good, too gentle to me, sir; I have deserved all the distress I feel.—Yet hear me, sir—If this must be—might not my brother, sir, dear as he is to me———

Sir *W.* My determination cannot now be alter'd; retire, my child.

Enter ROBERT.

Rob. Captain Lloyd, sir, desires to see your honour.

Sir *W.* Shew him up. [*Exit* Robert.

Har. Oh, sir!

Sir *W.* Leave me, my Harriot, leave me.
[*Embraces her.*

Har. My father! [*Exit* Harriot.

Sir *W.* My heart bleeds for her.

Enter Captain LLOYD.

Capt. I have crouded all the sail I could make, to come up with you, baronet; and now that I am here, I should be glad to know in what soundings we are, and whether we are to steer starboard or port?

Sir *W.* My letter, I believe, captain, must have given you to understand the reason, of my desiring to see you.---At present I am unhappily engaged, in a duel, and the opinion **I** have, both **of** your bravery and friendship, made me look upon you as the properest person of my acquaintance, to be my **second.**

Capt. As to that matter, Sir William, I think **I have** discharged as many broadsides as any gentleman in the navy---though I never yet drew a trigger, out of **the** line; but powder and ball, I suppose, do pretty much the same execution by land as by sea; though standing fair to the windward, is sometimes, of great use to us, baronet.

Sir *W.* It is of little consequence which **way** the wind sits at present, captain.

Capt. I can't **say** much to that, Sir William.---But I wish you had acquainted me with this business a day or two ago, **I** should have liked to have made a little will---But 'tis **no** great matter, neither------For if I should pop over, your daughter's husband will be my heir.

Sir *W.* There is not the least occasion for that precaution, captain, as your life will not be endangered.

Capt. How so? When the ship is once engaged, must not every man aboard her fight? All but the chaplain, and he should be busy, in his way, too.

Sir *W.* In this case, my friend, you need be no farther concerned, than to see that the laws of honour, are not violated.

Capt. Hold, hold, Sir William! this may do for some of your fresh water sparks; but Jerry Llody will never lie to, when the signal 's given for chace--- no lug-sail work for me; I shall come pouring down upon them. But pray, who is your antagonist? And what is the cause of your quarrel? Was it a drunken business?---I was pretty jolly myself, last night, but don't remember that I had words with any one except the waiter.

Sir W. I should be ashamed, captain, were I weak enough to run into one vice, from the consequences of another, or hazard my life this day, for having been guilty of excess last night.

Capt. Well! if that is not the case, I don't know what it is. For think you are not quarrelsome when you are sober,------But have you breakfasted? Though you may have no great appetite, my stomach has been ready for a mess this half hour, I can tell you.

Sir W. We shall find every thing prepared in the next room.

Capt. Let us make to the store-room directly; and while we are laying in our provisions, you may tell me who is your man, and all about it.   [*Exeunt.*

Enter Lord EUSTACE, Colonel EVANS, *and a* Servant.

Lord Eust. Let your master know that I am here.

Col. This is the most romantic affair, my lord, that ever I heard of. To set out determined to stand your enemy's fire without returning it!

Lord Eust. The wrongs I have done him, and his family, should be atoned and not increased, colonel; and were it now within my power, I would not take his life, even to save my own.

Col. There I think you are right, my lord; but I can't say I should carry my politeness so far as to make him a compliment of mine.

Lord *Eust.* There is something much higher than politeness in the question at present—justice, colonel —A man may dispense with the one but not the other.

Col. I am entirely of your opinion; but as your sentiments are so very delicate, and that you really love the girl, why may not I, as your second, step in, and save the explosion of gunpowder, and the lady's character, by preventing the duel?

Lord *Eust.* I will not suffer it.

Col. As you intend to offer her your hand, when this business is over, I don't see why you should run the hazard of losing life or limb; and if the father be a man of honour, as you say he is, I should think——

[*Harriot behind the Scenes.*

Har. I will not be restrained! No, I will rush be-tween their cruel swords!

Enter at the same instant, at opposite doors, Sir WILLIAM *and* HARRIOT.

Har. My brother here! then Heaven has heard my prayer.

Sir *W.* My son!

Col. My father!

Har. Will you not speak to me?

[*To the* Colonel *who turns from her.*

Lord *Eust.* Are you her brother?

Col. Yes, I have that dishonour—Ill fated girl!

Sir *W.* What can this mean? Are you come hither to abet the man, who has disgraced your sister?

Col. My father can't suppose it.

Sir *W.* Retire this moment, then, and take her with you——My lord, I am ready to attend you singly.

Har. You shall not go, for I will cling for ever here.
[*Falls at Sir* William's *feet.*

Lord *Eust.* I cannot bear this sight——Pray hear me, sir.

Sir *W.* Take her away. [*To the* Colonel.] This is no time for expostulation——Come, my lord——
[*To Lord* Eustace.

Col. Nay, then, sir, I must interfere——I cannot suffer you to turn assassin, even for her——Lord Eustace has not charged his pistols, nor does he mean to raise his arm against you——You cannot take his life upon these terms.

Sir *W.* Does he despise me, then?

Har. A little gleam of hope breaks in upon me.
[*Aside.*

Lord *Eust.* Your son can answer that, Sir William.

Col. With truth, my lord, I say you do not——Now, you must answer me. [*To Lord* Eustace.

Lord *Eust.* Your being perfectly acquainted with my intentions towards your sister, before I knew that you were related to her, should, I think, be a sufficient answer to any demand you can possibly have to make.

Col. By no means, my lord; though your tenderness for the weakness you have caused, may incline

you to repair her lost honour, I must and will be
guardian of my own ; and nothing but your meeting
me on fair and equal terms, can heal the wound you
have given it.

Sir W. Now, Harry, you are my son.

Har. Inhuman brother! will nothing but his life
content your rage? Let me die for him.

Lord Eust. My angel Harriot!—**But** since it must
be so, I am ready, colonel!   [*Aside.*

Col. I hope your lordship thinks **I stand** acquitted
of **my** obligations to you, by preventing your engaging, on such unequal terms, for that unworthy girl.

Lord Eust. You wrong her much ; it is I alone am
guilty.

Sir W. It is true, my son ; Harriot is innocent.

Col. If that be true, I have a double right to vengeance.

Lord Eust. You have a right to choose your reparation, sir, and I attend you.

Har. When shall my miseries end!

As Lord Eustace *and Colonel* Evans *are going off, enter*
Mr. **Frampton.**

Fram. I hope, this moment, madam.

Sir W. What can this mean?

Lord Eust. Frampton!

Fram. I have no sort of business with your lordship, my commission **is** directed to Sir William Evans,
and Lady Eustace.

Har. Do not insult me, sir ; I am not Lady Eustace.

Fram. That is a point, I think, that will not admit of being contested.

Col. You are mistaken, sir—but this is trifling.

Lord *Eust.* I am on the rack—explain yourself, my friend.

Fram. You must give me leave to speak, then—— When I saw the distress and anxiety of your mind, I was fully satisfied of your honourable intentions towards this lady, from the letter you intrusted me with, which yet remains unopened.—I determined, if possible, to preserve both your life and honour, for her sake, by preventing your duel with her father, and your marriage with Lady Anne Mountfort.

Col. The first event, sir, has been prevented, without your assistance, and I will venture to promise, that the second shall never take place.

Fram. I am quite of your opinion, sir. As I came this moment from Lord Delville, to acknowledge this fair lady as his son's wife—but this letter, Sir William, will more fully explain his lordship's sentiments.

Lord *Eust.* My generous friend! my guardian angel!

Fram. My lord, I neither desire nor deserve your thanks.—If I have been in any way serviceable to you, attribute it to my real attachment, to your truly amiable wife.

Col. I do not understand all this.

Enter Mrs. WINIFRED.

Mrs. *Win.* 'T is as I guess'd exactly.—All smoke, and no fire.——My nephew, here! Then something

Sir W. Lord Delville has behaved like a man of honour; but yet I must **inform you,** sir, that **the generosity** of his conduct cannot efface the baseness of his son—My daughter shall **never** be his wife—He has disgraced **her.** ·   [*To* Frampton.

Lord *Eust.* **Never, sir! Here** is my witness—this letter, which I now entreat my **Harriot to peruse,** will fully prove, that had I fallen by **your** hand, her honour would have been preserved.

Har. I will not read it.

Mrs. *Win.* I think that was behaving **like a** man of quality.

Fram. Let me entreat **you,** Sir William, **to** look it over, as I **can with** truth **and** honour, attest **the** sincerity of the **writer.**

Col. There need no **farther vouchers.** Let Harriot now determine for **herself.**

Har. The struggle is **too** great.——I cannot speak —Leave me, my lord——

Lord *Eust.* Never, whilst I have life, will I forsake you.

Har. It cannot be, my lord—Though I have the highest sense of gratitude, for Lord Delville's goodness to me, and though I believe you perfectly sincere in what you say at present; yet the humiliating situation, into which you **have** plunged me, the distress **you have** brought upon my family, your attachment to another lady——

Lord *Eust.* With shame I must confess my trifling with a lady, whom I could not have loved, even had

Col. I think I may venture to assure your lordship, that Lady **Anne** Mountfort will be very ready to forgive your want of passion for her, as her partiality for me might, perhaps, have been the cause of her blindness to your superior merits.

Lord *Eust.* I congratulate your good fortune, colonel; and am indebted to your generosity, for removing every shadow of difficulty on Lady Anne's account.

Mrs. *Win.* Nephew, I wish you joy—There will be one woman of quality, at least, in the family.

Har. Weak as I am, my lord, you cannot shake my resolution.

Lord *Eust.* I have no hope but in your interposition, sir : you are her father, and have been most offended ; yet you, perhaps, have the goodness to forgive !

[*To Sir* William.

Sir *W.* Aye, and give too, my lord ; the man who sincerely repents of error, is farther removed from vice, than one who has never been guilty—This letter is a sufficient and convincing proof of your contrition. Take her ; she is, and shall be yours.

Lord *Eust.* My wife! [*Embracing her.*

Har. The commands of a father must not be resisted.—O! my lord, how different are my present sensations from those I sustained, when I ventured to bestow this hand without his sanction!——But take it ; it is yours for ever now.

Lord *Eust.* Then every wish of my fond heart is accomplished.

Col. Joy to your lordship, and my dearest Harriot !

Fram. I sincerely wish your ladyship all the happiness which I well know you have deserved.

Lord *Eust.* And you, my friend, shall share it with us, who have steered my course to this blest harbour, through all the shoals and quick-sands of my folly.— You shall be happy too, if ought within my fortune or my power can render it so.

Fram. Continue to deserve your present bliss, my lord, and I am over-paid.

Mrs. *Win.* I think I have a right to partake in your ladyship's felicity, from the principal share I have had in bringing this event to pass. I hope that Lord Delville has been properly informed——

Enter Captain LLOYD.

——That man is my perpetual torment.

Capt. Why, hey day, Sir William! what wind's a blowing now? You seem to have cast anchor, when I thought you were puting out to sea.——Here is the whole crew assembled; Miss Winifred and all.—Do **women** fight duels? If I had them on board the Dreadnought, I 'd clap them all under hatches before she engaged.——But come along, baronet, you don't mean to slack sail now, I hope——I thought by this time we should have made a few eyelet holes, in the enemy's rigging.

Sir *W.* I hope, my good friend, you will excuse my seeming inattention to your impatient bravery, when I tell you that our contest has ended happily, and that you may now wish all this company, as well as Lord

Capt. He is to be married, then, it seems————I
hope, madam, you'll believe me another time.

[*To Mrs.* Winifred.

Mrs. Win. Yes, when you tell truth, captain—But
at present you happen to be a little out in your soundings, for the ship's name is not the Lady Anne, but
the Lovely Harriot———the country girl you talked of.

Capt. Well, well, all's one to me.—So she is bound
for the port of matrimony, I am content—and so I
wish your lordship, your ladyship, and all your ships,
a prosperous voyage to the island of happiness.

Sir William

They promise fair to reach that wish'd for port :
For virtue, though of winds and waves the sport,
By passions shaken, and by dangers crost,
On life's great sea, is never wholly lost.
Some power divine conducts her swelling sails,
And of her due reward she seldom fails.

EPILOGUE.

Written by the Author of the Prologue,

And spoken by Mrs. CLIVE.

I LONG *to know, dread sirs, with due submission,*
How you approve me as a politician ?
The thought was mine.—I told the scrib'ling dame,
This part of Winifred, *is much too tame :*
Ask but the town, said I, they 'll all agree,
That a tame character will not suit me :
I hate such lifeless, water-gruel stuff ;
Quicken her well with politics and snuff :
Small quantities of both will be but teizing ;
Give them enough, and set the town a sneezing.
Her scribbling vanity at this was stung ;
Would have disputed—Hold, says I, **you 're** *wrong,*
Do n't be so rash, to draw on me *your tongue ;*
I have a weapon, should I take the field,
A better never did a woman wield ;
You 'll find, when once my passion is afloat,
The soul of Cæsar, *in a petticoat !*
' *Aye, but,' says she ' in politics there 's danger,*
' *To courts, and state affairs, I 'm quite a stranger.'*
So much the better, thou most simple woman,

When you mistake, the town will think you clever,
Think that you mean great folks, and clap for ever;
Old England, like a boy, loves wicked fun,
Abuse your betters, and your work is done.
Small game the English spirit will not follow,
'Tis at the nobler chace you whoop and hollow!
O'er hedge and ditch you helter-skelter fly;
Start but a statesman—Yoax! the hounds full cry!
To pick up lesser game you will not stay,
While the fox runs, the hare may steal away:
Our auth'ress is the hare—who trembling sits,
'Till she escapes this dreadful pack of wits:
She hopes you will not hunt her, she's so small,
But hark to mercy as the noblest call.

EPILOGUE.

Written by HENRY JAMES PYE, Esq.

WELL! after much perplexity and rout,
At length the wish'd-for wedding's brought about.
A foolish girl! so near to throw away
Love, rank, and reputation, in a day.
And all for what? from prejudice, in truth,
Though christened delicacy, now, forsooth.
If (sentimental nonsense thrown aside)
*To **cards** and politics she had applied,*
For common cares, her soul had been too great,
*And only felt **an** ardor for the state ;*
Had glow'd alone with freedom's glorious flame,
And next to PAM's *had honour'd* PAOLI's **name.**

Twice in our annals, baffled France and Spain
Have wept the glories of a female reign :
With great success I think we now might try
The influence of a female ministry.
*In private life how well we 're used **to** sway,*
More husbands know, than you 'll persuade to say ;
*And **bow** finances properly **to** rule,*
All ladies learn, who ever kept a pool.
*Ye generous spirits, **who** approve my plan,*
And wish at least an equal sway with man,

(And some malicious wits so bold we find,
To say this comprehends all woman-kind)
In favour of a female bard, to-night,
Boldly assert a Briton's dearest right;
From man, from haughty man's tyrannic laws,
To your decision she submits her cause;
Rests on your candor, all her hopes and fears,
And only claims—a Trial by her Peers.

THE END.

THE

BROTHERS.

A

TRAGEDY.

By DR. EDWARD YOUNG.

ADAPTED FOR

THEATRICAL REPRESENTATION,

AS PERFORMED AT THE

THEATRE-ROYAL, DRURY-LANE.

REGULATED FROM THE PROMPT-BOOK,

By Permission of the Manager.

LONDON:

PRINTED FOR, AND UNDER THE DIRECTION OF,
GEORGE CAWTHORN, BRITISH LIBRARY, STRAND.

1797.

Dr. Edward Young, the son of Dr. Edward Young, dean of Sarum, was born at Upham, near Winchester, in June, 1681. He was placed on the foundation at Winchester College, where he remained until the election after his eighteenth birth-day; when not being chosen to New College, he, on the 13th of October, 1703, was entered an independant member of that society, and, that he might be at little expence, resided at the lodgings of the warden, who had been a particular friend of his father. In a few months, the death of his benefactor occasioned him to remove to Corpus, the president of which college invited him there for the same reasons as the warden of New College had before done. In 1708, he was nominated to a law-fellowship at All-Souls, by archbishop Tennison. On the 23d of April, 1714, he took the degree of bachelor of civil law; and his doctor's degree, on the 10th of June, 1719.

Two years after he had taken his first degre, he was appointed to speak the Latin Oration, which was delivered on laying the foundation of the Codrington Library. In 1719, he was received in the Earl of Exeter's family, as tutor to Lord Burleigh, with whom he was to travel, and might have secured an annuity of 100l. per annum, had he continued in that situation; but having been admitted to an intimacy with the witty Duke of Wharton, he directly attached himself to that nobleman, with whom he visited Ireland, and under whose auspices he became a candidate for the borough of Cirencester, in which attempt he was unsuccessful.

On the death of the Duke, Dr. Young took orders; and in April, 1728, was appointed Chaplain to George the Second. In July, 1730, he was presented by his College to the rectory of Welwyn, in Hertfordshire; and in April, 1732, married Lady Elizabeth Lee, daughter of the Earl of Litchfield, and widow of Colonel Lee. This lady died in the year 1740, and her death was soon afterwards followed by that of her daughter, an amiable young lady, whose husband, Mr. Temple, son of Lord Palmerston, did not long survive her. The loss of these three persons, for some time, threw a gloom over Dr. Young's mind, and gave birth to the *Night Thoughts*, a work by which it certainly was the author's wish to be distinguished, and by which his reputation has been established throughout his own and the neighbouring kingdoms. From this time he lived in his retreat at Welwyn, without receiving any addition to his preferment.

In 1761, at the age of fourscore, he was appointed Clerk of the Closet to the Princess-Dowager of Wales, and died in April, 1765.

He left the bulk of his fortune, which was considerable, to his only son, whom he had long excluded both from his roof and his protection. What offence occasioned this suspension of parental tenderness, we are not enabled to determine. Yet during his last confinement, even when the expectation of life had forsaken him, he continued strenuous in refusing to see his child, who repeatedly, but vainly, wished for his parting benediction.

Of the private habits of **Dr. Young** very few particulars are known. Singularity is said to have predominated in his most juvenile practices. The late Dr. Ridley remembered a report current at Oxford, that when he was composing, he would shut up his windows, and sit by **a lamp** even at mid-day; nay, that sculls, **bones, and** instruments of death were among the ornaments of his study. He rose betimes, and obliged his domestics to join with him in the duties of morning prayer. He read but little. While his health permitted him to walk **abroad,** he preferred a solitary ramble in his church-yard to exercise with a companion on a more cheerful spot. He was moderate in his meals, and rarely drank wine, except when he was ill, being (as he said) unwilling to waste the succours of sickness **on** the stability of health. After a slight refreshment he retired to bed at eight in the evening, although **he** might have guests in his house, who wished to prolong his stay **among** them to a later hour. He lived at a moderate expence, rather inclining to parsimony than profusion.

The remains of Dr. Young were deposited in his own church, with a plain Latin inscription over him.

We have now to give some account of the literary productions of this favourite of the Muses.

In 1704, he produced his celebrated Poem on the Last Day, which, as being the pious, as well as masterly composition of a young obscure layman, became presently a popular and generally-admired performance.

Soon after this he wrote the poem, entitled—The Force of Religion: or, Vanquish'd Love; which was likewise received with very flattering marks of distinction. Such was **the** success of **both** these juvenile performances, at a period when the noblest effusions of genius were daily issuing from the press—when, in fact, the literature of England seemed to have reached the zenith of its glory, that several of the first characters in the kingdom not only loaded him with applause, but actually courted his confidence and friendship.

Of all our Author's poetical performances, **the** Satires, entitled Love of Fame, the Universal Passion, have been generally considered as the most correct and finished, though written at an early period of life. By certain fastidious critics they have been stigmatized as a mere string of epigrams.

In 1719 our Author made his first appearance in the train of Melpomene; and though Busiris, his first effort in the line of tragedy, afforded but little pleasure in the representation, and is indeed frequently tinctured with the false sublime, yet, coolly examined in the closet, a reader of taste will discover in it a number of admirable lines of elevated sentiments.

His next, and confessedly the best of his tragic

compositions, (since it still continues a stock play at the theatres) was the Revenge. For the idea of this play, whih appears, from the Annals of the Drama, to have been acted in the same year with Busiris, our Poet is evidently indebted partly to the Othello of Shakspere, and partly to the Abdalazar of Mrs. Behn; on both which pieces he has indeed made many skilful improvements.

His last was the Brothers, a play written upon the plan of a French piece of great merit. The emoluments arising from the exhibition of this piece were generously allotted by the Author to the purposes of public charity.

Having followed Dr. Young through his dramatic career, let us now consider him as the moral and plaintive, the pious but gloomy, Author of the Night Thoughts; a work composed in a style so strictly peculiar to himself, that of the many efforts which have been made to imitate it, none have proved in any degree successful. Than the Night-Thoughts never was any poem received with applause more general or unbounded. " The unhappy bard, whose grief in melting numbers flows, and melancholy joys diffuse around," has been sung by the profane as well as the pious. These were written under the recent, the overwhelming pressure of sorrow for the death of his wife, and of his daughter and son in law: the former of whom, though distinguished by no name, he often pathetically alludes to; while the two latter he beautifully characterizes under the poetical appellations of Narcissa and Philander.

This sublime performance is addressed to Lorenzo, an infidel man of pleasure and dissipation ; in a word, a mere man of the world. By Lorenzo, if general report says true, we are to understand his own son, who, borne away by the passions **too** often fatal to youth, is well-known to have long laboured under the heavy punishment of a father's just displeasure. Whatever there may be in this, every page of the poem abounds with the noblest flights of fancy—flights which, especially in his description of Death, in the act of noting down, from his secret stand, the exercises of a Bacchanalian society ; in his epitaph on the departed World ; in the issuing of Satan from his dungeon on the day of judgment, and a few others, might tempt a reader of warm imagination to suppose the poet under the immediate inspiration of the Divinity.

Uniformly a friend to virtue, and an indefatigable assertor of the dignity of human nature against all the cavils, not of the rude multitude only, but of many well-disposed, tho' mistaken and discontented moralists, in 1754, under the patronage of Queen Caroline, our Author published his Estimate of Human Life ; a valuable tract, which, while it exhibits a striking picture of the writer's pious benevolence and charity, evinces him to **have** been alike qualified to shine in prose and verse.

This was followed by his Centaur not Fabulous, another of his prose pieces. When turned of eighty, our Author published (in the form of a letter addressed to his friend, (the celebrated editor of Sir Charles Grandison) his Conjectures on Original Composition; a performance which (it is more than conjecture to add) will for ever remain a singular monument, that even at that age of general imbecility and dotage, the intellectual powers of Dr. Young had apparently lost nothing of their wonted vigour.

PROLOGUE.

WRITTEN BY MR. DODSLEY.

THE tragic muse, revolving many a page
Of Time's long records, drawn from every age,
Forms not her plans on low or trivial deeds,
But marks the striking!—When some hero bleeds,
To save his country, then her powers inspire,
And souls congenial catch the patriot fire.
When bold Oppression grinds a suffering land;
When the keen dagger gleams in Murder's hand;
When black Conspiracy infects the throng;
Or fell Revenge sits brooding o'er his wrong;
Then walks she forth in terror; at her frown
Guilt shrinks appall'd, tho' seated on a throne.
But the rack'd soul when dark suspicions rend,
When brothers hate, and sons with sires contend;
When clashing interests war eternal wage;
And love, the tenderest passion, turns to rage;
Then grief on every visage stands imprest,
And pity throbs in every feeling breast;
Hope, fear, and indignation rise by turns,
And the strong scene with various passion burns.
Such is our tale.——Nor blush if tears should flow:
They're Virtue's tribute paid to human woe.
Such drops new lustre to bright eyes impart;
The silent witness of a tender heart:
Such drops adorn the noblest hero's cheek,

And paint his worth in strokes that more than speak :
Not he who cannot weep, but he who can,
Shews the great soul, and proves himself a man.
  Yet do not idly grieve at others' pain,
Nor let the tears of Nature fall in vain :
Watch the close crimes from whence their ills have grown,
And from their frailties learn to mend your own.

Dramatis Personae.

Men.

PHILIP, King of Macedon, - - - - Mr. BARRY.

PERSEUS, his elder Son, - - - - - Mr. MOSSOP.

DEMETRIUS, his younger Son, - - - Mr. GARRICK.

PERICLES, the Friend of Perseus, - - **Mr. BLAKES.**

ANTIGONUS, a Minister of State, - - Mr. BURTON.

DYMAS, the King's Favourite, - - - Mr. SIMSON.

POSTHUMIUS, } Roman Ambassadors, { Mr. WINSTONE.
CURTIUS, } { Mr. MOZEEN.

Women.

ERIXENE, the Thracian Princess, - - Mrs. BELLAMY.

Her Attendant, - - - - - - - MissHIPPISLEY.

THE BROTHERS.

ACT I. SCENE I.

Enter CURTIUS *and* POSTHUMIUS.

Curtius.

THERE'S something of magnificence about us
I have not seen at Rome. But you can tell me.

[*Gazes round.*

Post. True: hither sent on former embassies,
I know this splendid court of Macedon,
And haughty Philip, well.

Cur. His pride presumes
To treat us here like subjects more than Romans,
More than ambassadors, who, in our bosoms,
Bear peace and war, and throw him which we please,
As Jove his storm, or sunshine, on his creatures.

Post. This Philip only, since Rome's glory rose,
Preserves its grandeur to the name of King;
Like a bold star, that shews its fires by day.
The Greek, who won the world, was sent before him,
As the grey dawn before the blaze of noon:.

B

Philip **had** ne'er been conquered, but by Rome;
And what can fame say more of mortal man?

    Cur. I know his public character.

    Post. It pains me
To turn my thought on his domestic state.
There Philip is no God; but pours **his** heart,
In ceaseless groans, o'er his contending sons;
And pays the secret tax of mighty men
To their mortality.

    Cur. But whence this strife,
Which thus afflicts him?

    Post. From this Philip's bed
Two Alexanders spring.

    Cur. And but one world?
'Twill never do.

    Post. They both are bright; but one
Benignly bright, as stars to mariners;
And one a comet, with malignant blaze,
Denouncing ruin.

    Cur. You mean Perseus.

    Post. True.
The younger son, Demetrius, you well know,
Was bred at Rome, our hostage from his father.
Soon after, he was sent ambassador,
When Philip fear'd the thunder of our arms.
Rome's manners won him, and his manners Rome;
Who granted peace, declaring she forgave,
To his high worth, the conduct of his father.
This gave him all the hearts of Macedon;
Which, join'd to his high patronage from Rome,

Inflames his jealous brother.

 Cur. Glows there not

A second brand of enmity?

 Post. O yes;

The fair Erixene.

 Cur. I've partly heard

Her smother'd story.

 Post. Smother'd by the King;

And wisely too: but thou shalt hear it all.

Not seas of adamant, not mountains whelm'd

On guilty secrets, can exclude the day.

Long burnt a fix'd hereditary hate

Between the crowns of Macedon and Thrace;

The sword by both too much indulg'd in blood.

Philip, at length, prevail'd ; he took, by night,

The town and palace of his deadly foe ;

Rush'd thro' the flames, which he had kindled round,

And slew him, bold in vain : nor rested there ;

But, with unkingly cruelty, destroy'd

Two little sons within their mother's arms ;

Thus meaning to tread out those sparks of war,

Which might one day flame up to strong revenge.

The Queen, through grief, on her dead sons expir'd.

One child alone surviv'd ; a female infant,

Amidst these horrors, in the cradle smil'd.

 Cur. What of that infant?

 Post. Stung with sharp remorse,

The victor took, and gave her to his Queen.

The child was bred, and honour'd as her own ;

She grew, she bloom'd ; and now her eyes repay

Her brother wounds, on Philip's rival sons.

   Cur. Is then Erixene that Thracian child?
How just the Gods! from out that ruin'd house
He took a brand, to set his own on fire.

   Post. To give thee, friend, the whole in miniature;
This is the picture of great Philip's court:
The proud, but melancholy King, on high,
Majestic sits, like Jove, enthron'd in darkness;
His sons are as the thunder in his hand;
And the fair Thracian princess is a star,
That sparkles by, and gilds the solemn scene.

[Shouts heard.

'Tis their great day, supreme of all their year,
The fam'd lustration of their martial powers;
Thence, for our audience, chosen by the King.
If he provokes a war, his empire shakes,
And all her lofty glories nod to ruin.

   Cur. Who comes?

   Post. O, that's the jealous elder brother;
Irregular in manners, as in form.
Observe the fire, high birth, and empire, kindle!

   Cur. He holds his conference with much emotion.

   Post. The brothers both can talk, **and,** in their turn,
Have borne away the prize of eloquence
At Athens. Shun his walk: our own debate
Is now at hand. We'll seek his lion sire,
Who dares to frown on us, his conquerors;
And carries so much monarch on his brow,
As if he'd fright us with the wounds we gave him.

[Exeunt.

Enter PERSEUS *and* PERICLES.

Per. 'Tis empire! empire! empire! let that word
Make sacred all I do, or can attempt!
Had I been born a slave, I should affect it;
My nature's fiery, and, of course, aspires.
Who gives an empire, by the gift defeats
All end of giving; and procures contempt
Instead of gratitude.   An empire lost,
Destroy'd, would less confound me, than resign'd.

Peri. But are you sure Demetrius will attempt?

Per. Why does Rome court him? For his virtues? No.
To fire him to dominion; to blow up
A civil war; then to support him in it:
He gains the name of King, and Rome the power.

Peri. This is indeed the common art of Rome!

Per. That soure of justice thro' the wond'ring world?
His youth and valour second Rome's designs:
The first impels him to presumptuous hope;
The last supports him in it.   Then his person!
Thy hand, O Nature, has made bold with mine
Yet more! what words distil from his red lip,
To gull the multitude! and they make Kings.
Ten thousand fools, knaves, cowards, lump'd together,
Become all wise, all righteous, and almighty.
Nor is this all: the foolish Thracian maid
Prefers the boy to me.

Peri. And does that pain you?

Per. O Pericles, to death! It is most true,
Through hate to him, and not through love for her,

I paid my first addresses; but became
The fool I feign'd: my sighs are now sincere.
It smarts; it burns: O that 'twere fiction still!
By Heaven, she seems more beauteous than dominion!

  Peri. Dominion, and the princess, both are lost,
Unless **you** gain the King.

  Per. But how to gain him?
Old men love novelties; **the last arriv'd**
Still pleases best; the youngest steals their smiles.

  Peri. Dymas alone can work him to **his** pleasure;
First in esteem, and keeper of his heart.

  Per. To Dymas thou; and win him to thy will.
In the mean time, I'll seek my double rival;
Curb his presumption, and **erect** myself,
In all the dignity of birth, before him.
Whate'er can stir the blood, or sway the mind,
Is now at stake; and double is the loss,
When an inferior bears away the prize.

  Peri. Your brother, dress'd for the solemnity!

  Per. To Dymas fly! gain him, and think on this:
A prince indebted, is a fortune made. [*Exit* Pericles.

Enter DEMETRIUS.

  Dem. How brother! unattir'd! Have you forgot
What pomps are due to this illustrious day?

  Per. I am no gew-gaw for the throne to gaze at:
Some are design'd by nature but for shew;
The tinsel and the feather of mankind.

  Dem. Brother, of that no more: for shame, gird on
Your glitt'ring arms, and look like any Roman.

Per. No, brother, let the Romans look like me,
If they're ambitious.   But, I pr'ythee, stand;
Let me gaze on thee :—No inglorious figure!
More Romano, as it ought to be.
But what is this that dazzles my weak sight?
There's sunshine in thy beaver.

 Dem. 'Tis that helmet
Which Alexander wore at Granicus.

 Per. When he subdu'd the world? Ha! is't not so?
What world hast thou subdu'd? O yes, the fair!
Think'st thou there could in Macedon be found
No brow might suit that golden blaze but thine?

 Dem. I wore it but to grace this sacred day:
Jar not for trifles.

 Per. Nothing is a trifle
That argues the presumption of the soul.

 Dem. 'Tis they presume who know not to deserve.

 Per. Or who, deserving, scorn superior merit.

 Dem. Who combats with a brother, wounds himself:
Wave private wrath, and rush upon the foes
Of Macedonia.

 Per. No; I would not wound
Demetrius' friends!

 Dem. Demetrius' friends!

 Per. The Romans.
You copy Hannibal, our great ally:
Say, at what altar was you sworn their foe?
Peace-making brother! Wherefore bring you peace,
But to prevent my glory from the field?
The peace you bring, was meant as war to me.

Dem. Perseus, be bold when danger's all your **own**:
War now, were war with Philip more than Rome.

Per. Come, you love peace; that fair cheek hates a
You that admire the Romans, break the bridge [scar.
With Cocles, or with Curtius leap the gulph;
And league not with the vices of our foes.

Dem. What vices?

Per. With their **women** and their wits.
Your idol Lælius, Lælius the polite.
I hear, Sir, you take wing, and mount in metre.
Terence has own'd your aid, your comrade Terence.
God-like ambition! Terence there, the slave!

Dem. At Athens bred, and to the arts a foe? -

Per. At Athens bred, **and** borrow arts from Rome?

Dem. Brother, I've done: let our contention cease:
Our mother shudders at it in her grave.
And how has Philip mourn'd? a dreadful foe,
And awful King; but O the tend'rest parent
That ever wept in fondness o'er a child!

Per. Why, ay, go tell your father; fondly throw
Your arms around him; stroke him to your purpose,
As you are wont: **I** boast not so much worth;
I **am** no picture, by the doating eye
To be survey'd, and hung about his neck.
I fight his battles; that's all I can do.
But **if** you boast a piety sincere;
One way you may secure your father's peace;
And one alone—resign Erixene.

Dem. You flatter me, to think her in my power.
We run our fates together; you deserve,

And she can judge ; proceed we then like friends,
And he who gains her heart, and gains it fairly,
Let him enjoy his gen'rous rival's too.

   Per. Smooth-speaking, unsincere, insulting boy!
Is then my crown usurp'd but half thy crime ?
Desist; or by the Gods that smile on blood!
Not thy fine form, nor yet thy boasted peace,
Nor patronizing Rome, nor Philip's tears,
Nor Alexander's helmet ; no, nor more,
His radiant form, should it alight in thunder,
And spread its new divinity between us,
Should save a brother from a brother's fury.   [*Exit.*

   Dem. How's this? the waves ne'er ran thus high
Resign thee! yes, Erixene, with life.   [before,
Thou in whose eyes, so modest, and so bright,
Love ever wakes, and keeps a vestal fire.
Ne'er shall I wean my fond, fond heart from thee!
But Perseus warns me to rouse all my powers.
As yet I float in dark uncertainty ;
For tho' she smiles, I sound not her designs ;
I'll fly, fall, tremble, weep upon her feet ;
And learn (O all ye Gods !) my final doom !
My father ! ha! and on his brow deep thought
And pale concern ! Kind heav'n assuage his sorrows,
Which strike a damp thro' all my flames of love! [*Ex.*

Enter KING *and* ANTIGONUS.

   ' *King.* Kings of their envy cheat a foolish world :
' Fate gives us all in spite, that we alone
Might have the pain of knowing all is nothing.

' The seeming means of bliss but heighten woe,

' When impotent to make their promise good :

' Hence, kings, at least, bid fairest to be wretched.'

Ant. True, sir; 'tis empty, or tormenting, all ;

The days of life are sisters ; all alike:

None just the same ; which serves to fool us on

Through blasted hopes, with change of fallacy :

While **joy** is like to-morrow, still to come ;

Nor **ends** the fruitless chace but in the grave.

King. Ay, there, Antigonus, this pain will cease,

' Which meets me at my banquet ; haunts my pillow;

' Nor, by the din of arms, is frighted from me.'

Conscience, what art thou ? thou tremendous power !

Who dost inhabit us without our leave ;

And art, within ourselves, another self,

A master self, that loves to domineer

And treat the monarch frankly as **the slave.**

How dost thou light a torch **to** distant deeds !

Make the past, present ; and the future frown !

How, ever and anon, awake the soul,

As with a peal of thunder, to strange horrors,

In this long restless dream, which idiots hug,

Nay, wise men flatter with the name of life !

Ant. You think too much.

King. I do not think at all :

The **Gods** impose, the Gods inflict, my thoughts,

And paint my dreams with images of dread.

Last night, in sleep, I saw the Thracian Queen

And her two murder'd sons.   She frown'd upon me,

And pointed at their wounds. How throbb'd my heart!

How shook my couch! and when the morning came,
The formidable picture still subsisted,
And slowly vanish'd from my waking eye.
I fear some heavy vengeance hangs in air,
And **conscious** deities infuse these thoughts,
To **warn my soul of** her approaching doom.
The Gods are rigid when they weigh such deeds
As speak a ruthless heart; they measure blood
By drops; and bate not one in the repay.
Could infants hurt me? 'Twas not like a King.

Ant. My Lord, I **do** confess the Gods are with us;
Stand at **our side in ev'ry act of life**;
And on **our** pillow watch each secret thought;
Nay, **see** it in its embryo, yet unborn.
But **their** wrath ceases on remorse for guilt;
And well **I** know your sorrows touch your sons;
Nor is **it** possible but time must quench
Their flaming spirits in a father's tears.

King. Vain comfort! I this moment overheard
My jarring sons with fury shake my walls.
Ah! why my curse from those **who** ought to bless me?
The Queen of Thrace **can answer** that **sad** question.
She had two sons; but two: and **so** have I.
Misfortune stands with **her** bow ever bent
Over the world; **and he who** wounds another,
Directs the Goddess, **by** that part he wounds,
Where **to strike deep** her arrows in himself.

Ant. I own, **I think** it time your sons receive
A father's awful counsel; or, while here,
Now weary nature **calls** for kind repose,

Your curtains will be shaken with their broils :
And, when you die, sons' blood may stain your tomb.
But **other** cares demand you now :—the Romans.

    King. O change of pain! the Romans? Perish Rome!
Thrice happy they who sleep in humble life,
Beneath the storm ambition blows. 'Tis meet
The great should have the fame of happiness,
The consolation of a little envy ;
'Tis all their pay, for those superior cares,
Those pangs of heart, their vassals ne'er can feel.
Where are these strangers? First I'll hear their tale ;
Then talk in private **with my** sons.

    Ant. But how
Intends my Lord to make his **peace** with Rome?

    King. Rome calls me fiery : **let her find** me so.

    Ant. O, Sir, forbear! Too late you felt Rome's power.

    King. Yes, and that reason stings me more than ever,
To curse, and hate, and hazard all against her.

    Ant. Hate her too much to give her battle now ;
Nor **to** your god-like valour owe your ruin.
Greece, Thessaly, Illyrium, Rome has seiz'd ;
Your treasures wasted, and your phalanx thinn'd :
Should she proceed, and strike at Macedon,
What would be left of empire?

    King. Philip : all.
I'll take my throne. Send in these foreigners.

[*The Scene draws, and discovers* **a** *magnificent* Throne,
PERSEUS, DEMETRIUS, Courtiers, &c. *attending.*
POSTHUMIUS *and* CURTIUS, *the Roman* Ambassa-
dors, *enter.* Trumpets *sound.* The King *ascends the*
Throne.]

Post. Philip of Macedon, to those complaints,
Our friends groan out, and you have heard at large,
Rome now expects an answer. She sits judge,
And will have right on earth.

 King. Expects an answer!
I so shall answer as becomes a King.

 Post. **Or** more, Sir; as becomes a friend of Rome.

 King. **Or** Alexander's heir, to rise still higher.
But to the purpose. Thus a King to those
That would make Kings, and puff them out at pleasure:
Has Philip done amiss? 'Twas you provok'd him.
My cities, which deserted in my wars,
I thought it meet to punish: you deny'd me.
When I had shook the walls of **Marena,**
You pluck'd me thence, and took the taken town.
Then you sent word I should retire from Greece—
A conquest at my door, by nature mine—
And said, "Here end thy realm;" as ye were Gods!
And Gods ye shall be, ere Rome humbles me.
All this is done; yet Philip is your friend!
If this buys friendship, where can ye find foes?
In what regard will stern Rome look **upon** me?
If as a friend, too precious let her **hold**

    c

Her own esteem, to cast a stain on mine:
If as an enemy, let her proceed,
And do as she has done; she needs no more.

  Post. The Romans do no wrong; yet still are men:
And if to-day an error thwarts their purpose,
To-morrow **sets it right.** If Philip loves
Dominion, and the pride that waits on Kings,
(Of which, perhaps, his words too strongly savour)
Humility to Róme will lead him to it.
She can give more than common Kings can **govern.**

  King. Than common Kings? Ambassador! re-
    member
Cannæ—where first my sword was flush'd with blood.

  Dem. My Lord, forbear.   [*Aside to the* King.

  King. And Hannibal still lives.

  Post. Because he fled at Capua.

  King. There, indeed,
I was not with him.

  Post. Therefore he fled alone.——
Since thus you treat us, hear another charge.
Why here detain you, prisoner of your power,
His daughter, who was once Rome's good ally,
The King of Thrace? Why is she not restor'd?
For our next meeting you'll provide an answer.
What now has past, for his sake, we forgive.

              [*Pointing to* Demetrius.
But mark this well: there lies some little distance,
Philip, between a Roman and King. [*Exeunt Romans.*

  King. How say'st, unscepter'd boaster? This to me!

With Hannibal I cleft yon Alpine rocks;
With Hannibal choak'd Thrasymene with slaughter:
But, O the night of Cannæ's raging field!
When half the Roman senate lay in blood
Without our tent, and groan'd as we carous'd!
Immortal Gods! **for** such another hour!
Then throw my carcase to the dogs of Rome.

　　Ant. Sir, you forget your sons.

　　King. Let all withdraw.

　　　　　　　　[*Exeunt all but the* King *and his Sons.*

Two passions only take up all my soul;
Hatred to Rome, and tenderness for them.
Draw near, my sons, and listen to my age.
By what has past, you see the state of things.
Foreign alliance must a King secure;
And insolence sustain to serve his power.
And if **alliances** with Rome are needful,
Much more among ourselves. If I must bear,
Unmov'd, an insult from a stranger's brow,
Shall **not a** brother bear a brother's look
Without impatience? Whither all this tends,
I'm sorry that your conscious hearts can tell you:
Is it not most severe? Two sons alone
Have crown'd my bed; and they two are not brothers.
Look here, and, from my kind regards to you,
Copy such looks as you should bear each other.
Why **do** I sigh? Do you not know, my sons?
And if **you** do—O let me sigh no more!
Let these white hairs put in a claim to peace!

　　Per. Henceforth, my sole contention with my brother

Is this; which best obeys our father's will.

Dem. Father, if simple nature ever speaks
In her own language, scorning useless words,
You see her now; she swells into my eyes,
I take thee to my heart: I fold thee in it.

                        [*Embracing* Perseus,

Our father bids; and that we drank one milk,
Is now the smallest motive **of my love.**

King. Antigonus, the **joy their mother felt,**
When they were born, was faint to what **I feel.**

Dem. See, brother, if he does not weep! **His love**
Runs o'er in venerable tears. I'm rude;
But Nature will prevail—My king! My father!

Per. Now cannot I let fall **a** single tear.   [*Aside,*

King. **See!** the good man **has** caught it too.

Ant. Such tears,
And such alone, be shed in Macedonia!

King. Be not thou, Perseus, **jealous of thy** brother;
Nor thou, Demetrius, prone to give him cause;
Nor either think of empire till I'm dead.
You need not; you reign now; my heart **is your's.**
Sheath your resentments in your father's peace;
Come **to** my bosom both, and swear it there.

                     [*Embracing his Sons,*

Ant. Look down, ye Gods, and change me, if you can,
This sight for one more lovely! What so sweet,
So beautiful, on earth, and, ah! so rare,
As kindred love, and family repose?
This, this alliance, Rome, will quite undo thee.
See this, proud Eastern monarchs, and look pale!

Armies are routed, realms o'er-run by this.

King. Or if leagu'd worlds superior forces bring,
I'd rather die a father than a king.
Fathers alone a father's heart can know ;
What **secret** tides of still enjoyment flow,
When brothers love ; but if their hate succeeds,
They **wage** the war ; but 'tis the father bleeds.

[Exeunt.

ACT II. SCENE I.

Enter PERSEUS.

Perseus.

WHY loiters my ambasador to Dymas?
His greatness will not, sure, presume to scorn
A friendship offer'd from an heir of empire !—
But Pericles **returns.**

Enter PERICLES.

Is Dymas our's?

Peri. He's cautious, Sir ; he's subtle ; he's a courtier,
Dymas is now for you, now for your brother ;
For both, and neither : he's a summer-insect,
And loves the sunshine : on his gilded wings,
While the scales waver, he'll fly doubtful round you ;
And sing his flatteries to both alike :
The scales **once fix'd**, he'll settle on the winner,
And swear his pray'rs drew down the victory——
But what success had you, Sir, with your brother ?

Per. All, all my hopes are at the point of death!
The boy triumphant keeps his hold in love:
He's ever warbling nonsense in her ear;
With all th' intoxication of success.
Darkness incloses me; nor see I light
From any quarter dawn, but from his death.

 Peri. Why start at his death, who resolves on your's?

 Per. Resolves on mine!

 Peri. Have you not mark'd the Princess?
You have: with what a beam of majesty
Her eye strikes sacred awe! It speaks her mind
Exalted, as it is. Whom loves she then?
Demetrius? No; Rome's darling; who, no doubt,
Dares court her with your empire. And shall Perseus
Survive that loss?—Thus he resolves your death.

 Per. Most true. What crime then to strike first?
Or when? or where? O Pericles! assist me. [But how?

 Peri. 'Tis dangerous.

 Per. The fitter for me.

 Peri. Wait an occasion that befriends your wishes.

 Per. Go, fool, and teach a cataract to creep!
Can thirst of empire, vengeance, beauty, wait?

 Peri. In the mean time, accept a stratagem
That must secure your empire, or your love.
Your brother's Roman friendships gall no less
The King, than you: he dreads their consequence.
Dymas hates Rome; and Dymas has a daughter.
How can the King so powerfully fix
Demetrius' faith, as by his marriage there?
For Dymas thus, Rome's sworn, eternal foe,

Becomes a spy upon his private life,
And surety for his conduct.

Per. True—but **thus**
Our art defeats itself.   My brother gains
The favourite, and so strengthens in his treason.

Peri. Think you he'll wed her? No; the Princess'
Makes no such short-liv'd conquest. He'll refuse, [eye
And thus effect what I have strove in vain;
Yes, he'll refuse; and Dymas, in his wrath,
Will list for us, and vengeance.—Then the King
Will, doubtless, much resent his son's refusal;
And thus we kindle the whole court against him.

Per. My precious friend, I thank thee. I take wing
On ardent hope: I think it cannot fail.
Go, make thy court to Dymas with this scheme:
Begone—Erixene!—I'll feed her pride   [*Looking out.*
Once more, but not expend my breath in vain.
This meeting stamps unalterable fate,
I will wed her, or vengeance——

Enter ERIXENE *and* DELIA.

O, Erixene!

O, Princess! colder than your Thracian snows!
See Perseus, who ne'er stoop'd but to the Gods,
Prostrate before you.   Fame and empire sue.
Why have I conquer'd?—Because you are fair.
What's empire?—but a title to adore you.
Why do I number in my lineage high
Heroes and Gods?—That you, scarce less divine,
Without a blush may listen to my vows.

My ancestor subdu'd the world. I dare
Beyond his pride, and grasp at more, in you.
Obdurate maid! or turn, or I expire.

 Erix. If love, my Lord, is choice, who loves in vain
Should blame himself alone; and if 'tis fate,
'Tis fate in all: why then your blame on me?
My crown's precarious, through the chance of war;
But sure my heart's my own. Each villager
Is queen of her affections, and can vent
Her arbitrary sighs where'er she pleases.
Shall then the daughter of a race of Kings————

 Per. Madam, you justly blame the chance of war:
The Gods have been unkind: I am not so.
No! Perseus comes to counter-balance Fate.
Thrace ne'er was conquer'd—if you smile on me.
Silent! obdurate still! as cold as death!
But 'tis Demetrius————

 Erix. Prince, I take your meaning,
But, if you truly think his worth prevail,
How strange is your request!

 Per. No, madam, no:
Though love has hurt my mind, I still can judge
What springs controul the passions of the great.
Ambition is first minister of state;
Love's but a second in the cabinet:
Nor can he feather there his unfledg'd shaft
But from ambition's wing: but you conceive
More sanguine hopes, from him whom Rome supports,
Than me. You view Demetrius on my throne;
And thence he shines indeed! his charms from thence

Transpierce your soul, enamour'd of dominion.

Erix. Why now you shew me your profound esteem!
Demetrius' guilt alone has charms for me;
'Tis not the Prince, but Traitor wins my love.
Such insults are not brook'd by royal minds,
Howe'er their fortunes ebb; and though I mourn,
An orphan, and a captive, Gods there are——
Fear then an orphan's and a captive's wrong.

Per. Your cruel treatment of my passion——
But I'll not talk. This, madam; only this——
Think not the cause, the cursed cause of all,
Shall laugh secure, and triumph in my pangs.
No; by the torments of an heart on fire,
She gluts my vengeance, who defrauds my love! [*Exit.*

Erix. What have I done! In what a whirlwind rage
Has snatch'd him hence on ill! I frown on Perseus
And kill Demetrius.

Delia. Madam, see the Prince.

Enter DEMETRIUS.

Erix. Ah, Prince! the tempest, which so long has
Is now full ripe, and bursting o'er your head, [lour'd,
This moment Perseus' malice flam'd before me;
Victorious rage broke through his wonted guard,
And menac'd loud your ruin. Fly, O fly
This instant!

Dem. To what refuge?

Erix. Rome extends
Her longing arms to clasp you for her own.

Dem. Madam, 'tis prudent; I confess it is:

But is it loving as true lovers ought,
To be so very prudent in our love?
I boast not so much wisdom: I prefer
Death at your feet, before the world without you.

 Erix. In danger thus extreme——
 Dem. Oh! most belov'd!
Lov'd you like me, like me you would discern
That I but execute my brother's purpose
By such a flight.   At that his clamour, rage,
And menace aim: to chase a rival hence,
And keep the field alone.   Oh! shall I leave him
To gaze whole days; to learn to read your eye;
To study your delights, to chide the wind's
Too rude approach; to bid the ground be smooth;
To follow, like your shadow, where you go;
Tread in your steps; perhaps—to touch your hand!
O death! to minister in little things;
From half a glance to prophesy your will,
And do it, ere well form'd in your own mind!
Gods! Gods! while worlds divide me from my princess,
That, should she call, Demetrius might grow old
Ere he could reach her feet!

 Erix. If Perseus' love
Pains you, it pains me more.   Is your heart griev'd?
Mine is tormented: but since Philip's self
Is love's great advocate, a flat refusal
But blows their rage, and hastens your destruction.
Had I not that to fear! were you secure!
I'd ease my bosom of its full disdain,

And dash this bold presumer on his birth.
But, see! the grand procession.
  Dem. We must join it.

Enter the King, PERSEUS, Romans, ANTIGONUS, *&c.*

  King. Let the procession halt! and here be paid,
Before yon flaming altar, thanks to Heav'n,
That brings us safe to this auspicious day!
The great lustration of our martial powers,
Which from its distant birth to present time
Unfolds the glories of this ancient empire,
And throngs the pride of ages in an hour.
  Post. What figure's that, O Philip! which precedes?
                       [*Pointing.*

  King. The founder of our empire, furious son
Of great Alcides. We're ally'd to Heaven;
And you, I think, call Romulus a God.—
That, Philip, second of our name; and here,
O bend with awe to him, whose red right hand
Hurl'd proud Darius like a star from Heaven,
With lesser lights around him, flaming down,
And bid the laurel'd sons of Macedonia
Drink their own Ganges.
  Per. Give him his helmet, brother. [*Aside to* Dem.
  King. You lead the troops that join in mock en-
    counter:
And in no other may you ever meet! [*To his Sons.*
But march one way, and drive the world before you:
The victor, as our ancient rites decree,
Must hold a feast, and triumph in the bowl.

Dem. I long, my Lord, to see the charge begin:
The brandish'd faulchion, and the clashing helm,
Though but in sport, it is a sport for men.
Raw Alexander thus began his fame,
And overthrew Darius, first, at home.
We'll practise o'er the plans of future conquests,
While neighb'ring nations tremble at our play;
And own the fault in fortune; not in us,
That we but want a foe to be immortal.   [brother.

   Per. You have supply'd my wants: I thank you,
   King. [*Rising, and coming forward. Music.*] How
      vain all outward efforts to supply
The soul with joy! The noon-tide sun is dark,
And music discord, when the heart is low!
Avert its omen! what a damp hangs on me!
These sprightly, tuneful airs but skim along
The surface of my soul, not enter there:
She does not dance to this inchanting sound.
How, like a broken instrument, beneath
The skilful touch, my joyless heart lies dead!
Nor answers to the master's hand divine!   [joys

   Antig. When men once reach their autumn, sickly
Fall off apace, as yellow leaves from trees,
At ev'ry little breath misfortune blows;
Till, left quite naked of their happiness,
In the chill blasts of winter they expire.
This is the common lot. Have comfort then:
Your grief will damp the triumph.

   King. It is over.
Hear too; the trumpet calls us to the field,

And now this phantom of a fight begins.
Fair Princess, you and I will go together,
As Priam and bright Helen did of old,
To view the war. Your eyes will make them bolder,
And raise the price of victory itself.

[*All go out but* Perseus, *who has observed* Demetrius
and Erixene *all this time conversing, and stays behind,
thoughtful and disturbed.*

Per. Before my face she feeds him with her smiles:
The King looks on, nor disapproves the crime;
And the boy takes them as not due to me,
Without remorse, as happy as she'll make him.
Perish all three! I'll seek allies elsewhere;
Father and brother, nay, a mistress too.
Destruction, rise! Though thou art black as Night,
Thy mother, and as hideous as despair,
I'll clasp thee thus, nor think of woman more.
How the boy doats, and drinks in at his eyes
Her poison! O to stab him in her arms!
And yet do less than they have done to me.

Enter PERICLES.

Peri. Where is my prince? The nation's on the wing,
No bosom but exults; no hand but bears
A garland or a trophy: and shall Perseus——
Per. Vengeance!
Peri. Hear how with shouts they rend the skies!
                                    [*Shouts within.*
Per. Give me my vengeance!
Peri. Forty thousand men,

In polish'd armour, shine against the sun.

Per. Dare but another word, and not of vengeance,
And I will use thee, as I would—my brother.

Peri. Vengeance! on whom?

Per. On him.

Peri. What vengeance?

Per. Blood.

Peri. 'Tis your's.

Per. What God will give it me?

Peri. Your own right hand.

Per. I dare not—for my father.

Peri. You shall dare.

Per. Shalt thou dare give encouragement to Perseus?
Unfold thy purpose; I'll outshoot the mark.

Peri. Where are you going?

Per. To the mock encounter.

Peri. What more like mock encounter than the true?

Per. Enough—He's dead! 'Twas accident; 'twas
No matter what. Ten thousand share the blame. [error;

Peri. Hold, Sir! I had forgot: on this occasion,
The troops are search'd; and foils alone are worn,
Instead of swords.

Per. An osier were enough.
Who pains my heart, plants thunder in my hand,

Peri. But should this fail——

Per. Impossible!

Peri. But, should it,
The banquet follows.

Per. Poison in his wine.

Peri. Nay, should both fail, the field and banquet too,
All fails not; fairer hopes to fair succeed:
For **know**, my Lord, the King receiv'd with joy
The marriage-scheme, and sent for Dymas' daughter.

Per. Then there's a second bowl of poison for him.

Peri. Yet more; this ev'ning those ambassadors,
Which Philip sent to Rome, beneath the name
Of public business, but, in truth, to learn
Your brother's conduct, are expected home.

Per. Those whom I swore, before they parted hence,
In dreadful sacraments of wine and blood,
To bring back such reports as should destroy him:
And what if, to complete our secret plan,
We feign a letter to his friend the consul,
To strengthen our ambassadors' report?

Peri. That care, my Lord, be mine: I know a knave,
Grown fat on forgery; he'll counterfeit
Old Quintius' hand and seal, by former letters
Sent to the King; which you can gain with ease.

Per. Observe—This morning, at their interview,
The Romans, in effect, inform'd the King,
That Thrace was theirs, and order'd him restore
The Princess. This will give much air of truth,
If our forg'd letters say the Romans crown
Demetrius King of Thrace, and promise more.

Peri. My Lord, it shall be done.

Per. All cannot fail.   [*Trumpets.*

Peri. The trumpets sound; the troops are mounted.

Per. Vengeance!
Sweet vengeance calls; nor ever call'd a God

Such swift obedience : like the rapid wheel
I kindle in the course; I'm there already;
Snatch the bright weapon ; bound into my seat;
Strike ; triumph ; see him gasping on the ground.
And life, love, empire, springing from his wound.
When god-like ends, by means unjust, succeed,
The great result adorns the daring deed.
Virtue's a shackle, under fair disguise,
To fetter fools, while we bear off the prize.   [*Exeunt.*

ACT III. SCENE I.

Enter PERSEUS.

Perseus.

COWARDS in ill, like cowards in the field,
Are sure to be defeated.   To strike home,
In both, is prudence : guilt, begun, must fly
To guilt consummate, to be safe.

Enter PERICLES.

Peri. My Lord——
   Per. Disturb not my devotions ; they decline
The beaten track, the common path of pray'r——
Ye Pow'rs of darkness ! that rejoice in ill;
All sworn by Styx, with pestilential blasts
To wither every virtue in the bud ;
To keep the door of dark conspiracy,
And snuff the grateful fumes of human blood !
From sulphur blue, or your red beds of fire,

Or your black ebon thrones, auspicious rise;
And bursting through the barriers of this world,
Stand in dread contrast to the golden sun;
Fright day-light hence with your infernal smile;
And howl aloud your formidable joy,
While I transport you with the fair record
Of what your faithful minister has done,
Beyond your inspiration, self-impell'd
To spread your empire, and secure his own.
Hear, and applaud. Now, Pericles, proceed;
Speak, is the letter forg'd?

Peri. This moment; and might cheat
The cunning eye of jealousy itself.

Per. 'Tis well: Art thou appriz'd of what hath pass'd
Since last we parted?

Peri. No, my Lord.

Per. Then rouse
Thy whole attention: here we are in private:
Know then, my Pericles, the mock encounter
I turn'd, as taught by thee, to real rage.
But blasted be the cowards which I led!
They trembled at a boy.

Peri. Ha!

Per. Mark me well:
The villains fled; but soon my prudence turn'd
To good account that momentary shame.
Thus——I pretend 'twas voluntary flight
To save a brother's blood; accusing him
As author of that conflict I declin'd,
And he pursu'd with ardour and success.

Peri. That's artful. What ensu'd?

Per. The banquet follow'd,
Held by the victor, as our rights require :
To which his easy nature, soon appeas'd,
Invited me. I went not; but sent spies
To learn what pass'd; which spies, by chance detected,
(Observe me) were ill us'd.

Peri. By whom? your brother?

Per. No; by his sons of riot. He soon after,
Not knowing that my servants were abus'd,
Kind, and gay-hearted, came to visit me.
They, who misus'd my spies, for self-defence,
Conceal'd their arms beneath the robes of peace.
Of this inform'd, again my genius serv'd me.——

Peri. You took occasion, from these few in arms,
To charge a murderous assault on all.

Per. True, Pericles; but mark my whole address :
Against my brother swift I bar my gates;
Fly to my father; and with artful tears
Accuse Demetrius; first, of turning sports,
And guiltless exercise, to mortal rage ;
Then of inviting me (still blacker guilt !)
To smiling death in an invenom'd bowl;
And last, that both these failing, mad with rage,
He threw his schemes of baffled art aside,
And with arm'd men avow'dly sought my life.

Peri. Three startling articles, and well concerted,
Following each other in an easy train,
With fair similitude of truth! But, Sir,
How bore your father?

Per. Oh! he shook! he fell!
Nor was his fleeting soul recall'd with ease.
    Peri. What said he when recover'd?
    Per. His resolve
I know not yet; but see, his minion comes;
And comes perhaps to tell me. But I'll go;
Sustain my part, and echo loud my wrongs.
Nought so like innocence as perfect guilt.
If he brings aught of moment, you'll inform me.
        [*As* Perseus *goes off, he is seized by Officers.*

Enter DYMAS.

    Peri. How fares the King?
    Dym. Even as an aged oak
Push'd to and fro, the labour of the storm;
Whose largest branches are struck off by thunder:
Yet still he lives, and on the mountain groans;
Strong in affliction, awful from his wounds,
And more rever'd in ruin than in glory.
    Peri. I hear Prince Perseus has accus'd his brother.
    Dym. True; and the King's commands are now
     gone forth
To throw them both in chains; for farther thought
Makes Philip doubt the truth of Perseus' charge.
    Peri. What then is his design?
    Dym. They both this hour
Must plead their cause before him. Nay, already
His nobles, judges, counsellors, are met;
And public justice wears her sternest form:
A more momentous trial ne'er was known;

Whether the pleaders you survey as brothers,
Or princes known in arts, or fam'd for arms;
Whether you ponder, in their awful judge,
The tender parent, or the mighty King.
Greece, Athens hears the cause: the great result
Is life, or death; is infamy, or fame.   [*Trumpets.*

   Peri What trumpets these?
   Dym. They summon to the court.   [*Exeunt.*

The Scene draws, and discovers the Court, KING, *&c.*

   Enter DYMAS, *and takes his place by the* KING.

  King. Bring forth the prisoners.
Strange trial this! Here sit I to debate,
Which vital limb to lop, nor that to save,
But render wretched life more wretched still.
What see I, but Heaven's vengeance, in my sons?
Their guilt a scourge for mine: 'tis thus Heaven writes
Its awful meaning, plain in human deeds,
And language leaves to man.

Enter PERSEUS *and* DEMETRIUS, *in Chains, from different sides of the Stage;* PERSEUS *followed by* PERI-
CLES, *and* DEMETRIUS *by* ANTIGONUS.

  Dym. Dread Sir, your sons.
  King. I have no sons; and that I ever had,
Is now my heaviest curse: and yet what care,
What pains, I took to curb their rising rage!
How often have I rang'd through history,
To find examples for their private use?

The Theban brothers did I set before them——
What blood! **what** desolation! but in vain!
For **thee,** Demetrius, did I go to Rome,
And bring thee patterns thence of brother's love;
The Quintii, and the Scipios: but in vain!
If I'm a monarch, where is your obedience?
If I'm a father, where's your duty to me?
If old, your veneration due to years?
But I have wept, and you have sworn, in vain!
I had your ear, and enmity your heart.
How was this morning's counsel thrown away!
How happy is your mother in the grave!
She, when she bore you, suffer'd less: her pangs,
Her pungent pangs, throb through the father's heart.

　Dem. You can't condemn me, Sir, to worse than
　this.

　King. Than what, thou young deceiver? While I live,
You both with impious wishes grasp my sceptre:
Nothing is sacred, nothing dear, but empire.
Brother, nor father, can you bear; fierce lust
Of empire burns, extinguish'd all beside.
Why pant you for it? to give others awe?
Be therefore aw'd yourselves, and tremble at it,
While in a father's hand.

　Dym. My Lord, your warmth
Defers the business.

　King. Am I then too warm?
They that should shelter me from every blast,
To be themselves the storm! O! how Rome triumphs!
Oh! how they bring this hoary head to shame!

Conquest and fame, the labour of my life,
Now turn against me, and call in the world
To gaze at what was Philip, but who now
Wants even the wretch's privilege—a wish.
What can I wish? Demetrius may be guiltless.
What then is Perseus? Judgment hangs as yet
Doubtful o'er them; but I'm condemn'd already;
For both are mine; and one—is foul as hell.　[dear!)
Should these two hands wage war, (these hands less
What boots it which prevails? In both I bleed.
But I have done. Speak, Perseus, and at large;
You'll have no second hearing. Thou forbear.

　　　　　　　　　　　　　　　　　[*To* Demet.

　Per. Speak!—'Twas with utmost struggle I forbore:
These chains were scarce design'd to reach my tongue:
Their trespass is sufficient, stopping here.

　　　　　　　　　　　　　　　[*Shewing his arms.*
These chains! for what? Are chains for innocence?
Not so; for see Demetrius wears them too.
Fool that I was to tremble at vain laws;
Nor learn from him defiance of their frown;
Since innocence and guilt are us'd alike;
Blood-thirsty stabbers, and their destin'd prey;
Perseus, and he——I will not call him brother:

　　　　　　　　　　　　　　　[*Pointing at* Demet.
He wants not that enhancement of his guilt.

　King. But closer to the point; and lay before us
Your whole deportment this ill-fated day.

　Per. Scarce was he cool from that embrace this morn-
Which you enjoin'd, and I sincerely gave;　　[ing,

Nor thought he plann'd my death within my arms;
When, holding vile, oaths, honour, duty, love,
He fir'd our friendly sports to martial rage.
If **war**, why not fair war? But that has danger.
From hostile conflict, as from brothers' play,
He blush'd not to invite me to his banquet.
I went not; and in that was I to blame?
Think you, there nothing had been found but peace,
From whence soon after sally'd armed men?
Think you I nothing had to fear from swords,
When from their foils I scarce escap'd with life?
Or poison might his valour suit as well :—
This pass'd, as suits his wisdom, Macedonians,
Who volts o'er elder brothers to a throne.
With an arm'd rout he came to visit **me.**
Did I refuse to go, a bidden guest?
And should I welcome him, a threat'ning foe?
Resenting my refusal ; boiling for revenge!

  Dem. 'Tis false.

  Ant. Forbear——The King!

  ' *Per.* Had I receiv'd them,
' You now had mourn'd my death, nor heard my cause.
' Dares he deny he brought an armed throng?
' Call those I name ; who dare this deed, dare all;
' Yet will not dare deny that this is true.
' My death alone can yield a stronger proof;
' Will no less proof than that content a father?

  ' *Peri.* Perseus, you see, has art, as well as fire;
' Nor have the wars worn Athens from his tongue.'

  Per. Let him, who seeks to bathe in brother's blood,

Not find well pleas'd the fountain whence it flow'd :
Let him, who shudders at a brother's knife,
Find refuge in the bosom of a father :
For where else can I fly ? Whom else implore ?
I have no Romans, with their eagle's wings,
To shelter me; Demetrius borrows those,
To mount full rebel-high : I have their hatred ;
And, thanks to heaven ! deserve it : good Demetrius
Can see your towns and kingdoms **torn** away
By these protectors, and ne'er lose his temper.
My weakness, I confess, it makes me rave ;
It makes me weep—and my tears rarely flow.

 Peri. Was ever stronger proof of filial love ?

 Per. Vain are Rome's hopes, while you and I survive :
But should the sword take me, and age my father,
(Heav'n grant they leave him to the stroke of age !)
The kingdom, and the King, are both their own ;
A duteous loyal King, a scepter'd slave,
A willing Macedonian slave to Rome.

 King. First let an earthquake swallow Macedonia.

 Per. How, at such news, would Hannibal rejoice !
How the great shade of Alexander smile !
The thought quite choaks me up ; **I can no more.**

 King. Proceed.

 Per. No, Sir——Why have I spoke at all ?
'Twas needless : Philip justifies my charge ;
Philip's the single witness which I call,
To prove Demetrius guilty.

 King. What dost mean ?

 Per. What mean I, Sir ! what mean I !—To run mad :

For who, unshaken both in heart and brain,
Can recollect it?   .

  King. What?

  Per. This morning's insult.
This morning they proclaim'd him Philip's King.
This morning they forgave you for his sake.
O, pardon, pardon! I could strike him dead.

  King. More temper.

  Per. Not more truth; that cannot be!
And that it cannot, one proof can't escape you;
For what but truth could make me, Sir, so bold?
Rome puts forth all her strength to crowd her minion.
Demetrius' vices, thriving of themselves,
Her fulsome flatt'ries dung to ranker growth.
Demetrius is the burden of her song;
Each river, hill, and dale, has learnt his name;
While elder Perseus in a whisper dies.
Demetrius treats; Demetrius gives us peace;
Demetrius is our God, and would be so.
My sight is short: look on him you that can:
What sage experience sits upon his brow,
What awful marks of wisdom, who vouchsafes
To patronize a father, and a King?
Such patronage is treason.

  King. Treason! Death!

  Per. Nor let the ties of blood bind up the hands
Of justice; Nature's ties are broke already:
For, who contend before you?——Your two sons?——
No; read aright, 'tis Macedon and Rome.
A well-mask'd foreigner, and your——only son,

E

Guard of your life, and—exile of your love.
Now, bear me to my dungeon: what so fit
As darkness, chains, and death, for such a traitor?

 King. Speak, Demetrius.

 Ant. My Lord, he cannot speak; accept his tears—
Instead **of** words.

 Per. His tears are false as they————
Now, with fine phrase, and foppery of tongue,
More graceful action, and a smoother tone,
That orator of fable, and fair face,
Will steal on your brib'd hearts, and, as you listen,
Plain truth, and I, plain Perseus, are forgot.

 Dem. My father! King! and judge! thrice awful
  power!
Your son, your subject, and your prisoner, hear;
Thrice humble state! If I have grace of speech,
(Which gives, it seems, offence) be that no crime,
Which oft has serv'd my country, and my King:
Nor in my brother let it pass for virtue,
That, as he is, ungracious he would seem:
For, oh! he wants not art, tho' grace may fail him.
The wonted aids of those that are accus'd,
Has my accuser seiz'd. He shed false tears,
That my true sorrows might suspected flow:
He seeks my life, and calls me murderer;
And vows no refuge can he find on earth,
That I may want it in a father's arms;
Those arms, to which e'en strangers fly for safety.

 King. Speak to your charge.

 Dem. He charges me with treason.

If I'm a traitor, if I league with Rome,
Why did his zeal forbear me till this hour?
Was treason then no crime, till (as he feigns)
I sought his life? Dares Perseus hold so much
His father's welfare cheaper than his own?
Less cause have I, a brother, to complain.
He says, I wade for empire through his blood:
He says, I place my confidence in Rome:
Why murder him, if Rome will crown my brow?
Will then a sceptre, dipp'd in brother's blood,
Conciliate love, and make my reign secure?
False are both charges; and he proves them false,
By placing them together.

   Ant. That's well urg'd.   [me

   Dem. Mark, Sir, how Perseus, unawares, absolves
From guilt in all, by loading all with guilt.
Did I design him poison at my feast?
Why then did I provoke him in the field?
That, as he did, he might refuse to come?
When angry he refus'd, I should have sooth'd
His rous'd resentment, and deferr'd the blow;
Not destin'd him that moment to my sword,
Which I before instructed him to shun.
Through fear of death, did he decline my banquet?
Could I expect admittance then at his?
These numerous pleas at variance, overthrow
Each other, and are advocates for me.

   Per. No, Sir, Posthumius is his advocate.

   King. Art thou afraid that I should hear him out?

   ' *Dem.* Quit then this picture, this well-painted fear,

' And come to that which touches him indeed.
' Why is Demetrius not despis'd of all,
' His second in endowments, as in birth?
' How dare I draw the thoughts of Macedon?
' How dare I gain esteem with foreign powers?
' Esteem, when gain'd, how dare I to preserve?
' These are his secret thoughts; these burn within;
' These sting up accusations in his soul;
' Turn friendly visits to foul fraud, and murder;
' And pour in poison to the bowl of love.
' Merit is treason in a younger brother.

   ' *King.* But clear your conduct with regard to Rome.
   ' *Dem.* Alas! dread Sir, I grieve to find set down
' Among my crimes, what ought to be my praise.
' That I went hostage, or ambassador,
' Was Philip's high command, not my request:
' Indeed, when there, in both those characters,
' I bore in mind to whom I owe my birth:
' Rome's favour follow'd. If it is a crime
' To be regarded, spare a crime you caus'd;
' Caus'd by your orders, and examples too.
' True, I'm Rome's friend, while Rome is your ally:
' When not, this hostage, this ambassador,
' So dear, stands forth the fiercest of her foes;
' At your command, fly swift on wings of fire,
' The native thunder of a father's arm.

   ' *Ant.* There spoke at once the hero and the son.'
   Dem. To close—To thee, I grant, some thanks are
     due;   [*Speaking to* Perseus.
Not for thy kindness, but malignity:

Thy character's my friend, tho' thou my foe:
For, say, whose temper promises most guilt?
Perseus, importunate, demands my death:
I do not ask for his: Ah! no! I feel
Too pow'rful Nature pleading for him here:
But, were there no fraternal tie to bind me,
A son of Philip must be dear to me.
If you, my father, had been angry with me,
An elder brother, a less awful parent,
He should assuage you, he should intercede,
Soften my failings, and indulge my youth:
But my asylum drops its character;
I find not there my rescue, but my ruin.

Per. His bold assurance——

King. Do not interrupt him;
But let thy brother finish his defence.

Dem. O Perseus! how I tremble as I speak!
Where is a brother's voice, a brother's eye?
Where is the melting of a brother's heart?
Where is our awful father's dread command?
Where a dear dying mother's last request?
Forgot, scorn'd, hated, trodden under foot!
Thy heart, how dead to ev'ry call of nature!
Unson'd! unbrother'd! nay, unhumaniz'd!
Far from affection, as thou'rt near in blood!
Oh! Perseus! Perseus!—But my heart's too full.

[*Falls on* Antigonus.

King. Support him.

Per. Vengeance overtake his crimes.

King. No more!

E iij

Ant. See from his hoary brow he wipes the dew,
Which agony wrings from him.

  King. Oh, my friend,
These boys at strife, like Ætna's struggling flames,
Convulsions cause, and make a mountain shake ;
Shake Philip's firmness, and convulse his heart ;
And, with a fiery flood of civil war,
Threaten to deluge my divided land.

I've heard them both ; by neither am convinc'd ;
And yet Demetrius' words went through my heart.—
A double crime, Demetrius, is your charge ;
Fondness for Rome, and hatred to your brother.
If you can clear your innocence in one,
'Twill give us cause to think you wrong'd in both.

  Dem. How shall I clear it, Sir ?

  King. This honest man
Detests the Romans : if you wed his daughter,
Rome's foe becomes the guardian of your faith.

  Dem. I told you, Sir, when I return'd from Rome—

  King. How ! Dost thou want an absolute command ?
Your brother, father, country, all exact it.

  Ant. See yonder guards at hand, if you refuse.
Nay, more ; a father, so distress'd, demands
A son's compassion, to becalm his heart.
Oh ! Sir, comply.   [*Aside to* Demet.

  Dem. There ! there ! indeed, you touch me !
Besides, if I'm confin'd, and Perseus free,
I never, never shall behold her more.——
Pardon, ye Gods ! an artifice forc'd on me. [*Aside to* Ant.

Dread Sir, your son complies.   [*To the* King.

Dym. Astonishment!

King. Strike off his chains. Nay, Perseus too is free:
They wear no bonds, but those of duty, now.
Dymas, go thank the prince: he weds your daughter;
And highest honours pay your high desert.

        [*Exeunt all but* Dym. *and* Dem.

Dym. O, Sir, without presumption, may I dare
To lift my ravish'd thought?——

Dem. In what I've done,
I paid a duty to my father's will:
And set you an example, where 'tis due,
Of not with-holding your's.

Dym. My duty, Sir,
To you, can never fail.

Dem. Then, Dymas, I request thee,
Go seek the King, and save me from a marriage
My brother has contriv'd, in artful malice,
To make me lose my father, or my love.
Go, charge the just refusal on thyself.

Dym. What Philip authorizes me to wish,
You, Sir, may disappoint. But, to take on me
The load of the refusal——

Dem. Is no more
Than Dymas owes his honour, if he'd shun
The natural surmise, that he concurr'd
In brewing this foul treason.

Dym. Sir, the King
Knows what he does: and, if he seeks my glory——

Dem. In a degree, destructive of his own;

'Tis your's to disappoint him, or renounce
Your duty to your King.

  Dym. You'll better tell——

  Dem. Yes, better tell the King he wounds his honour,
By lifting up a minion from the dust,
And mating him with princes. Use your power
Against yourself. Yes, use it like a man,
In serving him who gave it. Thus you'll make
Indulgence, justice; and absolve your master.
Tho' Kings delight in raising what they love,
Less owe they to themselves, than to the throne;
Nor must they prostitute its majesty,
To swell a subject's pride, howe'er deserving.

  Dym. What the King grants me——

  Dem. Talk not of a grant:
What a King ought not, that he cannot give;
And what is more than meet from Princes' bounty,
Is plunder, not a grant. Think you, his honour
A perquisite belonging to your place,
As favourite paramount? Preserve the King
From doing wrong, tho' wrong is done for you;
And shew, 'tis not in favour to corrupt thee.

  Dym. I sought not, Sir, this honour.

  Dem. But would take it.
True majesty's the very soul of Kings;
And rectitude's the soul of majesty:
If mining minions sap that rectitude,
The King may live, but majesty expires:
And he that lessens majesty, impairs
That just obedience public good requires;

Doubly a traitor, to the crown and state.

Dym. Must I refuse what Philip's pleas'd to give?

Dem. Can a King give thee more than is his own?
Know, a King's dignity is public wealth;
On that subsists the nation's fame and power.
Shall fawning sycophants, to plump themselves,
Eat **up** their master, and dethrone his glory?
What are such wretches? What, but vapours foul,
From fens and bogs, by royal beams exhal'd,
That radiance intercepting, which should cheer
The land at large? Hence subjects' hearts grow cold,
And frozen loyalty forgets to flow:
But, then 'tis slippery standing for the minion:
Stains on his ermine, to their royal master
Such miscreants **are**; not jewels in his crown.
If you persist, Sir—But, of words no more!
To me, to threat, is harder than to do!

Dym. Let me embrace this genuine son of **empire.**
When warm debates divide the doubtful land,
Should I not know the prince most fit to reign?
I've try'd you as an eagle tries her young,
And find, your dauntless eye is fix'd on glory.
I'll to the King, and your commands obey.——
We must give young men opiates in a fever.   [*Aside.*
Yes, boy, I will obey thee, to thy ruin.
Erixene shall strike thee dead for this.   [*Exit* Dym.

Dem. These statesmen nothing woo but gold and
I'm a bold advocate for other love;   [power.
Tho' at their bar, indicted for a fool.
When reason, like the skilful charioteer,

Can break the fiery passions to the bit;
And, spite of their licentious sallies, keep
The radiant track of glory; passions, then,
Are aids and ornaments. Triumphant reason,
Firm in her seat, and swift in her career,
Enjoys their violence, and, smiling, thanks
Their formidable flame, for high renown:
Take then my soul, fair maid! 'tis wholly thine;
And thence I feel an energy divine.
When objects worthy praise our hearts approve,
Each virtue grows on consecrated love:
And, sure, soft passion claims to be forgiv'n,
When love of beauty is the love of Heav'n.   [*Exit.*

ACT IV. SCENE I.

Enter ERIXENE *and* DELIA.

Erixene.

'T is plain! 'tis plain! this marriage gains her father:
He join'd to Rome the crown. Thy words were true;
He wooes the diadem, that diadem which I
Despis'd for him. Oh, how unlike our loves!
But it is well; he gives me my revenge.
Wed Dymas' daughter! What a fall is there!
Not the world's empire could repair his glory.   [why

Del. Madam, you can't be mov'd too much! But
More now than at the first?

Erix. At first I doubted;

For who, that lov'd like me, could have believ'd?
I disbeliev'd what Pericles reported;
And thought it Perseus' art to wound our loves.
But when the good Antigonus, sworn friend
To false Demetrius, when his word confirm'd it,
Then passion took me, as the northern blast
An autumn leaf.   O Gods! the dreadful whirl!
But, while I speak, he's with her: laughs and plays;
Mingles his dalliance with insulting mirth;
To this new Goddess offers up my tears;
Yes, with my shame and torture, wooes her love.
I see, hear, feel it! O these raging fires!
Can then the thing we scorn give so much pain?

   Del. Madam, these transports give him cause to
      triumph!

   Erix. I vent my grief to thee; he ne'er shall know it.
If I can't conquer, I'll conceal my passion,
And stifle all its pangs beneath disdain.

   Del. The greatest minds are most relenting too:
If then Demetrius should repent his crime——

   Erix. If still my passion burns, it shall burn inward:
On the fierce rack in silence I'll expire,
Before one sigh escape me.—He repent!
What wild extravagance of thought is thine!
But did he? Who repents, has once been false:
In love, repentance but declares our guilt;
And injur'd honour shall exact its due.
In vain his love, nay mine, should groan in vain,
Both are devoted.   Vengeance, vengeance reigns!
Our first love murder'd, is the sharpest pang

A human heart can feel.

Del. The King approaches.

Enter the KING, *&c.*

King. Madam, at length we see the dawn of peace,
And hope an end of our domestic jars.
The jealous Perseus can no longer fear
Demetrius is a Roman, since this day
Makes him the son of Dymas, Rome's worst foe.

Erix. Already, Sir, I've heard, and heard with joy,
Th' important news.

King. To make our bliss run o'er :
You, Madam, will complete what Heav'n begins ;
And save the love-sick Perseus from despair.
That marriage would leave Rome without pretence
To touch our conquest ; and for ever join
To these dominions long disputed Thrace.

Enter DYMAS.

Erix. Tho' Thrace by conquest stoops to Macedon,
I know my rank, and would preserve its due.
With meditated coldness have I heard
Prince Perseus' vows ; unwilling to consent
Before restor'd to my forefather's throne,
Lest that consent should merit little thanks,
As flowing less from choice than your command :
But since the Roman pride will find account
In my persisting still, and Philip suffer,
I quit the lofty thought on which I stood,
And yield to your request.

King. Indulgent Gods !
Blest moment ! How will this with transport fill
The doubtful Perseus, after years of pain !   [joy

   Dym. My Lord, I've heard what pass'd, and give you
Of Perseus' nuptials, which your state requires ;
But for Demetrius'—think of those no more.
Far from accepting such a load of glory,
I bring, I bring, my Lord, this forfeit head,
Due to my bold refusal.

   King. Dares the boy
Fall from his promise, and impose on thee
Forc'd disobedience to my royal pleasure ?   [crime ;

   Dym. No, my most honour'd Lord, there, there's my
Fond of the maid, with ardour he press'd on ;
But should I dare pollute his blood with mine ?
But you, Sir, authorize it—still more base,
To wrong a master so profusely kind.

   King. That man is noble on whom Philip smiles ;
Come, come, there's something more in this—explain.

   Dym. Why am I forc'd on this ungrateful office ?
Yet can't I tell you more than fame has told ;
Which says, Demetrius is in league with Rome.
Why weds ambition then an humble maid,
But to gain me to treason ? What then follows ?
They'll say, the subtile statesman plann'd this marriage,
To raise his blood into his master's throne.
No, Sir, preserve my fame, let life suffice.

Enter PERICLES.

Peri. Sir, your ambassadors arriv'd from Rome—

                              [*Presents a letter.*

King. Ha! I must read it; this will tell me more.

                              [*After reading it.*

Oh, Princess! Now our only comfort flows
From your indulgence to my better son.
This dreadful news precipitates my wish.
To keep rapacious Rome from seizing Thrace,
You cannot wed too soon : my fair ally!
What if you bless me and my son to-morrow?

  Erix. Since you request, and your affairs demand it,
Without a blush, I think I may comply.

  King. Oh, daughter!—but no more ; the Gods will
I go to bless my Perseus with the news. [thank you.

  Dym. Thus the boy's dead in empire and in love.

                        [*Exeunt* King, Dymas, &c.

  Erix. I triumph! I'm reveng'd! I reign! I reign!
Nor thank Demetrius' treason for a crown.
Love is our own cause, honour is the Gods'.
I can be glorious without happiness ;
But without glory never can be blest.

  Del. 'Tis well : but can you wed the man you scorn?

  Erix. Wed any thing, for vengeance on the perjur'd.
I'll now insult him from an higher sphere:
This unexpected turn may gall his pride.
Whate'er has pangs for him, has charms for me.

  Del. A rooted love is scarce so soon remov'd.

  Erix. If not, the greater virtue to controul it:

And strike at his heart, though 'tis through my own.

Del. I can't but praise this triumph; yet I dread
The combat still. And see, the foe draws near.

Enter DEMETRIUS.

Dem. Erixene!

Erix. My Lord!

Dem. My pale cheek speaks;
My trembling limbs prevent my faultering tongue,
And ask you——

Erix. What, my **Lord**?

Dem. My Lord?—Her eyes
Confirm it true, and yet, without a crime,
I can't believe it. Oh, Erixene——

Erix. I guess your meaning, Sir; but am surpris'd
That Dymas' son should think of ought I do.

Dem. False are my senses! false both ear and eye!
All, all be rather false than her. I love!

Erix. She pass'd not, Sir, this way.

Dem. Is then my pain
Your sport? And can Erixene pretend
Herself deceiv'd by what deceiv'd the King?
An artifice made use of for your sake;
A proof, not violation of my love.

Erix. I thought not of your love, nor artifice:
Both were forgot; or, rather, never known.
But, without artifice, I tell you this;
Your brother lays his sceptre at my feet,——
And whose example bids my heart resist
The charms of empire?

F ij

Dem. This is woman's skill :
You cease to love, and from my conduct strive
To labour an excuse.   For if, indeed,
You thought me false, had you been thus serene,
Calm and unruffled ? No ; my heart says, no.
Passions, if great, though turn'd to their reverse,
Keep their degree, and are great passions still.
And she who, when she thinks her lover false,
Retains her temper, never lost her heart.

 Erix. That I'm serene, says not I never lov'd :
Indeed, the vulgar float as passion drives ;
But noble minds have reason for their queen.
While you deserv'd, my passion was sincere :
You change, my passion dies.   But, pardon, Sir,
If my vain mind thinks anger is too much ;
Take my neglect, I can afford no more.   [deaths !

 Dem. No: rage! flame! thunder! give a thousand
Oh, rescue me from this more dreadful calm !
This curs'd indifference ! which, like a frost
In northern seas, out-does the fiercest storm.
Commanded by my father to comply,
I feign'd obedience :—had I then refus'd——   [ful !

 Erix. I grant the consequence had been most dread-
I grant that Dymas' daughter had been angry.

 Dem. Ask Dymas with what rage——

 Erix. You well might rage,
To be refus'd.

 Dem. Refus'd ?

 Erix. He told your secret ;

Dem. Refus'd! false villain! Oh, the perjur'd slave!
Hell-born impostor! Madam, 'tis most false!
Warm from my heart is ev'ry word I speak!
The villain lies! Believe the pangs that rend me;
Believe the witness streaming from my eyes,
And let me speak no more.

Erix. I do believe
Your grief sincere. I've heard the maid is fair.

Dem. Proceed; and thus, indeed, commit that crime
You falsely charge on me. The crown has charm'd you.
How warm this morning did you press my flight!
The cause is plain: an outrag'd lover's groan,
And dying agony, molest your ear,
And hurt the music of a nuptial song.

Erix. Since your inconstancy persists to charge
Its crime on my ambition, I'll be kind,
And leave you in possession of an error
Of which you seem so fond.

Dem. Ah! stay one moment!

Enter Perseus *and* Pericles.

Per. Erixene!
Dem. Distraction! [*Starting*.
Erix. 'Tis well tim'd.
My Lord, your brother doubts if I'm sincere,
And thinks (an error natural to him)
I'll break my vow to you. You'll clear my fame,
And labour to convince him, that to-morrow
Erixene's at once a bride and queen. [*Exit*.

Per. When I have work'd him up to violence,

F iij

Bring thou the King, and pity my distress.

        [*To* Pericles, *who goes out.*

 ' *Dem.* On what extremes extreme distress compels
' In things impossible I put my trust: [me?
' I in my only brother find a foe;
' Yet in my rival, hope the greatest friend.
' When all our hopes are lodg'd in such expedients,
' 'Tis as if poison were our only food,
' And death was call'd on as the guard of life.'

 Per. Why dost thou droop?

 Dem. Because I'm dead; quite dead
To hope; and yet rebellious to despair;
Like ghosts unbless'd, that burst the bars of death.
Strange is my conduct!—Stranger my distress:
Beyond example both! Whoe'er before me
Press'd his worst foe, to prove his truest friend?
But though thou'rt not my brother, thou'rt a man;
And, if a man, compassionate the worst
That man can feel; though found that worst in me.

 Per. What would'st?

 Dem. Unclinch thy talons from thy prey;
Let the dove fly to this her nest again.

        ·[*Striking his breast.*

For, Oh! the maid's unalineably mine,
Though now through rage run mad, and turn'd to thee.
How often have I languish'd at her feet?
Bask'd in her eye, and revell'd in her smile?
How often, as she listen'd to my vows,
Trembling and pale with agonies of joy,
Have I left earth, and mounted to the stars?

Per. There Dymas' daughter shone above the rest,
Illustrious in thy sight.

Dem. Thy taunt, how false!——
I no less press your int'rest than my own.
Think you 'tis possible her heart so long
Inclin'd to me, the price of all my vows,
Purchas'd by tears and groans, and paid me down
In tenderest returns of love divine,
Can in one day be your's?—Impossible!

Per. If I'm deceiv'd, I'm pleas'd with the deceit,
How my heart dances in the golden dream!
In pity do not wake me 'till to-morrow.

‘ *Dem.* Then thou'lt wake distracted.   Trust me,
‘ She gives her hand alone. /   [brother,
‘ *Per.* Nor need I more ;
‘ That hand's enough that brings a sceptre in it.
‘ I scorn a Prince who weds with meaner views,
‘ Her duty's mine, and I conceive small pain
‘ From your sweet error, that her love is your's.
‘ I'm pleas'd such cordial thoughts of your own merit
‘ Support you in distress.'

Dem. Inhuman Perseus!
If pity dwells within the heart of man,
If due that pity to the last distress,
Pity a lover exquisitely pain'd,
A lover exquisitely pain'd by you.
Oh! in the name of all the Gods, relent!
Give me my Princess, give her to my throes!
Amidst a thousand you may chuse a love ;
The spacious earth contains but one for me.——

But Oh! I rave. Art thou not he, the man
Who drinks my groans like music at his ear?
And would, as wine, as nectar, drink my blood?
Are all my hopes of mercy lodg'd in thee?
Oh, rigid Gods! and shall I then fall down,
Embrace thy feet, and bathe them with my tears?
Yes, I will drown thee with my tears, my blood,
So thou afford a human ear to pangs,
A brother's pangs, a brother's broken heart.

 Per. Pardon, Demetrius; but the Princess calls,
And I am bound to go.

  Dem. Oh, stay!   [*Laying hold of him.*

  Per. You tremble.

  Dem. The Princess calls, and you are bound to go?

  Per. E'en so.

  Dem. What Princess?

  Per. Mine.

  Dem. 'Tis false.

  Per. Unhand me.

  Dem. What, see, talk, touch, may taste her like a bee,
Draw honey from her wounded lip, while I
Am stung to death!

  Per. The triumph once was your's:

  Dem. Rip up my breast, or you shall never stir.
My heart may visit her! Oh, take it with you!
Have I not seen her, where she has not been?
Have I not clasp'd her shadow? Trod her steps?
Transported trod! as if they led to Heaven!
Each morn my life I lighted at her eye,
And every evening, as its close, expir'd.——

Per. Fie! thou'rt a Roman; can a Roman weep?
Sure Alexander's helmet can sustain
Far heavier strokes than these. For shame, Demetrius;
E'en snatch up the next Sabin in thy way,
'Twill do as well. [*Going.*

Dem. By Heav'n you shall not stir.
Long as I live, I stand a world between you,
And keep you distant as the poles asunder.
Who takes my love, in mercy takes my life;
Thy bloody pass cleave through thy brother's breast.
I beg, I challenge, I provoke my death.

[*His hand upon his sword.*

Enter KING *and* DYMAS.

Per. You will not murder me?
Dem. Yes, you and all.
King. How like a tyger foaming o'er his prey!
Per. Now, Sir, believe your eye, believe your ear,
And still believe me perjur'd as this morning.
King. Heav'n's wrath's exhausted, there's no more to
My darling son found criminal in all. [fear.
Dem. That villain there to blast me! Yes, I'll speak;
For what have I to fear, who feel the worst?
'Tis time the truth were known. That villain, Sir,
Has cleft my heart, and laughs to see it bleed;
But his confession shall redeem my fame,
And re-enthrone me in my Princess' smile;
Or I'll return that false embrace he gave me,
And stab him in your sight.

King. Hold, insolent!
Where's your respect to me?

'*Dem.* Oh, royal Sir!
' That has undone me. Through respect I gave
' A feign'd consent, which his black artifice
' Has turn'd to my destruction. I refus'd
' That slave's, that cursed slave's, that statesman's
' And he pretends she was refus'd to me.   [daughter,
' Hence, hence, this desolation. Nought I fear,
' Though nature groan her last. And shall he then
' Escape and triumph?'

King. Guards there! Seize the Prince! [*He's seiz'd.*
The man you menace you shall learn to fear.

Dym. Hold, Sir! not this for me! It is your son:
What is my life, though pour'd upon your feet?

King. Is this a son?

Dem. No, Sir; my crime's too great;
Which dares to vindicate a father's honour,
To catch the glories of a falling crown,
And save it from pollution. But I've done.
I die, unless my Princess is restor'd; [*Pointing to* Dym.
And if I die, by heav'n, and earth, and hell!
His sordid blood shall mingle with the dust,
And see if thence 'twill mount into the throne.
Oh, Sir! think of it! I'll expect my fate.   [*Exit.*

King. And thou shalt have it.

Dym. How, my Lord; in tears!

King. As if the Gods came down in evidence!
How many sudden rays of proof concur

To my conviction ? Was ever equal boldness ?
But 'tis no wonder from a brother King ;
      [*Produces the forg'd letter.*
This King of Thrace—To-morrow he'll be King
Of Macedon——He therefore dies to-night.

Per. And yet I doubt it, for I know his fondness.
Thou practise well the lesson I have taught thee,
While I put on a solemn face of woe,
Afflicted for a brother's early fall—— [*Aside to* Dym.
Heaven knows with what regret—But, Sir, your safety—
   [*Presenting the mandate for* Demetrius's *death.*

King. What giv'st thou here ?

Dym. Your passport to renown.
You sign your apotheosis in that.
What scales the skies, but zeal for public good ?

Per. How god-like mercy ?

Dym. Mercy to mankind,
By treason aw'd.

King. Must then thy brother bleed ?   [*To* Per.
  [Dym. *seeming at* a loss, Per. *whispers him,*
    and gives a letter.

Dym. No, Sir, the King of Thrace.
      [*Looking on the letter.*

King. Why that is true——
Yet who, if not a father, should forgive ?

Dym. Who, Sir, if not a Philip, should be just ?

King. Is't not my son ?   [*To* Dym.

Dym. If not, far less his guilt.

King. Is not my other Perseus ?   [*To* Per.

Per. Sir, I thank you ;

That seeks your crown and life.

 King. And life?

 Dym. No, Sir;

He'll only take your crown, you still may live.

 King. Heav'n blast thee for that thought!

 Per. Why shakes my father?

 King. It stabs, it gnaws, it harrows up my soul.

Is he not young? Was he not much indulg'd?

Gall'd by his brother? Doubted by his father?

Tempted by Rome? A nation to a boy?

 Dym. Oh, a mere infant—that deposes Kings.

 King. No; once he sav'd my crown.

 Dym. And now would wear it.

 King. How my head swims!

 Per. Nor strange; the task is hard.

 Dym. Yet scarce for him. Brutus was but a Roman:

  [*Speaking as if he would not have the King hear.*

Yet like a Philip dar'd, and is immortal.

 King. I hear thee, Dymas; give me then the mandate.

   [*Going to sign, he stops short.*

 Dym. No wonder if his mother thus had paus'd.

 Per. Rank cankers **on** thy tongue! Why mention

 her?   [*Aside.*

 King. Oh, Gods! I see her now: what am I doing?

    [*Throws away the style.*

I see her dying eye let fall a tear

In favour of Demetrius. Shall I stab

Her lovely image stampt on ev'ry feature?

 Dym. His soul escap'd it, Sir.

 King. Thou **ly'st**; be gone.

[*Per.* and *Dym.* *in great confusion,* Per. *whispers* Dym.

Dym. True ; that, or nought, will touch him.

            [*Aside to* Per.

If, Sir, your mercy———   [*To the King.*

Per. O speak on of mercy!

Mercy, the darling attribute of Heav'n !

Dym. If you should spare him———

King. What if I should spare him ?

Dym. I dare not say—Your wrath again might rise.

King. Yes, if thou'rt silent—What if I should spare

  him ?   [you for it.

Dym. Why if you should, proud Rome would thank

King. Rome!—Her applause more shocks me than

Oh, thou, Death's orator! Dread advocate [his death.

For bowelless severity ! assist

My trembling hand, as thou hast steel'd my heart ;

And if it is guilt in me, share the guilt.

He's dead. [*Signs.*] And if I blot it with one tear,

Perseus, though less affected, will forgive me.

Per. Forgive! Sir, I applaud, and wish my sorrow

Was mild enough to weep.

   [*The* King *going out,* meets Demetrius *in mourning,*
    introduced by Antigonus. *He starts back, and*
    drops on Dymas. *Recovering, speaks.*

King. This, Fate, is thy tenth wave, and quite o'er-

  whelms me :

It less had shock'd me, had I met his ghost.

This is a plot to sentence me to death.

What hast thou done, my mortal foe! thrown bars

            [*To* Ant.

Athwart my glory? But thy scheme shall fail.
As rushing torrents sweep th' obstructed mound,
So Philip meets this mountain in his way,
Yet keeps his purpose still.

                    [*Perseus and* Pericles *whisper aside.*

Peri. I can't but fear it.

Per. I grant the danger great, yet don't despair.
Jove is against thee, Perseus on thy side.

Ant. The Prince, dread Sir, low on his bended knee—

King. This way, Antigonus. Dost mark his bloom?
Grace in his aspect, grandeur in his mien?

Ant. I do.

King. 'Tis false; take a king's word. He's dead.
That darling of my soul would stab me sleeping.
How dar'st thou start? Art thou the traitor's father?
If thou art pale, what is enough for me?
How his grave yawns! Oh, that it was my own!

Ant. Mourn not the guilty.

King. No, he's innocent:
Death pays his debt to justice, and that done,
I grant him still my son; as such I love him:
Yes, and will clasp him to my breast, while yet
His clay is warm, nor moulders at my touch.

Per. A curse on that embrace!   [*Aside.*

Dym. Nay, worse; he weeps.

King. Poor boy, be not deceiv'd by my compassion;
My tears are cruel, and I groan thy death.

Dem. And am I then to die? If death's decreed,
Stab me yourself, nor give me to the knife
Of midnight ruffians, that have forg'd my crimes.

For you I beg, for you I pour my tears;
You are deceiv'd, dishonour'd; I am only slain.
Oh, father!——

  King. 'Father! there's no father here.'
Forbear to wound me with that tender name:
Nor raise all nature up in arms against me.

  Dem. My father! guardian! friend!. 'nay, Deity!
'What less than Gods give being, life, and death!
My dying mother——

  '*King.* Hold thy peace, I charge thee.

  '*Dem.*' Pressing your hand, and bathing it with tears,
Bequeath'd your tenderness for her to me;
And low on earth my legacy I claim,
Clasping your knees, though banish'd from your breast.

  '*King.* My knees!—Would that were all, he grasps
    my heart!

'Perseus, **can**'st thou stand by and see me ruin'd?

                   [*Reaching his hand to* Perseus.

  '*Per.* Loose, loose thy hold.—It is my father too.

  '*King.* Yes, Macedon, and thine, and I'll preserve
    thee.   [Thracian?

  '*Dem.* Who once before preserv'd it from the
'And who at Thrasymene turn'd the lifted bolt
'From Philip's hoary brow?'

  King. I'll hear no more.
O Perseus! Dymas! Pericles! assist me,
Unbind me, disenchant me, break this charm
Of nature, that accomplice with my foes;
Rend me, O rend me, from the friend of Rome.

  '*Per.* **Nay,** then, howe'er reluctant, aid I must.

‘ The friend of Rome ?—That severs you for ever;
Though most incorporate and strongly knit;
As lightning rends the knotted oak asunder.
   ‘ *Dem.* In spite of lightning I renew the tie;
And stubborn is the grasp of dying men.—
‘ Who's he that shall divide me from myself?
   [*Demetrius is forc'd from the King's knees, on which,*
       starting up, he flings his arms round his father.
‘ Still of a piece with him from whom I grew,
‘ I'll bleed on my asylum, dart my soul
‘ In this embrace, and thus my treason crown.
   ‘ *King.*’ Who love yourselves, or Macedon, or me,
From the curs'd eagle's talons wrench'd my crown;
And this barb'd arrow from my breast.—'Tis done;
                               [*Forced asunder.*
And the blood gushes after it,—I faint.
   Dym. Support the King.
   Per. While treason licks the dust.
         [*Pointing at* Demetrius, *fallen in the struggle.*
   Dym. A field well fought.
   Per. And justice has prevail'd.
   King. ‘ O, that the traitor could conceal the son!’
Farewel, once best belov'd! still more deplor'd!
He, he who dooms thee, bleeds upon thy tomb. [*Exit.*
   Dem. Prostrate on thee, my mother earth, be thou
Kinder than brother, or than father; open
And save me in thy bosom from my—friends.
‘ Friends, sworn to wash their hands in guiltless tears,
‘ And quench infernal thirst in kindred blood;
‘ As if relation sever'd human hearts,

' Or that destruction was the child of love.

   ' *Per.* Farewel, young traitor: if they ask below,

' Who sent thee beardless down, say, honest Perseus;

' Whom reason sways, not instinct; who can strike

' At horrid parricide, and flagrant treason,

' Though through a bosom dearer than his own.

' Think'st thou, my tender heart can hate a brother?

' The Gods and Perseus war with nought but guilt.

' But I must go.   What, Sir, your last commands

' To your Erixene? She chides my stay.   [*Exit.*

   Dem. ' Without that token of a brother's love

' He could not part; my death was not enough.—

' I care for mercy, and I find it here.

' And death is mercy, since my love is lost.'

Alas! **my** father too; my heart aches for him.

And Perseus—fain wou'd I forgive e'en thee:

But Philip's sufferings cry too loud against it.

Blind author, and sure mourner of my death!

Father most dear! What pangs hast thou to come?

Like that poor wretch is thy unhappy doom,

Who, while in sleep his fever'd fancy glows,

Draws his keen sword, and sheaths it in his foes:

But, waking, starts upright, in wild surprise,

To feel warm blood glide round him as he lies;

To see his reeking hands in crimson dy'd,

And a **pale** corse extended by his side.

He views with horror what mad dreams have done,

And sinks, heart-broken, on a murder'd son.

ACT V. SCENE I.

KING, POSTHUMIUS, *&c. meeting.*

Posthumius.

WE, in behalf of our allies, O King!
Call'd on thee yesterday, to clear thy glory.
No wonder now that Philip is unjust
To strangers, who has murder'd his own son.
 King. 'Tis false.
 Post. No thanks to Philip that he fled,
 King. A traitor is no son.
 Post. Heav'n's vengeance on me,
If he refus'd not yesterday thy crown,
Though life and love both brib'd him to comply.
 King. See there.   · [*Gives the letter.*
 Post. 'Tis not the consul's hand or seal.
 King. You're his accomplices.
 Post. We're his avengers.
'Tis war.
 King. Eternal war.
 Post. Next time we meet——
 King. Is in the capitol, Haste, fly my kingdom,
 Post. No longer thine.
 King. Yes, and proud Rome a province.
      [*Exeunt* Posthumius, *&c.*
They brave, they make, they tyrannize o'er Kings.
The name of King the prostrate world ador'd,
Ere Romulus had call'd **his thieves** together,——

But let me pause—Not Quintius' hand or seal?—
Doubt and impatience, like thick smoke and fire,
Cloud and torment my reason.

   Ant. Sir, recall,
And re-examine those you sent to Rome:
You took their evidence in haste and anger.
Torture, if they refuse, will tell the truth.

   King. Go stop the nuptials, till you hear from me.

                     [*Exeunt* King *and* Ant.

Enter ERIXENE *and* DELIA, *meeting.*

   Del. Madam, the Prince, who fled from threaten'd
      death,
Attempting his escape to foreign realms,
Was lately taken at the city gates,
So strongly guarded by his father's pow'rs;
And now, confin'd, expects his final doom.

   Erix. Imprison'd, and to die!—And let him die.
Bid Dymas' daughter weep. I half forgot
His perjur'd insolence; I'll go and glut
My vengeance. Oh, how just a traitor's death!
And blacker still, a traitor to my love.

                     [*Exeunt* Erixene *and* Delia.

Scene draws, and shews DEMETRIUS *in Prison.*

   Dem. Thou subterranean sepulchre of peace!
Thou home of horror! hideous nest of crimes!
Guilt's first sad stage in her dark road to hell!
Ye thick-barr'd sunless passages for air,
To keep alive the wretch that longs to die!

Ye low-brow'd arches, through whose sullen gloom
Resound the ceaseless groans of pale despair!
Ye dreadful shambles, cak'd with human blood!
Receive a guest, from far, far other scenes,
From pompous courts, from shouting victories,
Carousing festivals, harmonious bow'rs,
And the soft chains of heart-dissolving love.
Oh, how unlike to these! Heart-breaking load
Of shame eternal, ne'er to be knock'd off,
Oh welcome death!—no, never but by thee'—
Nor has a foe done this.—A friend! a father!—
Oh, that I could have died without their guilt!—

Enter ERIXENE, DEMETRIUS *gazing at her.*

So look'd in chaos the first beam of light:
How drives the strong enchantment of her eye
All horror hence!—How die the thoughts of death!

Erix. I knew not my own heart. I cannot bear it.
Shame chides me back: for to insult his woes
Is too severe; and to condole, too kind.   [*Going.*

Dem. Thus I arrest you in the name of mercy,
And dare compel your stay. Is then one look,
One word, one moment, a last moment too,
When I stand tottering on the brink of death,
A cruel ignominious death, too much
For one that loves like me? A length of years
You may devote to my blest rival's arms,
I ask but one short moment. O permit,
Permit the dying to lay claim to thee,
To thee, thou dear equivalent for life,

Cruel, relentless, marble-hearted maid!

Erix. Demetrius, you persist to do me wrong;
For know, though I behold thee as thou art,
Doubly a traitor, to the state and me,
Thy sorrow, thy distress, have touch'd my bosom:
I own it is a fault,—I pity thee.

Enter Officer.

Offi. My Lord, your time is short, and death waits
for you.

Erix. Death!—I forgive thee from my inmost soul.

Dem. Forgive me? Oh! thou need'st not to forgive,
If imposition had not struck thee blind.
Truth lies in ambush yet, but will start up,
And seize thy trembling soul, when mine is fled.
O I've a thousand, thousand things to say!

Erix. And I am come a secret to disclose,
That might awake thee, wert thou dead already.

Offi. My Lord, your final moment is expir'd.

Dem. and Erix. One, one short moment more.

Dem. No; death lets fall
The curtain, and divides our loves for ever.

                [Demetrius *is forced out.*

Erix. Oh, I've a darker dungeon in my soul,
Nor want an executioner to kill me.
' What revolutions in the human heart
' Will pity cause! What horrid deeds revenge! [*Exit.*

                            [*Scene shuts.*

Enter ANTIGONUS, *with Attendants.*

Ant. How distant virtue dwells from mortal man !
Was't not that each man calls for others' virtue,
Her very name on earth would be forgot,
And leave the tongue, as it has left the heart.
Was ever such a labour'd plan of guilt ?
Take the King's mandate, to the prison fly,
Throw wide the gates, and let Demetrius know
The full detail.

Enter ERIXENE.

The Princess ! ha ! be gone ;   [*To the Attendant.*
While I stir up an equal transport here.
Princess, I see your griefs, and judge the cause :
But I bring news might raise you from your grave ;
Or call you down from Heaven to hear with joy.
Just Gods ! the virtuous will at last prevail.
On motives, here too tedious to relate,
I begg'd the King to re-examine those
Who came from Rome. The King approv'd my counsel.
Surpris'd, and conscious, in their charge they faulter'd,
And threaten'd tortures soon discover'd all :
That Perseus brib'd them to their perjuries ;
That Quintius' letter was a forgery ;
That Prince Demetrius' intercourse with Rome
Was innocent of treason to the state.   [with me ?
  Erix. Oh, my swoln heart ! What will the Gods do
  Ant. And to confirm this most surprising news,
Dymas, who, striving to suppress a tumult,
The rumour of Demetrius' flight had rais'd,

Was wounded sore, with his last breath confess'd,
The Prince refus'd his daughter; which affront
Inflam'd the statesman to his Prince's ruin.

 Erix. Did he refuse her?   [*Swoons.*

 Ant. Quite o'ercome with joy!
Transported out of life!—The Gods restore her!

 Erix. Ah! why recall me? This is a new kind
Of murder; most severe! that dooms to life.

 Ant. Fair Princess, you confound me.

 Erix. Am I fair?
Am I a Princess? Love and empire mine?
Gay, gorgeous visions dancing in my sight!——
No, here I stand a naked, shipwreck'd wretch,
Cold, trembling, pale, spent, helpless, hopeless, maid;
Cast on a shore as cruel as the waves,
O'erhung with rugged rocks, too steep to climb;
The mountain billows loud, come foaming in
Tremendous, and confound, ere they devour.

 ' *Ant.* Madam, the King absolves you from your vow.

 ' *Erix.* For me, it matters not; but Oh! the Prince—
' When he had shot the gulph of his despair;
' Emerging into all the light of Heav'n,
' His heart, high-beating with well-grounded hope;
' Then to make shipwreck of his happiness,
' Like a poor wretch that has escap'd the storm,
' And swam to what he deems an happy isle,
' When, lo! the savage natives drink his blood.
' Ah! why is vengeance sweet to woman's pride,
' As rapture to her love? It has undone me.'

 Del. Madam, he comes.

Erix. Leave us, Antigonus.

Ant. What dreadful secret this?—But I'll obey,
Invoke the Gods, and leave the rest to fate. [*Exit.*

Erix. How terribly triumphant comes the wretch!
He comes, like flowers ambrosial, early born,
To meet the blast, and perish in the storm.

Enter DEMETRIUS.

Dem. After an age of absence in one hour,
Have I then found thee, thou celestial maid!
Like a fair Venus in a stormy sea;
Or a bright Goddess, through the shades of night,
Dropt from the stars, to these blest arms again?
How exquisite is pleasure after pain!
Why throbs my heart so turbulently strong,
Pain'd at thy presence, through redundant joy,
Like a poor miser, beggar'd by his store?

Erix. Demetrius, joy and sorrow dwell too near.

Dem. Talk not of sorrow, lest the Gods resent,
As under-priz'd, so loud a call to joy.
I live, I love, am lov'd, I have her here!
Rapture, in present, and in prospect, more!
No rival, no destroyer, no despair;
For jealousies, for partings, groans, and death,
A train of joys, the Gods alone can name!
When Heav'n descends in blessings so profuse,
So sudden, so surpassing hope's extreme,
Like the sun bursting from the midnight gloom,
'Tis impious to be niggards in delight;
Joy becomes duty; Heav'n calls for some excess,

And transport flames as incense to the skies.

  Erix. Transport how dreadful!

  Dem. Turns Erixene?

Can she not bear the sun-shine of our fate?

Meridian happiness is pour'd around us;

The laughing loves descend in swarms upon us,

And where we tread is an eternal spring.

By heav'n, I almost pity guilty Perseus

For such a loss.

  Erix. That stabs me through and through! [love?

  Dem. What stabs thee?—Speak. Have I then lost thy

  Erix. To my confusion, be it spoke—'Tis thine.

  Dem. To thy confusion! Is it then a crime?

You heard how dying Dymas clear'd my fame.

  Erix. I heard, and trembled; heard, and ran distracted.

  Dem. Astonishment!

  Erix. I've nothing else to give thee.

    [*He steps back in astonishment; she in agony; and*
      both are silent for some time.

He is struck dumb:—nor can I speak.—Yet must I.

I tremble on the brink; yet must plunge in.

Know, my Demetrius, joys are for the Gods;

Man's common course of nature is distress:

His joys are prodigies; and, like them too,

Portend approaching ill. The wise man starts,

And trembles at the perils of a bliss.

To hope, how bold! how daring to be fond,

When, what our fondness grasps, is not immortal!

I will presume on thy known, steady virtue,

And treat thee like a man; I will, Demetrius!

Nor longer in my bosom hide a brand,
That burns unseen, and drinks my vital blood.

Dem. What mystery?   [*Here a second pause in both.*
Erix. The blackest.

Dem. How every terror doubles in the dark!
Why muffled up in silence stands my fate?
This horrid spectre let me see at once,
And shew if I'm a man.

Erix. It calls for more.

Dem. It calls for me then; love has made me more.

Erix. Oh, fortify thy soul with more than love!
To hear, what heard, thou'lt curse the tongue that tells

Dem. Curse whom? Curse thee!   [thee.

Erix. Yes, from thy inmost soul.
Why dost thou lift thine eyes and hands to Heav'n?
The Pow'rs, most conscious of this deed, reside
In darkness, howl below in raging fires,
Where pangs like mine corrode them. Thence arise,
Black Gods of execration and despair!
Through dreadful earthquakes cleave your upward way,
While nature shakes, and vapours blot the sun;
Then through those horrors in loud groans proclaim,
That I am——

Dem. What?—I'll have it, though it blast me.

Erix. Thus then in thunder—I am Perseus' wife.

  [Demetrius *falls against the* Scene. *After a pause—*
Dem. In thunder! No; that had not struck so deep.
What tempest e'er discharg'd so fierce a fire?
Calm and deliberate anguish feeds upon me;
Each thought sent out for help brings in new woe.

Where shall I turn? Where fly? To whom but thee?

[*Kneeling.*

Tremendous Jove! whom mortals will not know
From blessings, but compel to be severe,
I feel thy vengeance, and adore thy power;
I see my failings, and absolve thy rage.
But, Oh! I must perceive the load that's on me;
I can't but tremble underneath the stroke.
Aid me to bear!—But since it can't be borne,
Oh, let thy mercy burst in flames upon me!
Thy triple bolt is healing balm to this;
This pain unfelt, unfancy'd by the wretch,
The groaning wretch, that on the wheel expires.

  Erix. Why did I tell thee?

  Dem. Why commit a deed
Too shocking to be told? What fumes of hell
Flew to thy brain? What fiend the crime inspir'd?

  Erix. Perseus, last night, as soon as thou wast fled,
At that dead hour, when good men are at rest,
When every crime and horror is abroad,   [scream;
Graves yawn, fiends yell, wolves howl, and ravens
Than ravens, wolves, or fiends, more fatal far,
To me he came, and threw him at my feet,
And wept, and swore, unless I gave consent
To call a priest that moment, all was ruin'd:
That the next day Demetrius and his powers
Might conquer, he lose me, and I my crown,
Conferr'd by Philip but on Perseus' wife.
I started, trembled, fainted; he invades
My half-recover'd strength, brib'd priests conspire,

H ij

All urge my vow, **all** seize my ravish'd hand,
Invoke the Gods, run o'er the hasty rite;
While each ill omen of the sky flew o'er us,
And furies howl'd our nuptial song below.——
Can'st thou forgive?

   Dem. By all the flames of love,
And torments of despair, I never can.
The furies toss their torches from thy hand,
And all their adders hiss around thy head!
I'll see thy face no more.　　　　　　　　*[Going.*

   Erix. Thy rage is just.
Yet stay and hear me.　　　*[She kneels, and holds him.*

   Dem. I have heard too much.

   Erix. 'Till **thou** hast heard the whole, O do not curse
   me!

   Dem. Where can I find a curse to reach thy crime?

   Erix. Mercy!　　　　　　　　　　　*[Weeping.*

   Dem. [*Aside.*] Her tears, like drops of molten lead,
With torment burn their passage to my heart.
And yet such violation of her vows——

   Erix. Mercy!

   Dem. Perseus——　　　　　　　　*[Stamping.*

   Erix. **Stamp** 'till **the** centre shakes,
So black a dæmon shalt thou **never** raise.
Perseus! Can'st thou abhor **him more** than I?
Hell has its furies, Perseus has **his love,**
And, Oh! Demetrius his eternal hate.

   Dem. Eternal! Yes, eternal and eternal;
As deep, and everlasting, as my pain.

   Erix. Some God descend, and sooth his soul to peace!

Dem. Talk'st thou of peace? what peace hast thou
A brain distracted, and a broken heart. [bestow'd?
Talk'st thou of peace? Hark, hark, thy husband calls,
His father's rebel! Brother's murderer!
Nature's abhorrence, and—thy lawful lord!
Fly, my kind patroness, and in his bosom
Consuit my peace.

  Erix. I never shall be there.
My lord! my life!

  Dem. How say'st? Is Perseus here?——
Fly, fly! away, away! 'tis death! 'tis incest!

             [*Starting wide, and looking round him.*
Dar'st thou to touch Demetrius? Dar'st thou touch him,
Ev'n with thine eye?

           [*As he is going, she lays hold of his robe.*

  Erix. I dare—and more, dare seize,
And fix him here: no doubt to thy surprise——
I'm blemish'd, not abandon'd; honour still
Is sacred in my sight. Thou call'st it incest;
'Tis innocence, 'tis virtue; if there's virtue
In fix'd, inviolable strength of love.
For know, the moment the dark deed was done;
The moment madness made me Perseus' wife,
I seiz'd this friend, and lodg'd him in my bosom,

              [*Shewing a dagger.*
Firmly resolv'd I never would be more:
And now I fling me at thy feet, imploring
Thy steadier hand to guide him to my heart.
Who wed in vengeance, wed not but to die.

  ' *Dem.* Has Perseus then an hymeneal claim?

' And no divorce, but death?—and death from me,
' Who should defend thee from the world in arms?
' O thou still excellent! still most belov'd!
 ' *Erix.* Life is the foe that parts us; death, a friend
' All knots dissolving, joins us; and for ever.
' Why so disorder'd? Wherefore shakes thy frame?
' Look on me; do I tremble? Am I pale?
' When I let loose a sigh, I'll pardon thine.
' Take my example, and be bravely wretched;
' True grandeur rises from surmounted ills;
' The wretched only can be truly great.
' If not in kindness, yet in vengeance strike;
' 'Tis not Erixene, 'tis Perseus' wife.
' Thou'lt not resign me?
 ' *Dem.* Not to Jove.
 ' *Erix.*' Then strike.
 Dem. How can I strike?

     [*Gazing on her with astonishment.*
Stab at the face of Heav'n?
How can I strike? Yet how can I forbear?
I feel a thousand deaths debating one.
' A deity stands guard on every charm,
' And strikes at me.
 ' *Erix.* As will thy brother soon:
' He's now in arms, and may be here this hour.
' Nothing so cruel as too soft a soul;
' This is strange tenderness, that breaks my heart;
' Strange tenderness, that dooms to double death—
' To Perseus.
 ' *Dem.* True—but how to shun that horror?

' By wounding thee, whom savage pards would spare?
My heart's inhabitant! my soul's ambition!
By wounding thee, and bathing in thy blood;
That blood illustrious, through a radiant race
Of Kings and Herces, rolling down from Gods!

' *Erix.* Heroes and Kings, and Gods themselves, must
To dire necessity.   [yield

' *Dem.* Since that absolves me,
Stand firm and fair.

' *Erix.* My bosom meets the point,
' Than Perseus far more welcome to my breast.

' *Dem.* Necessity, for Gods themselves too strong,
' Is weaker than thy charms.   [*Drops the dagger.*

' *Erix.* Oh, my Demetrius!
         [*Turns, and goes to a farther part of the stage.*

' *Dem.* Oh, my Erixene!
            [*Both silent, weep, and tremble.*

' *Erix.* Farewel!   [*Going.*

' *Dem.* Where goest?   [*Passionately seizing her.*

' *Erix.* To seek a friend.

' *Dem.* He's here.

' *Erix.* Yes, Perseus' friend———
' Earth, open and receive me.

' *Dem.* Heav'n strike us dead,
' And save me from a double suicide,
' And one of tenfold death.—O Jove! O Jove!
            [*Falling on his knees.*

' But I'm distracted.   [*Suddenly starting up.*
' What can Jove? Why pray?
' What can I pray for?

' *Erix.* For a heart.

' *Dem.* Yes, one

' That cannot feel. Mine bleeds at every vein.

' Who never lov'd, ne'er suffer'd ; he feels nothing,

' Who nothing feels but for himself alone ;

' And when we feel for others, reason reels,

' O'erloaded, from **her** path, and man runs mad.

' As love alone can exquisitely bless,

' Love only feels **the** marvellous of pain ;

' Opens new veins of torture in the soul,

' And wakes the nerve where agonies are born.

' E'en Dymas, Perseus, (hearts of adamant !)

' Might weep these torments of their mortal foe.

   Erix. ' Shall I be less compassionate than they ?'

                    [*Takes up the dagger.*

What love deny'd, thine agonies have done ;

                    [*Stabs herself.*

Demetrius' sigh outstings the dart of death.

Enter the KING, *&c.*

   King. Give my Demetrius to my arms ; I call him

To life from death, to transport from despair.

   Dem. See Perseus' wife ! [*Pointing at* Erix.] let De-

  lia tell the rest.

   King. My grief-acsustom'd heart can guess too well.

   Dem. That sight turns all to guilt, but tears and

    death.

   King. Death ! Who shall quell false Perseus, now in

Who pour my tempest on the capitol ?   [arms ?

How shall I sweeten life to thy sad spirit ?——

I'll quit my throne this hour, and thou shalt reign.

Dem. You recommend that death you would dissuade ;
Ennobled thus, by fame and empire lost,
As well as life !—Small sacrifice to love.

  [*Going to stab himself, the King runs to prevent him;
    but too late.*   [*heart!*

King. Ah, hold! nor strike thy dagger through my

Dem. 'Tis my first disobedience, and my last.

             [*Falls.*

King. There Philip fell! There Macedon expir'd!
I see the Roman eagle hovering o'er us,
And the shaft broke should bring her to the ground.

         [*Pointing to* Dem-

Dem. Hear, good Antigonus, my last request :
Tell Perseus, if he'll sheath his impious sword
Drawn on his father, I'll forgive him all ;
Tho' poor Erixene lies bleeding by :
Her blood cries vengeance;—but my father's—peace.—

            [*Dies.*

King. As much his goodness wounds me, as his
  death.
‘ What then are both?—O Philip, once renown'd !
‘ Where is the pride of Greece, the dread of Rome,
‘ The theme of Athens, the wide world's example,
‘ And the God Alexander's rival, now ?
‘ E'en at the foot of fortune's precipice,
‘ Where the slave's sigh wafts pity to the prince,
‘ And his omnipotence cries out for more.
 ‘ *Ant.* As the swoln column of ascending smoke,
So solid swells thy grandeur, pigmy man !

'*King.*' My life's deep tragedy was plann'd with art,
From scene to scene advancing in distress,
Through a sad series, to this dire result;
As if the Thracian Queen conducted all,
And wrote the moral in her children's blood;
Which seas might labour to wash out in vain.
Hear it, ye nations! distant ages, hear;
And learn the dread decrees of Jove to fear:
His dread decrees the strictest balance keep;
The father groans, who made a mother weep;
But if no terror for yourselves can move,
Tremble, ye parents, for the child ye love;
·For your Demetrius: mine is doom'd to bleed,
A guiltless victim, for his father's deed.   [*Exeunt.*

AN HISTORICAL EPILOGUE.

AN Epilogue, through custom, is your right,
But ne'er, perhaps, was needful till this night:
To-night the virtuous falls, the guilty flies,
Guilt's dreadful close our narrow scene denies.
In history's authentic record read
What ample vengeance gluts Demetrius' shade:
Vengeance so great, that when his tale is told,
With pity some, even Perseus may behold.

 Perseus surviv'd, indeed, and fill'd the throne;
But ceaseless cares, in conquest made him groan.
Nor reign'd he long; from Rome swift thunder flew,
And headlong from his throne the tyrant threw:
Thrown headlong down, by Rome in triumph led,
For this night's deed, his perjur'd bosom bled.
His brother's ghost each moment made him start,
And all his father's anguish rent his heart.
When rob'd in black his children round him hung,
And their rais'd arms in early sorrow wrung;
The younger smil'd, unconscious of their woe;
At which thy tears, O Rome! began to flow;
So sad the scene: what then must Perseus feel,
To see Jove's race attend the victor's wheel:
To see the slaves of his worst foes encrease,
From such a source!—An emperor's embrace?
He sicken'd soon to death, and, what is worse,
He well deserv'd, and felt the coward's curse;
Unpity'd, scorn'd, insulted his last hour,
Far, far from home, and in a vassal's power:

His pale cheek rested on his shameful chain,
No friend to mourn, no flatterer to feign.
No suit retards, no comfort sooths his doom,
And not one tear bedews a monarch's tomb.
Nor ends it thus—dire vengeance to complete,
His ancient empire falling, shares his fate.
His throne forgot !—his weeping country chain'd !
And nations ask—Where Alexander reign'd.
As public woes a prince's crimes pursue,
So, public bleesings are his virtue's due.
Shout, Britons, shout ! Auspicious fortune bless !
And cry, long live—our title to success !